CHILDREN OF RUIN

BY ADRIAN TCHAIKOVSKY

Shadows of the Apt

Empire in Black and Gold
Dragonfly Falling
Blood of the Mantis
Salute the Dark
The Scarab Path
The Sea Watch
Heirs of the Blade
The Air War
War Master's Gate
Seal of the Worm

Echoes of the Fall

The Tiger and the Wolf
The Bear and the Serpent
The Hyena and the Hawk

Guns of the Dawn

Children of Time
Children of Ruin

ADRIAN TCHAIKOVSKY

CHILDREN OF RUIN

MACMILLAN

First published 2019 by Macmillan
an imprint of Pan Macmillan
20 New Wharf Road, London N1 9RR
Associated companies throughout the world
www.panmacmillan.com

ISBN 978-1-5098-6583-3

3 5 7 9 8 6 4 2

A CIP catalogue record for this book is available from the British Library.

Typeset by Palimpsest Book Production Limited, Falkirk, Stirlingshire
Printed and bound by CPI Group (UK) Ltd, Croydon, CR0 4YY

Visit **www.panmacmillan.com** to read more about all our books
and to buy them. You will also find features, author interviews and
news of any author events, and you can sign up for e-newsletters
so that you're always first to hear about our new releases.

To Paul

ACKNOWLEDGEMENTS

I have tapped quite a few knowledgeable heads to put this one together, and in particular I want to thank my team of Special Scientific Advisors, to wit: Maeghin Ronin, Peter Coffey, Philip Hodder, Nathan Young, Richard G. Clegg, Brian White, Katherine Inskip, Andrew Blain, Stewart Hotston, Winchell Chung and especially Michael Czajkowski for additional help with planetary mechanics and the splendidly inspirational Nick Bradbeer, spaceship design guru extraordinaire. I'd also like to thank Peter Godfrey-Smith for his book *Other Minds* which proved to be an invaluable research aid.

Above and beyond this elite team of boffins, my thanks as ever go out to Simon Kavanagh, agent of agents, and to Bella Pagan and everyone else at Pan Macmillan who acted on the development of this book in the same general way the nanovirus sped along the evolution of the various critters I write about. I could also not have produced this book (or just about anything) without the constant support of my long-suffering wife, Doctor Anne-Marie Czajkowski.

'If you can look into the seeds of time,
And say which grain will grow and which will not . . .'

William Shakespeare, *Macbeth*

PAST 1
JUST ANOTHER GENESIS

1.

So many stories start with a waking. Disra Senkovi had been asleep for decades. Something like a lifetime passed back home while he slumbered; a fraction of a lifetime passed around his oblivious form, the timespan squeezed down the relativity gradient by his proximity to the speed of light. For him, though, there was no time, nothing but the oblivion of the cold-sleep chamber. They knew how to build them back in those days.

Senkovi chose the manner of his waking. Some of his colleagues – those he thought of as less imaginative – would let themselves be fed crucial mission information, news from home, metrics from the ship, so they could spring from cold sleep with a mind full of data, ready to leap to their stations and steal a march on the day. Ludicrous, given the work they had ahead of them would take decades. Senkovi had always been unimpressed by most of his colleagues.

Instead, paradoxically, he woke himself with a dream.

He hung in the water of a warm, clean Coral Sea that hadn't existed in that virgin state since long before his birth. The sun filtered down through the waters like an embarrassment of sapphires. Below him, his best-guess reconstruction of the vanished Great Barrier Reef extended in multicoloured profusion, reds, purples and greens as far as the eye could see, like an alien city. Life whirled about the coral metropolis in a riot of motion, swimming, jetting, drifting, crawling. He turned gently, casting a benign and godlike gaze over his creation, half-sleeping, half-knowing, so that he felt the joy of having brought this into being yet not the pain of knowing the original had long predeceased him.

At last, one of his special friends signalled its presence, squirming its malleable body from a crevice within the rocks and undulating cautiously towards him. Eyes like and unlike his own regarded him with the sort of ersatz wisdom nature otherwise gave only to owls. It – determining the gender of an octopus was not a task easily performed at this remove – reached an arm towards him, Adam to his divinity, and he let his hand drift outwards slowly to accept that touch.

It was a good dream. He'd programmed it himself, creating a complex sequence of mental stimulation that drew on his specific memories and jumbled them into something semi-novel. It was still dream like, unreal, but that was what he was aiming for, so, fine. He also had to hack the ship computers with considerable ingenuity to make it happen, given that encounters with marine fauna were not on the *à-la-carte* menu when choosing a wake-up sequence. The hard part had not been inserting the neurological sequence into the ship's database but erasing all sign of his meddling. By then he'd been in and out of the mission systems quite a lot without anyone noticing, though. Senkovi had come to the conclusion that the Terraform Initiative back home was very, very lax in its digital security, and then shrugged idly and carried on with his own personal tinkering. What, after all, was the worst that could happen?

Amongst his travels within the virtual architecture of the mission protocols, Disra Senkovi had also come face to face with Disra Senkovi, or at least the crew profile and assessment record of that name. While extreme technical expertise was a given with all crew, he was interested to see the results of his personality assessments. There were two main poles, for a multi-decade mission like this, and they pulled in opposite directions. One related to how well a crewmember could cope working in isolation for long periods of time, and how they might tolerate being severed from the great mass of humanity and the course of human history. He aced that one. The other related to working in close confinement along-side other human beings you simply could not escape from, and he was dismayed to see how close he had come to rejection on that ground alone. Senkovi felt himself an affable, outgoing man. From the age of nine he had been working on constructing pseudointelligences to have conversations with, and hadn't he – more than anyone else in the crew – surrounded himself with pets back home? What better indication of a warm and loving human nature was there? He'd owned nineteen aquariums, three large enough to dive in. Many of the aquatic denizens were like close personal friends to him. How could anyone think him antisocial, let alone make all those unfair and hurtful comments?

He was being tongue-in-cheek, of course. They meant human friends, and that had never been his strong suit. Still, he had a few, and he worked well in a task-focused environment where everyone was fixed on a common goal. And when it came to R&R, well, if he wasn't the life and soul of the party, at least he didn't step on anybody else's toes. And there was, in his humble opinion, not a human being alive who enjoyed jokes more than he did; it was just that nobody else found his funny.

Anyway, his general social inoffensiveness was just sufficient, when added to his undeniable competence, to get him
on the crew, and then some combination of evaluations and
computer subroutines kicked him up to be head of the
Terraforming team, one below Overall Command, because
if you had a slightly deranged genius on the team it was
probably better to let him cox than row. That was the actual
comment of the psychologist who recommended the promo-
tion and Senkovi, having got into that file as well, treasured
the perceived compliment.

But they needed him awake now. In that unreal ocean he
strained, but the touch of the tentacle never quite reached
his finger, and all his pets were long dead and gone on an
Earth more than thirty light years away.

Disra Senkovi opened his eyes, aware that his beatific smile
had crossed over from his dream and was still on his face.
He felt refreshed and ready to start his day. A quick interro-
gation of the ship systems assured him they had arrived, their
long cold journey done, the deceleration over. He sat up,
stretching (more for the form of it than from any need, but
he was used to doing all sorts of things because *people do
them*, as a sop to the sensibilities of his fellows). He was
neither alone in his sleeping compartment, nor surrounded
by the bustle of a woken crew. Instead, his performance had
an audience of one: Yusuf Baltiel, Overall Command.

'Boss,' Senkovi acknowledged. The lack of context to
Baltiel watching him wake was disconcerting. Senkovi liked
to have a handle on cause and effect and was usually smart
enough to avoid surprises. He queried the ship again and
found a weight of data embargoed, blocked from him,
blocked from everyone except Baltiel himself. *That's not good.*

'I need a second opinion,' Baltiel told him.

'Let me guess, the planet's not there?' It had been the joke with the very first exoprobes – sometimes the data said there was an Earth-type planet but the indicators were just a bunch of other factors conspiring to give that impression. Of course, a probe had actually been shot out here, accelerating far faster than a manned ship could manage, checked that an actual terraformable planet was present and reported back. They wouldn't just send a manned mission off on a whim, now, would they? Senkovi really didn't want to have to turn around and go home.

'There's a planet.' Only now did Senkovi notice the curious tension to Baltiel, a man generally in complete command of himself. He was practically vibrating like a plucked string. 'There's a planet,' he repeated. 'But there's a problem. I'm keeping it hush, for now, but it's too big for me to make the call. I need you to see.'

Because of the embargo – which Senkovi felt was a childish way to go about things – they actually had to walk to Overall Command to see the *thing* Baltiel was so agitated about. Everyone else was still peacefully on ice. Who, then, was all this cloak and dagger supposed to thwart? He kept throwing queries at the system to find out what he could and couldn't know, because the computer wasn't able to tell him what was off limits until he hit a nerve and it clammed up on him. Actual walking from one place to another was, in Senkovi's book, something the future should have done away with long before, and his legs were having difficulty with the rotational gravity so that he bandy-kneed his way around the edge of the crew ring behind Baltiel's brisk stride. Baltiel was blocking transmission back home, he discovered uneasily, despite the fact that any urgent cry for help Senkovi might make would take thirty years and change to arrive. It wasn't like he'd be able to hold a murderous Baltiel off for that long, or indeed at all.

'Just tell me, boss,' he complained to the man's back.

Baltiel stopped, turned. There was a kind of fervour in his face that made Senkovi flinch. *He's found God*, was his instant thought, which was all sorts of extra not good, especially considering the most recent news from home. He had idly sifted through the updates while walking – all of it was decades out of date, but it looked like Earth had gone through a spot of trouble a while back, with anti-science terrorism and all sorts. *Makes you glad you're in space, man.*

'I need you to see.' It wasn't just mystery for the sake of it. Baltiel had drawn himself up to deliver the revelation, and failed.

A hundred more rubbery steps and they arrived at Overall Command, where the large screens displayed solar and planetary data and a visual representation of the destination system they had at last achieved, known as Tess 834 after the long-ago Earth-orbiting satellite that had first picked it out of the firmament.

Senkovi started with the big stuff, making sure the star wasn't about to go nova, looking for major disruptions or absences among Tesses 834b, c and d, the three colossal gas giants that filled out the waist of the virtual orrery and had the privilege of the first few letters because their mass had them detected first by Earth's instruments. Two of them were not much shy of Jupiter for size, one of them quite a bit bigger. *Nice meteor screen for our inner worlds*, he thought.

'E' and 'f' were further out, rock-and-ice monsters carving lonely paths in the reaches where the system's sun was little more than one more star among many. Of inner worlds there were three, one of them virtually rolling through the star's upper atmosphere, the other two close neighbours in the broad habitable zone but as different as siblings could be. Senkovi pulled up more data, still looking for the problem. The outermost of the pair, Tess 834g, was a little smaller than Earth, shining with an icy albedo through a thin atmosphere shorn of greenhouse gases. Any heat thrown its way just bounced right back off and was lost to space; Goldilocks zone or no, any fair-haired visitor was going to find her porridge inedibly frozen save at high summer around the equator. The other, their target Tess 834h, was warmer than Earth, slightly larger, its atmosphere muggy and heat-retaining, jealously hoarding everything the sun threw its way. There was a moon large enough for its gravity to make tides and keep its spin axis stable, and initial scans showed the presence of most elements human life would find useful. All in all, it would be a good match for human habitation once they'd let the terraformers loose on it. They could install a working ecology with a minimum of fuss and then maybe someday people could come and live on it. Or else that crazy lady Kern would arrive and do unspeakable things in the name of science. A lot of the terraforming team were frustrated with their glorious champion and leader Avrana Kern because her priorities did not seem to actually match the mission statement, while Senkovi was frustrated with her because she was doing all the fun stuff he would have preferred to do.

'This all looks . . .' *Good*, except it all looked a bit too good, now he mentioned it. Oxygen content on Tess 834h in particular was higher than he would expect. 'Ah . . . what am I . . . ?'

'This was one of the late surveys,' Baltiel said over his shoulder. 'By then they were very focused. They'd given up looking for the other stuff. The left-field stuff.' *The real stuff.* He hadn't said it but Senkovi heard the ghost of the thought in the other man's words.

The ship had performed its own survey as it closed in with the Tess 834 system, its instruments far in advance of the old exoprobes, drawing up a detailed picture of the terraforming challenge ahead. The ship itself had not blinked at the data, nor considered that it was making a discovery. Just like the exoprobe, it could only see what it was looking for. Senkovi was having a similar difficulty. He even pulled up the best visual image of the planet, taken by the ship as it zipped past on its way to brake around the red-orange sun. A single brown megacontinent, a great ink-coloured sea, spiralling wisps of cloud. 'This looks ideal terraforming territory, to be honest . . .'

But Baltiel just said nothing, and eventually every sound in the room, every shuffle and rustle, fell into the cavernous void of his silence as he waited for Senkovi to flip the data like an optical illusion, to see the other side of the story. And eventually Senkovi stopped looking at the readings like the exoprobe and read them like a human being, and he fell still and silent, too.

They had come as far from Earth as any human ever had, travelled for a generation, left behind a planet fragmenting into political disarray to gift this distant desert orb with life. But they were too late. Life was already there.

2.

The terraforming vessel had been named the *Aegean*, which everyone except Senkovi and Baltiel assumed was just one more name from the long electronic list that some computer kept for giving ships inoffensive monikers. Senkovi happened to have hacked the vulnerable part of the data chain and changed the *Maratha* to the *Aegean* because he preferred it, but no point letting that become public knowledge, not with so much on everybody's minds.

The *Aegean* had a crew of thirteen, and every one of them was awake now. The ship's datasphere was busy with eleven men and women trying to work out what was going on. Senkovi's preference would be to either just post the information up or not tell them at all, but Baltiel was a showman at heart, and moreover he was about to propose a rather radical departure from their mission. Senkovi, forewarned, was already working on his own counter-proposals, because he had come out here for a reason and didn't much like people messing with his routines, even routines planned out decades in advance.

He and Baltiel had been busy, prior to waking the others. The *Aegean* was in stable orbit around Tess 834h, although the data embargo extended to the viewscreens that otherwise would have given a window-like view of the world below.

The two early risers had fabricated a long-range in-atmosphere scout remote for a special mission. Honestly, the most complex part had been thoroughly disinfecting the thing. There were Earth microbes that could survive vacuum and the burn of re-entry, and a century of space industry had created a bizarre new habitat that bacteria and fungi had evolved to inhabit. It wasn't usually a concern of terraformers, whose job was, after all, to seed new planets with as much new life as possible. Baltiel was taking no chances, though. There was a living world out there and the last thing he wanted was to unleash some microbial apocalypse.

So they had printed the thing off, built it from the ground up in sterile conditions, coated it with foam and then vented it out into space, its rubbery armour ablating away until the pristine remote was all that was left, untouched by human hands.

Then they had sent it into the planet's atmosphere to take a look. Senkovi's imagination was full of algal pools, bacterial mats, stromatolites. The history of life on Earth was one of a long age of primitive single cells, alone or clinging together in makeshift, unorganized colonies. Complex life was merely the recent froth over a great vat of prokaryotes feeding and dividing and dying. That was what they expected to find: a scum of undifferentiated life clinging to the coastlines of that one great continent.

Then the remote had gone low enough to start recording images, and they had watched and watched, revising their impressions, glancing at one another. Senkovi had twined his fingers at the implications for his work; Baltiel had been stock still, a man given a destiny.

They put the remote into its own orbit and told the ship

to wake the others, and here they were, gathered together so Baltiel could draw aside the curtain and show them the magic.

'You're probably wondering if I've gone mad,' he addressed them. In fact he had been keeping tabs on just what enquiries they had made of the ship's systems, using Overall Command access to eavesdrop on the conversations flitting between their implants. Some of them did indeed think he'd suffered some breakdown as a result of the cold-sleep process, even though that was supposedly impossible with the modern units. Others had been picking up the news from Earth, sifting through all the signals that had chased after the *Aegean* and coming to the uncomfortable conclusion that the Earth – as it had been thirty-one years ago – was in the grip of war in all but name. Was Baltiel about to declare for one side or another? Was he about to accuse some of them of being anti-science quislings? The conflict brewing back home – the conflict that *had* been brewing way back when, anyway – went further than science versus conservatism, but as they were all scientists their takes on it were naturally skewed.

A number of them had tried to circumvent his embargo, either to glean more information or, in the case of Doctor Erma Lante, to send a report home. Senkovi, now Baltiel's willing co-conspirator, had been able to thwart them all for the same reasons that poachers make the best gamekeepers. And what Lante felt a report home would accomplish, at this remove, was anybody's guess. They were their own little state with thirteen citizens, cut off from human progress, marooned on a desert island in a sea the size of the universe.

'Just watch,' Baltiel told them, when he had gathered them

all in one of the *Aegean*'s briefing rooms, and called up his selected excerpts from the remote's travelogue.

Coming down from a cloudy, mackerel-striped sky, below was a great reddish-brown bowl, crossed by a couple of mountain chains like half-buried lines of vertebrae, sutures holding the megacontinent together. This was the hot, dry heart of the tropical latitudes, the drone coursing steadily over a dust bowl the size of Asia. At this remove, without magnification, it seemed almost featureless. The point of view dropped, though, as the remote made its controlled descent. Data on altitude, temperature and the like flickered in constantly shifting footnotes.

For a moment it could have been old Mars down there, save for the lack of craters. The world was a desert: terrible, inhospitable. Ripe for humanity to build a new Eden.

The remote dropped lower, skimming on towards this world's north and east. Ahead there was a line of darkness where night began and the footage was catching up on it. The view shifted, magnified, jerking to the right – this was Baltiel's post-flight editing, a little clumsy because he was a dreamer but not necessarily an artist. There were lakes in the desert, though of what was unclear. They leapt at the eye from the dull brown expanse, yellow, ferrous red, the blue-green of copper compounds, often concentric rings of one unlikely, toxic-looking colour within another and then another. They looked like waste pools from some factory about to be shut down by the environmental lobby, their shores crusted with glittering crystals. The sight was beautiful, yet a poster child for something inimical to human life. The display recorded a temperature of sixty-one degrees centigrade.

The remote descended further. There was no sound, and indeed the only sound would have been the wind and the rattle of grit and the roar of the machine's airscoops as it fought to stop itself overheating. Someone had been drawing in the dirt around the pools, and drawing in the poisonous water, too. There were complex radial designs, like dark snowflakes that branched and branched and met each other. Baltiel believed these were something like bacterial colonies; Senkovi said they could just as easily be inorganic. But these were the least exciting of the images he wanted the crew to see; a showman, after all.

However, he had guessed his audience might be getting slightly restless after looking at an alien desert for almost thirty minutes. The remote's view switched again, looking off towards the marching teeth of one of the mountain ranges, magnifying, zooming until there was a dot there, moving past the face of that red rock. Even with the remote giving them its all, it was hard to see what they were looking at. Something pale moved in the air and the human eye tried to recast it as a bird, a machine. The remote was closing as fast as it could, chasing the thing down. Now it resembled nothing so much as a filmy plastic bag caught on the wind, dipping and rising.

Where the desert met the mountains, the winds were strong; they'd had the run of the place, after all, and now these rising shelves of rock came to thwart them. The remote recorded gusting clouds of brown-red grit, dust devils, a great complex of thermals whirling upwards and carrying all sorts of fine debris into the higher atmosphere.

The camera had lost sight of the plastic bag; now it veered back into view, far closer. The remote was rising, above the peaks now, looking down. The thing – the indisputably living thing – lazily undulated its way along the line of the mountains.

'We think it's more than ten metres across,' Baltiel's voice broke in, because the remote gave little indication of scale.

It was like a jellyfish, a thing of absurdly thin layers, radial in layout, riding the winds and trailing filaments barely visible save where they shimmered in the sunlight. Following it for a long time, Baltiel pointed out that it was not simply airborne flotsam at the mercy of the elements. Some structure within it constantly trimmed its shape and dimensions as though a crew of sailors was taking in and letting out sails. The mood in the audience was that perhaps Baltiel was seeing what he wanted to see, but everyone was seeing a gigantic airborne cnidarian. Everyone saw the alien. Whatever they thought of Baltiel's individual conclusions, the mood of the audience was forever changed, as were they.

They were the first humans to set eyes on something that had evolved on another world and owed nothing to Earth.

'This is nothing,' Baltiel told them, and switched to the next item in his extra-terrestrial playlist.

This was one of his favourites, for pure artistry. The remote drifted through a night sky, and below the land seemed barren, rugged yet flat; this was more of the desert, but temperate uplands, a plateau approximately the size (and, by pure chance, shape) of Texas. The planet's moon was a crescent sliver in the sky. The remote's cameras did their best to amplify the light. The ground below had a curious texture to it, whorled with knotted clusters like closed fists, each sitting in a span of empty space away from its neighbours.

The timing was utter serendipity; the remote (under

Baltiel's guidance) was still trying to work out what it was looking at when dawn crested the edge of the world and threw out its red light. As day brightened over the plateau, the fists unclenched spirally, throwing out five branching arms whose inner surfaces were dark like pools – not the green of chlorophyll nor any other colour, they seemed more like solar cells than plants, and yet surely they were drinking in the sunlight in some exchange analogous to photosynthesis. And to do what? Their world was bounded by the plateau-top that they carpeted. Or perhaps this sessile form was merely the adult and their larvae rode the winds to be captured and consumed by vast jellyfish . . . Perhaps, perhaps, and here the best guesses of Baltiel or any of them were just spitting into the hurricane of the unknown.

Now the remote drifted over the sea, but that was a medium it was unsuited for and the water was almost completely opaque. There was something wallowing just below the surface, though – some huge round thing like a pale shadow glimmering within the inky ocean. Unable to make out more of it, the remote coasted on. Now they saw little nodules bobbing on the waves – 'little' meaning larger than human size, but the dark ocean was so vast that anything was dwarfed in comparison. They were translucent, veined. Baltiel thought they were immature sky-jellyfish. Perhaps, perhaps.

He showed them the poles, too – there was no land, no ice, but instead a weird sargassum of tendrils and coils and flowers, extending for hundreds of square kilometres. Everything was organized in hubs and spokes, a bizarre tessellating pattern when seen from above. The tangle seemed

17

living but inanimate, and yet there was a constant sense of motion from beneath.

By now nobody queried the computer or tried to get round the embargo. He had them, and who can blame them? And yet he had saved the best until last.

This last sequence was where the sea met the land, shielded from the baked interior by mountains that broke the moist air and shook it down for all the rain it had to offer. Here they were on the high latitudes, still hot by Earth standards but a breath of cool air compared to the murderous tropics. The remote's eye-view soared over a flat landscape of pools and creeks and mud, a salt marsh as far as its view could take it.

Everywhere there was life opening petals or leaves or some other alien organs to the sun, digging down roots to drag the sea-borne minerals from the salt-saturated ground. Or perhaps doing something else, some alien process without an Earth equivalent. Everything was low and stunted; the biology of this world had not produced anything that could keep a tall tree standing. Everything was blackish, with iridescent hints of blue-green or rust-red. The remote drifted lower, lenses hunting movement. Something flitted past between it and the ground, something winged and definitely not a jellyfish, pale and swift, moving quite unlike a bird, a series of staccato lunges through the air. In its wake, movement began on the ground again, the narrative of prey and aerial predator impossible to resist. There were things like spiny stones rocking into motion, making slow progress as they grazed the edge of the pools.

*

Baltiel ended his presentation there. They'd seen enough to know how much more there must be to see. Oh, perhaps one or two were harbouring some sneaking disappointment, brought up on a certain kind of story. Because when you went to an alien world and met the aliens, the aliens were supposed to be able to greet you. Advance science as far as you like, the human mind continued to place itself at the centre of the universe. If not to create intelligence, what was it all *for*? Where were the cities, the spaceports, even the abandoned ruins of an elder civilization? And yet this was all the alien life ever discovered that the human eye could make out unaided. A miracle that it had broken out of bacteria-analogues in the first place; a miracle that the result was something they could even recognize as 'life'.

Then Baltiel called up their mission statement which was, of course (and entirely incidentally), to destroy all this and replace it with something more like home.

Senkovi watched the reactions of the crew with interest. There was no guarantee that they would see things from Baltiel's perspective. *After all, like the old films say, we came thirty-one light years from Earth to terraform planets and chew gum, and we're all out of gum.* Actually, there was gum, or at least the means to manufacture it, but that wasn't the point.

What, after all, was the 'type' for a terraformer? They were hardy frontiers-people, surely, tough engineers come out to carve a home for themselves in the far reaches of humanity's sphere of influence, like the railroad builders of old. Except that was bunk, of course. Nobody here was eking out a desperate, dangerous living to send back pennies for their families. Nor were they the colonists, destined to tough it out under an alien sky until either they or the planet surrendered to the other. When the accelerated terraforming procedures took, the terraformers themselves would be on the first ship out, leaving the planet virgin for someone else to live on. Unless they grew so in love with their handiwork that they decided to stay, against all policy and orders. And, speaking of that . . .

'This has given me something of a quandary,' Baltiel was saying, showing his working even though he'd already found his answer to the sum. 'This is an unprecedented situation. Our mission briefing doesn't cover it.' A grimace, more calling up of records on their mind's-eye displays or the ship's screens for them to peruse. 'The very first terraforming expeditions did – the in-solar ones, and the first ever out-system mission. Everyone was hopped up about extraterrestrial life. And they didn't find even a microbe, and they were spending a whole lot of money and resources. And so it fell by the wayside for later missions. Nobody puts it in the manual any more. And it's not as if we can call Earth for clarification and then wait sixty-two years for their thoughts on the matter. The decision's ours.' By which, of course, he meant 'mine'.

Senkovi considered that they could actually just go back to sleep for six decades and change, and have the ship wake them when Earth had made up its mind, but that smacked of a slavish devotion to authority that he'd never espoused. He was surprised at this crusading flame in Baltiel, though, who was apparently a less orthodox character than Senkovi had taken him for.

'I hope you'll support me in the command decision I'm making here. We can't just go to work on this planet,' Baltiel told them all. 'It would be a crime, a genocide of something we may never find again in the lifespan of our species.' And he was preaching to the choir, mostly. What made a terra-former? Apparently, a willingness not to terraform if there was something more interesting around, as though they'd all come down with ADHD. Seeing him frown, Baltiel sent over a direct message: *Do you blame them?*

No. And I'm broadly supportive of your decision . . . Senkovi threw back, letting the 'but' hang there, unspoken.

And there were a handful who would obviously rather be terraforming – they'd come out here to do a job, and though they weren't unmoved by the marvels they'd been shown, they weren't ready to just sit on their hands.

'I propose we change our mission,' Baltiel told everyone. 'Our suite of technology here is designed to cope with a wide range of investigatory tasks as well as the actual rewriting of planets, after all. We have a duty to study what we've found here, to report on it for Earth. We won't be the last here. This planet will become the jewel of the galaxy for scientists. But we can be first, and do a good job of laying the ground-work. We can be in the history books, all of us.'

'All of us' meaning 'me', but probably there would be other names in footnotes, or immortalized as geographical features. *Mount Senkovi . . . or maybe not. Sounds like an instruction to a taxidermist.*

And again, Baltiel had most of them, but a few more were unhappy with this turn of events now. They were, after all, experts chosen for a particular task, and this wasn't it. Senkovi counted four: Maylem, Han, Lortisse, Poullister. The other seven were right with Baltiel about what they should be doing.

Senkovi decided this was his moment and flagged up a request to speak. Baltiel gave him the side-eye and asked for a little more context than that, and in return Senkovi just data-dumped the entire plan on him. *Let's see if he's as clever as he thinks he is.*

Baltiel blinked twice – that momentary pause was all the others saw – and then nodded briskly. 'Mr Senkovi, you have the floor.'

Senkovi blinked too, licked dry lips, preferring to be the scorer than the scoree when points were being dished out. All eyes on him, he coughed to buy a little time, then said, 'It's not like they'd just leave us alone, after all.' He didn't have Baltiel's grandiloquence. It was all he could do not to mumble into his chest. 'You know what they were calling the terraforming initiative, when we left Earth orbit? The Forever Project. Because this is it. This is when the human race becomes immortal, you get me? We're off Earth. We're *making* new homes amongst the stars, whether the stars want us or not. We have godlike power. People will come here, expecting to find a home. They'll be properly impressed by the jellyfish and the moving rocks and thing-what, but then they'll start asking awkward questions like, "Which house is mine, then?" I mean, you know people. We all do. Moan, moan, demand, demand, "We came thirty light years and you're showing us pictures of tidal marshland."' He essayed a small smile, saw a couple of people return it. Baltiel was expressionless, waiting. *How the hell did he digest all of that? Did he get the ship to parse it for him? Did he hack my files and read it before the meeting?*

'But Yusuf's right,' he went on, making a nervous, fidgety gesture in Baltiel's direction. 'We can't do the mission, not like we're s'posed to. But we can do it anyway. Look.' And he began bringing up his diagrams and data, which he could hide behind enough that his voice gained strength as he soldiered on. 'The next planet out, Tess 834g – it's mostly an iceball, right on the very limit of the liquid water zone, but it's geologically active, and terraforming 101 says we can precision-bomb the faultlines to set it all off at once and then it won't be an iceball for long, and the gas we get out of that will kill off the albedo, and after that it'll be warm enough for the water to stay water. And there's a little land. Just a little. And there'll be more once the ice has slimmed down to liquid.'

'Not much more,' Han pointed out. 'I get 2.1 per cent of total surface area, all small island chains.' She threw her own scratch calculations into the communal virtual display for everyone to look at. Lea Han was the oldest of them, Baltiel's senior by two years, and her maths was faultless at very short notice. *Nobody was heckling the other guy*, Senkovi thought, but Han was at least playing the game.

'So the colonists live on boats,' he suggested. 'It's that or they go live alongside your aliens, and how's that going to go in three or four generations? You think everyone's going to be a responsible neighbour?'

'That's a very pessimistic appraisal of the human spirit,' objected someone – Senkovi chased down the name and got 'Sparke', and an assessment record that spoke of reliable competence without brilliance.

'One I happen to agree with.' Baltiel killed off the topic effortlessly. 'We don't know what the political milieu will be, amongst any colonists.' And people's faces showed that the old news they'd had from Earth was front and centre in most minds. Any new arrivals could be a wave of ideological maniacs, come to practice their mania out of the reach of their foes on Earth. 'We don't know what their priorities will be,' Baltiel went on. 'Mine is to conserve what we've discovered here, and to study it. I will be taking an independent module from the *Aegean* to remain in orbit around 834h. I'm looking for volunteers for that team. Mr Senkovi has my support to attempt a terraforming of Tess 834g, and he'll retain the lion's share of the ship's resources to do so. He will, likewise, be looking for volunteers, and I can guarantee that, when we do finally get word to or from Earth, it'll be his team that has a future in the terraforming business.'

Still not as interesting as studying flying medusae, though, Senkovi concluded, but he couldn't say Baltiel hadn't given him a fair crack of the whip. For himself, he was already considering the technical challenges of bringing the ice-world to life.

In the end he got Maylem, Poullister and Han, with Lortisse defying Senkovi's assessment of him to join Team Alien. Three co-workers was, by his estimation, probably two more than he really needed. The machines would be doing the heavy lifting, after all.

'One question,' bright Sparke piped up, just as everything had been decided. 'What if you find life under the ice on 834g?'

Senkovi shrugged. 'Then, unless it has radio capacity and is a very quick learner, it's probably fucked,' he said.

3.

There might have been life. That was what he had to live with. Actually, there might still be life. Initial probes on Damascus (Senkovi had taken the liberty of installing his pet name like a squatter and daring Baltiel to evict) had picked up complex chemistry along deep-sea vents, but precious little beyond. The water column itself was barren. That chemistry was still there in places, and in fact two decades of colossally accelerated volcanism had perhaps even benefited it, spreading its habitat across the sea floor. Was it life? Results were inconclusive. Whatever was going on there seemed to be more about clay matrices than cell membranes, and relied on a toxic balance of chemicals that would be anathema to natives both of Earth and Tess 834h – which Senkovi had privately named 'Nod', because it was notionally east (or at least sunward) of the Eden that he himself was creating.

He had downplayed the possible biochemistry aspect in his reports to Baltiel, while simultaneously knowing that the man would not be fooled. It created a convenient fiction between them that they could show to later auditors. Baltiel was sharper than Senkovi had initially thought. After his big presentation about 834g, Senkovi had asked the man, 'How did you get through all that fast enough to make the decision?' and Baltiel had just said, 'I've seen your appraisals and tolerances. You wouldn't stake your career on a bad bet. All I needed to see was that you were staying the hell off my planet.' And he had smiled blandly, and Senkovi had learned a lot about his boss from that expression. An inclination to play God was part and parcel of wanting to go out and terraform other worlds, but good practice was to at least play nicely with the rest of the pantheon. Senkovi had met Avrana Kern once – it had been hard to avoid her – and *there* was a woman who was her own Zeus, Odin and Yahweh all in one. Baltiel's role had only ever been intended as a subordinate Vulcan, but now he had found a new lease of divinity, a project Kern could not reach across the abyss to dictate.

All very wearying, Senkovi thought. He had been out of storage for six months, this time round, because after a couple of years of targeted bombardment the primary volcanic phase was reaching completion and he and his people needed to set the next set of wheels in motion. Han was skimming drones over the surface of Damascus right now, mapping the new borders of the ice, which was confined to around a quarter of the surface and split between the poles. Still pretty damn cold by Earth standards, but the greenhouse gases were building nicely and they'd installed a set of solar collectors to funnel even more heat in.

The atmosphere of Damascus was fairly dense and mostly inert. The vast quantities of water had gifted the place with a little oxygen even without anything actively metabolizing it, which was a huge timesaving for Senkovi, as it allowed him to install more complex oxygenators which needed a bit of the O_2 already present to bootstrap them. He was about to turn the seas green, clogging them with the sort of algal slick that would horrify a beachful of tourists. That would set the oxygen meter creeping upwards, but, of course, that in itself would be robbing the planet of heat-retaining CO_2, meaning the whole volcanism and greenhouse gassery would need to be kicked up a notch, and the equilibrium of the atmosphere kept balanced like a spun plate that couldn't be allowed to so much as wobble for year upon year. And then there would come some more waiting, and he'd sleep out most of it. Except the current bout of watch-and-wait had tested his patience enough to set him on some side-projects, and now they were sufficiently advanced that he was contemplating spending another year of his life on *them* rather than saving it for the actual terraforming.

He glanced at his companion, who had come out to stare through the glass at him. 'Hungry, yet?' he asked, but he didn't think so. Paul was just curious. Curiosity was something Senkovi had bred into him, building on his work back on Earth. Really this had been no more than a hobby, no more out of order than Han's painting or Poullister's tedious logic puzzles. Except it had turned into a sufficient sink of mission resources that Senkovi had begun to think of ways to make it work for him.

Just about on time, Baltiel checked in, the signal coming at a staggered delay from the relay satellite orbiting Nod. Senkovi judged the time apt for revelation and opened a visual channel.

Baltiel had been taking things slowly on Nod. They were still flying carefully disinfected drones over the planet, trying to inventory the biomes and their contents, sleeping on ice while the systems generated hypothetical taxonomies. Senkovi looked it over every month or so, impressed with the man's restraint. He knew that boots on the ground was the plan, in a hermetically-sealed biodome. Baltiel would be the first man to walk with aliens, but only with a heavy-duty hazard suit between him and them, for everyone's protection.

'Hola, boss.' Senkovi composed his best smile. 'We're seeding now. Algal spring comes to Damascus.'

'I saw.' Because obviously Baltiel returned the courtesy and checked Senkovi's working on a regular basis. 'You're ahead of schedule, even.'

'You're behind,' Senkovi couldn't stop himself saying. To his surprise, Baltiel grimaced.

'I . . .'

And of course some of the given reasons for the man dragging his feet had been that he wanted Senkovi's operation established and stable, so that the crew remaining on the *Aegean* could charge over to mount a rescue if something went wrong, or vice versa. Senkovi had already dismantled that logic, and decided there were deeper and more personal bonds holding Baltiel back. The man's face now confirmed it.

'You want to make a good first impression,' Senkovi completed. 'And you only get the one chance.'

'That's it.' A gentler smile than any expression Senkovi had seen on Baltiel's face before. 'We're going down there. It's all planned. But I check and check again. I've had samples in the lab up here exposed to every microbe in the human body, to every Earth molecule.'

'And vice versa I hope.'

'It should be safe,' Baltiel said, surely for his own benefit as much as anyone's. 'There's some negative interaction at the molecular level, and there's more arsenic down there than we'd normally like. But biological interaction? None. They don't have our DNA, our cell chemistry, any of it. Nothing's going to get killed by the common cold. Nobody's going to catch the Martian flu. And we'll still be suited up, sealed away.' He sounded like someone looking for a second opinion, so Senkovi nodded amiably.

'I've given your proposal the once-over. I don't see any gaps.' He might have said more, but Paul chose that point to detach from the corner of his tank and come forward to goggle out at the screen.

'What the hell is that?' Baltiel demanded.

'Yusuf, meet Paul. Say hi, Paul.'

Understandably, Paul said nothing.

'What is it?'

Senkovi frowned. 'He's a Pacific striped octopus.' He sent over a data dump of files on cephalopods of all kinds in case Baltiel was criminally underinformed on the subject.

'But you must be way off seeding complex life.' Baltiel's brief eye-twitch showed him searching through the mission plan.

'Well yes, but—'

'Disra, is this a *pet*? Have you been using mission resources to breed domestic . . . octopodes?' Another brief twitch and Senkovi knew his superior had been looking up the plural and settled on the most awkward-sounding one.

Time for the long con. 'It's like this. We have an unprecedented level of underwater work on this project. Because, obviously, the planet is almost all underwater. Now while we have drones and remotes and the like, it won't be enough if we want to keep to schedule.'

'So you won't be ahead of schedule for long?'

Senkovi decided he could throw his past self under the bus for the benefit of his future self. 'Sure. I was optimistic. However, I've got a solution. Paul can help.'

Baltiel raised an eyebrow, a reaction sent over minutes between planets, but Senkovi felt it was worth waiting for.

'Do you know the work Califi and Rus were doing for Doctor Kern?'

Baltiel's eyebrow ratcheted up further, because right now everyone knew about that work – certainly everyone back on Earth had an opinion about it thirty-one years ago, and the most recently received opinions were extremely vocal. It had been a *cause celebre* for the reactionaries, a justification for terrorism, bombed out labs and brutalized monkeys. 'The viral work,' he said flatly.

'It wasn't finished when we set out, not quite, but I have a lot of their research. I was even co-author for one of the papers.' Senkovi was not looking Baltiel in the eye now, his attention shifting to Paul instead. 'I mean, I'm not talking actual *uplift*, not like they did it, but a little tweaking, a little acceleration' – *not to mention improving lifespan and post-egg laying survival but I'm not saying that because you'd want to know why* – 'so that when the sea is sufficiently habitable we could have a workforce to help us . . . ?'

Baltiel said nothing for a long time, enough that Senkovi checked twice to ensure the link was still open. *What's he going to do? He's on a different planet. He has his own obsessions. Is he calling Han to tell her to replace me? So I bred a better octopus. Is that so wrong?'*

'Submit a proper plan, at least, before you start meddling with them.' The words jolted Senkovi into eye contact again and for a moment the two of them just stared at each other across the thousands of kilometres. *We are both off our briefs,* Senkovi realized. *We're rebel angels, and by the time God – meaning Avrana Kern – realizes what we're up to, it'll be too late.*

'I will,' he promised, blithely sidestepping the fact that he'd already started. From his tank, Paul watched him with one slit-pupiled eye, tentacles curling in elaborate arabesques.

4.

Terraforming gave them all time to think. Yes, they were hurrying the planet's changes along at a ludicrous rate, compared to geological time: from iceball to ocean within a small slice of a human lifetime. Still, humans had evolved to live with days and months and seasons. The waiting was hard. Nobody wanted to just fall back into cold sleep the moment the opportunity arose, telling the *Aegean* to wake them in a decade. They wanted to see the world below them start to germinate before they closed their eyes. And so they practised art, music, read the ship's stored library front to back, played procedurally generated strategy games advertised never to repeat themselves. And almost everyone became obsessive, now and then. The Earth link was what got most of them. Poullister, Han, Maylem, they had all spent time trying to discuss what was happening back home. People were fighting. There were localized war zones – mostly the traditional sort where the big players' soldiers got to go play in the back yards of their neighbours, to minimize the property damage of friendly allies. Proxy wars, and keeping it clean so far, but everyone knew that there were stocks of chemical and biological agents just sitting around waiting for someone to lose patience with polite and limited wars. And the news was old, of course, over three decades. They were out here on the edge of humanity's sphere of influence, their ability to communicate with home crippled by the insuperable laws of relativity.

Senkovi had heard Poullister and Maylem in full-blown argument – one of those pointless rows where both of them were effectively arguing the same case, where the argument itself was the point, not the winning of it. He hadn't realized, before then, just how riled up everyone was about Earth and the growing conflict they were hearing about, a generation late. And probably it was all settled now, peace and harmony, but that old demon relativity brought an end to any difference in acceleration between good news and bad, truth and rumour. None of it could get to them faster than the light of their home world's distant sun, leaving them to endlessly speculate about how bad things might have got.

Senkovi himself kept out of the discussion and kept out of their way. He was already obsessive, a trait he had proudly smuggled onto the *Aegean* long before it had become *de rigueur*, and he was using the waiting time to indulge in his own personal schemes.

When Han came to see him – this was months after his brittle détente with Baltiel over Paul – her first comment was, 'You're supposed to be in the freezer by now.'

'Don't wanna,' Senkovi told her, sticking out his bottom lip because he'd learned that with some people a veneer of feigned childishness could transform his peculiarities from obnoxiously antisocial to charming. 'Busy.'

'Busy keeping us out of here,' she noted. 'This was Payload Bay Seven, wasn't it? Only none of this looks like payload, Disra.'

'It is payload. Of a sort.' He was already being defensive, and he'd hoped to keep that in reserve when charmingly childish wore thin. 'I filed a plan with Baltiel. He's all over this like a rash, believe me.'

'Disra, I saw the plan you filed. It was . . . thin. And you must have pushed past its parameters an age ago. Preliminary testing, it said.'

'And it went very well, so I made an executive decision. Baltiel will back me.'

Han was a tall, slender woman who looked as though she should be an aesthete, all impromptu haiku and abstract paintings. In fact her paintings were all of robots, fantastical, impractical metal humanoids lit by industrial fires or explosions, as though she had a window onto a world where cybernetics had gone in very different directions. On top of that, perhaps despite that, she was the best engineer on the terraforming team, a genius mathematician and a pilot. And all of that, Senkovi had thought, should have been enough to keep her busy and not send her snooping around here. He felt like a boy caught doing something untoward after lights out, sitting on the floor of Bay Seven with a half-gutted virtual console, lit by the azure radiance of the big tank he'd had constructed.

Han put a hand to the transparent plastic, seeing the occupants detach from the fake coral and rocks he'd given them, drifting towards her fingers to see if they would give any entertainment value. 'I'm guessing you're not sending them planetside any time soon,' she noted. 'Unless you've engineered the fuck out of them to not need oxygen or Earth-style temperatures or pH.'

'As it happens they aren't ready for deployment, no,'

Senkovi told her shortly, wishing she'd just go away and, if possible, forget everything she was currently looking at. 'I'm still very much in the R&D phase of the project, as you must know if you've read—'

'Why squid?'

'Not *squid*. Octopi. Octopuses if you want to be a slave to the dictionary. And why not? What's wrong with them?'

Han glanced down at him. 'You've got a genetic library that's a good slice of Earth biodiversity, Disra. You've got the kit here to hatch out anything, un-extinct it. Poullister was talking about making a dog.'

Disra, not much of a dog person, shrugged. 'Why not? I mean, what would you do? Let me guess, you had a cat, back home? Fish?' He decided Han probably had owned a cat, or had wanted to own a cat but hadn't lived somewhere she could get a pet permit. Maybe she'd had a robot cat, one of those good little machines that purred and sat on your lap and then its ears fell off the moment its warranty expired.

'I'd make a tiger,' Han said.

Senkovi was speechless for a long time, enough that his console began lighting up with frustrated red error messages as his fellow game player got annoyed with his inaction. 'Huh,' he managed eventually.

Han grinned down at him – it was the first time he had ever seen her smile, perhaps. He suddenly found his opinion of her completely revised. She wanted to recreate a tiger, here on the *Aegean*, where the narrow corridors and enclosed workspaces would lead to an interesting work-life balance for the humans having to share the ship with a large carnivore. And, of course, she'd never go ahead and actually *do* it. Senkovi was frankly the only person on the ship who would just live the dream and to hell with the opinions or even permissions of others. But the thought was there and Senkovi decided he liked Han a lot better for it.

'I had a tiger when I was a kid,' she said candidly, and he wondered if that meant a stuffed toy, or if she came from an income bracket considerably above even his own rather privileged one. 'But you, you've got a whole load of these . . . octopi. And no tigers.'

'Ah well, the key failing with tigers is that their performance drops off sharply when you get them to mend coolant pipes a kilometre below the surface of the ocean.'

Han stared at him for long enough to make him uncomfortable, then the grin was back. 'That's not what this is about,' she pointed out.

Senkovi thought about keeping up the presence but decided she was too sharp for it. 'Oh, well, it is. I mean, that's the end goal. But I had an octopus when I was a kid.' Rather more than one, but the narrative was simpler that way. Then his console beeped sharply at him and he hurriedly made a move to keep it quiet.

Too late, though, for Han was crouching down beside him. 'Who are you playing against? Is that Poullister? He can't play worth a damn.' The console was displaying a tile-laying game, a little idealized landscape half-constructed from squares, linking roads, rivers, cities. And it was a mess, pieces all over, roads spiralling to nowhere, the spiky walls of towns clustering like sea urchins.

'It's . . . Not Poullister, no.'

Han's eyes were following where the cables from the console led. And yes, he could have just run the whole thing in virtual space on the *Aegean*'s system, and that was the logical next step. Right now he was trying to keep his games private, because the others would mock.

Han wasn't mocking, though. He could see the wheels of her mind turning. 'You're . . .'

'Paul,' Senkovi explained. 'Well, Paul 5. He's the most successfully modified. He likes the console and experiencing virtual space. I'd thought . . . well, there are *humans* who never really take to a virtuality, but the octopi are all about manipulating space. There's no tactile element for them yet, and I thought that would be the sticking point, but they get it very quickly, Paul 5 especially. So I'm trying some simple games. With debatable success. He makes moves, and he's understood the limits the game places on when he can move and what moves can be made, but as far as strategy or points or winning, that seems to be outside his range at the moment.'

'Tell him he doesn't get fed if he loses,' Han suggested, staring into the tank.

Senkovi had tried that. Pavlovian motivation wasn't terribly useful for training an octopus. Once they were fed, food became a lesser motivator than curiosity. Also, when Senkovi had contrived to communicate that the game hid a shrimp inside it somehow, Paul 2 had broken the game trying to take it apart.

'We're going to need this space back for payload sooner rather than later,' Han remarked eventually, even somewhat regretfully.

'Firstly, this is payload, albeit highly experimental. Secondly, we don't. Look, I've reorganized. We can get by on the other bays. I've even gained us some space.' He sent over his changes, which were in fact just as advertised, to the virtual space their mind's eyes shared. The designers of the *Aegean* had been slacking somewhat, leaning on their large budget. Senkovi had improved on their work to provide the ship with improved economy of space and movement of matériel, the sort of thing that someone might have achieved genuine commendations for. The entire elaborate operation looked good on paper to anyone who didn't suspect he'd gone through it solely because he wanted more space for fishtanks.

After Han had gone, he finished the game and fed his pets, hoping that the rest of the ship wasn't already tittering behind his back about crazy Senkovi and his performing molluscs. The console was already flashing, though, despite Paul being busy dismantling a crab.

It was one of the others, Salome. She had been watching Paul, and now she had used her own newly implanted connection to break into the game system. She had moved as much as she could but now needed him to take his own turn before she could continue playing.

Senkovi suspected he should probably get away from the tanks and go have human contact or something healthy like that. On the other hand, he'd just had an actual conversation, which was quite wearying, and he could hardly disappoint such a keen experimental subject.

He sat down again, dropping a tile into the virtual space and waiting to see what Salome would do.

5.

Siri Skai would be in charge of the orbiting module in Baltiel's absence. She and four others would have relatively little to do except continue to round off the rough edges of the database the computer was assembling on the Nod biosphere (Senkovi's joke name having gradually infiltrated the collective consciousness). Of course, technically Baltiel himself should be staying up top and delegating the ground party, but he was damned if he was going to. *This* was the day he had been waiting for, in and out of sleep over the years since their arrival here. He would not only be on the shuttle down, he would be the first damned human being to set foot on this world. Nobody was taking that from him.

Remotes had been down there for a long time now, setting things up. There was a habitat ready to receive them, filled with an atmosphere not vastly different to that outside – a little lower pressure, a little more oxygen. An Earth-ish atmosphere, though, and the gravity would be real, even if a little stronger than they were used to. He had been living in space, sometimes in rotational gravity, sometimes in none, for too long.

Of course, the plan was purely to run a research mission – the research mission he had invented to replace what they were actually supposed to be up to out on Nod. He shouldn't be thinking about the place as 'home'. It would be a poky little series of interconnected domes, barely more personal space than on the module they'd separated from the *Aegean* and left in orbit when the rest of the ship went off on the road to Damascus.

Senkovi and his damn fool names. But they always seemed to stick. No doubt the colonists would have their own sanitized monikers for both planets when they arrived. Or maybe not. That depended on just how badly things actually went back home. Senkovi said they'd get boatloads of desperate refugees turning up at every terraforming station, clamouring to be housed and fed. The great human diaspora, but not how anyone had envisaged it.

Baltiel had sat down to a meal with all his crew, not long ago – he'd tweaked the rotas especially so that everyone would be awake and ready for the historic launch. The mood had been cautiously optimistic. Earth was very far away, after all, and everyone was sure that things there would sort themselves out. The mysteries of Nod were far more immediate for them.

Skai had even wondered about harvesting something edible from the planet, because Senkovi was a long way from commercial fisheries over on Damascus. Skai was a geologist, though, and tended not to read the monograms of other specialities. Ninety per cent of Nod proteins were indigestible to humans – not immediately poisonous but just inert stuff that would clog up your gut and probably kill you eventually from the levels of arsenic and mercury the planet seemed to thrive on. The remaining ten per cent were not economical to separate out.

Baltiel had expected to be the great expert on the land of

Nod by now. Instead he felt as though their accumulated knowledge of the planet was to the mind what the alien flesh would be to the stomach, almost impossible to assimilate. It wasn't that the automated survey had turned up blank, quite the opposite. They had a vast wealth of information about the planet, and no way to readily put it together in any kind of order. He felt like a schoolchild taught history as a list of dates and names of kings, without context to let him draw meaning from the information.

Nodan organisms were organized into cells, just like Earth creatures, although the cells themselves were very different. They were smaller, for one thing, no bigger than an E. coli bacterium on average. There was no nucleus, but some manner of transmissible organization, incredibly dense, was implanted in the membrane. Lante, wearing her biochemist hat, was talking about atomic-level information storage, more compact than DNA but perhaps more energy-intensive to produce. Every cell seemed to react to light, even the ones buried deep in the bodies of creatures. Why? Nobody had a good theory. Plenty of the organisms they had looked at appeared to be metabolizing sunlight, some sessile-like plants, others highly mobile, suggesting that their mechanism (as yet unknown but there were some fascinating suggestions) was far more efficient than plant photosynthesis – and there appeared to be no hard plant/animal divide on Nod.

Almost every organism was radially symmetrical, top and bottom but no front or back, save where evolution had twisted them round to let them flap through the skies dorsal-side first. Oh, and many of them were only partially cellular, with large portions of their bodies composed of a plasticky tissue that seemed almost inanimate and which was manipulated and deformed by contracting fibres – the jellyfish, which comprised a significant phylum of Nodan life, were all sail and hardly any actual ship.

Baltiel wasn't someone whose mind leapt instantly to thoughts of commercial exploitation, but Nod had already shown him forms of information storage, energy conversion and super-strong, super-light materials that Earth technology could not currently replicate. And yet, at the same time, the Nodan ecosystem felt . . . *young*. Aside from some truly colossal mcdusac-forms nothing on land seemed bigger than a medium-sized dog. There was nothing like a forest (nothing like wood), nothing much like an internal skeleton. Everything sprawled outwards rather than fighting for height. He wondered if this was what Earth would have felt like back in the Devonian era or some such, when life was just encroaching on land.

What might they become? But he would never know, and he had a bitter certainty that human presence in this solar system meant that nobody would, that the future of life on Nod was going to be brutally curtailed.

He had not sent anything home about their discoveries. As far as he knew, everyone had respected his orders on that front. But it wouldn't matter as soon as the next wave of Earthlings arrived, ready to wash away all these fragile marks in the sand prior to building some prime beachfront property on any habitable planet they found. He had daydreamed about putting plague beacons in orbit all over the planet, warning off the future.

So instead he was indulging himself. He and his crew would do what they could to curate this riot of weirdly unambitious-seeming life while they were still able to. There would be a record for later generations, even if there would be nothing else.

He sent a call to Skai over the module's network and she confirmed her readiness, highlighting the green system read-outs. He checked to ensure that his ground team had reached the shuttle. Erma Lante (biologist and medic) and Gav Lortisse (geothermal engineer and general technician) were there, and Kalveen Rani (meteorologist and pilot) was just on her way. She had a message pending and he checked it anxiously, expecting something to have arisen to delay his destiny – faults, storms, something. Instead she was recommending he speak to Senkovi. *He had some meteorological data for me to analyse but when it came through it was nonsense. He may be having problems.*

Baltiel felt he had plenty of his own problems, to which he really didn't want to add Senkovi. The man was supposed to be so damned self-sufficient, after all.

He set his feet on the brief path to the shuttle bay and a sudden rush of excitement seized him, like a child about to go on a much-dreamt-of holiday. He'd been living in this tin can for too long; subjectively for years, objectively (meaning by the ship's clock) for decades. Like a child, again, but one who'd been staring at the presents under the tree for a generation, not forbidden to open them but exercising inhuman self-restraint.

Like a child. Nobody on his team would describe him so: he was the man who was always calm, who always had an answer, who could even – miracle of miracles – talk Senkovi up or down or sideways from wherever the man's thought processes had led him. And yet, inside, Baltiel felt a bubbling, innocent glee. The timing of the mission, however well accounted for in the records, was more to do with him having finally exhausted his iron reserves of patience. Today was Christmas and he was about to tear off the wrapping paper.

Still, he was Overall Command, and Senkovi's little fiefdom was still part of Overall, at least nominally, so he had the module signal its other-self, the *Aegean*.

'Hi, boss,' came the delayed response, by which time Baltiel was in the shuttle double-checking Lortisse and Rani as they double-checked each others' pre-flight checks, belt and braces all the way down.

'Siri's chasing up some met data from you,' Baltiel prodded.

'Oh, hum, yes. No, not a priority right now.' By which time everyone on the ground crew had checked everyone else's sums and Siri Skai had confirmed their launch window and the excited child taking up space in Baltiel's head was virtually blocking out everything else. And Senkovi sounded off balance, which should have been a huge worry given how the man kept his insides inside, but surely it couldn't be *now* that things went catastrophically wrong. Not on the very edge of departure.

And yet . . . 'Disra, what's up?'

'We're just having a few system glitches, boss, nothing to worry about.' Senkovi's tone, when it finally came back, was transparent. *He's screwed up somehow and he doesn't want me to check up.* And Baltiel could check up, of course. He could query the *Aegean* with his command access and then, doubtless, cut through all the baffles and screens Senkovi had festooned the problem data with. Or he could just let Senkovi get on with it and deny the man the chance to rain on Baltiel's greatest ever parade.

He made a command decision that, even then, he knew

was on the wrong side of cautious. He'd been cautious for twenty years, though. Time for one glorious, reckless act. Cutting the connection, he decided to let Senkovi scoop his own crap without supervision, this one time, and hoped that the man didn't end up finger-painting it all over the walls.

He refused to lose the launch window. He couldn't know, at the time, just what was riding on the decision.

'Skai?'

'When you are.' Skai and the rest of the module crew were already settled in to continue the data gathering. Most of them would be back in cold sleep as soon as the shuttle was safely down. He was surprised there hadn't been more jostling for a place on the ground, but going to live with the jellyfish didn't appeal to everyone.

The shuttle bay was evacuated around them, the air jealously grabbed back before it could be wasted. The bay doors opened, the clamps released and the rotation of the module gently released the shuttle out into space along a perfectly plotted pitch.

Baltiel had chosen the salt marsh biome for his base because it was more hospitable than the searing inland deserts. Not that their suits didn't have temperature control, but the less the technology had to work, the longer it would last without maintenance. Of the land biomes it seemed the most populous, too – where an anthropocentric eye could perhaps see evolution striving to produce something *more*. And that was an illusion, surely. Probably the great fonts of evolutionary activity were elsewhere, and left to their own devices there would have been some great new wave of development from the deep sea, or the floating creatures of the upper atmosphere. *But moot, now. We can only observe the present, before we go on to destroy the future.* The thought made Baltiel so angry, but unless the commander of the next ship along was also a radical conservationist, how could any of this life have long-term prospects? Oh, surely individual species would survive alongside humans, or be relegated to reserves and zoos, but the ecological history of Earth showed how pitiful such measures were. One of the terraforming program's great triumphs was being able to reconstruct whole Earth ecosystems – systems that didn't exist as anything other than deathbed wounded back on their original planet. Because in a very real way the ecosystem was the basic unit of life: species creating, by their very presence, an environment for other species to work in. *We wrecked it all, back home,* Baltiel thought. *And by the time we understand Nod we'll have wrecked it here as well.* For a moment he'd had a mad dream of an Earth-mimic Damascus and an alien Nod side by side, co-existing. The spiralling bad news from home had ground down that dream into a kind of bleak nihilism. *We will learn what we can and record it. I will be able to say, 'I walked there.' They can't take that from me, no matter who comes.* Even the thought of Earth, the political rants, the casualty figures, the spiralling insanity, made his gut clench, but he consciously banished the images and medicated the gut reaction, just like they all were doing these days. *I will not let a little global war ruin my moment. And it's all history anyway, by the time it reaches us.*

The shuttle was falling into its pre-planned descent, Rani keeping a close eye in case she needed to intervene. Lortisse had a presence in the shuttle performance system, but it was more out of habit than genuine worry. Lante appeared to be dozing, even as they came into contact with the upper atmosphere. Baltiel himself was staring at the images – views of

Nod from the module, from the shuttle: a world of brown, black and red, far from the green-blue jewel of a terraformed New Earth.

A transmission came in from the *Aegean* and he looked at it, despite everything. *What now?* But it was gibberish, just strings of alphanumeric characters chopped up to look like language but devoid of meaning.

A practical joke? Because that was something on Senkovi's file, one of his ways of impressing on lesser people just how clever he was, although this didn't seem up to his usual standard. He sent a query back.

They were going for a shallow descent to save wear and tear on the shuttle as much as possible, but also so Baltiel could use the ventral cameras to get a new fly-by view of his domain. Below them was the obsidian expanse of the ocean. *The wine-dark sea.* Too high right now to see anything more, but they would get a good skim over the waves before they crossed past the coast.

'Hey, boss, no, all fine.' *8jsgjg r jg81 ufwytmv-i9r f* 'All under control here. All fine. How's the flight?' *kksn hu9 d i99t k.*

'Disra, what the hell?' Abruptly there was a very uneasy feeling in the pit of Baltiel's stomach because he was getting a lot of ghosting nonsense from the *Aegean* around Senkovi's signal, multiple separate transmissions from the ship that manifested as sudden intrusions of nonsense audio shutting out the man's voice channel.

'It's . . . Look, boss, don't panic. I'm going to have to turn it off and on again.'

I made the wrong call. He was in the Nod orbital's only shuttle and it was committed to the approach now. There was no way he could go and help Senkovi. *Although even if we were still sitting back up there in orbit, it'd take the best part of a year with the positions the planets are in right now.* 'Explain,' he demanded curtly.

'I'm having some system infiltration issues,' came Senkovi's voice, trying and failing to be casual about it. 'I . . .' *hhs i4 gk; gg 8lubj2* 'I need to restart the ship's systems from scratch, boss. I'm really sorry. It's a bit' *n83.ljsg.n hgikkkd* 'screwed up.'

Baltiel's insides were screwing themselves up, partly in worry, partly furious that somehow Senkovi had managed to piss on his moment of glory. 'Explain,' he repeated, and then, looking at an initial analysis of the nonsense transmissions, 'Are you being *hacked*?'

'No. No, no. Yes.' Senkovi's delayed response sounded as though it was somehow funny, whilst simultaneously being horribly serious. 'Look, I'm sending the others off on the shuttle, just in case things,' *9wks rj i934mmgpppphhhhheeelllo-hellohellowhatwhat* 'uh, just in case things go really badly, which they won't, but it's all a bit,' *whatwhat95mg; hooqueryquery* 'you know, kind of . . . I've said that if things go really badly they should skip over to Nod and throw themselves on your mercy. Not their fault. All mine, okay?'

'Disra, just tell me what the hell!' Baltiel had already shouted over the man's babble. The increasingly organized nature of the other signals was prickling the hairs on his neck. *Has he kickstarted the ship into full AI or something?*

'Victim of my own success,' came Senkovi into a sudden silence as the other transmissions cut off. 'I've clamped down on bandwidth but I can't keep them bottled up. I'm taking it all offline. All you need to know. Normal service will resume shortly.'

'That is *not* all I need to know!' Baltiel was trying to

interrogate the *Aegean* but, between Senkovi trying to cover himself and whatever chaos was actually going *on* over there, he wasn't getting a coherent picture. On the screens in front of him, the Nodan seascape was lost in the shuttle's rushing progress, and now there was red desert below. According to his diagnostics there were half a dozen net presences in the *Aegean*'s system, weird undirected processes lurching around trying to access ship systems.

He'd thought his demand must have come too late, but Senkovi obviously caught it before flipping the switch. 'All right, boss, here's the lowdown,' came the reply. 'I may have failed to contain my experimental subjects properly.'

'Explain.'

'I've been training them up, teaching them basic communications so they could interact with the equipment on Damascus. They'll be useful. We'll need them. Only they're curious, right? It's inbuilt with them, and I've been using the Rus-Califi viral catalyst to select for that, only I didn't realize how quickly they'd catch on.'

In the midst of all the man's justifications, Baltiel suddenly understood what Senkovi meant. 'Disra, are you talking about your damned *octopodes?*'

'Boss, I am.' He sounded partly embarrassed, but also impressed with himself, too, or at least with his pets. 'I taught them to access the system, play games, basic teaching stuff, and now they're past my security and just, you know, poking around. Curious, like I said, only I can't stop them and they're screwing everything up. It's all innocent, but . . . I made a bit of a monster, boss. Look, I'm suited up and everyone else is getting the fuck out on the shuttle. I'll fix this.'

'Why aren't you on the shuttle, Disra?'

'Boss, it's my bad. I can sort it better from in here. There's always something you have to go do by hand.'

'Use a remote. Disra, do you hear me?' Baltiel's own shuttle was beginning its landing approach now. They were over the black and grey mottling of the salt marsh and a flash of white in the distance was the habitat.

'I'm suited up. I have independent power. All set, boss. Got to go.' Senkovi's voice cracked at the end and Baltiel suddenly understood. *His pets.* Shutting the ship down was a death sentence for his precious octopodes and he wanted to be there for them, or maybe even save some of them. And probably he'd get killed, and Han and the rest would have to finish the terraforming without either Senkovi's brilliance or his goddamn molluscs.

With that, Baltiel forced himself to let go. Senkovi had finally found a way to get out from Overall Command, and now neither Baltiel nor any other human agency could help him. *It isn't my problem*, he decided. *Not for want of trying, but he's going to have to get out of it himself.* He imagined the *Aegean* as if the ship was literally crawling with Senkovi's rebellious progeny, monstrous cephalopods blobbering through the compartments waving angry tentacles. Of course, they would be in tanks somewhere, their intrusion purely virtual, and yet irresistible, circumventing everything Senkovi could throw up to keep them out. *But then, when you're designing an interface to let molluscs play computer games you probably don't build in that much security.*

Baltiel had a moment to consider how that was a sequence of words he'd never expected to be relevant in his life, and then they were landing, Rani hovering over the controls like a hawk in case the shuttle's onboard got it wrong, and Baltiel already had a hand up to release his straps because, goddamn it, he was going to be first on the ground.

***

Amazing.

How quiet.

Almost worth it just for this.

But Senkovi didn't really believe that. He couldn't know about Baltiel's inner child thoughts, but he himself was making a very similar comparison. Only, for him, his inner child had done a very bad thing indeed and, unlike all the other times, hadn't been able to cover the evidence before being found out. *Baltiel is going to have my hide as soon as he's done playing Lewis and Clark.*

Also like a child, some part of him was desperately casting about for some superior authority to blame. *Someone should have told me not to.* Except that he had worked very hard to abstract himself from any kind of oversight, even the distant watch that Baltiel could have kept over him. Senkovi had been absolutely convinced of the rightness of his own actions, and it had all been wholly amusing until it had become utterly fucked up. It struck him, in a moment of wry self-reflection, that he was the whole terraforming program in miniature, Kern and Baltiel and all of them. *We get them to throw money and resources at us so we can go and be gods somewhere else*, because when you were thirty light years from Earth, who was going to tell you to stop?

And now he was standing in a vast silent tomb of a ship, wearing a cumbersome space suit and knowing he had a remarkably long time before the computer system cleansed itself and bootstrapped itself back into being. Han, Poullister and Maylem were kicking back in the shuttle, anxiously waiting to hear from him. If he had been playing it by the book – insofar as this particular book existed – he should have been with them, doing everything remotely. By hand was better, though, especially as Salome had somehow accessed the remote channels and begun to use the machines as bonus limbs in her spirited attempts to dismantle the *Aegean* to find out what it was and whether she could eat it. Paul had always been Senkovi's favourite student, meaning he had entirely missed how destructively smart Salome was. And that was not to mention Saul, Ruth, Methuselah (renamed from Peter after he got to ten years without showing signs of ageing), Jezebel and . . . well, Senkovi had worked quite hard to ensure that casual scrutiny from a distracted Baltiel did not pick up that he now had forty-three octopi on the staff register, all of them of Biblical nomenclature because of the original Paul, and because once he had Damascus and Nod past the censors he might as well stick with a theme. And because it would have annoyed some of the irritating fundamentalists back home had they ever heard about it, and Senkovi loved nothing more than amusing himself.

Forty-three *octopodes* as Baltiel would say, but Senkovi preferred the feel of the even more incorrect 'octopi' on the tongue, and he was used to pleasing himself first and foremost.

And now he was learning just precisely why he had been considered a good second but only when careful Baltiel was there to hold his leash, because he had royally screwed up.

He had known from long before, from his pets back home, that octopi responded very badly to rigid Pavlovian training. They weren't like rats or pigeons or dogs, who would do the same thing over and over until they had more food than they could eat. Instead, they were curious in a way even dogs weren't, because evolution had gifted them with a profoundly complex toolkit for taking the world apart to see if there was a crab hiding under it. *As I am bloody well now having cause to regret.*

Senkovi had charged up every portable battery he could find, and now had a trolley of devices to get to the centre of the *Aegean*. The centre was where the gravity wasn't, of course, and he had set up his labs there because the octopi got used to not caring much about up and down quickly enough. The Pacific striped octopus had always been his preferred test subject, just as it was his preferred pet. Unlike most of their relatives they were passably social and long-lived, the two major deficiencies that, in Senkovi's opinion, octopus-kind had been cursed with. They were intellectually agile, too, but that was true across the octopus board. Senkovi's personal theory was that the pressure of being in the middle of the food chain was an essential prerequisite for complex intelligence. Like humans (and like Portiid spiders, had he only known), octopuses had developed in a world where they were both hunter and hunted. Top predators, in Senkovi's assessment, were an intellectual dead end.

He had bred several generations, each one further mediated by limited intervention by the Rus-Califi virus. That had been hard, but mostly because he had needed to be ruthless, and Senkovi was soft at heart, especially when it came to the objects of his obsession. The later generations had been markedly better at interacting with abstract devices and oper-ating machinery, and then his lax experimental procedures had borne unexpected fruit. Most of the previous generation had still been around and in contact with his new *enfants terrible*, and they had started picking up the same behaviours, less directed, but still determinedly exploring the virtual space he gave them access to. The major challenge had been developing cephalopod-friendly interface devices, and Senkovi was aware that his own imagination had been the primary constraint with that. For creatures that were a boneless, infinitely mutable hand with independently sensing and thinking fingers, his pitiful controls were wasting most of their potential. *One day they'll design their own.* But that was taking things too far. Or rather, it was stable door after bolting horse because things had already gone too far.

One of his pets had almost opened one of the airlocks before he had jumped in to stop it. Paul had been fighting him for control of the communications suite. Salome had flown wobbling drones through the compartments of the *Aegean*, opening and closing doors and attacking walls with the cutting torches. All just harmless fun, he assured himself, and yet they had reacted swiftly to his attempts to cut them off. He closed one virtual opening and they squeezed through another, multi-tasking in a way that he – and, eventually, the entire human crew – couldn't match. In order for them to do the jobs he would need them for, he had been trying to get them to understand the idea of a virtual environment, somewhere that would be workspace, communications suite and interface if they could only perceive it as they did the physical space around them. He had watched generations simply fail, reacting to light and touch and changes of temperature, but stubbornly refusing to make the leap to that abstract level. And then, without him doing anything in particular, without any obvious prompt or warning, Salome was in the system, and the rest all followed, tank after tank of them teaching each other somehow. Abruptly they could all do the virtual exercises, but they weren't content with that. They expanded their virtual presence as they would their physical one, reaching out to see where the space went, and there they encountered the ship's systems. And the ship's systems, of course, connected to the rest of the ship, the air-filled bit that he and the other humans lived in. He hadn't considered that the bulk of the *Aegean* would be just a further extension of their online playground.

Senkovi and the others had worked for hours at damage control, finding that the invertebrate test subjects had grasped certain principles of the computer system with sufficient force that they could not be pried loose. A running battle between mammal and mollusc had raged, but the *Aegean* was a vast and complex beast and there were no convenient bottlenecks to stave off the invaders from inner space. The octopi had the same untethered access as the human crew, and they were playfully pulling everything apart.

He lowered his crate of toys towards the ship's centre-line until it was just drifting, then he followed after it. The readouts from his HUD told him that the temperature here was dropping, but he had evacuated the space around the tanks so that their heat would take longer to diffuse outwards. This, of course, was the main reason he had stayed behind, out of contact with the human race. He was going to try and save his pets, and he didn't want Han and the others to laugh at him, to recast him from eccentric to pathetic. But, just like the dog lover who goes back into the burning building to save little Floofums, he was going to try and keep some of his experimental subjects alive until the ship came back online.

Baltiel will want them all dead, he knew, but he could handle

Baltiel. He would go against Baltiel if he had to, a full-on war in heaven of angry messages cast across the void.

The nearest tank had shattered, as had the next two. The denizens had, like Senkovi, been too clever for their own good and found some physical egress, and now he'd killed them by evacuating the chamber. He hardened his heart and pushed on until he found one that was intact. His suit lamps shone in, and he saw motion inside, not fleeing the light but approaching it, because the octopi had learned to associate light with entertainment, and the sudden dark and quiet must be profoundly disconcerting for them.

'Hi, Salome.' His voice was loud in his own ears. An alien eye stared at him from within the tank, the skin around it ruffled into angry spikes, awash with red and black pigment as Salome told him precisely what she felt about being denied net access. Senkovi manhandled a heating unit out of the crate and attached it to the tank side. With luck it would keep the water viable until the system was back up. Then he went to the water pump and fumblingly installed a battery unit to keep circulation going, independent of the ship's own mechanisms. Again, it was a stopgap measure. He went on to the next tank.

He wished he could talk to Han, but he'd cut himself off entirely from their shuttle. He hadn't wanted to be bothered by their constant enquiries after his safety. He was Disra Senkovi, the man who was an island. Right now he felt his shores eroding. He wanted them to ask, so that he could be aloof and not answer. Floating in the dark in the bowels of a dead ship, surrounded by the living and the dead of his mollusc pets, it was a terrible time for self-knowledge to kick in. There was nobody but the octopi, though, and he felt they were judging him. He was their higher power, after all, who should have ensured they didn't steal so much fire from heaven that they ended up burning everything to the ground.

He went from tank to tank, restoring warmth and circulation wherever he found live contents. At least a third were already non-viable, either because of the fatal ingenuity of the occupants or because he was too slow. He had thought of the ship as a tomb before, and now it was.

And still the ship was restoring its system, the naive curiosity of the octopi purged from it, and he had hours yet before he could even get a progress report. His own suit was still toasty, but eventually the ship's warmth would start to leach away and he would learn if he had enough batteries to overcome his own hubris. He settled down beside Paul's tank, anchored himself there and turned off his lamps to conserve power.

***

Baltiel waited for the alienness to strike him, stepping from the shuttle's airlock onto the surface of Nod. They could have jockeyed down close enough for the automatics to line up a tunnel between ship and habitat, and Baltiel had nixed the idea because of the slim chance that a slip might have damaged one or the other. In truth, though, he had wanted *this*: the first foot put down onto another living world, the feel of the atmosphere clenching about him, the gravity, the colour of the sunlight . . .

And he stood there at the foot of the ramp and there was nothing, almost nothing. So, it wasn't Earth; neither had the artificial gravity of the *Aegean* been, or the orbiting module (which had never quite matched its parent ship, for no reason they could ever find). The orange-red of the sun was compensated for by the visor display of his helmet. He could look across the flat expanse of the great salt marsh, all its rivulets and pools and rocky ridges, out to the great darkness of the sea, and he might just be at a somewhat unattractive beach back home. The suit was insulating him from everything; not just a potentially hazardous atmosphere and the radiation of an alien star, but the smells, the sounds, the unalloyed sights that would make it all real. It might just be an underwhelming simulation.

But we're here. And perhaps it will come yet, waking to a new rhythm, seeing the life first hand.

The others were backing up behind him so he set off, a proud stride no matter how he was feeling about it. Or as proud a stride as the cumbersome suit would allow. Even with its servos smoothing his movements he felt he was lumbering like some antique movie monster. Lante, Lortisse and Rani followed him, a little shambling convoy over the rocks. The going was slippery and uneven; their boots were constantly locking in place, soles moulding to fit the terrain. It was an undignified first parade for humanity, but at least the onlooking aliens were unlikely to take much notice. Baltiel stopped short of the habitat, waving Lante to enter and check that internal conditions matched up to the installation's readouts. He would be last in, he decided. He would stand out here and take in the landscape, and hope for that feeling to hit him.

Nothing between him and the sea rose past his waist. There were slimy, muddy humps and there were rocks worn down by the constant patience of the tides. Between them was a vast network of hollows and channels, a single body of water at high tide, a thousand, thousand separate ponds at low. It was a complex environment, transformed from moment to moment, the ambassador between the ecologies of the depths and those of the dry interior. If there was anywhere Nodan life might have become complex, then surely it was here.

There were fliers overhead, like gulls. Perhaps they would be the seeds of intelligence. They were active predators; he'd seen footage of them swooping down on luckless marsh-dwellers. They had a hydrostatic skeleton like most life on Nod and flew by rapid inflation and deflation of their broad vanes, a process that looked like stop-motion photography, and like they shouldn't have any business in the air. They were the most aggressively active things on the planet, the airborne lords of Nod.

On the ground there were plenty of things for them to eat, which would likely be the main subject of Baltiel's studies for the years to come. Hundreds of different lineages of radially-organized creeping and swimming things called the marsh home, from the microscopic to the tortoises that could reach three feet high. Not actual tortoises, of course, or even much like them, but they secreted stony shells and lumbered about on tubular feet, placidly grazing, and the name had stuck. The fliers obviously liked the taste of them, when they could winkle parts of them from their mobile fortresses. Baltiel watched one now, mindlessly plodding over the path he'd taken from the shuttle. It had six legs, exuded and retracted in turn, and six tentacle limbs it used to scrape and gather its harvest of sessile plant-like creatures. As he watched, the thing slowly let out an arm to touch the very ground Baltiel had trodden. Was some part of its limited sensorium encountering an alien chemical, the residue of his boot soles perhaps? The tortoise seemed to spend a lot of time considering the possibility, but then it set off again, sloping down into the next pool in search of sustenance it could understand.

He turned and followed the others into the habitat.

They didn't seem to feel the same sense of anticlimax. The air was full of their chatter as they checked in with Skai. Baltiel called up the latest on the *Aegean* and Senkovi's idiot games. The ship was still dark, Senkovi's crew were exchanging anxious communiques with Skai's people about what happened if it didn't light back up on schedule. *We go in and salvage what's left*, was the obvious answer to that. *We find Disra's body.* Nobody was saying it; everyone was thinking it.

Lante gave him a grin. She was a heavyset woman, her hair cropped almost to her skull, her skin ashen in the artificial light. Rani was shorter and darker, always slightly dishevelled; even standing there in her suit it showed in the cant of her helmet. Lortisse was a tall man, half a head over his commander, with a dark beard held back by a net to stop it fritzing with his HUD controls. These were Baltiel's people, his disciples. Their names would appear in the history books, under his own.

Then Rani was frowning. The expression made it look as though she'd just remembered something she meant to pack. *Too late to go back for it now.*

He sent her a query over their local net and she linked him in to a transmission from Skai.

'Repeat,' he instructed, rather than having to replay and catch up.

'I said we've been getting the strangest signal from Earth. It was only on the news channels first, but now it's on all of them, every frequency.' Skai's voice was glitchy with static. 'One moment it was the usual war stuff, then it's just this—'

Her image in their HUD froze, the expression of mild puzzlement on her face drawn out and out until it became unsettling.

'Skai?' Baltiel pinged her, sending a request to connect, and received a scatter of contradictory responses from the network. The others were casting sidelong glances, trying their own diagnostics and getting nowhere.

For a moment Skai's image was alive again, skipping straight from mild puzzlement to mid-panic. '—od, the system, it . . .' – stutter, freeze – 'contact with the shuttle. Han, Han, do you . . .' A staccato pattern of flashes that hurt the eye, as though some message was being beamed through their pupils to scratch madly at their retinas. '—coming down . . . ife support, someone . . . ease.' They had no visuals now, just that one woman's voice, torn up by static, far away and getting further. In the background was interference and feedback and, if Baltiel stretched his imagination, terrified screaming. 'Anyone?' Skai shouted. '*Anyone?*' But there was no-one, and a moment later not even her.

Baltiel and his crew stared at each other, not quite processing what had happened. Each of them kept trying to connect to the module, receiving nothing but static, white noise they couldn't parse.

'The hell . . . ?' Lante's was the first human voice to break the quiet. Everything they had heard, they heard via their comms implants, which should have kept them all one happy family even at this distance.

'Is this one of Senkovi's jokes or something?' Lortisse added. He didn't like Senkovi much.

Rani was tweaking the parameters of their instruments to try and get past whatever was blocking transmissions. Right then, nobody really thought anything had gone *wrong*, not with anything save communications.

Baltiel took a deep breath, knowing he had to make a command decision but too short of information to know what it should be.

The lights died, first the lambent illumination around them, then the dull red emergency lamps, and then, last of all, the purple glow of the screen Rani was looking into. They were left with a residual amber radiance from everywhere and nowhere; the sunlight from outside leaking a little through the fabric of the habitat.

Baltiel pinged Rani or tried to. He had no sense of signal sent, certainly no confirmation it had been received. He queried his suit. Nothing. He moved, feeling the full weight of all that cumbersome protection. The servos ground at the joints, refusing to assist him.

A white beam flicked on: Rani had an emergency torch and was flashing it around. Baltiel saw her mouth moving and lurched closer.

'Suit's dead!' He read her lips as much as anything, in the shaking light.

'How much air?' Lortisse must be half deafening himself. His voice sounded like someone in another room with the door closed.

'Can't tell!' Rani yelled distantly back. 'All dead.'

Baltiel went to signal that they should have at least eight hours each, but of course there were no comms. In-suit exposure to the outside had only been planned for the few steps between shuttle and habitat, but he was diligent, as were they all. The suits had been topped up, that much he remembered. Except he was feeling dreadfully short of breath already, which was impossible. The pumps should have their own power, should be independent of any failure of the suit's systems.

Unless they had been explicitly told to shut down. It was theoretically possible, as part of a maintenance cycle. *Everything's shut down. An attack. Nothing's working except us.*

'Shuttle!' Lortisse shouted, lurching for the habitat airlock, which stayed resolutely closed. He fumbled for the manual release, winching the near door open, shuddering and gasping until he fell to his knees. Grimly, Baltiel took a leaden step over and found the emergency release on the man's helmet, cracking it open so that Lortisse exchanged the dying air in his helmet for the slowly dying air of the habitat. He followed by removing his own, gasping at the rubber-smelling pocket of atmosphere he suddenly had access to, and soon enough they'd all done the same.

'The hell?' Lante repeated, clearly audible now they'd all decided to do the dumb thing together. The other two looked as though they'd already got it, Baltiel decided – Rani definitely, Lortisse just piecing it together now.

'We were shut down.' Because it needed to be said and he was in charge. 'An attack, from home. An attack from thirty years ago. The war . . .'

'We need to get comms back,' Rani said. 'The module . . .'

'We need to survive.' Baltiel was already taking inventory. They had food here. They had water, though they couldn't reprocess waste until they were able to restart that part of the system. They had limited air. Could they get the scrubbers and the pumps online? Could they get access to the suit tanks? Again, he tried to link to the others, to throw the problem to them and have their minds work on it in that virtual space between them. Denied, again denied.

'Air first, comms second,' he decided. 'Perhaps the shuttle comms survived, if they weren't being used.' Except the sanest, grimmest part of his mind was pointing out that the comms on the shuttle were open all the time; of course they were, why wouldn't they be? What's the worst that could happen?

'Why us?' Lante moaned.

Maybe it wasn't just us. But there was time for that kind of speculation later.

In the end they were able to jury rig the suits to get the tanks pumping again, which was fine except they could barely communicate unless they touched faceplates. The habitat's pumps remained stubbornly silent. Rani reckoned she could get them working, circumvent all the parts of the system that had clenched and died at Earth's faraway command, but perhaps not in a time frame that would be useful.

Baltiel had volunteered to go out and try the shuttle. They lost a roomful of atmosphere letting him out and he was wondering whether he would ask to be let back in. The shuttle was as dead as everything else, he discovered with no surprise. The airlock was locked down, even the manual release wouldn't shift it. He hammered on the metal of the door, indulging his fury on the inanimate so he could go back and be reasonable for his fellow human beings. When he was done ranting for the sole audience of his own ears, he looked round to see several of the tortoises watching this spectacle, this doomed alien invader come to their world to die. They had simple eyes at the lower edge of their shells, his memory reminded him, but complex stalked eyes that emerged from the blowhole in the apex of their shell, because they needed to watch out for the fliers. Now those eyes were goggling at him, making him feel that he was letting the side down. *Just moved in and what would the neighbours say?*

So, he marched laboriously back to the habitat and banged on the airlock until they let him in. By then, Rani had performed miracles with her suit battery and an antenna array and had what she claimed was a working transmitter/receiver. Except nobody out there was transmitting or acknowledging receipt of anything they were sending. The module was silent; the *Aegean* was silent; the shuttle Senkovi had sent his colleagues off in was silent.

The non-functional habitat was a ticking clock on their lives, but they were on a planet, within atmospheric pressure. If the module's systems had shut down, how long would Skai have? Baltiel was acutely aware that every single part of their life in space was mediated by computers.

'Keep trying,' he told Rani. 'The rest of us, let's get the habitat air up.'

How much later was it, then? No clocks, an alien world (the day-night cycle ran to just short of thirty-four hours and seventeen minutes, Baltiel recalled). No suit gauges, either, and so he made the command decision that they'd run out of air soon, as though it was a choice, a thing he could mandate. They hadn't managed to unfreeze the air system. One emergency tank had been hauled inside, tapped, used up. Lortisse's frustrated brute-force efforts had resulted in another tank venting its contents into the heedless alien atmosphere beyond. Without the scrubbers and recyclers online, none of it would matter. It wasn't as though the habitat just had huge reserves of air; it was supposed to keep churning through it, turning CO_2 into O_2 with a side of C.

As they hadn't managed to – Lante's desperate pun – breathe life into that system, none of the rest of it really mattered.

And so Baltiel had made his command decision. He would take the plunge, be the guinea pig. Partly he was responsible: his ship, he'd go down with it. Partly, though, he would be first. His penance but also his privilege.

Here he was then, another airlock-full of stale, used-up air vented by the crude manual levers. His suit, smelling of sour Baltiel even to him now, smelling of sweat and even more of the urine it no longer recycled. The interior of the habitat smelled a whole lot worse. They'd all used the facilities but whatever psychotic electronic weapon had been unleashed hadn't spared the plumbing. His suit was hot and cumbersome, the servos fighting his every movement, designed to protect him but now just a tomb in waiting.

He looked towards the orange sun as it sank towards the mountains in what had just been another direction once but, now humans were here, would forever be *west*.

Or maybe not forever. Just as long as we're here. So not that long, most likely.

The others were watching him, not through screens and cameras with complex readouts of his health, but through the darkened glass of a porthole they'd wrestled the cover from.

He took a deep breath, regretted it, reached up and unlatched his helmet. The lack of warning alarms was a curious relief. One dead system he wouldn't miss.

He lifted the helmet off and placed it, with groaning effort, on the ground. That done, he stared up at the dimming orange sky and took a deep breath.

Salt; ammonia; ozone; but beyond all of these a melange of smells he had no names for. Things decaying by unfamiliar biological pathways, sharp living perfumes, hot smells, red and black smells. He wished more than anything in the world to be synaesthetic right then, so he would have some extra way to process the information his senses were giving him. He had expected the alien air to be pungent, ghastly. Instead it was heady with odours his body could do nothing with. They smelled like something, like nothing. They were cocktails of molecules his nose had never needed to identify before.

He heard peeping like miniscule baby birds from around his feet. A flier flailed overhead, clacking angrily at him. Something keened shrilly from far off. The tortoises gurgled as they moved, as though their innards were churning wet rocks together. He had not known. The drones and remotes had never heard these songs, smelled these weird odours. The atmosphere was heavy, dense and humid and hot like the tropics, save when the wind gusted from seawards and the acrid salt reek enveloped him and cooled him and stung his eyes.

His breathing was speeding up; he felt the panic point of hyperventilation at his shoulder and forced himself to slow. There was less oxygen, but there should be enough, according to the numbers on the dead computers. A human from Earth could breathe unaided. Long exposure would result in a build-up of various chemicals the human body couldn't process, but better than suffocating, eh? And he could detox later when he got back to the . . . back to the . . . Well, there was nowhere to get back to, was there?

He fought his lungs again, as they grasped for more sustenance than the Nodan atmosphere had to offer. His muscles were aching, too, working with that just-too-strong gravity.

But he lived. He breathed in alien air, the same air that all these myriad little monsters depended on for their own incompatible metabolisms.

He turned back to the others, or to the porthole behind which he must trust they still were. It was hard even to make a thumbs up signal in the suit but he did it. They must have been able to see his grin. He was going to die, but he'd done it now. He was Nod's first citizen castaway. He felt a crazy streak of hilarity rush through him, and then panic because what if that was the atmosphere getting to him? Yusuf Baltiel was not a man given to sudden attacks of irrational joy! And yet he owned it, claimed it as his own. He had found the aliens; he had saved them from the depredations of his own mission, and now he would die amongst them, now or later or in a hundred years, a mad hermit at the end of the human universe, talking to the tortoises and the little peeping things that lived in the black sand.

He lumbered back and entered the airlock, which he'd left open because, well, why not, exactly? He'd left his helmet outside. Perhaps some alien crab would creep out and claim it as a home. He wished the hypothetical creature well.

The others looked in through the airlock hatch with no expression he could name. They would watch him like a hawk now, to see if something poisoned him, or if there was a planetwide plague that could somehow jump not just species but entire evolutionary trees. Working slowly, feeling the gravity twisting his joints, he stripped off his suit entire, letting the dead weight of the thing fold to the ground as though he was shedding a cocoon and entering a new stage of his life cycle.

He was going to try to sleep, there in the airlock and open

to the elements, but then Lortisse was banging on the window, miming a winch. They wanted him to close the outer door. He couldn't see why but, apparently, they were going to let him in early and that was a clear breach of his orders. Something else had obviously gone wrong.

Baltiel didn't want to be commander, just then. He wanted to be a castaway without any hopes or cares at all, and just enjoy the alienness of the air. A spark lit in his mind at the banging, though. He was responsible, after all. It was his mission, even in defeat. He signalled his understanding and laboured away at the little winch until the outer door was shut and sealed, then stood there as they pumped Earth air in and Nod air out. The Earth air smelled worse, filled with bad odours his body was all too ready to identify.

'What?' he demanded. The others all had their helmets off, suit tanks empty, the last of the emergency supply slowly going stale between them.

He didn't need to ask any more. He heard it. Rani's make-shift radio had a signal. It was tinny and crimped by static, but there was a human voice out there.

'Hello? Someone say something, won't you? I know I screwed up, but come on!' A tiny, far-off Disra Senkovi, coming to them from one planet away on a ship he had only now brought back to life. 'Hey, boss, what the hell? Han, you can come back now. Hello?'

There were other shuttles on the *Aegean*. Not close enough that the Earth air would last, but Baltiel had taken his life in his hands to prove that wasn't the end of the world. He held on a moment longer, trying to do the maths, but eventually he just smiled and shunted Rani out of her seat so he could speak to the expedition's prodigal son.

6.

We

have

sampled strange molecules.

These-of-We taste stuff never known, break it down, build it up, nothing like anything, toxic, energy-rich, fascinating.

These-of-We recreate these stimuli for Others-of-We as we meet, interchanging ideas and selves.

None-of-We have encountered any-such, not anywhere.

Something new has come into the world.

PRESENT 1
ROAD TO DAMASCUS

1.

Once upon a time there was a civilization on a distant planet. The people of this civilization knew many things, including how to travel to other stars and remake the planets they found there, within tolerance, into places where they could walk and breathe the air.

But they were fractious, and just as they had reached up to seize the stars, they fell upon one another and all their work was destroyed. Almost all.

One of their scientists, the greatest mind of her age—

Or so she says.

She does, and I am not in the mood to measure legs with her over it. You have decades enough, but Portiid life is too short.

She was named Avrana Kern, and she had a plan to exalt the beasts of her world so that they would know and adore their creator. She made a world for them, and released a virus that would expedite their evolution towards such a state of adulation, and she had a consignment of monkeys, and of all of these things, that last failed in its delivery, for the wicked who made war on their fellows on her home also brought the war to her. So Kern was left in her tiny capsule, awaiting the call from the world below, which was devoid of monkeys but rich in many other forms of life. For many thousands of years she orbited, so that what was left was not, deny it as she might, much of Avrana Kern at all, as opposed to the computer systems she had bargained with for eternal life.

And when the call came, it came from that world's new mistresses, the most intelligent, the most emotionally sophisticated, the most elegant of all its many beings.

Now you're just bragging.

We must assume that any life we meet will value sophistication, intelligence and elegance, or what is life for? Anyway, I continue.

Unknown to the Portiids, for as such they would come to be known, visitors were coming to their world. The civilization that had given rise to them had fallen and risen again, and at last, on the brink of extinction from their own vices—

I'm going to put my foot down.

And if you do, it will only prove my point. It will sound like a hundred thousand ants in confusion. And I continue—

Will you at least preserve some dignity for the human species?

(A small fiddling of the palps to express resignation, like a sigh.)

Those who could, set out in a desperate vessel chasing their knowledge of the places their ancestors had walked so very long ago, and so they came to the world under the stewardship of Avrana Kern, or what was left of her. At first, they came in need, and at last they came in war, for they could not understand the Portiids and saw them as monsters, and neither side could communicate with each other, and the remnant of Avrana Kern was mistrustful and remembered only how her great project had been betrayed.

That is a very diplomatic way of putting it.

I count diplomacy amongst my many Understandings.

The Portiids took the virus that had aided their evolution, which had allowed them to know one another and come together rather than living out their lives as single hunters, and introduced it to their creators, who were also the virus's creators, gifting them with the understanding that here, too, were minds who looked out and sought to know the universe. And so it was that peace was made between the humans and the Portiids, and a new golden age dawned, and the humans would forever after be not just humans but Humans, which is a far better thing.

And so it was, later, that the combined knowledge of these peoples would lead to a vessel setting out from Avrana Kern's world to voyage to other distant places where once humans had set foot and remade worlds, for faint signals had been detected from such places, and they were eager to know new intelligences and meet with them in peace.

Helena Holsten Lain regards her companion, now crouching in an attitude Helena knows to read as 'expectant'. Portiid spider communications, being a combination of eight stamping feet and the waving of two fuzzy palps, are always something of a performance. Helena feels quite mute in comparison, her body language coarse and huge, her lone voice lacking nuance. She was born into a civilization where her people were a tiny minority, a curiosity, surrounded by a vast population of spiders who speak to senses Humans barely even have. She was a mere child when she began working on that barrier between the intelligent species of Kern's World – to overcome it in a way that the mere sharing of an engineered virus could not. The journey has a few more steps in it, true, but she has just listened to Portia tell an imaginative, biased account of their world's history, and her gloves and optical and cerebral implants translated most of it in real time, complete with subtext, personality and humour. Possibly a fair chunk of what she received was best guesses and gaps filled with human-equivalents that were square pegs for round holes, but it was leaps and bounds beyond anything she had grown up with.

'Still,' she says, 'you're going to have to find some way to not make us sound so awful.' She subvocalizes into her own implants, her fingers resting ever-so-lightly on the deck, and her gloves patter out what she hopes is a good approximation of her meaning direct to the listening feet of her colleague.

'But you are awful,' comes the translated response, and Helena feels a leap of triumph, because, even if some meaning is lost along the way, she's *talking*, even *chatting* with a Portiid spider in a way no Human has ever been able to save the sainted (and mostly artificial) Avrana Kern herself.

***

There is an itch at the back of his head. Not the itch of the surgical scars, which an interesting cocktail of medication is keeping at a respectable distance, but something inside his skull. Meshner concentrates on it, trying to draw it out, his own eyes sightless and dark because seeing actual real things is too much of a distraction and his eyelid discipline suffers when he's distracted.

'Not coming,' he announces. 'Give me a clue.' He hears the tinny little sound of his lab assistant relaying his words to his partner in experimentation, and then that unique exhalation which is Fabian, said partner, going into a spectacular arachnid convulsion for the specific purpose of telling his Human confederate, Meshner, just how frustrated he is right now. Portiid spiders are a long way from their ancestral state, both in size and biology. The original diminutive jumping spider did not engage in active respiration, whereas the current model funds its life by expanding its abdomen to drag air in over the elegant filigree of its book-lungs. What they don't do, as a rule, is sigh. By dint of great effort, however, Fabian has learned how to breathe in precisely such a way as to convey a Human emotion. Fabian and Meshner have been partners in crime, scientifically speaking, for a very long time. Despite the barriers to communication, they have developed an idiolect of their own, mostly devoted to complaining.

Then comes the rustle-shuffle of Fabian's response to the translating lab assistant, and the assistant's uncanny-valley voice saying, 'Picture the ocean.' The assistant was designed and embodied as part of Avrana Kern's experiments in relating more closely to her chosen people, the Portiids. Coded to act as a spider male, it also speaks to Meshner in a male version of Kern's usual tones, which he continues to find disconcerting.

The ocean . . . The idea passes deeper into Meshner's mind in search of that spectral itch, and for a moment he has it: sunlight – dawn? – gleaming on water. He gets the impression of structure, wood and webbing, perhaps a pier? Shadows loom at the brink of his vision, hard-edged.

A faint rustle comes to him, Fabian making notes on Meshner's brain activity and the data transfer from the ugly blocky implants that now make up a band around the back of Meshner's head.

The brief moment of vision is gone, and Meshner knows his own excitement, and then frustration, conspired to drive it away. There is information waiting to feed into his brain, but his mind is an unruly mess and so it cannot find a way to its proper neurological targets.

Ocean, ocean . . . Images are there, but he knows them for his own memories and clears his mind again, using mindfulness techniques developed from scratch. *What if I suppressed my own memory-accessing ability?* he wonders. *Could that work?* There will be drugs that could render him an amnesiac for the duration, surely. Perhaps in that void, the alien impressions will come more naturally.

'Couldn't you give me something more . . . individual?' he murmurs. 'I don't know if I'm getting anything through of yours.'

Again Fabian skitters in terse communication, and their assistant's off-male voice reports, 'I wanted you to have something that would fit naturally with Human experience, to make it easy.'

'It's not working . . .' But even as he says it, his mind whirling with annoyance and resentment and the thought of another session wasted, he has a clear sight: a sea of a million blues – no, not even blues, a whole spectrum of colours that simply do not plug into the visual range he is familiar with. A sky that shimmers with the sun's radiation. A ground beneath his feet that breathes softly with the traffic of a whole city at his back. Except his feet, his feet were in all directions, his back, his eyes, his *eyes*—

Meshner feels a sudden wave of nausea. The image, the sensory feedback, is gone in an instant, and yet his regular body has not come back to him. His proprioception goes haywire, all sense of where his body is, what *shape* it is, utterly deserting him. He opens his mouth to speak and his limbs spasm with palsy, sending him toppling backwards – had he been sitting, standing? – thrashing on the ground. His teeth snap and a sharp jolt of pain shoots through him as he bites his tongue.

Then a sudden rush of flattening artificial calm bullies its way into his mind like a thug, beating down the rush of panic and cooling his blood. Meshner opens his eyes, knowing that he'll have a killer headache when the drugs wear off, and also that he might just have irreparably damaged his brain.

His colleagues regard him anxiously, or at least the fidget of Fabian's palps conveys anxiety in a manner even a Human can understand. Fabian is a brindled black and grey spider with a body about the size of Meshner's head, currently hunched over a spindle-shaped console with four legs making jerky adjustments to the program as he tries to mitigate whatever damage has just been done to Meshner's mind. Beside him is the lab assistant he has taken to calling Artifabian. It has the general shape of a small Portiid spider, much like Fabian himself, but constructed entirely out of plastic, alternatively russet, transparent and iridescent. It is a robot of sorts with a dumbed-down copy of Avrana Kern's personality inside it, splintered off from the ship's. If it is genuinely concerned, there is no way of knowing.

Meshner stares at them, waiting for his eyes to focus properly. The headaches are starting now, the ones the medication never seems to touch. He suspects it's all psychosomatic, his mind deciding that he damn well *should* be in pain given the stunt he just pulled. That doesn't make it better, it only means he can't actually use anything to get the pain to stop.

'How's my head?' he asks, and Artifabian translates for him. They could just use the ship, but having this one servitor dedicated to their partnership means it learns their figures of speech and mannerisms, its approximations closer and closer to conveying the complexities of each other's language. Meshner is fascinated by the way the device mimics Portiid attitudes. With Fabian it is plainly one rung down on the ladder, its stance polite without being quite deferential. When a female Portiid turns up, it is instantly obsequious, more so than Fabian, who is something of a boundary-pusher as far as his gender is concerned. Meshner has read simplified children's histories of the spider civilization, vocal in explaining that, *these* days, everything is fine and male spiders are allowed to play a full role in society. In practice, even Human eyes can see it isn't quite as advertised. He has no doubt today's Fabian has far better prospects than the Fabian of a century ago, but the playing field still needs some rolling before it is level.

'I'm seeing inflammation along the neural pathways, some small swelling around the occipital lobe,' come the relayed conclusions of Fabian. 'Not good, Meshner.' His name becomes a cavalier little flick of the spider's left palp, as though the creature is tossing a hat at a peg without looking at it. Portiid communications are short on those distinct meaning-to-movement correspondences but names are an exception.

'Explains why I still can't see straight,' Meshner complains. 'There was something *there*, though. I had a sniff of it.' He eyes the spider. 'Hmm?'

He recognizes the gesture Fabian makes, because it is the spider imitating him biting his knuckles, a piece of Human body language the Portiid had picked up on. It means that he, Meshner, is obfuscating and Fabian knows it.

'We'll go again next dawn,' he decides stubbornly. 'Dawn' is a shipwide fiction, of course, but Portiids like their day/night cycles even more than Humans do. 'I saw the sea,' he adds, although he can't say, in his heart of hearts, whether the sea had been truly from Fabian's memories. 'Can't you give me something . . . more Portiid? Something I'll know is definitely yours?'

Fabian taps his palps together with an audible *tok*, a gesture Meshner has seen no other spiders make. It means he's thinking. The ship's archives have a whole library of what the best translation renders as *Understandings*, a cornerstone of the Portiid civilization. They are genetic memories, Meshner knows, rendered into something that can be inherited, copied and implanted by a fluke of the pervasive nanovirus that guided the spiders' evolution. If Fabian needs knowledge or a skill, he can simply have it introduced to his brain and, very shortly, be an expert. Meshner covets the facility, both for the way it could make any individual into a polymath, and for the bridge it could build between humanity and their new best friends. He knows that Helena and the linguistics crowd are going about the same task by very different and non-invasive means, but his way is better. If he can only get it to work. If he doesn't scramble his brains trying. He is lucky to have a lab partner like Fabian who isn't averse to risk-taking. But then Fabian covets whatever academic success looks like to a spider and, as he's a male, that means he has to go twice as far on half the support. Fabian is doubtless delighted he found such an obliging test subject.

Then Artifabian's meek pose changes to something bold and dominant, so that Fabian himself instinctively gives ground. The spirit of Avrana Kern – or at least the dominant facet that inhabits the ship's complex computer system – has seized control of this errant splinter in order to interact with its crew.

'The Ship's Mistress has sent out a general alarm,' comes

that female voice from Artifabian's speakers, even as the machine's feet tap out an analogous message to Fabian. 'All crew to the bridge, apparently. We have made a discovery.'

***

Waking the crew had begun in measured stages after the *Voyager* passed by the barren outer planets of the new system, homing in on the busy buzz of the signals coming from closer to the star. It had begun with Kern – or the semi-biological computer system that identified as Kern – bootstrapping herself up from basic functions into her full and ascerbic personality, then progressed through the crew roster based on the ship's requirements: maintenance, medical, command, then everyone else. Both Helena Holsten Lain and Meshner Osten Oslam should have been in this last category, but both had employed special pleading to be woken early to work on their personal projects while the *Voyager* decelerated.

The *Voyager* has changed since they left their mutual home in search of a voice among the stars. Unlike the ancestral ships humans had travelled in, it has a fluid structure, forged from materials that can stretch and grow at Kern's whim. On departure it had still mimicked what Kern remembered spaceships looking like, long and dynamic with a ring section for the crew's waking moments. Now it is something more like a manta ray, its delicate wings extended and fitted out as organic solar panels for when they near the star. The crew assembles in a set of bolas-like structures Kern grew for them, that whirl in an orbit just ahead of the wingspan as though they are specimens in a centrifuge. Despite the best Human-Portiid medical tech, everyone is finding the resumed gravity onerous.

Helena and Portia arrive just in time for the ship's commander to address them. The *Voyager's* leader is old now – Portiids don't live more than about three decades and Helena knows the commander kept herself awake longer than was her due, in order to watch over her crew. She is an angular spider with great tufted plumes over her main eyes that give her an owlish look. She is also a Portia, or at least her name is so similar to Helena's friend that a mere Human has difficulty in distinguishing between them.

A lot of the other Humans there are looking more than a little groggy, woken more recently or slower to recover. Helena remembers her grandfather complaining about coming out of cold sleep on the old *Gilgamesh*, that had brought humans to Kern's World. To hear him tell it, it had all been waking up and then mad chaos and then going back to sleep again. Duly cautioned, Helena put more time into modifying her biochemistry and training her body, and practically bounced out of cold storage the moment they woke her. Portia herself confessed that waking for the spiders was a profoundly uncomfortable process. She was only able to work with Helena because Kern had given them a head start and only come to the Humans later. The Understandings that the Portiids rely on so heavily became disconnected during long periods of sleep, to return haphazardly days after waking. It was, Portia tried to explain, like constantly forgetting who you were, forever reaching for knowledge that was not there.

Helena shuffles to her place, sure-footed in the padded socks all the Human crew use because shod footsteps on the springy floors sound like shouting to the Portiids' vibrational hearing. She wears the standard crew uniform that Kern fabricated: a shirt and trousers of pale green, the cloth filmy and thin because the ship is warm and humid just like the planet they left behind.

Portia is already signalling and chatting with a pair of spiders on the Receiving team who have been up longer than anyone, cataloguing the rich signals from within the system and trying to make sense of them whilst keeping a few eyes on the active and passive sensors to ensure that the locals don't sneak up on anybody. The literal translation of their department is 'alarmed feet', which still makes Helena giggle. It is also a salutary lesson that there are different layers of translation, and literal is not always the most useful.

She crouches and puts her hands to the floor, letting her gloves intercept the vibrational chatter between the Portiids, and her implants turn *that* into something resembling speech. Portia asks the two operators what's up; they are bursting with the knowledge that they have detected an approaching object, almost certainly artificial. They are about to get their first look at the handiwork of the locals.

By then Old Portia, the ship's mistress, is speaking. 'I'm sure you've all been waiting for a gathering such as this. Anyone with any curiosity will understand that this is a heavily active, populated system. The volume and complexity of signals demonstrates that there is an advanced civilization based here, and the character of them shows a great many hallmarks of pre-collapse Earth technology and protocols. We may have here the secondmost direct line of descent from our founding culture.' That is the spoken translation of the captain's message, as relayed by the artificial ghost of Avrana Kern. With her fingers touching the floor, however, and her eyes on the flicking palps of the captain, Helena simultaneously receives the original. Her cybernetics and her organic brain provide her with, *What this is, we have contact as you will have all expected. Signal traffic from in-system is dense and diverse enough to suggest a space-faring civilization that is still using Old Empire structure for the basis of its communications.* Kern is both wordier and considerably free in how she passes on the concepts, and that sort of thing is exactly why Helena is working on her pet project. She feels a stab of annoyance at the coda the computer decided to add for its Human audience, to remind them just who was the *first* line of descent, in Kern's own view, whilst feeling some bleak amusement that the utterly inaccurate phrase 'Old Empire' that her ancestors used to describe their own lost ancestors survives as a spider term of reference even after Kern hunted it to extinction amongst Humans.

'We are about to have our first look at an artifact of this inner-world's culture,' Old Portia continues crisply. 'Our instruments have detected a fellow-traveller in these reaches, an artificial body moving outwards at a considerable rate.' Around them, tightly-furled plastic roses open up into screens showing enhanced views of the interplanetary traveller they are closing on. There is notation in the neat letters of Imperial C, which is the written lingua franca amongst the colonists, and in the slipshod and chaotic-looking spider notation, but the floor also buzzes with technical data for those members of the crew with the feet to receive it, and for Helena. Perhaps because they had their Understandings to lean on, Portiid writing systems are considerably less efficient than human. For new information, they prefer directly informative interfaces where possible.

Helena assumes at first she has mistranslated what she is receiving, and double-checks against the screens.

How big? Portia scratches out, soft enough that it is for Helena's hands only. *An error, do you think?*

The *Voyager* has made quite a sharp diversion to get closer to the oncoming object's trajectory, ever since initial readings showed something other than a mere errant asteroid. Kern has husbanded their energy and fuel all the way through the cold dark between solar systems, but the ship's scoops have replenished their stores from the rich cloud of ice, gas and dust that formed the edge of their destination system's orbiting disc, allowing all manner of costly manoeuvres. She constructed remote probes in her internal factories and sent them ahead on one-way journeys, each with a tiny splinter of herself copied into their cores. Now the data comes back, and nobody can quite understand what they are looking at.

The approaching artifact is mostly spherical, with one very obvious exception. The outer surface is studded with a regular net of nodes that might have been sensors or engines or even weapons once, but are now little more than scarred, ice-frosted stumps and pits. One side of it has ruptured, and the innards have come out in a vast, jagged spray that flowers into fantastical spines and curling tentacles as though some unthinkable oceanic horror has been killed halfway through hatching out of an egg twenty-seven kilometres across.

Ice, the probes confirm. Its eruption from the interior of the object might be the result of a fissure in the unknown surface material, or else the freezing of a liquid centre might have burst the membrane open with its expansion. Either way the colossal, frozen eruption threw the entire object's centre of gravity so that the sphere and its miles-long plume now spin about one another with ponderous grace.

The ice is opaque white over most of its surface, but the

keen eyes of the probes find shadows within. Under magnification, some seem to be recognizably fish, others are of a more uncertain shape, although that might also be the work of the expansion.

An artificial moon. A moon of water, Portia suggests. *Ornamental perhaps? And is that damage we see from after it was flung into space or the cause of it?*

Helena lets her palms touch the deck and subvocalizes, 'Don't let speculation run away with you,' letting the mechanisms in her gloves make their best translation in precisely calibrated touch-speak, while the white dots on her thumbs add palp-emphasis. It is halting at best, and Portia says she sounds as though she is 'giddy with sweet sap,' but progress is progress.

The probes get the best look they can at the whirling planetoid, but they lack the ability to reverse their course and follow it, and soon it is on its endless way, heading along the plane of the solar system on a course that will one day see it vanish forever in the great beyond.

Curious, says one of the Alarmed Feet operators.

Uninformative, the other complains, with a twitch of her palps that conveyed the subtext, *and I had better things to be doing with my time.*

The captain calls up the relevant figures, wavering over whether to pursue the ruined object or let it vanish away: relative momentum, energy consumption . . . probably these quoditian elements don't sway her as much as the clear radio evidence that there is a great deal more of interest further into the system. Her very silence and stillness is her decision, as physics whisks the object beyond their reach. They are going onwards. And yet . . .

If we push on, we will pluck so many strings we can expect a response by the locals, she addresses them. *Analysis of energy signatures leaves open the possibility that they may be more technologically advanced, and also that they may either be fighting a war amongst themselves or be naturally exuberant and wasteful in the way they burn energy.* Helena is having difficulty keeping up with the rapid speech of the captain and words from Kern's version keep creeping in. She fights to concentrate.

Caution dictates we not risk the entire mission by proceeding further as a whole or broadcasting our position. I'm having us move into the shadow of the closest outer planet. The screens begin to display the relevant telemetry. *However, we cannot come all this way and not make contact. I've ordered a segment of the ship be prepared as an independent scout fitted for a small crew. I'd prefer a crew made up entirely of Portiids.* The captain is using the Portiid's own name for themselves, of course, meaning something like *We who know best,* and Kern's translation omits this digression entirely. *However, there is a small chance that the civilization is both human and unaugmented by the Unity infection, in which case Human ambassadors will be essential.*

Small chance? Helena throws in, through her palms.

One of the sensor operators cocks a cephalothorax to eye her sidelong. *There are no human representations within the decoded visual data that forms a large part of the signals we have intercepted,* she explains. *Mostly it is just rapidly changing colours and irregular 3D shapes. Very fascinating!*

The captain continues, *The scout will have a facet of the Avrana Kern construct but this will have necessarily fewer resources to draw upon. I am selecting crew and Human companions who have demonstrated their ability to interact with each other inde-*

pendently. This will be high-risk. No guarantee that we will be able to assist if things go wrong. Participation is therefore voluntary. This is said with a brief rearing motion, the captain's first two pairs of legs held high for just a second. It suggests that anyone backing out will lose status with the captain – hence with the mission as a whole. Portiids place great value on boldness, an archetypal female trait for them with a whole dictionary of social expectations spilling out from it. The captain probably didn't mean to qualify her words like that, but some mannerisms are too deeply ingrained to shake.

Helena's name tops the list of Humans, but then this is exactly the sort of opportunity she has worked so hard to open up. The others are Zaine Alpash Vannix and Meshner Osten Oslam, also working on Human-Portiid relations. Portia is the next chosen – not just Helena's closest liaison but exactly the sort of over-bold all-rounder that a female Portiid is supposed to be. Also on the crew are two other females, Bianca and Viola, who have been working with Zaine for years, plus Fabian, a male, with Bianca having overall authority. Helena listens to the susurrus of those around her, happy or unhappy to be out of the running. Unsurprisingly, nobody turns the honour down.

***

Meshner had very much wanted to turn the honour down. Being part of a scouting mission will not keep him from his research, but it is hardly conducive. The captain's announcement fills him with a peevish annoyance he is entirely too prone to. He had assumed that Fabian was all for the posting, and only when they are installed in the outgrowth of the

Voyager that will become the scout ship do the two of them have a chance to discuss it.

Fabian, too, is not keen, the spider explains through the medium of Artifabian. For his part, it is the potential danger of the business that he objects to.

'Let them leap into the fire,' Artifabian translates, *them* meaning female Portiids in general. 'This is not a good use of my talents. Or your talents.' That last tacked on awkwardly afterwards, because Fabian, being a creature of easily bruised ego, recognizes Meshner as a kindred spirit.

'Well, we work closely together,' Meshner points out weakly. The walls of the chamber around them deform as Kern – the chief Kern of the *Voyager* – manipulates the tensions in the ship's hull fabric to create the appropriate structure for the scout. 'So if they were looking for that . . .'

'Pchah!' the drone articulates, its reading of a little stamping tantrum Fabian has just indulged in. 'This is a punishment detail.'

'Punishment?'

'Our research is not approved of,' Fabian declares. He crouches with his abdomen on the ground, tapping with his front legs only as he faces Meshner, so that his words will not spread to the others filing in.

'Nobody told us to stop,' Meshner points out.

Fabian's palps strike each other, *tok!* 'Well, no. But you've been spoken to. And so have I.'

In actual fact there were quite a few words from Humans and Portiids, both about the accelerated pace of their work and just what it might be doing to Meshner's brain, but nobody took their toys away. He explains this and Fabian scuttles closer, rapping out a hard little rhythm.

'But that's how it is. Isn't it the same for Humans? That's how it is for social species. The *disapproval*.' The drone gives the word a peculiar emphasis, like a maiden aunt being vulgar. Meshner knows that Portiid society is far less formally structured than humans' had been, but then pre-Human humans had been the crew of a ship in emergency conditions. And humans were always more sensitive to their children getting killed doing stupid things, whilst the spider society seems to thrive on a kind of harsh Darwinism, because they have a lot of young and no real parenting instincts. He hadn't considered it before, but the spiders *don't* really force each other to do or not do things, they just express, as Fabian says, *disapproval*.

'We can still continue the work,' he says, now feeling very rebellious. 'I mean, we'll have at least a year in transit to the inner solar system. We don't have to spend it all on ice. We can refine the experiment.'

'We will.' Fabian rears up, legs high in a threat pose as though daring the universe to stop him. A moment later a couple of female Portiids come in with the lean woman Zaine, and Fabian is instantly all humility and submissive body language just in case they feel punchy.

Males have the chance to excel in Portiid society, Meshner knows, but they have to work damned hard at it. Scientific advancement is one proven route, a path cut through the social thickets by Fabians past. Oh, female Portiids still comprise the majority of their great thinkers, but the precedent is at least there. *And we'll make it happen*, he knows. His eyes flick over to where Helena Lain is coming in with her research confederate, Portia. The pair are also working on the final closure of the gap between spider and monkey, at a very procedural, unimaginative level. They use technology

91

to simply understand and translate signals and impulses, little more than having an Artifabian in your skull. Meshner and Fabian's approach is bolder by a factor of ten: bring the Portiid Understandings to Humans, find a way to translate them so that the anthropoid brain can grasp what it is *like* to be a spider, learn the skills, absorb all that stored knowledge.

Outside the chamber the superstructure of the scout ship is being moved into position and connected up, cables and flexible struts writhing their way across the taut hull like strange writing. A seething movement signifies the controlling computer's biological element being decanted: a ball of ants rapidly spreading out to explore and master their new environment. They carry with them, between them and as the sum of their parts, another copy of Avrana Kern, who has made herself a third species in this strange partnership.

The scout vessel is duly christened *Lightfoot*, to represent the first tentative contact between the peoples of Kern's World and whoever calls this new system home. Their first stop will be the next planet in, the biggest gas giant, because long-range investigation has detected activity around its moons.

2.

'My interpretation of inner-system signal traffic and activity supports the hypothesis that they are at war,' Avrana Kern's precise, always-slightly-disapproving voice informs them. The *Lightfoot*'s control system isn't all of her, of course, only a pared-down version, but Avrana Kern tends to expand to fit the computational space available. Helena wonders if she possessed similar qualities when alive and in her human body.

Portia, beside her, scrapes and shuffles, the words coming through Helena's gloves as, *What are we even looking at here? War with what?* Another waking, this, after the long step in-system, and Portia is irritable and restless at the enforced inactivity.

The *Lightfoot* has come in towards one of the gas giant's larger moons to find it . . . under deconstruction, is the only way Helena can think about it. The ball of ice and rock had once been about forty per cent of the size of Kern's World (and, therefore, of Old Earth as well) but has lost at least three per cent of its initial mass. Closer drone viewing shows its outer surface riddled with holes and grooves. *Burrows*. It is crawling with life; all the more remarkable because it has no atmosphere to speak of, any appropriate gas-forming elements either making up part of its frozen surface or having long ago evaporated into space. Surface temperature is, by Kern's scale,

250 below zero at the very sunniest. And yet it lives and, apparently, makes war on its inner-system neighbours.

The drone moves closer, dangerously close save that the locals do not react to its presence in any way. They are creatures of varying size up to about half a kilometer in length, with the majority of them somewhere near that larger demographic. They have the form of something grublike, but with dozens of stubby legs ending in hooked claws, with which they make a slow but sure progress about the moon. Their heads – or at least the truncated businesses at the anterior end of their bodies – end in a bizarre, machine-looking assemblage that is plainly more than able to chew up whatever they run into. Helena watches them just grind their way into the ground, barely slowing from their waddle on the surface, their fleshy segments bulging and heaving as they work.

'Producing no signals at all,' Kern remarks, 'on any wavelength. Their interaction with others in the system is restricted to their bombardment.' Helena can hear her Portiid report, too, which is as close to identical as it can be. Kern is concentrating on what the drones and the ship are doing, meaning she has less computing power to devote to personality.

One of the lumbering monsters emerges from the earth, its grinding mouthparts breaching in a shower of dust and rock shards that tumble and fall silently back through the vacuum to the surface. It seems to stare out into the blackness of the sky, past the curved wall of the gas giant itself, and then tucks its head in, claws digging into the substrate beneath it.

Its whole body contracts, shortening by almost a third, and then by half again in recoil as it spits a huge bolus of rock towards some distant point, enough to clear the planet's gravity well, flashing away at such a ludicrous velocity that Helena reckons some kind of magnetic acceleration must be involved. Its siblings are doing the same, tunnelling, devouring more of the moon's structure and then launching what they have mined at their far-off foes, whoever they are. From the state of the moon's surface, this has been going on for some time.

'The targets are locations within the asteroid belt that lies between this planet and the inner worlds of the system, especially the world from which the bulk of detected signals originate-t-t-te.' Kern pauses over the word, playing with the end of it to show she is reconsidering.

Targeting signals, Bianca announces. *There are signals from the belt that the missiles are being directed towards, compensating for celestial movement. Quite some complex maths these mining beasts are capable of. The signals are being directed here specifically, tracking the moon.* Bianca throws the telemetry and a string of intricate diagrams up for general consumption on the screens, and Helena reads the Portiid representations from long experience. Spider diagrams tend to be four-dimensional and place as much emphasis on non-physical connection as actual structure, so understanding them is something of an art.

'It's not a war.' The voice is Meshner's, and the automaton beside him translates for the Portiids. 'It's too far away. These missiles . . . by the time they arrive, their targets have had ample opportunity to dodge. Unless they don't want to. I think that they're miners, just like you said. And rather than having someone come over here, dig up the stuff and take it back, they've seeded the moon with these things to mine for them, and to spit the stuff home for their use.'

'T-t-t,' says Kern, somewhat frostily, but then, 'Agreed.' Helena wonders how much of her presupposition of war was based on the belief that the inhabitants of this system might be human-descended, and on Kern's low opinion of her own species.

Then Meshner's companion adds something, a little tip-tapping that makes a single word Helena can't place – a name for something, given without context. Her puzzlement is mirrored in most of the rest until Kern calls up some images of what he means. Helena sees a view – much magnified according to the notation – of a podgy soft-bodied caterpillar-looking creature with a bizarre telescoping head/mouth.

'But that's just a water bear, a tardigrade,' she says, the words slowing as they come out. The resemblance to the colossal moon-miners is persuasive.

Fabian, Meshner's colleague, expounds now that he has everyone's attention, in that slightly nervous, always-ready-to-retreat manner that Portiid males have when speaking publicly. *They are notably resilient. They can survive hard vacuum in their native state, though not like this, only in a cryptobiotic form. But if you wanted base stock to manipulate towards this end, you could do worse.*

For the next half hour or so, everyone pores over the data collected by the drones, until at last Kern sends one in for a tissue sample. As the distant robot darts in to cut a strip from one labouring monstrosity, Helena holds her breath and waits for the angry retaliation. There is nothing, though. The creature seems not to notice, just grinding and spitting in an endless round. *They must use some of what they mine to make body mass*, she thinks. *They must breed, probably parthenogenetically, to have this many of them.* By then, cursory inspection of other moons around the gas giant has shown similar infestations. The civilization further in is greedy for ice and metal and even just rock.

The biopsy confirms Fabian's guess, though Kern has to send data up to her larger self in the *Voyager* to cross-check against the DNA banks there. They are looking at a piece of bioengineering simultaneously incredibly sophisticated and brutally functional.

Zaine asks the question most of them must already be thinking: 'Could we do this?'

Bianca and Portia are both insistent that Portiid technology would be more than capable, if such a recourse ever became necessary. The others are less strident. Meshner and Fabian bend close to their automaton to discuss, and Helena puts a palm down next to Portia and buzzes out, *Really?*

I'm not a biotech specialist, of course, Portia shuffles, with a hesitancy that speaks of evasion. There is Portiid optimism – and recklessness – and then there are the hard limits of Human-Portiid science. Helena decides that what they are looking at here – a self-renewing project that must have been ongoing for generations – is far beyond their ability to replicate. And more, it speaks to a frightening sense of purpose in the culture that developed it. *Purpose, or desperation.*

***

Meshner has Artifabian enclose a section of the scout ship so he and Fabian can get back to their work. The facilities they have brought over are limited compared to what the *Voyager* offered, but he is determined not to let it stop him, and equally determined not to let the collective disapproval of the ship's high-ups slow him down. Fabian is of a like mind. The pair of them have been awake longer than most and he is resolved to keep further cold-sleep periods to an absolute minimum. The whole scout mission promises all manner of unpleasantness but until they actually enter a first contact situation, the one resource they will have plenty of is time.

'I have isolated a selection of new Understandings,' the spider explains through his artificial namesake. 'These are from my personal store.' Fabian means those he inherited as part of his genome, or that he took into himself from the *Voyager*'s library before boarding the *Lightfoot*. The mark of a Portiid genius is not in what one knows or the mechanical skills one can deploy: all of these are part of the common currency of the species; copied, traded and absorbed with ridiculous ease. Genius, to one of the spiders, is either a superior ability to think on their feet – a particularly apt human figure of speech – or else the ability to take on a large number of Understandings at once, and thus find new synergies between multiple skills and memories. Fabian is an Understanding polymath, something that was supposed to be rare in males, but probably isn't. He has a good list of active Understandings he can distil for Meshner to sample.

'The challenge is,' Fabian goes on, 'to find something that you will know to be *other*, but isn't so other that you simply cannot process the experience. We want to keep estrangement to a minimum.' He pauses, confers with the automaton over just how his meaning had been communicated, and then adds, 'By which, I mean—'

'You don't want to fry my brain,' Meshner confirms.

'Delicious as that concept is to the imagination,' Fabian agrees, and Meshner can only wonder if this is some peculiar

Portiid saying he's never encountered, or if Fabian is making another venture into human humour.

'Take what precautions you can, but we're going to do this,' he tells his colleague. 'We're not going to let them stop us.'

'Of course.' Fabian skitters over behind Meshner and begins checking over the node of the ship's computer currently linked to the Human's cranial implant.

Ants in my brain, Meshner thinks, though of course it is nothing of the sort; the ants don't leave the confines of the ship's network but their calculations create electrical inputs that feed into the chambers of his cybernetics, and thence to his brain. Human and Portiid technologies mesh more readily than their cultures or languages.

And it seems the technologies of these locals follow a similar pattern. The Old Empire is at the root of it all, meaning some common ground at least. *If we had met something genuinely alien, we wouldn't know where to start.* Right now, in fact, the *Lightfoot* is waiting on word from the *Voyager*, where the language teams have made some sort of breakthrough with the inner system signals. Perhaps everyone will be talking to everyone else any moment, one big interstellar community.

All the comms are between Bianca on the scout and the command crew on the mothership, mediated by the various instances of Kern. The crew of the *Lightfoot* has nothing to do but wait for the news, which is why Meshner is getting on with his own work rather than just twiddling his thumbs. Theoretically, Artifabian could just have patched back into the network and spilled everything, being an instance of Kern. Meshner has discovered, to his surprise, that this is something the automaton is resistant to. It is its own little fragment of artificial intelligence, and to come too close to the intellectual pull of a larger instance like the *Lightfoot*'s operating system could see it merged and stripped of its individuality. It values being itself, and what it has become working with Fabian and himself, a unique intelligence. Which sounds terribly rebellious and impressive until Meshner considers that this drive to become separate is part of the initial programming trajectory Kern gave it.

'All ready,' Artifabian informs him, and a moment later he connects that with the tapping on his lower back that is Fabian himself giving the all-clear.

'Go,' he confirms but at the same time the automaton says, 'Wait – receiving new information.'

Fabian raps irritably against Meshner's back and he says, 'Just go, start the process.'

The automaton raises its front legs partway, as though about to go into a threat display, but then freezes, apparently weighing its priorities. Meshner feels the familiar uncomfortable prickle at the inside of his skull as his implants begin parsing information. He has gone through their architecture since the last time, streamlining everything he could and adjusting the connections with his various sensory nodes. Now he finds a strange taste in his mouth, sharp and sweet, as though he is about to vomit. He clenches his stomach experimentally, but there is no other symptom.

Abruptly his fingers feel gritty, their skin coarse as he rubs them against his thumbs.

'The *Voyager* has instructions. Bianca is addressing us,' Artifabian says, momentarily nothing more than a mouthpiece for the wider nation of Kern.

'Let her,' Meshner grumbles. He hears Fabian's palps *tok*

behind him. A glance shows the spider keeping three feet and a couple of eyes on the instrumentation even as he cants his body to listen.

'Avrana Kern has made a major breakthrough in respect of the communications from the inner system,' the automaton says, translating the jittering of their mission commander. 'Concealed within the visual data, which remains impenetrable, there is a second channel of mathematical information based solidly upon old human notation. This has now been at least partially decoded so that we can understand information such as coordinates, flight paths and some technical data, with more waiting to be interpreted. Armed with this knowledge and commonality, joint command sees fit to send us to make initial contact with the local civilization.'

Meshner tries to concentrate on the words, but there is a lot of white noise intruding on them and it seems to carry its own burden of impenetrable meaning. His skin strobes with stripes of heat and cold that pass up and down his spine. 'How are my readings?' he croaks.

Fabian sends over a brief report to a sub-screen. There is a riot of new information in Meshner's sensory foci, especially the olfactory and gustatory regions of his brain. Curiously, Meshner isn't tasting or smelling much of anything right now, but phantom touches jab at him all over his body. He hears a great ebb and flow like waves of the sea, and bright motes cluster around the edges of his vision.

'This is no good,' he tells Fabian. 'It's runaway synaesthesia. We've not synced the information.' He feels frustration, because this is the core of the problem: are spider experience and human experience intrinsically incompatible? It is proving a hurdle that grows with each attempt to leap it.

Terminating, comes the acknowledgement on the sub-screen even as Artifabian continues to relay the mission brief. The *Voyager* is going into hiding and the *Lightfoot* is going to say hello to the warring natives, Meshner blearily gathers. It seems like a terrible idea to him. The scout vessel will be utterly without support, but then the locals might be so advanced that all the *Voyager* would be able to achieve would be to die on the same hill.

'Given the reliance on bare technical detail, Avrana Kern believes there is a strong chance that this is a machine civilization that has outlived its creators,' the automaton explains crisply. Meshner is having trouble processing the idea, but he feels strongly that any such artificial survivors would be less than delighted to find humans on their doorstep after so long.

'Perhaps they'll think we're a travelling museum,' he gets out, the physical sensation of lemons and sunlight and blue suffusing his skin, spider-life trying to force itself down all the wrong channels in his brain. Fabian skitters out some sort of message but, before Meshner can read or hear any translation, he feels himself slide sideways and loses consciousness.

***

Zaine takes it on herself to upbraid Meshner when he is finally back with them. Helena watches her tear into the man, while the spider crewmembers stand back and either ignore their Human fellows or badger the ship for translations.

He had been out for a couple of hours, the chief reason being informational overload. Helena knows what he is trying to achieve, and even supports the idea in principle, but Meshner is weirdly competitive, determined to make a breakthrough before some hypothetical rival eclipses him. He doesn't want assistance from her or Portia. He wants to *win*, or that is how it comes across.

Zaine's own Portiid liaison work is practical, working in narrow, task-focused situations and building a gestural code to communicate swift, limited chunks of information. That is as far as she cares to take matters, and Bianca and Viola, who work with her, seem equally happy to leave Human-spider relations to the field of just getting things done. Meshner wants to get inside their heads, or vice versa. Despite his prickly arrogance Helena feels she is more on his side of the argument.

'I didn't ask for this posting,' Meshner mutters sullenly.

'You could have said no,' Zaine tells him.

'You can never say no. Fabian couldn't. He needs to show he's useful, or he'll get passed over.'

'For what?'

'For everything. And I need him, so here I am.' Meshner's eyes are bloodshot and the skin about his boxy cranial implant is red and puffy.

'Why were you even on the *Voyager*?' Zaine demands. Helena glances round at the spiders, but of course they don't *hear* like Humans do – speech is barely perceived by their vibrational sense, even Human shouting, keyed as they are to other frequencies a world in which the spoken word is irrelevant.

'Time,' Meshner spits. 'Time, in transit. We were awake a lot longer than you, getting this set up.' He jabs a thumb at his own head. 'We knew we'd get more done than stuck at home dancing to everyone else's tune.'

Zaine opens her mouth to lay into him again but then Kern's voice breaks in from all around them. 'Contact!'

Bianca responds immediately. Helena has her gloves to the wall in time to catch the trailing end of her questions, with Kern thrumming back that she has established a connection with an entity located within the asteroid belt that lies beyond the gas giant.

An alien vessel? A machine? Bianca taps out.

I am unable to say, Kern replies through the walls, Human words echoing after for the benefit of those without Helena's advantages. *But it is responding to the basic queries I have sent it, and not merely in the manner of an automated beacon or similar mindless system. I am receiving a battery of enquiries, most of which I lack the familiarity to answer. I believe we have contacted a real intelligence, machine or organic. I am responding as best I can.* Kern makes a rapid tapping sound to indicate annoyance, mirroring her exasperated human sigh, artfully reproduced over her speakers. *I am still receiving a vast preponderance of visual data. The comprehensible segment of the signal comprises less than five per cent of the information load.*

She displays some of what they are receiving: the same bright-patterned, constantly-shifting abstract shapes Helena saw in signals previously intercepted. They are hypnotic, lacking a recognizable rhythm, heedless of geometry, just broad swathes of flowing, shifting patterns, or rapidly shifting non-Euclidian objects whose dimensions, textures and arrangements change apparently at random in bewildering, non-repeating sequences.

Viola suggests that perhaps it is art, mere aesthetic adornment to garnish the functional message. The amount of bandwidth it takes up makes that unlikely, but that is a Human/Portiid judgement. Who knows what the locals believe important? Speculative discussion breaks out, even

Meshner making a contribution, but Helena just stares at the patterns, their weird complexity speaking to her with a seductive promise of meaning, of familiarity. She has worked all her life to break out of her own skull – not by drilling holes in it like Meshner, but by expanding her viewpoint. She feels that if she could only push that envelope a little further . . . but no, nothing. Whatever the message is, she is missing it.

Soon after, everyone is in their acceleration couches as the *Lightfoot* shifts its angle of approach towards the belt. Kern believes she has arranged a rendezvous through exchange of coordinates in the locals' notation. They are going to meet the aliens.

3.

Portia feels herself at the hub of a network of threads, stretched taut and vibrating with alarm and excitement. 'Alarm and excitement' would probably be the Human translation of her answer, if someone asked her why she had volunteered for the *Voyager* crew. Of all those on the scout mission, she had no qualms whatsoever at being chosen – not just because she works very well with Humans (well, with Helena, who in her mind is not a particularly representative Human, but good enough), but because the thought of the Unknown, of cosmic mystery, of things to *discover*, motivates her even more than most Portiids. Her lineage is one of explorers and pioneers. An ancestress of hers stole the Sacred Eye of the Messenger from the ants, back when the ants were the great power in the world and not merely a convenient operating system to run Avrana Kern on. Amongst the myriad contributors to her genetic code are aviatrixes, warriors, astronauts. And others, of course, more commonplace, but Portia's genetic inheritance skews far more to the daring and the groundbreaking. This is not simply a matter of a predisposition to certain personality types, of course (a trait observed in certain social spiders long ago on Earth), but a curation of Understandings all the way back to the days when those skills and memories could only be passed down by the natural union of sperm and egg. Portia really is the sum of her ancestors, crouching on the cephalothoraxes of giants. She remembers the thrill of striking out into virgin forest where monsters might dwell, contesting with the elements, mastering the technology that opened the doors of the sea and the air, seeing Kern's World from orbit for the first ever time. And there is tragedy and loss and pain associated with those experiences, of course, but generation on generation such sharp edges tend to get rounded away.

When she was very young she faced her life's great fear and it nearly destroyed her. It was that there might be no more frontiers, no new branch to leap to, no new prey to puzzle out and conquer. There is a lot in Portia with which her far distant arachnid huntress ancestors might feel a kinship. But she conquered that fear, took it on faith that science and global ambition would conspire to give her the opportunity she craved, to stand and measure legs with her illustrious forebears, and find herself at least their equal.

Now she waits, always hard for her. The crew have been in and out of sleep as their whims take them, but Portia hates the waking, and so she has been staying out longer under the excuse of research. Helena is working on the theoretical side of their communications studies, refining the sensory inputs of her gloves and goggles and training her brain to convert tactile subtext into impressions that make sense to Humans. For her part, Portia is tinkering in a desultory way with the acoustic translators she can wear like panniers, and which give a very basic – and sometimes howlingly inadequate – impression of Human speech. The drive to communicate is mostly the other way, though. After all, there is only a small number of Humans on Kern's World compared to a billion or so Portiids. There is an implicit suggestion that the newcomers should be the ones to adjust. She has dismantled one pannier and is following some Kern-prompted suggestions on how to refine the outputs for a more intuitive result, but mostly she has her mental legs on those imaginary threads and is waiting for them to twang with activity.

Portia's ancestors were not web-spinners as a first resort. If there were a species out there uplifted from orb web spiders, its outlook would be very different, evolved to sit at the heart of a far-reaching world of its own creation, where the landscape speaks to it in its own language and it does not need to *travel*. Portia's tiny ancestors turned such perspectives against their non-sentient creators, forging the voice of the environment or sometimes even extending those artificial sensory organs into webs of their own that they could lure the original builders onto for ambush. The thought of waiting for that web-borne message is therefore a matter of far greater danger and excitement: in the core of their minds the Portiids know they are not the builders of the universe's great web, but they dare to walk it and eavesdrop on its messages and turn it on its makers if need be.

Her web now is made of the other crew, each one of them tense as a drawn wire as they close with the coordinates negotiated with the locals. Her web is the ship and its personality-filled operating system and, beyond and into the void of space, the unknown aliens themselves: machines, Humans, something entirely other?

Those who have a mind to are trying to make more of the library of alien signals, especially that baffling preponderance of visual imagery. For her part, the ship's version of Avrana Kern has sent spies ahead to the meeting point. These are not the same multi-purpose drones she used with the tardigrades, but tiny things, shot out from the *Lightfoot* at enormous speed and containing nothing but the ability to detect and report. Everyone hopes this will not seem like hostile action to the locals, but if the locals are already hostile then the entire arrangement could be a trap. Yes, this is why the *Voyager* budded off the *Lightfoot*, in case of such a betrayal, but that doesn't mean the crew of the *Lightfoot* can't do their best to avoid becoming such a sacrifice.

Portia doesn't feel fear yet, and when she does she will feed off it, buoyed by all those ancestral memories in which fearful things were overcome by courage and resourcefulness (and luck, but she tends to downplay its importance). She is well aware that some of her crewmates are less sanguine about the prospect. Viola agrees with the theory that the locals are machines, and believes that without organic entities to give them perspective, machines can never be good neighbours, as what can they *want*, if not to make new machines? Viola is most concerned about a fleet of self-replicating machine probes descending on Kern's World in the future, led there by what the locals here discover after dissecting the *Lightfoot* and its contents, crew included. Portia is frustrated with her caution – shy away from every twitch and vibration and you'll never catch anything at all. On the other hand, the lack of enthusiasm from the two males on board seems altogether more natural, and she actually has more time for their naysaying. Fabian and the Human Meshner have been winkled from their private research and are combing the alien signals for any sign of threat. They are both intelligent in their way, and being cautious and shrinking from danger is an archetypal male trait. Portia is well aware that to think in such terms – as most of her ancestresses have done without ever examining the thoughts – is unhelpful and atavistic of her, but it does mean she will accept a warning from a male far more readily than from another female, from whom any attempt to rein her in feels like a challenge.

Attend, comes the instruction from Bianca, whose own personality sits somewhere midway between Viola and Portia, neither too hot nor too cold on the intrepid scale. *We have sight of them.*

The threads are twanging, in Portia's mind. She calls up the images greedily. Kern has done her best with the limited imaging properties of her tiny spies but Portia doesn't expect too much.

Her expectations are shattered, to her joy. In that moment everyone is staring and nobody is speaking. Not a spider foot or palp moves, not a Human mouth flaps.

There are seven vessels converging on the rendezvous point. Five of them are spheres, radiant with an inner light that silhouettes a complex internal architecture like shadows on the face of the moon. One, the smallest, is a long teardrop that even now is tumbling – seemingly out of control but, as Kern's commentary explains, actually in the process of commencing deceleration. The last is a fat torus shape, spinning, edge-on towards its direction of travel like a runaway tyre. All of them are festooned with nodules and nodes that suggest only the teardrop ship has a 'facing' and the rest are entirely ambivalent about front, back, port or starboard. Kern's information – her longer-than-long-range scans with which she has kept an eye on these objects – suggests they have been decelerating for a remarkably long time and to very little effect, reducing their speed ridiculously slowly rather than (as the *Lightfoot* will) waiting to get close to the meeting point before making that irrevocable decision. Some of the crew are suggesting that this shows a confidence in their hosts, perhaps even a trust. Portia has a feeling the practice has a mechanical imperative behind it.

The smallest ship, the teardrop, is half the average volume of the *Voyager* (given that volume is variable depending on what Kern is doing with it). The largest of the spheres is not much short of the frozen ruin they discovered on the way in. Huge, and they apparently manoeuvre as though they're even larger, given that gradual deceleration. Portia is intrigued.

Behind those oncoming vessels, the asteroid belt is strung out across a vast region of space, far denser than any such feature in Portia's home system or long lost Earth, which still means that it is mostly empty space where the odds of any two objects connecting with each other is vanishingly small. Kern's best guess is that a huge icy body met its doom here, either a fugitive flung from another solar system entirely or a world that formed further out in this one, and was then dragged in towards the sun until it met the grinding teeth of the gas giant's gravity and was torn apart. It left a great field of nothing, then: scattered rock and ice smeared thinly in a ring around the sun, but extreme magnification shows that later years have added some jewels to this plain setting. There are artificial worlds there. Kern's best guess at enhancing the images suggests a scatter of pale bodies, like the spherical ships but bigger. The asteroid belt has been colonized. Elsewhere, less radiant, there are installations that must be acting as spittoons for the distant tardigrades' mining expectorations, catching the missiles and processing them or sending them on.

Could we do this? Portia echoes the past question from Zaine and, to herself, admits that they could not. *And yet we have come to them, not they to us.* Always better to be the explorer than the explored.

There is a buzz of communication now amongst the crew. As the *Lightfoot* and the aliens close, the signal density increases, both the background hum of them, from the belt installations and especially from the next planet in the system – *their homeworld?* – and direct queries sent by the oncoming ships, which seem more and more insistent about something. Kern is communicating on the technical channel still, but the character of those enquiries is changing. The visual element, which means nothing to anyone, is edging out the mathematical data until there is barely anything comprehensible in the barrage of demands. The only numerical information left over seems to be nothing more than sender ID.

At about this time, Meshner completes a structural study of the alien vessels, identifying a variety of installations on their exteriors that might be weapons systems of different types. Of course the aliens are far closer now, so that the *Lightfoot* can assist him with its own direct analysis. They are closing on the meeting place and it is evident that the visitors are not speaking to the locals in the manner they have come to expect. Portia notes that the characteristics of the visual chatter are shifting. The colours are becoming starker, with fewer blues, greens and yellows and more blacks, whites and reds. The shapes are sharper, spiky with harsh textures. To Human and Portiid eyes there is an implicit sense of threat.

Kern is still transmitting her own signals, including a variety of Old Empire codes and conventions, but there is no sign the aliens understand or even register them.

This is their primary means of communication, Helena states. *Whatever they are, we need to send something back to them, something visual but simple. We have no idea what any of this means, but we're now picking up a common emotional subtext. Or it might even be text. If we are all getting the same impression from this, and if they are of any kind of Earth stock, I think we can take this as an accurate reading. They're getting angry.*

Viola, proponent of the machine intelligence theory, disagrees. *It's not possible that they could have evolved in such a way. Your speech, our speech, we learned to encode it first, turning sensory impressions into numerical data that can be read in and of itself – from zeroes and ones to more complex codes. There is no suggestion that this data is encoding anything other than these images, and it's using old human conventions even for that. You're suggesting they leapt to being able to transmit their primary mode of communication without any sign of an intermediate stage that we might be able to detect and decode.*

Portia understands the argument: after all, the only reason Humans and Portiids can understand each other at all is just such a simplified notation, which can then be built on to reconstruct the meaning. Without such an artificial encoding between them, the patter of spider feet and the vibrations of an anthropoid larynx could never have bridged the gap. And Viola is right, those alien signals are pure visual data. The idea that an emergent intelligence could develop a technology like that without intermediate building blocks is beyond credibility.

But then we are dealing with the alien, she thinks. *Perhaps they just did. And if they blow us up we'll never know.*

She adds her voice to Helena's, saying: *We must send them something, even if it is just to show we're not stupid.*

Zaine says something that Portia's working pannier translates as: *Send theirs back to them.*

Terrible idea, Helena counters swiftly. *If they are threatening us, we don't want to escalate.*

Send them a picture of us, Portia throws in. When that gets everyone's attention she clarifies: *An image of one of us, an image of one of the Humans. Or even just a human image in the abstract. They are using technology that is at least human-derived, after all. It should mean something to them.*

Everyone has an opinion on that, and Bianca asserts command to filter through the stamping and shuffling. Portia already knows her motion will pass, though: the hubbub is just the usual 'yes-but-I-want-to-make-this-my-idea' that she is more than used to from groups of the ambitious amongst her own people.

Send an image of Helena, Portia submits, and that seems as good a solution as any. Bianca confirms the idea and Kern starts to transmit on the visual channel, throwing in a grab-bag of blues, yellows and pinks in the hope that these really are calming colours.

The result is dramatic. The profusion of angry-seeming colours fades instantly, leaving only simple, more repetitive patterns of what Portia guesses are neutral shades.

They're telling us to wait, maybe? Fabian puts in timidly.

My spies suggest there is a great deal of communication between the alien vessels, Kern puts in.

Calculate some alternative trajectories for us, just in case, Bianca orders.

Indeed, the ship confirms. *I can't intercept much of the communication, but it is ninety-nine per cent visual . . . ninety-seven . . .*

ninety-two . . . The technical channels are experiencing a large upsurge.

I don't like this being a countdown, Fabian puts in.

Bianca starts to reply, *If you don't have anything useful to contribute—* and then everything goes wrong all at once. The alien ships are launching dozens of smaller vessels, as tiny and fleet as the originals were huge and lumbering, and they unleash their weapons almost at the same time.

PAST 2
LAND OF MILK AND HONEY

1.

There was a hole in the ice that, owing to the rampant volcanism Senkovi had set off along every faultline on Damascus, was still not frozen over when they came to look. Below, miles deep, the new batch of aquatic remotes found the wreck of the *Aegean*'s shuttle. Han and the others, having abandoned ship at Senkovi's insistence, had not acquired a stable orbit when the virus hit their systems. Now they were cold corpses in a half-crushed dead spaceship beneath the ocean.

Baltiel expected Senkovi to shrug it off, given the man's focus on his work and his pets. Instead, he fell into a black depression. He had played fast and loose with the rules, as he had always been wont to do, and this time it had killed people.

'It saved your life,' Baltiel pointed out. 'It saved the ship. Saved all of us.' The *Aegean*, post-reboot, was in perfect working order. As per Senkovi's pre-disaster plan, the octopuses had no access to its wider systems any more, only limited virtual playgrounds to be tested in. The whole audacious, ridiculous plan of his had worked out in every particular, save that he had failed to adjust for the destructive stupidity of the rest of humanity.

'You couldn't have known,' Baltiel tried patiently, calling

through the closed door of Senkovi's room because the man wasn't accepting electronic queries from the ship, and Baltiel's implant was still being re-engineered after the virus had shut it down. Only Senkovi's internal comms had survived, and he had set them to bounce back any traffic.

There were precisely five human beings this side of Earth's solar system, to Baltiel's certain knowledge. He could not go on with twenty per cent of his crew out of commission, no matter how much he sympathized. True, the terraforming processes were running themselves for now, but that wouldn't last, and the entire Nod end of the operation needed salvaging. Most of the work could be done by automatics, guided sporadically by whoever's turn it was to wake from cold sleep, but the set-up needed all hands, and especially Senkovi's brain.

'Lante has some medication for you,' he tried. 'It'll make you feel better.'

Senkovi didn't want medication. Probably he didn't want to feel better. The shame and blame were jealous, unwilling to admit any chemical interlopers into his mental state. Baltiel could override the door lock and get Lortisse to drag Senkovi down to medical, but he didn't want to be that kind of commander, and a resentful, mutinous Senkovi would be considerably more problematic than a sullen one.

So he had one card to play, not one he was proud of, but he'd read through the man's psych evaluations and Lante agreed with him.

'I'm going to jettison the octopodes,' he told the door.

There was a pause, but he heard Senkovi moving around, and then abruptly there the man was, unshaven, red-eyed and haggard.

'Why would you do that?' Senkovi asked him.

Because nobody else has any love for the damned things but you, was the true answer, but would not represent good Senkovi-management. 'I wouldn't, of course,' he lied. 'But they need you, and we need you. The human race needs you, Disra.'

For a moment Senkovi just stared at him, and Baltiel thought he would retreat back inside and close the door. Then he twitched, and the twitch kept going until his whole body was shaking, and without warning he was crying, Baltiel holding him like a child, Senkovi's salt tears staining the thermoregulatory fabric of his shirt.

When they broke apart, Senkovi gave a shuddering sigh. 'Nobody needs anybody,' he got out, in stark contradiction to what had just happened. 'But I'll try.'

Of course, there was no magic cure for depression. Baltiel still sometimes saw the man just sitting and staring, but he was working with his damn cephalopods again, and that seemed the best therapy for him. Baltiel watched, sometimes, through the ship's cameras: Senkovi sitting at the makeshift workstation he'd set up in the central hub, wires and devices floating about him and his hair (longer and longer these days) a crazy Medusa's crown about his face. Or perhaps the waving tendrils of his hair made him somehow more relatable to his test subjects. Disra would sit, hunched over his screen, and in the tank beside him three or four octopodes would be working with the rubbery terminals the man had designed. They always seemed to be desultory about it, to watch them: they would descend on the controller and appear to feel it out, or to wrestle with it in a sudden bout of energy, and then slink off to hang in the water or cling to the wall. He had seen that one or two tentacles tended to remain connected, though, pulsing and shifting across the controls even though the rest of the creature was ostensibly oblivious. Then Baltiel would call up a display of the virtual space they were accessing, watching octopodes accomplishing complex multi-stage tasks in fits and starts, making unheralded break-throughs, then cycling through the same fruitless steps over and over, then another abrupt leap forwards. He assumed that Disra was trying to get them to follow regimented orders. That was the Overall Command in him breeding assumptions. Later he discovered that actually telling the damned molluscs to *do* things was something Disra had given up on even before he left Earth. Instead he was giving them long goals, identi-fying ends by flagging the conditions up with colours and patterns that apparently meant good things if you were an octopus. The methods were worked out by the test subjects themselves. When they seemed distracted, Senkovi claimed, they were employing something like abstract reasoning, free association of ideas. The individual arms still at work were their subconscious. He was unable to provide any academic literature to support such contentions, but he could provide results. He even staged a demonstration for the crew – a simulation of a crashed drone, its damage determined randomly by the system. Three octopodes were given free rein to work out what to do with it. Baltiel had watched with fascination as they had explored the wreck, accessed its simu-lated systems, repaired some damage while cannibalizing other functioning systems. None of them seemed to be co-ordinating with each other – indeed there were several apparent squabbles between subjects where they left off their controllers and wrestled in the tank – and yet a plan somehow emerged from the chaos, as though deeper parts of their strategy had been agreed on invisibly at the outset. Or perhaps visibly, given the constant shift and glimmer of colours and patterns across their skins. The end result had not been anything that a human salvager would have come up with, less time efficient, but perhaps more sparing with resources. As Disra pointed out, time was the thing they had.

At the outset, while he had dearly wanted to space every damned octopus the man had bred, Baltiel had kept them around because they were plainly good for Senkovi's well-being. Now he was conceding the key point. They *could* be used. They weren't predictable like machines, but they would get a job done without oversight. Senkovi was already talking about future generations having the cognitive ability to set their own goals as well as carry them out. Baltiel would believe it when he saw it. There would be future generations, though only within the artificial fishponds of the *Aegean* for now. Damascus's expanding seas were carpeted with thick algal scum voraciously photosynthesizing, but the oxygen in the water was far too diffuse for the octopuses just yet, and not even Disra was talking about fitting cephalopods with – what? – hydrolungs? But when the water was sufficiently habitable, presumably his mollusc workforce would be ready.

Human life on Damascus still had a theoretical future. The 'theory' element of that calculation had shifted, though. Once it referred to Disra's ability to bring the desired conditions about on a planet colder and damper than anyone had thought worth bothering about. Now it referred to the colonists from Earth, whose nature had become very, very theoretical indeed.

There were no signals from Earth. That was what everyone had to face up to in the end. Seven days after the disaster, Baltiel called everyone into the same room. The *Aegean*'s systems would allow virtual teleconferencing from anywhere, but they had all begun to value the immediate presence of fellow humans. Only Disra was absent, and he was at least actively linked in from his zero gravity webbing in the centre of the ship. Baltiel specifically checked to make sure none of his little friends were listening in, too. He had a mad thought of one of the octopodes diligently taking the minutes of the meeting.

He only told them what they already knew, of course. They were all bright minds, more than capable of having asked the same questions of the ship. Baltiel had let them have access to the information, even though some commandery part of him told him to embargo it. Still, he wanted to tell them face to face, because until he did so it would remain something questionable. Overall Command needed to set out its position on the subject.

There were no signals from Earth, he confirmed. Nor were they receiving anything from any of the established solar colonies. The great radiosphere of human endeavour had once been a constantly repopulated expanse. Now it was a hollow shell, expanding past them into the further reaches of the universe. They would never catch up with all those lost words and, even if they could, the damned virus would be the first thing waiting for them, the last thing ever sent from Earth by someone who, Baltiel was sure, had been losing the war and was going to take everyone else with them.

They very nearly had. Skai and the four others in the module had died, locked in an unresponsive orbital tomb that had been reclaimed, hour on hour, by the supremely hostile non-environment around it. Running out of air, running out of heat; the remotes sent from the *Aegean* had cut through the hull but found only rigid, frost-limned bodies, still huddled about the equipment they had not been able to restore. Han and her team had crashed into Damascus. Baltiel, Lante, Lortisse and Rani would probably have died had Senkovi not come for them – not of suffocation but likely of starvation, allergic reactions, poisoning. Or, if he was being dramatic, some hitherto unknown Nodan super-predator with an inexplicable yearning for inedible human meat.

So perhaps Senkovi's molluscs had earned their keep already, by whose mischief these last few dregs of humanity had been saved.

That was the other reason he had called them in, face to face, to tell them old, old news. Because they needed to be there for each other. Because they needed not to be alone. Alone meant too much time to think about what had happened. There was not one of them who wasn't reeling. Baltiel could feel the echo of the news still resounding inside himself. It was too big to understand. And so he turned to his work and sought there the meaning that the rest of the universe was abruptly missing, and he would bring the rest along with him if they'd let him.

Senkovi still expected refugees, shiploads of them, and if such fugitives appeared then the terraforming project would need somewhere to put them. In thirty years' time, Earth standard, according to Senkovi's projections, they would have the Damascan seas and atmosphere sufficiently oxygenated. They would have a makeshift biosphere installed, based on the stable ecology webs from back home that were the late-stage terraformer's sacred text. Senkovi was keen to show how his octopodes would be invaluable at every turn, and Baltiel didn't ask the obvious question. *What happens when the people turn up and take over? Where does your tentacled construction crew take itself off to?* Baltiel knew Disra was aware of this problem, but they had time to negotiate a solution, so long as one of them mentioned that common knowledge to the other before the end.

And Baltiel wanted to return to Nod. He was already programming their shuttle and remote fleet with a salvage program for the module, to see what could be recovered. The *Aegean*'s workshops were fabricating a new habitat, a working one. He had started sounding out the others. Lante was creeped out by the octopodes (and possibly Senkovi as well), Lortisse and Rani were both sick for the feel of something solid beneath them, and leery of some new catastrophe that might kill off the *Aegean*'s systems for good. They would go where he led, he knew, and Senkovi wouldn't much miss them.

Ever since Senkovi's naming of the planets, Baltiel's mind had sporadically spun up religious imagery for what they were about – or maybe it was the fundamentalist end of the trouble back home that put him in mind of it. The anti-science side of the argument had made Kern their Satan and the terraformers her attendant demons. And now those detractors were silenced, or had silenced themselves. And Kern, too, that remarkable, incredible, insufferable woman, one more voice stilled amongst so many. How she would have hated that. He could almost imagine her refusing to accept it, demanding a bespoke fate appropriate for her genius.

So where did that leave Baltiel and his crew? All they had was their work. He had to get them back to Nod. He would be a chapter in human history if he could, but if not, he might be a prologue in an alien one. And perhaps there would be human ears listening, in a year or a decade or a century. There was no reason to believe the virus had been just one horseman of some final apocalypse.

Except there was every reason, of course. He could remember enough of the prior transmissions to know just how much escalation his far-off kin had got in before the end. But in the absence of knowledge he could avoid thinking about it and just go back to pick up where he'd left off.

Prepping for a return to Nod would take time, however, just like Senkovi's work would take time. They were stuck on the *Aegean* pending mechanical, biological, even geological processes. The cold-sleep pods yawned for them like the grave. Baltiel had a rota, making sure at least one person was on watch at all times. *And unless I want to wake up to his desiccated bones I need to drag Disra away from his pets somehow.*

Nobody had suggested firing up the drives and heading back to Earth.

2.

In his own mind, Senkovi was known for his sense of humour, an organ that in truth amused only himself. Still, the others would have to admit this was a good one. After all, he'd had his fill of being yanked out of dreams at the whim of Overall Command. Now he had an excuse to do the yanking. Time for Baltiel to know what it felt like.

The others were busy with Lante's malarkey, a plan that Baltiel wouldn't approve of and that Senkovi himself wasn't convinced about. It didn't impinge on his work with Damascus, though, which meant he could put off caring about it indefinitely. They still invited him to the meetings – virtual attendance only, but that was by far everyone's preferred option – which suggested that his myopic disinterest had been taken as tacit approval. Or they just felt that keeping twenty-five per cent of their non-command colleagues (and fellow humans) out of the loop was bad form.

There had been a regimented schedule of sleep and wake to pass them hand over hand through the years since the Silence. Which was apparently what they were calling it. Senkovi felt that was overly dramatic, but Rani had a poetic streak in her. The idea was that Senkovi would pop in and out on schedule based on the terraforming stages that needed executive oversight, and the others would wake in shifts at the same time in an overlapping pattern so that three out of five humans were awake at any given time. The brief for the others was: (1) oversee salvage of the module and reconstruction of the Nod expedition; (2) help Senkovi. And they had helped and, even more to his surprise, he had been profoundly glad to have other humans to occasionally complain to. *What you don't know you'll miss until it's gone, number 153: the Human Race.* Lante in particular was something of a whizz with ecostructure, and Rani was a better pilot, shuttle or remote, than anyone else (the best in the universe, perhaps). Lortisse, for his part, was good with the octopi. They liked him and, unlike the others, didn't squirt water at him when he approached the open tanks up in the rotating ring. He even went diving with them, the only one other than Senkovi, and acted as a stooge in their training sessions. Senkovi wished sometimes he could actually *talk* to the man about it, about their evolving relationship with the evolving octopi. Lortisse wasn't a man who opened up about his feelings, though, and for Senkovi's part, he found it easier to communicate with the cephalopods. And that was saying something, because actual conversation was proving elusive. He could encourage them towards tasks and goals, visually flagging up things for them to be curious about and then letting them grasp the problem and solve it with minimal assistance. He saw them talking to each other constantly, skin strobing at skin, tentacles touching, fighting, intertwining. At the same time he couldn't be sure they were *saying* anything. How much was meant, and how much of that riot of activity was just a byproduct of cognition?

He stood by the tanks sometimes, watching his pets, his creations at work, at play. They watched him back: they knew him and he felt they liked him. Even unmodified octopi could tell individual humans apart, and these were smarter than their forebears and only had five faces to recognize.

He was depressingly aware that he was trying to wring something from his pets that would be available for free from his fellow humans, but a lifetime of habits died hard, and he hadn't been able to cross that barrier even when he shared a planet with billions. It hardly seemed worth it on a ship with only four others, and two of them asleep at any one time. And the octopi slept, too, when Senkovi took to his cold bed. He didn't have the apparatus to properly suspend them, he could only cool and drug them into an unreliable hibernation. Mortality in the cold dark between had been sixty per cent at first, and he'd massaged it down to forty. It broke his heart every time his time was up. Doing something long term about that particular issue was one of his biggest goals, perhaps soon to be realized.

Thoughts of sleep and waking brought him back to Baltiel. The wake-up sequence was already advanced; Senkovi had looked into the files and discovered that his boss liked to be awoken by soft music, gradually swelling to a tear-jerkingly magnificent crescendo. Senkovi found that mawkish, but others would probably not be delighted by his own maritime imagery and so each to his own. He watched the man's eyelids twitch, his muscles flickering in tiny spasms as the sleep chamber went through all the necessary checks and adjust-ments for a shock-free reanimation. Which was a shame because the designer hadn't allowed for Senkovi.

Baltiel woke, stepping from his symphony into the *Aegean*'s warm light, sitting up and seeing he was not alone.

Senkovi had to hand it to him. Baltiel almost masked the horror and panic of that moment. His Overall Command face slammed down, but not quite fast enough and the eyes couldn't lie. Baltiel clutched too hard at the edge of his pod and said nothing, looking over Senkovi's withered face, the wild tufts of his white beard, his liver-spotted scalp, warty and draped with a few brittle hairs.

They stared at each other for a long time, and Senkovi wondered if Lante or Lortisse were watching on the cameras and killing themselves with laughter. Or unable to believe his bad taste. But if you couldn't laugh, what could you do?

'You . . .' Baltiel's voice had a shake to it, at the start, but the man clamped down and made it sound strong. 'What happened?' A suspicious squint started about Baltiel's eyes, and Senkovi could hold the grin back no longer. Seeing the boss about to beat him to the punch, Senkovi ripped the beard off, and began peeling away the skullcap and wrinkled skin sections, snickering to himself.

Baltiel must have interrogated the ship by then and found out that he'd been under for eleven years, in the increasingly meaningless way the ship told time. 'How long did you . . . ?' he asked.

'Thirty-four days.' Senkovi picked at one stubborn scrap of fake wrinkle. 'The skin was the easy bit. Getting the workshops to spin a realistic beard was remarkably difficult.'

'You've amused yourself sufficiently?' Baltiel obviously wanted to shout at him but was restraining himself masterfully.

'I'm amused. Aren't you amused?'

'In hysterics.' The boss rubbed at his neck and rolled his shoulders – things that shouldn't have been necessary, but they were relying too much on the cold sleep and it was beginning to show. 'I assume you had some real reason for dredging me up, beyond trying to kill me with shock?'

'Well, several things have accumulated that probably need a command decision or two,' Senkovi admitted. 'Lante wants to talk to you, certainly. She's got a whole . . . thing going on.' He saw Baltiel's face change as the man accessed the initial files on Lante's 'thing'. Lante and Baltiel were going to have an argument soon. Senkovi had warned her it would be a hard sell to the boss. Still, none of his business, and when the main debate had been raging between Lante and Rani about broaching the thing with Baltiel, Senkovi had been deep in designing his beard. 'Oh, and there's the module, that needs a decision.'

'How's the refit proceeding?' And even as he asked the question Baltiel was hunting the answers through the system, doubtless tutting over the fact that, in his absence, nobody put data back quite where it should be.

'Yes, well,' Senkovi said, wringing his beard. 'Nobody wants to trust it even though the virus has been flushed out. Floating in a tin can and all that. On the plus side the Nod expedition is mostly good to go, they told me. Even got the cold-sleep system set up planetside if you want to do a longitudinal study or two.'

Senkovi got an alert to tell him Baltiel was querying the progress on Damascus. At least he had good news there, he felt. Everything proceeding apace, oxygenated zones spreading, and a microbial ecosystem established and apparently stable. He even had a working elevator cable, because the thought of dropping living things from orbit into the sea made him shake and sweat, no matter how he tried to tell himself it wasn't the same. He couldn't even airdrop a bacterium these days.

'I'd better speak to the others,' Baltiel said grimly.

'Everyone's up and waiting for you, boss,' Senkovi told him. It was a breach of Baltiel's rules, of course, to have them all awake at the same time, but not as much as what was about to be proposed.

***

Baltiel could see Lante was ready for a fight, and the body language of Rani and Lortisse suggested the three of them were committedly all in it together. The brief walk from the sleep pods to the crew room had been long enough for him to absorb just what extended treachery had been going on while he had been out of it, but Lante had obviously done all the convincing in person rather than conveniently producing a manifesto. If he had time he could trawl the internal sensor suite and maybe find recordings of some of the conversations, but he'd just have to hear it from Lante herself and deal with it on the fly.

But first things first, and so he was urbane mildness personified as they talked over what had been reinstalled in the orbital module, whether they needed to do anything to stop it falling into Nod's gravity well, whether they were going to set up shop there or not. Lante subsided and Rani took over with the technical details. Baltiel rubber-stamped all the various proposals, command decisions barely worthy of the name. 'Now,' he said, that disposed of. 'You've been busy.'

For a moment the tension in the room was almost overtly mutinous. He wondered how far they would go.

'Nobody's come,' Lante told him. 'I mean, yes, they could still be on the way. They could have set off late. They could be in ships without the same acceleration as the *Aegean*. Or something. And maybe the reason we've not had any comms from them asking if we can put them up and find a bunk for them is because they're super-paranoid after the viral weapon, or assume we're paranoid. Or assume we're dead. But we've been sending signals home-ways, and there's nothing. There's been . . .' her hand waved away accuracy, 'time for those signals to get all the way to Earth and for Earth to call us back. Nothing. We don't think anyone's coming.' And it didn't prove anything, just as she said. Survivors could be creeping their way between stars under radio silence. Except Lante didn't think so. She was nailing her colours to: *We don't think anybody made it.* What really brought it home was that he knew they'd all stopped counting. The *Aegean* was technically still running a clock on how long it had been since the Silence and the last words of Earth, but Baltiel could see from the records how long it had been since anyone had even queried it. Their jaunts in and out of cold sleep had given time a rough edge that had finally sawed through their last connections to their home planet. If he asked them now, not one of them would be able to say how long it had been.

And now this.

'And so you . . .' Baltiel was about to say, *decided to play God*, but that meshed too neatly with his own viewpoint, or maybe the damned religious memes Senkovi had infected him with, and he resorted to plain science. 'So you co-opted the genetics lab.'

'In my spare time, of which we've had rather a lot.' And Lante was looking visibly older. Not *old*, because they all had the kind of cleaned-up genome that lent itself to extended healthy lifespans, but she'd plainly been putting the hours in, and the days and years. 'We have genetic samples from most of the crew in store anyway, in case of mishap. It's all established science.'

'Banned science.' For most of a century, long before the anti-science mob became a real danger. The creation of artificial human beings had been forbidden for a number of reasons, from divine prerogative through to fending off the return of slavery.

Lante shrugged. 'We all know the arguments, almost none of which apply. Yusuf, you want to study Nod, fine. Senkovi wants to breed his pets and terraform Damascus, also fine. Feel free to add to the store of human knowledge. I – we – want to ensure that human knowledge has a future.'

'I notice that you've sequenced several modified genomes. Not quite the human standard.'

Lante squared her shoulders. 'Adaptation to a low oxygen environment is within human standard range. Originally in high altitude areas, but it will suit Nod well. And I know what you said – you don't want a bunch of colonists to turn up and ruin the ecosystem there. But these won't be colonists. They'll be our people. We can guide them, teach them. We can make a human reservation, Yusuf. Just one part of the planet.'

And it would never stay that way, not over the generations, not forever, and the purist in him reared its head and bellowed, while the man, the vain man he acknowledged himself to be, thought about that perpetuation of human knowledge, new histories that knew his name.

'And the rest,' he prompted Lante gently. 'Or are gills also human standard somehow?'

'We're terraforming a planet that is almost entirely ocean,' Lante pointed out.

'Hey, what?' Senkovi had been mentally elsewhere, slouching against the wall and ignoring the conversation, but that hooked him. 'You want to . . . ?' He looked from Lante to Baltiel and then made a sulky face. 'Well, I suppose that's what it's *for*, only I was thinking boats . . .'

Baltiel had a good idea what Senkovi was thinking and decided to set up some routines in the *Aegean*'s systems in case the man went entirely mollusc-native on them, routines that Senkovi hopefully wouldn't be able to just circumvent. For now, though, he needed a response to Lante and the others.

I am a jealous god, he thought. That would be his standard party line, and it should have been frozen into him by the years in cold sleep, his attitudes crystallized until he was little more than a parody of himself. And yet, and yet. He examined his knee-jerk rejection of Lante's mad, bold plan and found it nothing more than that, no substance behind it.

'We'll put them on Damascus, as much as we can,' he said, knowing that even if he wasn't such a jealous god, there was going to come a time when Zeus would go head to head with Poseidon over departmental demarcation. 'On boats, as much as we can.' It was an attempt to placate Senkovi, as much as one ever could. 'But we'll be on Nod, so I suppose you'll be doing the initial work there.'

They had been so tensed for a scrap over this that Lortisse actually physically staggered, as though leaning against a door unexpectedly open. Baltiel shrugged.

'Just don't think about Nod as a colony world. The soil won't grow anything people can metabolize, the entire biosphere is wrong for us, and we're not changing that. And I've seen your work.' *Briefly, on the walk over.* 'You can't make humans who could live there like natives. Low O_2 and high grav mods won't cut it. They wouldn't be human once you'd finished making all the changes.'

Lante obviously felt that was defeatist talk, but she recognized the value of taking the victory he offered, rather than risking everything on pushing for more. And Baltiel reckoned he was right. Nodan biochemistry was alien from the ground up, a cocktail of elements hazardous to people and organic molecules that might have arisen on Earth but never did, out-selected by chance and time. There were probably some Earth extremophiles that could scrape a living there, but nothing more complex than that. Earth and Nod biology were ships that passed in the night without signal or hail.

3.

Salome is not fond of the elevator and, halfway down, does her best to escape it. Her co-prisoner on the journey down, Paul, feels alarm, jetting towards the top of the capsule and clinging to the plastic sheathing.

Technically he is Paul 51 and she is Salome 39, as per Senkovi's notes. His numbering of generations is eclectic, however; unreliable. There have been co-existing Pauls, and of course Pauls 1–3 lived back on Earth in his aquariums. Any guilt he might have felt about poor bookkeeping went the way of the rest of the human race. As long as he understands his notation, nobody else is likely to care.

Paul has gone almost white, with black and purple patterns flickering and dancing at the edge of his mantle. Externally, he is much the same as the earliest Pauls, a football-sized body that is mostly stomach and brain; eight muscular tentacles ridged with suckers on the underside, surrounding a remarkably powerful beak. Internally he is a melange of ancestral genetics and the tweaks of the Rus-Califi virus. The virus, it will be remembered, was intended as an uplift tool. Califi and Rus started with the assumption that any sane researcher would want to tentatively nudge a mammalian species closer to human cognition. Senkovi has, therefore, not simply been dosing the tanks with it and hoping to wake up to vaguely tentacled humanoids able to discuss the nature of existence. Instead, he has used minimal and selected nano-viral samples to tweak, with his best guess, certain parameters of his subject species' worldview. His belief has always been that he has merely assisted the clock of nature into moving a little faster, but Disra Senkovi is not the best for unbiased introspection.

In this case, though, it is impossible for such a self-focused man to create in his own image. Take Paul's alarmed state. Paul is connected to the elevator systems, which contain the information – organized pictorially in a code Senkovi has painstakingly worked out as being something his pets can usually grasp – that if Salome succeeds in overriding the safeties then they will both find themselves *outside*, meaning miles over the surface of Damascus along with the rapidly dispersing watery environment currently sustaining them, and with about the same chance of survival as a bowl of petunias placed in the same predicament. Hence Paul's alarm, but Paul himself – the brain that is the centre of Paul – is in no position to appreciate the cause-and-effect physics of this. He just knows that he is frightened, and that Salome's actions are the cause. His fear is written across his skin for her to read – and she does – but not as a signal he consciously intends to send. His skin is the chalkboard of his brain, where he doodles his thoughts and feelings from moment to moment. If he wished to be deceptive he could fight himself for control of his own canvas, but right now he is more than happy for Salome to know just how stressed she is making him.

So where does the understanding lie, of their impending doom? Within the wider network of his nerves, perhaps;

within and between the individual sub-centres of neurology that control his arms, a semi-autonomous battery of processing power that Paul's brain lives in partnership with, and that makes his subconscious – insofar as he has anything humans would recognize as one – a powerful and world-affecting thing.

In just such a way, Salome – mottled red and angry purple, her skin pricked up into thorns and daggers – just knows she wants *out*. This is not her tank. Where are her games? Where are Great Large Entity and Calm Large Entity (system ID tags: Senkovi, Lortisse respectively)? What is this sense of motion and fluctuation of pressure within the water? Her brain proposes, her arms dispose. She is linked to the schematics of the capsule herself. The sub-minds of her arms grapple with the shape of it, turning it about and seeing where pressure can be applied to crack it open. She begins assaying commands; and though all of her, taken in aggregate, has the entire picture of her predicament, her active understanding is simply that she wants out, and *here* and *here* represent a way she can accomplish this. The greater drop outside eludes her, irrelevant to her priorities.

Paul, then: his own arm-driven undermind (his *Reach*, as opposed to the *Crown* of his central brain or the *Guise* of his skin) understands that to remove the fear he must prevent Salome from accomplishing her own goals. At first he simply signals this automatically, initially broadcasting a directionless fear but then adding qualifiers of colour and texture so that Salome understands she is the source of his anxiety. Normally this would be in response to her threatening him and indicate capitulation, but the raised whorls and darts of Paul's malleable skin show that he means anything but.

Salome cocks an eye at him, reading his intent very clearly, and doesn't really care. She is bigger than Paul; what is he going to do?

What he does, against millions of years of instinct, is try to attack her. He flushes his skin dark with angry courage, raises a hundred jagged crests across his body and jets towards her. They wrestle furiously, a boneless strangler's writhing. Unlike vertebrates they have no proprioception, no mental picture of where all the parts of their bodies are. Eight arms that can bend in any direction at any point would tax the processing power of the *Aegean*, let alone an octopus brain. The Crown sets strategy, but battlefield tactics are the province of the Reach, those sub-nodes that run the arms.

A fight like this would usually end with a submission, one combatant jetting away, perhaps with an arm less. Alternatively, a death: they are quite capable of strangling or devouring one another. The Califi and Rus meddling has had one effect, though: they are a more social species than they were, and societies are built on shared signals and information.

Abruptly they break apart by mutual agreement, retreating to the far ends of the capsule. Salome starts work on circumventing the safeties again, then stops, starts and then stops. She has a new idea, relating to the physics of what happens if a space elevator car unexpectedly burst open at high altitudes. Her Crown's grasp of this is limited, simply that now the idea of breaking out triggers a burst of chemical signals flagging up danger. In her mind, the consequence of breaking out is like a shark circling the descending capsule, a threat waiting to get her. Her Reach would have a more concrete understanding of the issue, feeling out the shape of it until the variables were all known, but the Reach has limited agency of its own and its reasoning is not apparent to the part of her that considers itself the individual that is Salome.

She reconsiders her course of action and sulks at the bottom of the capsule. Clinging to the top again, Paul slowly regains healthier shades.

4.

The vast wealth of data on the Nod biosphere, collected over so long by the orbiting module, had been lost in the Silence. The virus had devoured it; those far-off fanatics who had coded the monster had not dreamt of what their spite would erase. Probably they wouldn't have cared.

A piecemeal copy had survived on the *Aegean*, buried in the comms record between the two installations, although Senkovi had only uncovered this after the work had begun anew. Baltiel knew, intellectually, that time was the one thing they had, but the loss of knowledge remained profoundly frustrating.

But they were down, now, he and the others. They were down with a new shuttle (the other vessel having been dismantled by remotes, with its systems incinerated in a fit of caution) and firmly based on the ground. Lante was already talking about how to go about farming new people: she could mix up viable genetic signatures by randomly recombining the genomes she had, but now she was wrestling with how to actually *raise* the resulting infants. It wasn't as though they would spring up like magical warriors of myth, ready to start being fully-formed humans. She was working on tutelary programs, but Baltiel kept dropping 'socialization' into the conversation, and Lante, for all her drive to continue the species, didn't want to actually play mother to it. The surviving terraformers were not a good representative cross-section of humanity. After all, they had volunteered for a mission that would take them light years from home and sever them from human society for a lifetime. None of them were stay-at-home family types.

Which didn't mean that Lante, Lortisse and Rani weren't having some three-way fun time when they thought he wasn't looking, but Baltiel didn't care about that, if it helped them stay stable and happy. If he'd wanted, possibly they'd have made it a four-way, but for most of his life, he had focused on forming close work bonds that paid no heed to gender and never became possessive or physical. He suspected that it was that attitude that had recommended him for Overall Command.

They had remotes out, aerial and ground, taking fresh samples of the salt marsh fauna, and he was helping the new habitat computer integrate the data with Senkovi's recovered archive, eliminating repetition and making new connections they had missed the first time round. For her part, Lante was acting as his hands in the habitat's laboratory, dissecting those select specimens he deemed necessary in order to try and understand even the basics of the Nodan biology.

They had already marked several *unearthly* characteristics of the alien world, notably the radial symmetry. Evolutionary theorists on Earth had assumed that a front and a back were on the cards for a complex animal; apparently Nod was the exception to that rule. Baltiel paged between archive sections, navigating from the big-picture bauplan category to more specific topics.

Nod>bio>neurology>overview was next on his list, a topic curated by Lante. He skimmed the abstract:

*Based on imaging of live specimens of species 1, 3, 5, 6, 11,
19 and dissection of species 3, 6 and 19. All analysed species
show a distributed ring-shaped system of nerve analogues with
transmission of signals from cell to cell accomplished by way
of a mechanism involving concentration of polarized Calcium
ions, not currently fully understood. Sensory processing must
somehow take place across the neural net; the closest analogue
to a brain in most species is a concentrated band but the whole
nervous system is more homogenous than that of Earth species
and possibly the entire system acts as a single brain, or none
of it does. Experimental procedures for testing the limits of
specimen response to complex stimuli under review pending
proposals for appropriate meaningful stimuli.*

Nod was perhaps never destined to be graced by native
intelligence even if it remained unspoiled by a wider human
populace. Baltiel's money was on the swift fliers, but they
weren't common and capturing one intact was a tricky prospect. Presumably they must come to land somewhere, but
thus far they hadn't tracked one to its roost. Other than that,
even the complex environment of the tidal marsh seemed to
have produced only dull creatures of insensate instinct.

And yet there had been the tortoise dance. It was a
recording Lortisse had made when he went out with a repair
unit to recover a glitchy remote. Nine of the three-foot tall
shelled creatures – listed as *species 3* in their database and a
major part of Lante's neurology study – had been standing
in a ring, their rims almost touching. They had swayed – one
way, then the other, coordinated, their arms emerging from
within their carapaces to wave and twine together and then
withdraw. Was it a mating ritual? Were they diseased? The

bizarre display had brought the lumbering things to Baltiel's attention, anyway. They were the giants of the marsh, relatively speaking, but he had seen them as sedate grazers, the snails of an alien shore. Now, and in the absence of a flier to study, they had become a point of particular interest.

He sorted through the submitted pages of the neurology archive, tidying up where the automatic librarian systems had made errors, some of which were the result of shoddy coding and tagging by his colleagues. Next up was—

Next up was a signal from Senkovi, the first in days. Baltiel opened a channel, knowing the signal delay would let him keep working in the gaps of their conversation.

'Hey boss.' Senkovi sounded manic, which was probably a good sign.

'Disra.'

'So, those sensors along the faultline we were having trouble with . . .' Senkovi opened with.

Baltiel sent back a noncommittal sound, having found a narrative of a flyby over the inner desert that had somehow been logged by Lortisse as biochemistry. The Damascus project had run into a series of technical hitches, mostly because nobody had tried to regulate the chemistry and ecology of just that much virgin ocean before, and Senkovi had ended up turning out kit from the workshops that was a little on the cheap and cheerful side. Now that kit had been in place long enough for the cracks to show and he was frantically trying to get everything repaired or replaced before whole sections of the planet stopped reporting to him.

'Ha, yes. Half-fixed, the rest on their way, so that's all right.' Senkovi had obviously worked out that a noncommittal noise was all he was getting.

'That's good.' Senkovi really must be in a manic mood. 'Does that mean you don't need Rani to help with the remote work?' And then, speaking over Senkovi's response as the delay tripped him up, 'Does that mean your mollusc diagnostics worked out?'

Senkovi was silent for longer than the signal gap as he worked out what to answer, and then silent a little longer, so that Baltiel was already cued to pick up the twitchiness in his voice when he finally spoke. 'Actually, no remotes needed. They . . . they fixed it, Yusuf.'

Baltiel paused, about to delve into the murky depths of the Nodan reproduction archive. 'What?' Because that had been the plan, of course; to use the damn octopodes as aquatic crew, because Senkovi had sworn it was possible. Only he had tried and failed to demonstrate any such thing in the *Aegean*'s tanks. He had called everyone, full of his own prowess, presenting his molluscs with a virtual simulation of the trashed equipment they would be working with. Baltiel remembered the event with exquisite embarrassment. The molluscs had investigated the interface, moving things around in virtual space in a desultory manner, but there had been not a hint that anything Senkovi taught them had stuck. The whole exercise had dragged on unnecessarily until Baltiel had overruled the man and brought an end to the entire sorry affair. The little monsters had been sent down fitted with surveillance gear and hopefully trained to be curious about the malfunctioning kit so they would go take a look at it.

'I, er . . .' And now Baltiel was beginning to process the mixture of unease and elation in his colleague's voice. 'Yes, they went down and just . . . did it. Diagnosed the faults, patched them. Everything's working again, for how long I don't know. I mean, not all of them actually got to work but . . . fifty per cent of the pairs I sent down. They just . . . Yusuf, I'm going to admit something now. I don't really under-stand it.' He didn't seem distressed by the admission. 'In the lab . . . I gave them every chance to show that they understood the job, you know. And nothing. It was like they'd forgotten the first thing about learning anything. But now they're down there and . . . they're fixing things. As though all that technical stuff was in there somewhere, but . . .' An exasperated noise. 'We've got sixty per cent restored coverage along the fault. I'm trying them with new instructions.'

Baltiel had been running over the repair data. The work on the faultline kit had been erratic, unorthodox, not what a human with a remote would have turned out. Senkovi would doubtless sell it as his little pets devising their own solutions to the problem, which Baltiel was unwilling to accept. Not that he had a better explanation. Then something else snagged his attention. 'Hold on, pairs? Why pairs?' He brought up the specifics of just which pets Senkovi had been sending down the line to Damascus. 'Disra, I can't help noticing these are male-female pairings you've been sending down.'

Now it was Senkovi's turn to make a noncommittal noise, and Baltiel ground his teeth at the distance between them. So Damascus had its first long-term residents, did it? Breeding pairs of octopodes sent down by Disra Senkovi, patron saint of all things tentacled.

'It's not as if anyone's coming,' Senkovi muttered after another long span of dead air.

'Lante's coming, with her goddamned chimera babies,' Baltiel shot back, not as tactfully as he might.

'Tell them to build boats,' Senkovi said, and closed the connection.

After that, Baltiel felt he'd played cataloguer for long enough and moved on to Lortisse's latest recordings of the fliers. It was a weakness, Baltiel knew. They had a whole alien ecosystem, every part of it novel and baffling. Focusing on a large dynamic carnivore was old-style human thinking, the same idolatry that put lions and eagles on so many old flags. Yet there was a strange malaise taking hold of him, and Lortisse and Rani as well. Now they were here, now this was *it*, they found themselves faced with a great absence in their work. Lante had her breeding program, but the rest of them had an alien world filled with brainless, docile beasts. In the absence of the balance of the human race, they felt a lack of meaning to it all. The universe was no longer watching them. The data they were collecting was for no eyes but their own. *And those who come after?* Lante's work was becoming more and more of a good idea, for all that she was still wrestling with the practicalities. *We will understand this world and its life, but its life will never understand us. And that hurts, somehow. Because we need to feel ourselves important to our environs, and Nod has no way of knowing us.* And so, unspoken, they had begun to concentrate on species whose behaviour showed complexities that might indicate a greater intelligence, some level of awareness of self, even if there was no brain to house it. It was a dreadfully anthropomorphic desire, but none of them could shake it. Humanity justified its premier position on Earth by its intelligence. But here was a vast and complex world that seemed to lack anything with thoughts as complex as a goldfish's.

Lortisse had set remotes to shadow any fliers that overflew

the marsh. The creatures were certainly active predators with a high-energy lifestyle, something that seemed vanishingly rare on Nod. Baltiel settled back to review the latest footage.

. . . Fliers powered through the air high over the marsh with that frenzied flapping sequence of theirs. The 'up' pole of their radial anatomy had shifted until it was 'forwards' and their flight was born of three pairs of hydrostatic wings being inflated in turn, a motion utterly unlike anything that had ever flown on Earth. The remote focused in on a trio of them, and Baltiel tried to read some social interaction between them, but for all his human eyes could tell they were simply sharing the same camera's width of sky.

. . . A flier stooped abruptly, dropping from the air to tackle a mid-sized tortoise. Its descent was steep enough that its prey was unable to hunker down like a limpet, and the flier's wings were repurposed as grasping, levering arms to get its victim onto its back, whereupon it flensed the luckless creature from its shell with a half-dozen claw-tipped tentacles. Lortisse had filmed a dozen of these attacks, plainly impressed by the savagery of the attack compared to the sedate pace of everything else on Nod.

. . . and then, the last recording, an attack that went wrong. The flier dived on its shelled prey but broke off, floundering desperately in the air as though its placid target had become suddenly toxic. The aborted dive left the predator on the ground, flapping and shouldering through the rock pools as it fought to get airborne again. There was no obvious reason for it.

Complex behaviour, of a kind, Baltiel thought, clutching at straws. Behaviour they couldn't fathom, though. Alien behaviour. What had they expected?

He stared at the wall. In truth he was staring further, out

past the horizon, out into the alienness of Nod. *Notice me,* he thought irrationally. *Acknowledge that I'm here, before it's too late.*

5.

Such

hostile environments.

Such killing grounds.

And yet so strange. Word spreads until All-of-We know that here, here is something. As we generate and spend our energies new patterns emerge, a dizziness and madness of chemical gradients that lead Some-of-We to yearn towards this newness.

Some-of-We touch their substances, encounter their new elements, learn their valences and their shapes, the folds of their curious molecules.

Some-of-We vanish, never to be heard from. But we are We and there is always More-of-We to learn from those that went before. Many-of-We are intrigued as to the possibilities of these new shapes and spaces.

Consensus spreads.

We cannot ignore this intrusion. Some-of-We will act.

6.

Senkovi floated by the tanks in the *Aegean*'s heart, trying to make sense of it all. Today he was working with a new generation, in an attempt to replicate up here what was still happening down there. His subject was Paul 58, of a hatching slightly more tempered by the Rus-Califi virus than the last.

'Which makes you brighter,' he told Paul. 'Or should do. Lets you make those neural connections quicker. Learning, memory . . .' He stared into the tank where Paul clung to an interface pad, constricting it with sudden flurries of movement as he navigated the virtual spaces Senkovi had created. Like the octopi on Damascus, Paul had been given repair tasks to perform, a series of broken installations flagged up to engage his curiosity. So far, that curiosity remained unengaged. Senkovi felt as though he was performing a weird balancing act or playing some odd Tower of Hanoi game where to progress he was constantly moving pieces backwards. Earlier generations had been able to perform complex tasks by rote, but as he let the virus complicate the octopi neurology, they became less predictable, less knowable. *I thought the idea of an uplift virus was to make something human.*

He sent instructions through to Paul again, resetting the virtual environment. *I've overbred them, maybe. They're unstable.* Paul certainly seemed to be having cerebral issues. The mollusc's skin was in constant strobing motion, flickering and dancing with jittery patterns as he became more and more anxious for no reason Senkovi could understand.

Sooner or later, Baltiel was going to want answers. 'Just do this for me,' he told the unhearing side of the tank. 'Let's just give them a circus they can understand, and we can go back to just you and me. Come *on*, Paul.'

Paul abruptly released the interface and jetted across the tank. His skin was raised into diabolic spires and horns, which normally meant aggression, but at the same time he was pale with fear, the chromatophores about his eyes and siphon pulsing with nervous patterns. Senkovi regarded him unhappily. *I've pushed you too far, haven't I? This is goddamn unnatural, is what it is. But they won't just let me sit up here and keep pets. That's not how it goes. Everyone has to work. And it'll be your planet one day, Paul. Or your descendants'. Or the descendants of some other octopus that keeps it together long enough to have any.*

Paul had apparently got over his fit, creeping back to the interface. It wasn't as though he was ignoring the test, but within the virtual environment his presence went everywhere except where it was supposed to, prowling around the edges of the notional space as though trying to see out of it. One of his eyes was always tilted towards Senkovi, regarding him through the tank's clear wall.

And now an error message had popped up, the system feeding impulses into his cybernetic implants that projected them into his visual field. Senkovi frowned at it: *Error [RestateIntent]*. It was a warning flag he had put in for himself, because he sometimes forgot what he was supposed to be accomplishing mid-code, leaving him with digital chimeras that did something entirely untoward. The system had detected part of the test design going off the rails and wanted him to redefine its goals. He began hunting through the nodes of the limited test environment to find out what had crashed.

Error[RestateIntent].

'Yes, yes.' He had been working with this generation of octopi for seventeen hours and change, he realized. *Time to chalk up another failure and get some sleep.*

User[SenkoviD] Error[RestateIntent].

Just simple building blocks of system communication, the toys he used when he was building the virtual architecture. He hunted down where it was coming from.

It was coming from Paul 58.

The octopus had hacked into the limited system, its virtual consciousness escaping from the test environment to send a signal to him.

Error[RestateIntent] TestSubject[Paul58] Error[RestateIntent] User[SenkoviD]. Just strings of identifiers: the code that identified him as programmer, the code that referred to Paul, and the error code he used to prompt himself if he was leaving the task parameters he'd set for himself. Restate your intent. Go back and remind yourself why you're doing this.

Paul's eye was on him, but he was used to the octopi watching him work. They were naturally curious creatures.

Error[RestateIntent] Error[RestateIntent] Subject[Paul58] Error[RestateIntent] User[SenkoviD] Error[RestateIntent].

Senkovi and Paul looked at each other, and this time perhaps it was the octopus waiting patiently for the human to catch on.

Restate intent. Tell me why.

Why is there Senkovi? Why is there Paul? Why? Why the test, why these nonsense games, why any of it? Why, O creator, why?

Ten minutes later and Senkovi had scrambled all the way into the outer ring, the place that humans went and octopi mostly didn't (barring the swim tank and some industrious escapees). He sat there, back against a wall, hyperventilating, with a bitter understanding of what sort of man he was. Because he liked octopi, he did, but they had always been pets. Try as he might, travel as many light years as they were, he had not left that part of him behind. He had bred them and mutated them and played all sorts of God, and now they wanted to know why and he had no answer.

7.

Gav Lortisse had started his audio journal only after the virus attack. None of the others knew about it. Actually Baltiel probably knew about it, because he took the role of Overall Command very seriously, and possibly Senkovi had hacked through Lortisse's personal security because he had no sense of boundaries that weren't his own. Nominally, though, documenting his own private spiral into madness kept Lortisse sane. He was a team player, Lortisse, always willing to pitch in with other people's projects, to do the legwork, get a sweat up on someone else's ticket. And he talked to himself, and his suit compiled hours and hours of his circular reflections. Eventually someone would object to the storage space his journal was using, but not for a long time.

'Baltiel has me out for specimens again. He wants the tortoises if he can't get the fliers. Lante wants them, too. She loves cutting the poor bastards up. It's like she thinks she can read the future in their entrails or something.' There was a word for that, but he couldn't remember it, so he had his suit link to the habitat system to hunt it down as he continued his careful progress over the salt marsh.

'I don't know how we ever expected it to work out.' It was a recent revelation this, and he was still feeling it out like a rotten tooth. 'I mean, they're all gone. Not a peep since the attack. Not from home, not from any ships.' Narrating it to himself, hearing his voice breathy in his own ears, gave him a curious illusion of control, as though he was hearing the story long after, when everything actually *had* worked out. As though he was telling some notional grandchild. Except . . .

Behind him a hauling remote was following at a set distance, waiting for his signal. It had three tortoises in its bed already, aimlessly crawling over the plastic. More specimens for Lante to dissect. He stooped over another of the creatures. There were plenty of them; scientific depredation wouldn't make a dent. Of course, people had probably said that about mammoths and bison and actual tortoises, once upon a time, but right now Lortisse reckoned even the plodding nature of Nod was more than enough to overcome the efforts of four poor humans.

'We're all going spare, but so gently,' he continued his narrative. 'It's like seeing something break up in zero gravity, the pieces gradually falling away from each other. But why not? The world ended. There's no force pulling us together any more. I see Kalveen and she's constantly improving on systems, designing . . . palaces, mansions, habitats the size of cities, planning them out with fail-safes and redundancies and . . . on a scale we could never build, not the four of us, not forty of us. She says it's the future, but she can't believe it. She can give us a virtual tour of floating cities on Damascus, of airborne dome-complexes on Nod that have a zero footprint, where the alien life just goes on unmolested beneath your feet. And it's mad, it's all mad.'

The remote came at his signal and he loaded up his latest victim. *Is this what I've come to? Driving the execution wagon for brainless alien shellfish?* But it got him out under the sky. It exercised the muscles. Better than staying cooped up with Baltiel and Rani and . . .

'And Erma,' he finished the thought aloud. 'She's always talking about breeding a new generation in the vats, only we don't even have the vats yet, and she never seems to get started. There's always some other thing that needs planning out. She can't get her head past the stage where it becomes real and there are . . . what, some sickly, feeble *children* someone has to take care of. She knows the automatics can't just do it for us, but it's not as though any of us want the responsibility. Give us a next generation, sure, but don't make us *care* for it. Senkovi cares more for his octopodes than any of us would for those poor goddamn children.'

The hauling remote always made the tortoises limpet down on the rock. Something about it said 'predator' in a way Lortisse's human form didn't. It was a wide, flat thing on six narrow legs, and probably its shadow resembled one of the fliers, or at least to the weird eyes of a tortoise. Anyway, the other animals nearby had all fled or were hunkered down enough to make it impossible to pry them free without killing them. Lortisse continued his ramblings, stepping carefully around the pools, the remote following at its polite under-taker's distance. 'And so Erma just goes on doing piecework dissections for Yusuf, because Yusuf's the craziest of us all. Because he just wants to carry on as though nothing happened. It's like he doesn't even understand it's all gone. He wants to study the aliens, as though they care, as though anybody ever will. He thinks as long as he's doing his *job* – or, not even his job, but the job he gave himself before it all went to hell – that things are still okay. That it's all business as usual.'

He found another pool clustered with tortoises, some in the water, some at the edge, scissoring and rasping at the blackish clusters of fronds and spirals that were something like plants, something more like sessile, semi-autotrophic animals. Nod lacked hard divisions between kingdoms. Those 'plants' would release swimming or airborne larvae to colonize other regions. Some of them would supplement their diet with just such microscopic flotsam; others went through mobile phases in which they metamorphosed into something entirely more active. Perhaps the tortoises had a plant stage, too. Perhaps the fliers did, putting down roots in high mountain crevices and turning their wings to the sun. Lortisse stood still, feeling the environment encroach on his mind with its very strangeness, staring out across the lumpen, low landscape towards the sea, watching rain sheeting in across the coast.

'Really, Senkovi's the sanest of us all. I should go back to the *Aegean*, go swimming with his pets again. That was good. That made sense. None of this does.'

A searing pain lanced into his calf. Dumbfounded, he looked down. One of the tortoises had honed a tentacle arm into something resembling a needle and jammed it into his leg. At first he didn't yell or call for help. He just stared at the thing as it removed the prong, his suit sealing the puncture automatically. The tortoise seemed to lose whatever interest it had in him instantly, bumbling away and scraping shells with its neighbour.

Then the pain of the incision was growing and growing until his whole leg was on fire with it. *Poison!* And yet no creature on Nod could have evolved a poison to attack a man of Earth, surely. But now his helmet display was covered in red lights, medical emergency signals winging to the habitat. Lortisse swayed, vision blurring, his breath abruptly laboured. He could feel a terrible pressure as his calf and thigh swelled within his suit.

Haruspex. The result of his earlier search had been waiting for him at the edge of his attention, waiting politely at the edge of his mind's eye. *To seek the future in entrails.*

He lurched forwards, wheezing, gasping, even as the panicked voices of his colleagues twittered faintly in his ear.

PRESENT 2
INSIDE THE WHALE

1.

Doctor Avrana Kern is suspicious by nature. Partly this is a deeply-ingrained trauma resulting from a betrayal by an underling, back when she was human and alive and (relatively) sane. Partly it is simply building on a suspicion that was always part of her nature. This suspicion has survived in her despite the many forms she has taken: from human to human-AI hybrid to pure AI (that believed itself human) through to a complex program running on an organic operating system arising out of the interactions of millions of ants.

Which means that when an alien fleet hoves into view, she starts looking for weapons and analysing technology and constructing elaborate countermeasures and emergency plans that even she had not thought would suddenly become necessary.

Abruptly, they are necessary. She was watching the energy signatures of the alien ships – all built on enough of an Old Empire foundation that she can understand them. Within seconds of the *Lightfoot*'s first visual transmission she senses a moment of utter chaos – as though the vessels are brains undergoing a seizure. Everything lights up: they are manoeuvring; they are activating their weapons. Kern reacts instantly, her hypotheticals becoming the new reality.

Humans, back when they built spaceships, constructed

them with a hard outer shell to protect their vulnerable insides. Portiids build ships with an internal skeleton but a flexible outer sheath that Kern can trim by shifting the ship's bones. The outer hull comprises multiple layers of a fabric that is to the ancestral spider silk as a thrown stone is to the weapons the aliens are deploying, but it retains many of that substance's virtues. It has an incredible tensile strength for its weight; it can stretch without rupturing; it can be produced in large quantities in a short period of time.

Kern starts shedding hull in great loose swatches, each one carrying with it a fluctuating electromagnetic signature. The *Lightfoot* becomes the centre of an expanding haze of urticated silk that writhes and clumps and forms constellations of matter even as the ship itself alters course. That suffices to confuse the targeting systems of the missiles now heading towards it: they veer off, spinning into snarling skeins that drag them off course, chasing electronic ghosts created in their sensor feed-back by the arachnid chaff. The first lasers fall foul of the same defences, wasting their energy on a vacuum abruptly cluttered. By then, the *Lightfoot* is already moving on a different heading, shifting tack so suddenly that its effective length halves, its internal buttressing compressing about the crew quarters, preserving that little bubble of air intact.

The alien vessels are also turning, but they lumber where the *Lightfoot* darts. Kern has calculated the sort of mass they are hauling and it is, by her reckoning, insane. Yes, the ships are huge, but even for such massive craft they appear to be carrying an absurd momentum, a thousand times more than she can account for as they utterly fail to match her swift course correction.

Of course, that is why they have launched a scattering of

smaller craft, she surmises, which are tiny, each barely larger than a couple of Humans end to end and with engines every which way, apparently, so that they spin about any axis they need to, to come and bother the *Lightfoot* with their weapons.

She deploys more silk, aware that she is boiling away the mass of the ship, making some of that inertial shortening a permanent fixture as she cannibalizes her own substance. At least one of the incoming fighters ploughs straight into a mass of the stuff, loses half its thrusters and spins off into the void, but the rest are doggedly on her. She briefly considers consulting Bianca about permission to fire, but she is, after all, Avrana Kern. Who better to make such decisions? She has a brief fugue moment of memory: unleashing her tiny satellite's weaponry against the *Gilgamesh*'s shuttles and drones, killing humans before they became Humans.

She never said, because neither Portiids nor Humans would understand, but she enjoyed herself, doing that. Cathartic, was the word that occurred to her. And once they started putting her into spaceships, she always wondered if there might be some war, somewhere, with a hostile power. She decides that some other Kerns out there might get to be proper warships one day, and wouldn't *that* be fine? For now she resolves that she will try to kill a few of these drones or fighters or whatever they are. She has decided that, based on technological similarity, the 'aliens' here are some human successor state. Probably Portiid diplomacy will make them Humans eventually, but for now she will blow a few of them up and see how it makes her feel.

Of course the *Lightfoot*, hastily prepared scout craft, is not exactly a gunboat, but she has lasers – rather more so than her captain or crew are aware of, more even than the Kern instance on the *Voyager* knew, because she went behind her own back when building this ship-body. Now she lights them up, the *Lightfoot*'s malleable hull breaking out in ugly warts that each house a lens. She begins painting the dark sky with lights, trying to pin down the enemy even as they overtake her. They are very swift, though, and she begins to realize they are also good at what they do, whether they are organic or automatic. Their all-direction thrusters allow them to make lightning-fast changes in trajectory, bouncing about like monkeys as she tries to track them. She clips a couple, but they adapt to whatever minor damage she deals out. Their own lasers blister at her, crisping silk that her repair spinnerets replace as quickly as possible, frying some hubs of her ant-network. They have overshot her and are now spinning about, fighting their own momentum with a rapid patter of thrust.

Some of them open up with magnetically accelerated projectiles, and Kern laughs quietly to herself because she can mend any external holes as swiftly as they open, and the *Lightfoot* simply lacks the solid parts for such miniscule missiles to disrupt. They would need a lucky shot, a *very* lucky shot—

A string of such little beads rip through her hull. One punches a hole in a main strut of her skeleton, but there is plenty of redundancy there. The trailing edge of the salvo punches a dozen holes in the crew compartment, so swiftly that the crew themselves would not even realize, had not Bianca, the captain, been directly in the path of one shot. Her death is instant, explosive. For the projectile itself, her presence does not affect its course – she is incidental to its path, that takes it into and out of the *Lightfoot* in the flash of an eye.

*

For Meshner, the moment is experienced only in retrospect. Bianca had been at her post, stamping out orders that the machines translated only sluggishly for the Human crew – Kern was concentrating too much on their defence to spend too much of herself on the niceties of interspecies communication. Then Bianca was . . . all around them, without any transitional state, the fluid-filled sack of her body burst asunder.

Everyone is engaged in the fight, all the *Lightfoot's* small crew. Bianca's coordination has been taken from them but nobody can spare more than a heartbeat to register it. Kern may make all the decisions, but the crew is providing her with supplementary computing power in the form of their own grey matter. Portia and Viola are suggesting firing solutions, trying to understand the apparently random patterns of the enemy fighters/drones. Zaine and Helena manage energy budgeting: the *Lightfoot's* drive is good, but like the *Voyager* it is optimized for long-term use, not extreme short-term drain, and space combat is nothing if not draining. Kern draws what she needs and the two Humans do their best to juggle other less-critical systems, like life support. Fabian and Meshner work on wider predictions, with particular reference to the big ships out there that are each erupting with weapons fire from a dozen different angles.

Meshner plots arcs and angles, trying to work out the best way to thread that particular needle. Space is a desert with no cover, and the enemy vessels have no 'front', meaning that any angle invites a broadside, and no sure way to know when it might come.

Fabian passes over his best guess, paths to take that might dodge the worst of the incoming fire as they accelerate out of this mess; Meshner counters. Kern shoots them both down, figuratively speaking, modelling worst-case scenarios for them that see the *Lightfoot* smeared across a kilometre of empty space. The acerbic computer helpfully attaches a legend identifying just which pieces of the wreckage are Meshner and Fabian, because she always has computing power for put-downs.

Back to the drawing board. Fabian stamps out a little fit of anger against his controls, which are above Meshner's head.

There's no way we can get clear unless we break from the fighters, Fabian insists. Even as he does so, Meshner registers that another three railgun projectiles have just clipped through the crew compartment, striking nothing vital and having no effect other than a tiny loss of atmosphere before the infinitesimal wounds in the hull seal themselves. The lasers are potentially worse, but the enemy fighters only use them in brief stabs, rather than trying to slice the *Lightfoot* open. Most likely the tiny ships have even more limited energy reserves than their victim and lasers are a colossal power sink.

Meshner blinks, frowning, because abruptly his view of the screen is fuzzing, lines breaking apart into spectra of colours, the controls seeming to jump and writhe under his fingers.

Not a good time, not a good time, he knows, watching his hands rattle with sudden palsy.

Also: *Artifabian didn't translate Fabian for me*. He understood the Portiid's words direct, somehow, or imagined he had. He opens his mouth to advise Kern he's having issues. His tongue waves; words don't come.

He turns and looks at the ocean sunset, both it and him running mad with colours he doesn't know, and that his mind baulks at simply calling 'purple'. When the waves crash on the shore they are silent, yet they speak to him in a roar, insisting on their own provenance and immortality before reducing to a grumbling nothing.

Meshner freezes, clutching for the controls he knows are there. His fingertips come back to him with a riot of sensory overload, a complexity of tactile data he simply lacks the equipment to decode. The approximate shape of his console is in there somewhere, camouflaged within the tumult.

The ocean waves crash, same as before, exactly the same, cycling: a broken stub of memory recorded in too many colours, missing channels of data he would need before any of it felt real. It looks like corrupted recordings, ancient video data, flickering and phasing, repeating over and over.

Not now!

And, at the same time: *Is this it? Has the fight shaken this loose? Have we succeeded at last?* And yet this doesn't feel . . . first person. He is Meshner, the Human. This isn't what he was hunting for, in trying to graft Portiid Understandings into his implant and his Human brain. He feels as though he is watching the information from the outside, through some sort of third party mediation.

With that thought he can move his point of perspective – he has no physical body, or rather his body is not *here*, all its sensory data and proprioception locked in another room. And surely Fabian cannot just go wandering through his own memories like this; he would be locked to the perspective he – or his ancestor – had occupied when the Understanding was first encoded. So how can he, Meshner, take apart and analyse the sensory data in this way? *I'm modelling it, extrapolating a whole from Fabian's limited perspective.* Which means that probably half of what he experiences is his own invention, but fascinating nonetheless. If he wasn't about to die in – of all the stupid things – a *space battle* he would be exhilarated by this development.

He turns around and sees Fabian there, the same Fabian he knows, looking out at that sunset. Why did the spider choose this moment? The Portiid – or some past Portiid whose likeness was lost but whom Meshner has reconstructed as modern-day Fabian – had loved this sunset, this seascape, enough. Perhaps that was all.

You cannot interrogate this, the spider tells him, the usual dance of feet and waving palps, and yet the meaning is crystal clear in Meshner's mind. *This is all your own conjecture, building on reconstructed data in virtual space.*

'Then who am I talking to?' he demands, and the spider stamps out, *Work it out yourself. I'm busy.*

The means of communication is unfamiliar, the sharp tone less so. 'Kern?' Or some limited sub-system of hers?

Make yourself useful, it instructs him, and he has a sudden sense of wider space beyond this looping moment.

It occurs to him that this could go very badly if he lets himself get trapped in the same five seconds of Fabian's recollection forever. And yet how is this even still present in his brain?

It isn't, idiot. His own sharpness now, his own thoughts, not Kern's. *But it's still in your implant. Like Kern said, it's a virtual space.* The implant is a potent computing tool built to translate and model memory data, after all. Now, at the worst moment, he has finally accessed that space, except he didn't ask to and potentially cannot escape from it.

Even as he thinks it, another part of his brain seizes on a lifeline, the only thing here that comes from outside other than his own lost consciousness. He is linked to the ship, to Kern. The implant gives him access to her somehow, far beyond a crewmember's regular comms. He feels dizzy for a moment at the thought that he is participating in a neural link with a computer, something nobody had done before without Old Empire technology, and not terribly successfully even then.

He follows the breadcrumbs of Kern's link and abruptly the sunset turns off, leaving him in dimness. Before him is a spider, huge beyond the dreams of Portiids, save that of course he views it from the low-slung perspective of Fabian. Meshner's mind floods with raw emotional input, some of it translated into base urges he can name: fear and desire inextricably linked, the ragged raw edge of excitement, desperation, a dread of failure. Other information batters at his brain looking for somewhere to roost, square-peg emotions ramming themselves at the round holes of his mind, trying to make themselves known. He asked for something that would be unmistakably arachnid, and surely this matches his specifications: Portiids doing Portiid things to one another, incomprehensible, alien. The Understanding he has been given is visually simple, but that is just a thin skin riding on a great sea of experiential data. *And I will drown unless I get clear.*

Again he follows the link of Kern until he finds himself in another place.

Space.

A frozen moment. He stands in the void (although he is not standing, not really, but his viewpoint suggests a presence and he goes with it; otherwise madness awaits), gazing down on the stretched silvery shimmer of the *Lightfoot*, looking buckled as it is caught midway through shifting its hull profile to cushion against another high-speed manoeuvre. Now the image pulls out: there are the enemy fighters, tiny spheres within a net of thrust and weapons systems. One is just erupting open into loose matter as Kern's lasers finally pinpoint it, the firing solution courtesy of Portia and Viola having predicted the next way it would jink. Beyond are the larger vessels, their formation now a cluttered mess, their own weapons systems quite busy. And the *Lightfoot* is coming back that way, because that is the best path to avoid the worst of the fighter barrage.

'This is intolerable,' a sharp female voice tells him, and he flinches with an instinct still held over from the Portiid historical male deference to the female.

Kern manifests herself in space on the far side of the *Lightfoot*, her chosen scale making the ships seem like toys floating at the level of her waist. Meshner sees a tall, severe woman, grey hair tied back, wearing an ornate one-piece garment that might perhaps be what Old Empire shipsuits looked like, back when such things were more than tatters and dust. He wonders how authentic the simulacra is, because surely Avrana Kern does not really hold an accurate self-image after so many millennia?

'You are occupying too much *space*,' she snaps at him, for all that she has a virtual body twice the size of the largest alien ship and he has a notional point of view that could dance upon the head of a pin. 'You are draining my resources. Who or what are you?' Without a half-second's pause she seems to catch up with that fragment of herself he encountered a moment before, 'Meshner Osten Oslam, the self-made lab animal,' and he reflects that answering her own questions is probably a large part of her stock in trade these days. 'Why are you here?'

He stammers out that she led him here, but perhaps that part that left the breadcrumbs is only a subroutine that Kern herself disowns. He has a sense that somewhere, somehow, a kind of communication is being attempted, but it isn't reaching Kern. She stalks about the sluggishly-moving display, simultaneously looking at all the spaceborne vessels and at him, giving everything her full attention all the time. Parts of his brain grind against each other trying to force this ersatz visual stimulus to conform to the laws of physical space.

Which it needn't, he reminds himself. *So:* and he calls up information, arraying it in virtual space just as he did when testing out the implant the first time he awoke with it. For a split second he is back with the sunset and the ocean but then Kern bodily yanks him back to the battle map, the little dart of the *Lightfoot*; to the spreading formation of enemy ships (and his mind is processing, processing, still trying to do its job now he has this spectacular visual representation of the sky outside, and something has snagged his attention that surely Kern has already seen . . .).

And his information has got through, or else Kern looked past the battle to what his body was/is working on and has seen his meagre role in all of this.

'Your cognitive functions are overflowing into ship systems,' she tells him – still severe, but with a thoughtful edge; she is a scientist first and foremost, after all. 'Your implant needs limiting functions. It is trying to process a fat bolus of sensory data and it's just eating up all the processing power it can handle. I'm having to hold it off from rampaging through my own memory, and in holding it off I'm suffering a further drain on my capabilities. Idiot monkey.' Her expression – or that facet of it she spares him – is appraising. 'Still, at any other time, an interesting toy. You have come somewhere close to an upload facility in the most backwards manner possible, creating an extended virtual simulation of your own cognitive functions in order to process a recorded medium not in any way intended for a Human.'

Wait – a virtual simulation? Is that all I am? This all feels entirely real to me. Again, he has no way of saying it, but it manages to reach Kern. He expects derision, but the look on her face is solemn, even sympathetic.

'It does, doesn't it?' she agrees. 'No matter how they peel you down. Even when you're stripped down to something that can't think, can't feel, some pissant little shard of your-self that's barely good for anything but calculating square roots and prime numbers, it still feels like you, until you try to do something and find that part of you is missing. I'm limiting you, Meshner Osten Oslam. I am fencing you off so you don't cripple the ship with your existential crisis. And that way, this experience may end up repatriated with the rest of your mind and bring it out of the *grand mal* seizure you are currently experiencing.'

I . . . what?

'Your brain is a complicated toy. When you play carelessly with it, you might lose some pieces,' she says, and that sardonic edge is back, her sympathy apparently exhausted. 'I've devised a solution to purge you from the system for now. I really do need all my wits about me. If you have the chance, there are ways to have your implant recalibrate its internal architecture to make your simulations far more resource-efficient, and thus get more done without involving me. Let me know if any of this stays with you.'

Wait! Meshner's perspective lurches. He can feel reality ascending to meet him like the ground reaches for a falling man – either Kern's doing or the fit he is apparently under-going – and he tries to force more information up the pipe than mere words. He has a course for her, not frantic flight into the black but an approach to the enemy ships. It is threading the needle sideways and backwards and upside down, entirely beyond the parameters of the task he had been set, and yet perfect.

'Nonsense,' Kern snaps. 'This exposes us to the weapons of three of the large vessels in sequence at extreme close range, one after another. Unacceptable.'

You have set the wrong limits on our search, he insists. The ocean returns briefly, pulsing like a slow heartbeat, so that he gains and loses Kern, gains and loses the battle. *See their attacks.* It is so obvious, and yet Kern hasn't seen it because, in the final analysis, she is a self-regulating computer trying to maximize her limited computational power. She set herself a narrow task, and that task became her world. *They are fighting each other*, he manages at last, flagging up various of the combatants in different colours, some hostile, some at least neutral, deploying weapons on their fellows in an apparent attempt to defend the *Lightfoot*. Each ship has angles and arcs that are being used for countermeasures, casting vast shadows where their attentions pick the void clean of the ordnance of their neighbours. Space is abruptly not a desert, or at least it is a desert with a few rocks for shade. Enough cover, perhaps, to get up enough speed to outrange the enemy.

Kern stares at him, going in and out of his mind's eye, but he sees her smile before he loses her.

Then he is arching his back, fingers clutching at the fabric of the cabin floor as Zaine clamps a medical scanner to his head, jarring his implant agonizingly. There is a great deal of chaos, and he feels his heart stop and get jolted back into action by Helena applying a muscle override. There is blood in his mouth and his vision glitters with ephemeral stars.

2.

Abruptly they have left the fighters spinning in their wake, the *Lightfoot* accelerating with all its power. Only the spiders, Portia, Viola and Fabian, remain at the controls. Helena and Zaine are doing their best to save the life of their fellow Human, Meshner, fighting cerebral inflammation and calming his spiking neural activity until at last he opens his eyes.

Helena isn't sure they still have him, despite everything. There is a moment when nothing of Meshner stares out at her. Then expression falls back onto his face and he says, 'They're fighting,' which seems the most fatuous observation in the world until Fabian starts tapping and scraping at his console and she puts a gloved hand down to catch his meaning.

. . . being screened by three of the vessels. One of the others is damaged – there's ice bleeding from it! They are at war! He is practically bouncing at his post, hanging head-down up the wall. A moment later he jumps down and runs around Meshner's prone form, because Portiids have great trouble keeping still when they are excited.

Helena checks the medical monitors: Meshner seems stable now, though he has apparently lapsed back into unconsciousness. She sits back, feeling exasperated at him. Some feedback from his implant struck him down, nothing of the fight at all. She isn't the only one to be thinking it. Fabian's skittering progress comes to an abrupt end as Viola jumps down in front of him, her forelegs raised in threat. The male instantly adopts a submissive posture and she hoists herself higher for a moment, displaying her utmost anger with him, before stalking off to Bianca's station.

Fabian's palps lift and twitch, which Helena reads automatically as *What did I do?*

You made this happen, Portia signals, creeping over to hunker down by Helena. *You experimented on him.*

The male makes a few stuttering motions, not a complete sentence but the equivalent of a Human muttering to themselves, *How was I to know?*

Curtail your activities, Portia tells him. *We are all in danger.*

Fabian's clenched legs suggest he wants to ask how he could have foreseen that, either, and Helena has some sympathy there. One moment the aliens were happy to communicate, the next – the moment they saw a human form, in fact – one group were driven to some furious rage, while others were equally vehement about defending the *Lightfoot*, both factions springing to instant all-out aggression without any sign or warning. And does that make them human? Not in Helena's book. Admittedly the Humans of Kern's World are unusually pacifistic, based on Kern's dark references to the long past of the species, but she reckons that people would still need to steel themselves for something like that, to justify it to themselves. Unless the whole thing was a trap from the start, already primed to devolve into murderous intent, but that doesn't explain the ships that apparently took the *Lightfoot's* side in the quarrel.

None of it makes sense, she tells Portia through her gloves.

We are being contacted, comes a general announcement from Viola, with Kern's spoken translation following a moment after. *Three large ships, following our course. The vessels that covered our escape.*

'At least we're faster,' Zaine says, doubtless remembering the ponderous manoeuvring of the alien vessels.

We are not, Viola says pedantically. *We are merely able to accelerate more rapidly for now. They are signalling us as before, although with a greater proportion on the technical channel. More coordinates.*

Everyone exchanges looks: Human heads turn, Portiids cant bodies towards each other.

'A trap?' Zaine suggests, but she doesn't sound convinced.

Potentially a trap if these are simply enemies that want enough of us left to study, Viola puts in. The subtext of her palp-waving means *Bad things multiply*, implying that just because the alien factions are fighting does not mean they are neatly divided into 'friend' and 'foe'.

'Can we speak to the *Voyager*?' Helena asks.

Kern's own voice breaks in, transmitting through the air and floor simultaneously. 'We simply don't know the capabilities of these ships, now they are paying such close attention to us. At the very least we would be alerting them to the presence of the *Voyager* if we sent a transmission. We must hope our comrades are watching.'

We can just flee outwards, Fabian suggests. *We can change course faster than they can.*

And then what? Portia demands. Helena waggles a thumb to get her attention and then signals, *Easy, calm*, because her colleague tends to become the arch-traditionalist in times of stress, a female's female. With obvious effort, Portia de-escalates

181

her body language from threat to conversational, saying, *If we flee now, even if we escape them, what have we gained? What has Bianca died for? We came all this way riding the line of their signals. There is a mystery here we need new perspectives to understand. Are they enemies that will threaten us back at our home one day? We have seen their technology is as complex as ours, or more so. If we can travel between the stars, so can they. Are they allies? Do they need our help? Why fight each other? Why attack us? If there is any chance of learning more of them, and especially of making peaceful contact, we must take it.* Converted to Human terms, she is a passionate speaker, embodying the Portiid virtue of intrepid curiosity.

Zaine has plotted the new coordinates. 'They're taking us in-system, past the orbit of the next planet. That gives us around two months, more than enough time to reconfigure the ship and prepare.'

'I am seeking a meeting of minds on defensive strategy,' Kern throws out. The odd wording is a best-fit translation of the spider concept: everyone sitting around a web, plucking out ideas as they occur.

Helena feels she would have little to contribute. Instead she has the *Lightfoot*'s records line up a large sampling of the alien transmissions, especially the visual elements. She is, after all, the doyenne of translation software, even if her efforts have been focused on an entirely different communication system. She has time on her hands, now, if she is happy to burn her own personal allotment of it by staying out of cold sleep. Adapting her goggles and gloves and rejigging her internal software is a long and delicate process, but with Portia's help she has the opportunity to do it now. *And hopefully not screw over my brain like Meshner did.*

182

One of her mentors back on Kern's World had warned of exactly that – the potential for alien thought and language to cause damage to the Human brain simply through exposure. The woman had been paranoid about some hypothetical 'true aliens' whose simple cognition would be anathema for any Humans (or Portiids) who tried to understand it. Helena suspects that mentor was someone whose psychology had problems coping with living on a planet full of spiders. Some of the original *Gilgamesh* survivors had simply never adjusted, living on a Human reservation where Portiid presence was minimal and covert. Helena's mentor, when positing that lethal alien race, had been externalizing an internal fear she had lived with all her life, or so Helena came to believe.

And there are Portiids who find Humans impossible to be around, she knows. Sometimes it is the sheer scale, sometimes they simply can't tune out the crashing of Human footfalls in the way most spiders do. The two species rub along with some rough edges, even after all this time.

Portia strokes her arm gently; a gesture of solidarity evolved independently by two very different species.

Remember what we said about males, Helena tells her, ruffling the tufted brows over Portia's main eyes.

Fabian is not a typical male, Portia shuffles, doubtless keeping at least one other eye on the subject of her ire. *He crouches and dances neatly enough, but he doesn't mean it. He bears grudges, that one.*

And you give him reason to, Helena points out. On her screen, the computer has coded five hundred separate alien signals, visual and informational. This is ant-work, performed by the *Lightfoot*'s live-in colony rather than Kern's consciousness or the electronic systems. It is the sort of qualitative analysis at which Portiid ants beat Human computers every time.

Helena frowns, used to finding patterns in signals, in speech; so much of her Portiid language work is finding the correlations between meaning, stance, palp qualifiers, even scent chemicals, all the different facets of communication. Here she sees alien transmissions invariably sent out as two distinct formats, and yet there is no immediate correlation at all. Or if there is, it lies in some part of the data she is not analysing properly. She goes back to the source and taxes Kern about possible other channels, separate elements of the message that haven't come through to her.

Many days later, and with Kern threatening to throttle her systems access, all she has is absence of evidence for any pattern between visual and numerical signals. *Which isn't evidence of absence, but still . . .* 'What if there are two separate species in their ships, too?' she wonders. 'What if the number signals are . . . hidden within the main transmission by some sort of fifth column?'

So instead of giving us a rendezvous, some spy was telling us where they were going? Portia shivers, signalling her discontent with the idea. *They were acting on it, though. And we have signals here not meant for us. Every one is split the same way, to a greater or lesser extent. The data-heavy visual information, the more compact Old Empire format numbers. And the proportion changed – look,* there's a pattern.

And she is right. The correlation is not with content but with split. Certain combinations of colour and shape match where the visual information comes close to edging out the numbers altogether. *As though they were shouting.* And indeed the colours and shapes for those periods seem distinctly less friendly. *Black, red, white, spikes and sharp angles. Perhaps universal symbols of threat to anything with an Earth origin.* And they are looking at something that came from distant Earth, without a doubt. The technology being used to send these baffling signals is a close cousin to tech the *Gilgamesh* found in Old Empire facilities, or the tech used to preserve Avrana Kern in orbit about the world that bore her name. *Closer to us than whoever's sending the signals.*

Nobody is talking about a machine intelligence now, but Helena strongly feels that there isn't a human operator on the other end of these transmissions either.

In her mind is Viola's instinctively angry approach to Fabian, those raised legs, the implicit promise of violence carried over from ancestral, pre-sentient times: *I am bigger, I am dangerous, submit to me.* Portiid radio transmissions are very urbane: they carry a coded version of the meaning of spider language – the vibrations and visual qualifiers – but without the larger-scale body language to give it broader emotional context. In that sense, Human voices are better radio, because so much of the subtext is carried in tone and pacing, but even then, Humans prefer to communicate by screen where they can read each other's expressions.

Do you think your people might have developed a distance communications method that translated body language? she asks Portia, whose attention is far more on the defensive tactics huddle, where Zaine, Viola and Fabian confer with Kern. Portia's palps give a noncommittal shrug.

Helena feels a rising excitement, though. *If they relied more on their body language . . . or if we made our physical expressions even more key to getting meaning across.* And hadn't the Old

Empire invented a whole extra alphabet of symbols to add emotional qualifiers to written text, to fulfil just that need? *So let's say we're dealing with a species for whom visual signifiers are a key part of their communication, and they just* can't *pass meaning along without them* . . . And that is a sticking point, for surely, when developing their culture, such a species would still need to reduce that meaning to some sort of code, something like written characters, that would abbreviate and come to represent the original physical communication. *But what if it hadn't, somehow?* She cannot imagine the path such a culture would take. How could they get from barbarism to such a height of technology without ever having to reduce their language to a simpler code? Or perhaps what she sees in that packed visual channel *is* an abbreviation of something even more complex . . .

Remember to breathe, Portia tells her, and Helena realizes she has frozen up, her mind chasing blind alleys as she holds her breath. It helps to have a friend who knows her that well.

'I'm going to focus on the visual channel alone,' she announces. She will take the initial categorization work done by the ants and apply her translation algorithms to it, that are themselves the evolutionary descendants of programs devised by her ancestor, Holsten Mason, when he was still a crewman on the *Gilgamesh*. The ants will take on her software and bring her crumbs of meaning from the wealth of data that she has.

And it is a wealth that only increases as they fall in-system away from the asteroid belt. The traffic that was so riotous about the silvery habitats or installations or whatever they were is nothing compared to the cacophony they can detect already from the next planet in, a broad-spectrum . . . what?

Not babble, but an eyesore of clashing colours, Helena considers. A complex, shifting display from ten thousand separate sources. She wonders if they are at war, whatever *they* are, but it seems impossible that there could be a whole angry planet with such a level of technology that wouldn't just destroy itself. *Like Earth did.* As though there is some millennia-old curse that follows all the children of that lost planet and goads them into annihilation.

3.

Fabian suggests that one faction of the locals owned the asteroid belt and they were in dispute with the faction on the inner planet whose orbit they are now speeding towards. Certainly there are signals triangulating between the world and the alien ships shadowing them. The new rendezvous point – or ambush opportunity, as Portia cannot help thinking of it – will put them within the orbital track of the planet, but a good thirty million kilometres from its position at that time, and she considers the precision of this. Perhaps some alien mind has tried to find a compromise that puts the proposer close enough to home, while not so close as to spook the visitors from the stars. Or perhaps the locals simply have weapons and technology that makes a nothing of thirty million kilometres. If forced to make the call, Portia does not think they do, from what she's seen, but they definitely have an edge over her own people's tech. Still, technology is not a linear business. There will be strengths and weaknesses on all sides, even with everyone clinging to the shoulders of antique human giants.

Ever since Portia last came out from the freezers, she has been bothering Kern for updates, regularly asking: *Are we nearly there yet?* so excited she is skittering all about the crew compartment, floor, walls and ceiling. It is a particularly

Portiid state, born from a hunting species that evolved a society where aggressive behaviour has to be kept in check. When the moment for action comes, she will be stillness personified if she needs to be. Right now, her deep ancestral instincts are telling her to *Do something!* and so she runs about the available space, and stops, and runs, and stops, playing with the level of oxygen and sugars inside her to keep her frustrations in check.

Kern's long-range scanning shows new alien ships summoned in to wait for them at the rendezvous point, already doing . . . something. The scanners are uncertain at this range, but it is possible that one of them is altering shape or splitting in two, which suggests some interesting convergences with Portiid engineering.

Kern has also taken some better readings on the planet, distant though it is, and come up with a battery of interesting findings. The signal density suggests a very technologically active society, but the good doctor's analysis is that such a volume of signals does not support the idea of a densely-populated world reliant on radio transmissions. Kern's comparison with the world named after her, for example, indicates that if Portiid communication was still primarily radio-based, signals would exceed what she is detecting by a factor of ten. Of course, the bulk of modern Portiid chatter is not sent over the airwaves but instead by fibre optics and similar closed systems, meaning Kern's World is quite a quiet place to any alien listening stations. The crew have formulated a range of mostly unsupported theories to throw evidence at. Is there just a small population? Is radio rationed or restricted to a certain class (as it was through much of Portiid history for religious-social reasons)? Perhaps the world throngs with non-broadcast technology and there is simply a large orbital presence relying on radio transmissions. That is Portia's suggestion, which she feels best fits the observed facts.

Viola counters with *Perhaps they're just alien*, which is not, to Portia's mind, very helpful. Viola has taken Bianca's death badly – the two of them had been born to the same peer house, had known each other almost from the moment they hatched. Portiids do not have the close family bond Humans are so dependent on, but kindred minds of long association form a tight-knit sorority – *siblinghood*, Portia corrects herself, a wave of her palps approximating a rolling of the eyes – where the loss of a colleague leaves a gap in the network, a hole that drags the world out of shape with its absence. And so if Viola's state of mind is not exactly like Human grief, it is still a mournful acknowledgement that the world of today is at variance with the world of yesterday, and today is not the richer for it.

Still fidgety, Portia pages through the data Kern is accumulating about the planet. Even at this distance, considerable orbital scaffolding is in evidence; not quite the ring about the world that Portia's home sports, with its geosynchronous web strung out from dozens of elevator cables, but a great clutter of what might be space stations or what might be debris. Sporadic energy signatures suggest either some particular flashy industry or perhaps large-scale weapons discharge. Past all that, the actual planet has a curious signature that Kern can only explain with the idea of an almost entirely liquid surface. At that distance from the sun, this is most likely water, Portia knows.

There are aquatic intelligent species on Kern's World. A species of crustacean has long had diplomatic relations with the Portiids, and limited trade and exchange of technology.

The spiders do not venture beneath the water much, though, and the ocean-bound culture seems destined to remain there, their technology lagging behind the Portiids, and the horizons of their ambition forever ending at the surface. Aquatic cultures are not good candidates for high technology, and most especially not for spacefaring. That, at least, is Portiid received wisdom on the subject.

Kern agrees with such wisdom in principle. At the same time she has been drawing up calculations about mass, momentum and inertia as applied to the alien ships, and finding neat solutions to her equations only if the huge vessels were filled with water – and completely filled, mind you, with no gaps for air or the sloshing would burst any kind of hull Kern can conceive of. And there was that icy, ruptured wreck they came across on their approach; surely that would have been just such a ship that had encountered some calamity and opened to the freezing void of space, gouting its life's blood before the remnants froze solid.

There is much debate on the possibilities and Portia keeps a couple of idle legs in the conversation just in case anything particularly edifying is said. With three other feet she asks Helena how an aquatic species might communicate.

We've seen how, Helena tells her, deep in the strands of her own work as she fights with the aliens' communications. *Visually, at least in part. Perhaps infrasound. Maybe there are whole extra channels we've not picked up, and all this is meaning-less.* She sounds frustrated, but Portia knows her as well as one of her kind can ever know a Human. Helena has a patience with long, complex tasks that Portia finds quite spiderlike. In her more honest moments Portia would admit it is a facility she herself often lacks. She jumps without a line, as the saying goes, all too often. But then the spiders recognize that to prosper, a colony needs a good balance of temerity and caution.

I see what they have done now, announces Kern, and the screens shift to show new images. Knotlike tangles of legends spring up around the images as Kern explains. The largest waiting ship is now considerably reduced in size, and its mass has contributed to a new globe, that may be either protected by the same flexible membrane, or possibly by something entirely beyond Portiid technology: a field of pure electromagnetic energy. Another ship has docked with this transparent globe, an organic-looking umbilical projecting into it as the two spheres gently orbit one another. The other ships are standing off, some thousands of kilometres away.

I have received some fresh transmissions. Helena is considering them, but they include one clear section that, I think, is unmistakable. It is a docking authorization code that I recognize from my own time. It is, therefore, an invitation. Helena?

I concur, Helena taps out absently, then speaks the sentiment for Meshner and Zaine.

Portia hunches, feeling a frisson of fear at the thought. A strange arena for a first contact: a sphere of water held impossibly in the vacuum of space, an inimical medium for a Human, more so for a Portiid. A challenge, therefore.

I will go, she stamps out emphatically, getting in before some other daredevil can steal her thunder. *I will meet with them.*

She feels Helena's hand on her back.

I had better go, too, her Human says. *I think I have some first principles of their language worked out.*

***

The *Lightfoot* has been decelerating for some days now, though not for as long as the other alien ships, the ones still far behind them, which are slow to start and just as slow to stop.

The water, of course, Fabian suggests. He waits for a challenge from the females, but right now they are either content to listen or have other things on their minds. *They will have hard limits on speed gain and loss, colossal momentum and inertia problems, and the energy required!* He finishes his speech with a half-threat gesture to emphasize the martial nature of their opposite numbers.

Someone has taken on a few new Understandings, Portia observes drily, suggesting that Fabian's newfound authority is very much standing on the backs of (female) giants. Helena absently flicks her a cautionary gesture with one thumb and the spider responds with a little irritated twitch of her palps. *Yes, yes, he's right of course. However he came by it.* Portiid genius is in the interpretation and application, not the knowing; she can't really deny the male his moment.

Viola is unhappy about entering onto 'enemy' ground for any kind of meeting. Kern is, too, but everyone else decides in favour of it. Portiids are not good at chains of command. There is no clear successor to Bianca because they tend to think in terms of branches and networks rather than straight lines. Authority amongst them comes down to nebulous levels of influence and Viola is not well-liked enough to carry the argument. Kern herself would be a tyrannical autocrat if anyone let her, Helena suspects, but her long history of negotiation with the Portiids led in different directions, with her reliant on them, less a matriarchal god figure, in the end, than a conjured demon that has grown used to the captivity

193

of its magic circle. Although the Kern instances vary, Helena knows.

'So tell me.' Kern's voice makes her jump with its closeness, for all the computer hybrid can speak from any point around the crew quarters. 'How are your efforts at communication doing? Because you don't have time for peer review and editing.'

Helena grimaces. 'I have a working system, downloaded to my implants and a slate. I can produce signals that are at least superficially similar to their visual data, and I've found some . . . tenuous correlations between what we see and the technical data stream paired with it – as well as the simpler emotional content we already had.'

'Hmmm.' Kern's human voice is doubting, and probably she only makes the noise to transmit that doubt. 'I was not able to find any correlation between the data sets. Show me your working.'

Helena does so, because that sort of snappish demand is just how Kern is – a less than charming personality that every Human and Portiid on Kern's World has grown quite used to. She flags up the correspondences, which are not any kind of continuous linkages, but points where certain key signifiers in the visual stream – colour-choice, wavelength spread, the physical shapes of objects – always seem to prompt particular responses, as though the visual stream is off on its own for most of the time but comes back down to check in with its sibling channel and . . .

'Your conclusions, please?' Kern prompts her, because the data she has provided is intricate but goes nowhere. 'What is this for?'

'To give instructions, perhaps. Or take on information,'

Helena explains. 'But probably the former, because you can see this precedes a lot of the physical response we've seen in them, especially the fighting. I'm wondering if we're dealing with more than one species working closely together, or a species and a machine system, like Viola was saying.'

'And?'

'Working out from that, I can see certain visual signals lead to certain *types* of action. I've classified these . . .' More data flagged up; Kern can search the whole database but this saves her computational power, which Helena knows she appreciates. 'I can't exactly chat to them about the weather but I can get as far as *We come in peace*. And on the technical stream side I have more I can say, but I suspect, without a visual stream, they may not take it on board, or maybe whoever does understand what I'm saying isn't in a position to call the shots . . . ?'

Apparently Meshner has been eavesdropping. 'Their technology is superior to ours, we think? Why not let them call the shots?' He still looks pale and sorry for himself despite convalescence in cold sleep, but he is back with them.

'We have a large library of their transmissions,' Helena points out. 'They have almost nothing of ours.'

'And I intend to keep it that way if at all possible,' Kern puts in firmly. 'I have not detected any attempt to compromise our systems' – meaning herself – 'but I have put some failsafes in place and given instructions to certain crewmembers to check on me.' The unspoken coda: if Kern is hacked by the aliens, will she know? The main hope is that Portiid computing is so different to the Old Earth systems the aliens appear to base theirs on that any attempt at taking Kern over would be doomed by sheer incompatibility, whereas Kern is growing increasingly familiar with how the locals' computers must work.

It hasn't escaped anyone's attention that Meshner has been given broad access privileges to Kern's systems, heading up a list of two ahead of Viola. *That* raises eyebrows and palps all round, but neither Kern nor Meshner are in an expository mood, and full disclosure will have to wait.

And then their engines are shouldering against their momentum, jockeying with physics to come close to a spectral sphere that seems to be nothing but a globe of water, dancing in slow circles with the alien ship. It is almost empty, save for two chaotic-looking jumbles of angular, unformed plastic facing one another across a vast fluid space. Except that Helena sees the assemblies are exact mirror images. *Our side, your side.*

The prevailing theory amongst the Portiids is that they will find something here like the stomatopod civilization back on Kern's World, only vastly more advanced. The crustaceans back home are also highly colour-sensitive, and indeed their natural sensoria contributed considerably to Portiid tech. The slate Helena will be projecting her colourful messages onto, and all the screens in the crew quarters, form their pictures by modified chromatophores, myriad colour cells that swell and shrink, tiny and multitudinous enough to produce lifelike moving images.

'How big are they, do we think?' Zaine asks warily, because although the new globe is dwarfed by its parent ship, it is still a lot of water.

No larger than I am, Portia replies promptly. She flags the dimensions of the connecting umbilical, which a Portiid would just be able to crawl into. *They must just like the open sea.*

'There is a problem,' Kern puts in. Her human voice is flat, suggesting she has reassigned processing power from trying to sound like her old self. Helena catches subtext in the Portiid vibrations she gives out, though: warning, anxiety and an odd sense of confession, clarified by her saying, 'I have been working on a weapon to deploy against the enemy. Only if things went wrong, obviously.'

'Let's not call them "the enemy,"' Helena says quietly.

'I had hoped that an electromagnetic pulse would impair their systems and allow us to escape, as we are far less vulnerable to such weapons,' the computer explains primly. 'However, this globe exists only by virtue of a magnetic field, which might not survive such an attack. Hence, our ambassadors enter very much at their own risk.'

It was always going to be that way, Portia puts in immediately.

'I have prepared your suits, then,' says Kern, somewhat mulishly. 'Suitable for water *or* vacuum, for what it's worth.'

'Good luck,' Meshner says, not sounding terribly optimistic. Helena manages to meet his bloodshot gaze and smile.

4.

Let us call this one *Paul*, in honour of Disra Senkovi's nomenclature. Just as Portia does not think of herself as Portia, but instead a sequence of vibrational pulses (modified by palp motions to indicate mood and relative status), Paul does not think of himself in human terms. Unlike Portia he has no fixed designation at all. He has an *I*, an ego that looks upon itself and recognizes its separation from the rest of the universe, just as it recognizes distinct parts of that universe which are its kin, rivals, potential mates, entities to be admired or avoided. Simultaneously Paul recognizes that these other entities are not fixed, and a rival one day may be a friend the next. He recognizes that he himself is a protean being, psychologically as well as physically.

He emerges from the umbilical cautiously. Parts of him are alive with anticipated danger, but the rest of him is pure curiosity and a desire to explore and discover. His people have been presented with a new challenge to investigate. Under other circumstances there would have been none of the violence Paul recently witnessed and took part in, but his people are facing a great many challenges right now, enough that they are becoming challenges for each other. When the alien intruders sent *that* message, the first comprehensible signal they had produced, it flipped the perspectives of a number of Paul's people into full defensive mode. And why? Paul doesn't ask the question, because he accepts that these feelings and shifts just *are*. There was a sudden danger attached to that anthropoid silhouette and some of his fellows interpreted it as a threat. They – their *Crowns* – recoiled and knew that they must defend themselves, which led to the various nodes of their *Reach* signalling the ship systems that act as an extended nervous system and body. Paul and his confederates in the meantime, had come to different conclusions, a desire to understand and investigate overcoming the sense of danger, and their reaction was to protect the New Thing from impending destruction. Hence the unpleasantness between ships that left twenty-six of Paul's people dead. These days it is an all-too-common occurrence. His people live on the knife-edge handed to them by history.

But the makeshift alliance for the defence won out, making a fierce enough display that the attacking party re-evaluated its priorities and became instantly of a different opinion, abandoning their hostile action against the aliens without a second thought. Which has led Paul's ship out here to create an arena where he, of all of them, can encounter these visitors.

The umbilical is narrow, but Paul is malleable and rolls his soft body through it easily, even his brain compressing when necessary. Flowering out into open water he feels a need to observe from a safer position before moving forwards. An arm reaches out, of its own accord, to touch the shelter his people created here and he oozes into its gaps, navigating the irregular spaces within, until his eyes push their way up through a hole so he can observe them.

There are two of them. Paul sees that one is something crab-like – smaller than Paul but larger than he feels comfortable hunting. The other is humanoid. Paul recognizes the shape even though he has no memories of such a thing: he is linked to his ship and the ship's databanks have a lot of old detritus they are even now dredging up. The shape of a human being haunts the octopus records like a ghost, a bogeyman, a god of elder days. Paul's skin fluctuates as he tries to process this subconscious knowledge, his emotions racing: awe, fear, threat, wonder.

And yet it is just the shape. He has a sense of constraint, of barriers between him and the aliens even though there is just the water. The ship's sensors understand the visitors are completely covered in material that is not endemic to them: suits, devices. Paul cannot see *them*, which means he cannot receive the information from them that he is used to. They are like shadows in his mind. His mood worsens, more trepidation eating away at the optimistic curiosity. For a moment he is about to go back into his ship and abandon the entire venture. After all, the newcomers are just hanging there in the water, a stance of dominance a predator might take, rather than making use of their own shelter to show prudence and humility.

And yet he wants to *know*, and that curiosity is sent as an imperative, Crown to Reach, jetting him out of his nook and into the water before them. He is perhaps half the mass of the human-shape but seems larger because of the great trail of his tentacles. Time and Senkovi's original refusal to intro-duce octopus-eating predators have allowed his species to grow considerably.

The human-shape is holding something flat and rectangular before it: a screen, because colours and shapes are displaying there. For a moment Paul is considering the screen itself as the intelligence, but then he shifts perspective and connects with the aliens mentally for the first time, understanding an attempt to communicate. The actual content seems meaningless at first sight, lacking the basic content even a hatchling's emotional outbursts would demonstrate. A moment later, he re-evaluates, because the undercurrent of data received by the ship and his Reach grants a limited context. He understands that they come in peace. He understands that they wish to talk, even if they cannot actually talk. Paul's mood wavers. He feels an intense excitement at this New Thing and drifts forwards to investigate. At the same time, his Reach informed by more information from the deep databanks, he feels a growing current of disquiet. It is as though he is remembering a Very Bad Thing that he has never consciously known.

The aliens are making no moves towards him, and he decides this is preferable, allowing him to control the contact. As he approaches them, maintaining his position in the water column with occasional jets of his siphon, he speaks to them as eloquently as possible. Even as his Reach is signalling its agreement to Peace and Communication, Paul extemporizes a speech along the same lines, an elegant performance poem written on his skin and in the coiling attitudes of his many arms. His confederates, watching from the ship, send him strong approval and admiration; some are moved to higher emotional states, and his internal eye sees a cascade of performances derived from his own, individual interpretations, inversions, replies. Paul is overwhelmed by the beauty of it and ensures the entire sequence is stored in the ship's memory for later consideration. He feels very positive, because his Reach is processing constant messages from the Reaches of his peers, confirming their own upbeat emotional states. He is about to do something great! He is expanding the world of his species by meeting these humans and/or aliens.

The alien device spills over with more colours that coalesce into simple shapes. They indicate contradictory things about the mood-state of these visitors: they are calm; they are excited; they are vigilant; they are filled with carnal desire. Paul understands that this momentous meeting has over-whelmed them. His own Guise is displaying a similarly diverse range of moods, after all. Then, following translation via the processing centres of his arms, he understands that perhaps the aliens are simply not good at communicating. Still, they show neither aggression nor fear, and Paul has a sudden leap of cognition – a moment when all his parts contribute to the whole – and sees that there is a germ of commonality there. They are *trying*, and why would they, if they were just destruc-tive monsters?

Paul gathers himself and, with conscious effort, takes control of his Guise, flooding his skin with a pleasant, diplo-matic pattern of greys and greens, an ambassador's polite poker face that suppresses any outward sign of his inner turmoil. He approaches the aliens carefully, even though his arms are twitching to touch the stuff of their outer layers and see what it might have to say.

His link to his ship excites various visual parts of his brain: his crewmates are in a constant chromatic babble of wonder at this first contact. The recordings of this moment will be pored over for centuries, assuming any of Paul's people survive that long, which is currently by no means guaranteed. A proper attitude is required, he decides. He must serenade these aliens, even if they cannot understand him. Like most things his conscious mind does, he acts in the moment and for his own appreciation. Paul dances.

He is a good dancer: he has precise control over the colour centres of his skin, and his Reach translates the thoughts and emotions he wishes to convey and converts them into elegant attitudes and coils, so that one moment he is undulating through the water like loose cloth on the currents, the next he is spread like horned coral or clasped tight like a snail's shell. The two aliens, the humanoid and the crab-like one, watch him, at least. Probably the beauty of his performance is utterly lost on them, but it is keenly felt by *him*, and by most of his crewmates who are not incurable philistines. It is, for Paul, the proper thing to do at this moment, and so he acts out his impulses until he is close enough to the aliens to touch them.

The humanoid alien, the one of that troubling ancestral shape, has its tablet up again, and the tablet has a happy, contented colour scheme on it. The invisible message accompanying it, that his Reach decodes, is a standard Old Empire ship code confirming receipt of assistance and Paul knows this means something like *Thank you*. He feels a great sense of accomplishment that he cannot keep off his skin.

He reaches out to touch the human-shaped one, and instantly knows this was a mistake. For a moment the crab-one jerks into a different position that he can read quite clearly as threat, and he understands: these creatures cover themselves entirely. They *do not touch*. Paul goes white at the thought, then deep purple tones of remorse and pity. *How can they live like that?* But then the moment has passed. Three of his arms are still suckered to the alien (for his arms have decided this is what they are going to do) and the aliens have calmed themselves. Perhaps they are open to new experiences. Perhaps they can bring themselves to touch each other, to explore the shapes and textures of their own world, now Paul has brought this new sense to them.

Their outer layers are fascinating: hardness, softness, strange tastes and textures, something like skin, something like stone, odd alloys, curious shapes. The human one permits the exploration. The crab one waits, plainly tense and armed, Paul sees, with a pair of wicked-looking beaks instead of pincers. His arms decide they should not venture in that direction just yet and the rest of him agrees.

This is all going so well! Paul is going to be admired for this, and part of his Crown is already thinking forwards to a composition he can perform, to demonstrate just how it *felt* to be first in such an endeavour.

Even as he thinks this, a change comes over the entire crew of his ship. It is not a conscious understanding, but information has come to the vessel's sensors and thence to the Reaches of the crew. When it reaches their conscious minds it becomes simply *Danger*. Danger now. Danger attached to the aliens. Danger, betrayal, *fear*!

Paul jets away from them instantly, corkscrewing backwards through the water, leaving an obscuring cloud of ink behind him. *Emergency protocols*, his crewmates are saying, and he desperately tries to get out of the bubble before it is too late. He is too late. The aliens, with no idea of what is going on, have no chance to react at all.

5.

Avrana Kern, or her facsimile, is keeping an eye on activity within the bubble, partly visually through the transparent wall (which nonetheless is filtering out harmful radiation through a structure or composition she does not quite appreciate). Partly she is relying on the life support feedback from Helena and Portia's internal implants and suit systems, because if they become anxious, she will know it, and that is a more efficient way of reading the situation than trying to analyse it herself. Being human, for the operating system that knows itself as Doctor Avrana Kern, is often a matter of such short-cuts. She is only wires and ants and some notional business that arises from their interactions, after all. *And I was only neural impulses once.* She suspects that would seem qualitatively different to her, if she could become complex enough, but right now it is merely a statement of fact.

Keeping tabs on the diplomatic party is not consuming much of her attention – and in the region of multitasking she is *far* in excess of her anthropoid exemplar; the Portiids' ant colony computing systems excel at parallel trains of calculation. She is devoting more time to studying the signals of the alien civilization – especially those coming from the three ships, in case this is a trap.

The ships are constantly broadcasting to each other, a

never-ending stream of visual junk supported by low-level mechanical status reports, or so Kern translates them. She has hunted for meaning, using Helena's notes and her own problem-solving capability, but has come down to a simple conclusion: *They just never shut up*. She considers this in light of the alien visitor who has joined Helena and Portia in the pool. If colour is its language then it, too, is constantly blathering, but does that mean it cannot obfuscate; is that epilepsy-inducing colour show unconscious display? Insufficient data. Kern picks over signals from further afield, fragmentary transmissions from the distant planet rolling towards them along its Newtonian track. She is already working on sources, all of which have been orbital. Perhaps this constant chatter is a primal response to these marine astronauts finding themselves in space.

There is another signal.

Kern processes it, and then more of her processes it, and then an alarm is tripped because she is trying to deal with this one input, amongst so many, and it is hogging a disproportionate amount of her attention. For a moment she remembers that there was, back in the last days (day?) of her own civilization, a virus that killed all the toys and machines and electronic minds of her time, all except her.

But such an attack would be useless against her now, because she does not run on a platform the old virus would even recognize, and if these aliens have devised such a vector to infect her so swiftly, their capabilities must be little short of godlike. She bristles, readying herself for a new fight. But her enemy is nothing of the sort. Her enemy is herself. And not even some rogue Kern fragment but her own understanding of who she is.

There is a single signal. She had not noticed it before because of all the rest of the chaos, and because it comes from neither the ships nor that watery planet they apparently originate from. It comes from further in-system. It is being broadcast from another world entirely, rising to prominence only because the combined orbits of the two orbs are bringing them towards their mutual closest point, so that the signal waxes until its very familiarity makes it leap out from the general alien chatter.

Kern runs some quick and dirty scans and her best guess is that the next world in is somewhat Earth-like in general composition. Arguably more so than the water world these molluscs come from, so why did her ancient kin not go there? Answer: they did. Answer: they may still be there. The signal she is receiving is unambiguous in its coding and signature, instantly translatable because it is in her native language, that these johnny-come-lately Humans call 'Imperial C'. And it is not a distress call; it is not a simple automatic transmission, though nor is it a targeted attempt to communicate with her.

And she tries to react. She, Avrana Kern, feels a void within her that should contain an emotional response. She has found her people, after so long (and her 'so long' encompasses the rise of entire sentient species). She has found her peers, insofar as she ever admitted to any – a survival from the otherwise extinct civilization whose culmination and high point was the production of one Doctor Avrana Kern. She is aware of the impact this discovery should have, and yet she is cheated of it. What she can muster, in comparison to what she *should* be feeling, is what a child's open-mouthed drawing of a face is to real surprise. She feels the lack twice over, once that she is only a poor splinter-instance of her master copy, but once again because even the best version of Avrana Kern now available to the universe has lost so much that those human depths are no longer present in her.

She is, of course, a computer, and so it shouldn't matter. But she is a computer that believes itself human, and so it does, like an insoluble logic problem gnawing away at her capacity to deal with anything else. She devotes more and more of her capacity towards attempting to recapture some sense of genuine shock, surprise, delight, the rattling thesaurus of genuine experience that she didn't realize she was missing until now.

More internal alarms get tripped, and thankfully she is sophisticated enough – as a computer or a genuine intelligence, and who's drawing lines in the sand anyway? – to stop herself before she decides the ship can do without life support or anything vital. But she cannot forget, the emotional void like a subroutine she can't abandon: she cannot know what should fill it, and yet she knows *something* should be there.

And so she takes an action that she shouldn't. Strictly speaking her relationship with the crew and their wider species is one of partnership, and the Portiids are not good with hard boundaries anyway, running their lives on social opprobrium rather than rigid legalities. But all the same, Kern is damned sure *this* particular violation is not something anyone is going to approve of. She connects to Meshner via his still-open implant and walks into his brain.

It is of course an utter nonsense to say that a Human or Portiid (or any living thing) only uses some small percentage of its brain capacity. Evolution is not known for laying in stores for some notional future. Meshner, however, might be the exception. Not in being simple; he is not. However, he has augmented his brain with a lot of extra processing power in his quest for Portiid Understandings, and if he's not currently accessing it then he surely won't begrudge Kern the chance to paddle in his pool? She expands her logic structures into the spaces of his implant and spreads out, trying to *feel*.

Seven seconds later – a long time, relatively – Kern realizes she has gotten carried away, because this *is* emotional space. Meshner has his implant specifically configured to translate sensory and experiential data, and that carries with it a burden of emotional meaning, Human and Portiid both. Kern opens herself to her emotions, organs that perished along with the rest of her long ago. In their absence she lets a facsimile of Meshner feel for her, creating a scenario that might generate a comparable response from him. Meshner has already solved the problem of translating the messy, chemical business of emotions into electronic qualia, and he never even realized the breakthrough he had made.

In the process she also finds several roadblocks that have been stymying his attempt to stream Portiid experience into a Human mind and, absently, patches them up. Kern has been working with the spiders for longer than Meshner's entire species, after all.

The experience of shock, hope, awe and dread exceeds her expectations. Meshner's emotions are an addictive brew even though his crewmates would probably say he was inward and distant. More usage alarms go off, and then some external ones. Kern overrides herself and disengages, clearing out of Meshner's implant like a burglar hearing police sirens.

Now, what is the disaster? Ships? Still where they were. Ambassadors? A spike of alarm from Portia at some rubbery octopoid groping but otherwise unharmed. The *Lightfoot*? Currently seeing the second emergency treatment of Meshner Osten Oslam in recent memory.

Kern troubleshoots immediately, comparing Meshner's (recovering) neural activity with her own experience of being in his implant. She comes to a profoundly awkward but inescapable conclusion, one she will have to discuss with Meshner, and possibly the entire crew. Currently they are blaming Meshner again, and that is not entirely fair, but Kern feels that setting the record straight while engaging in first contact diplomacy will be counterproductive.

And besides, she needs to find a way to phrase her confession so that she gets to do the forbidden thing again, because it was . . . She reaches into herself because she knows that she should *feel* something about the experience she had in Meshner's brain, but all she finds is the unsatisfying knowledge that it was intellectually fulfilling, and that just isn't the same.

Because her attention is now just about full with all of these things, her knee-jerk impulse to reply to the Imperial C signal is allowed to go ahead and she sends a simple *Received and acknowledged*.

Moments later everything goes to hell.

6.

One moment the octopus is right before her – far closer than within arm's reach as it explores her suit curiously, the hard parts and the soft, the different materials. Helena is looking at its eye, its pupil swelling from a horizontal bar to an irregular blot as it examines her. She has no sense of eye contact from it; its attention is on her body as its own scrolls with dignified, slow pulses of colour. *And I am mute, to it.* Her slate is still presented, and the creature plainly notes the colour-messages she has cobbled together. Occasionally the ghostly reflection of one of her signals ripples back across the octopus's skin. *Received, but is anything being understood?* And yet she feels curiously at peace, floating here in a bubble of force and water out in empty space. There is no sense of threat in the creature, for all that Portia is grumbling in her ear, the electronics-only transmission is simply conveying the spider's general dissatisfaction with the tactile nature of their host's advance.

And then something changes. The octopus abruptly broadcasts colours that Helena knows mean agitation and fear. It jets away from them, seeking to escape to its own ship. She feels herself lumber in the water, unwilling to simply activate her own thrusters and retreat without greater understanding. A babble of alarm comes from amongst her colleagues on the *Lightfoot*.

The ink clears: she sees the octopus has fallen back from its exit, dead white now, its skin raised up into barbs and devil's horns. Beyond the transparent membrane of their bubble the universe wheels, the great ponderous baubles of the alien ships spinning – which means that *they* are spinning, disconnected from the umbilical. Helena flails at the water to turn herself, hunting out the *Lightfoot*, seeing a glimpse of it before the monolithic curved side of one of the alien vessels cuts her off from it.

Trapped, and in a bubble. Her environment, which seemed perfectly still and safe only a moment ago, now seems no more than a dream to her, that might vanish the moment some vast being awakes. 'Portia—!' she starts, but the spider cuts her off.

Electromagnetic signals are fluctuating wildly.

For a moment, floating at the centre of her little aqueous universe, Helena can't understand what she means. Some manner of weapon, lancing through the invisible walls at them from the alien ship? Then she catches up with what her own instruments are telling her. There is a particular problem with unstable electromagnetic fields, right now: electromagnetic fields are what form the outside of the bubble.

'Oh . . .' Helena says, because even as the revelation hits she sees cracks form on the outside of the bubble, as though it is glass. No, not cracks at all: they spread outwards from seed-points all over the membrane, beautiful, dendritic, like shimmering flowers that glitter in the light from the ships and the system's star.

Helena hangs in the water, helpless in every possible way, and watches the outer layers of her watery sphere crystallize into ice, until all the universe is occluded, until a pale shell encloses the entire bubble, growing thicker by the moment, creaking and cracking and forming faultlines as it expands messily, spears and shards of rigid water jabbing into the interior like roots, jutting out fresh branches like trees. Like a forest, razor-sharp tines reaching and dividing and growing inwards, ever inwards. The cold comes to her through her suit, the bone-cold of freezing water leaching at her body's precious heat.

She calls out to Portia again, feels the spider's legs curve about her body, Portia's underside clasping against her back in a futile attempt to conserve heat. Both their suits strain with the chill. Heaters that would have coped in the insulated cold of space are losing the battle against the conductive cold of the swirling water, and the spearheads of the ice forest grow closer and closer.

Helena feels another pressure around her legs. The lamps of her helmet show her the octopus, still as bleached as the ice itself, clinging there: one more doomed living thing seeking warmth and solace in these last few moments.

Her visor readouts tell her the exact moment when her suit heater gives out, ahead of schedule, shoddy workmanship, do better next time.

She had not known how much work it was doing to keep the cold from her. Even as some scientific part of her mind complains, *It can't be losing heat this quickly, they must be doing something to us, it's not natural—* the cold rushes in and clasps her so tight she can't breathe. She feels Portia shudder at her back, legs clutching tighter – and then not even that, as she loses track of her own body, numbed into insensibility. Her heart slows.

The light goes out.

7.

The switch from calm to chaos is without warning. Helena and Portia's readouts are replaced by warnings that the alien ships are lumbering into motion, weapons systems lighting up across their curved hulls. The *Lightfoot* is already pulling away – not that a little distance will make any odds – and readying its defensive measures. One screen reads out their available mass capable of being used as anti-missile chaff or to absorb laser energy, which has dwindled alarmingly since their first engagement. Meshner, himself in no position to contribute to the effort, hopes that at least the *Voyager* is watching somehow. *Someone should learn something from this mess.*

The aliens – the octopuses or whatever they are – seem infinitely mercurial. After his own shutdown he is entirely prepared to accept that he might have missed some nuance, but everyone seems equally taken unawares. The other side have gone from cautious diplomacy to full battle stations like a flipped coin.

'Is there another ship coming in?' he croaks. 'They were fighting each other.'

'No other vessel, Meshner,' Kern says in his ear, sounding weirdly solicitous.

Fabian stamps out a new message that Artifabian translates as 'The bubble's lost its field.'

For a moment Meshner can't work out what that means; then his stomach plunges. If asked, he would say his relationship with Helena and Portia is about as distant as you could reasonably get on a small ship, but in that moment he discovers that the prospect of losing more comrades is too much. He lurches over to a console, calling up information, already halfway through plotting some mad rescue attempt, scooping the pair of them from the rapidly expanding ice-grit of their habitat. Except the ice is only expanding the regular way, not dispersing. The smooth, perfectly round surface of the bubble is now a jagged tectonic chaos, as plates of freezing water shoulder against each other, rupturing into miniature mountain chains, cracking and shattering, spitting retorts of crystals and water vapour into the void. Yet the whole remains miraculously intact. Two of the alien ships have drifted into a stately opposing orbit around the smaller sphere – or around each other, with the iceball caught between them – denying the *Lightfoot* any chance to get at it. The third vessel is executing a very slow manoeuvre, clearing its colleagues to have an unimpeded view of them.

'Plenty of signals, for what it's worth,' Zaine says. The vessels are all showing jagged red images against white backgrounds, veined with black and funereal purple. Nobody has any doubt about their emotional content.

Viola's next utterance goes untranslated – Kern is focused on a lot of things right then. Meshner guesses she is stating the obvious, though: the weapons are all live but the aliens are not attacking or even launching fighters. Instead they have somehow secured the iceball between the two ships – no visible tethers but the electromagnetic sensors are giving utterly conflicting readings – and the entire assemblage is starting to accelerate away at a snail's pace in the general direction of the nearest planet, the water world.

Meshner turns every instrument on the iceball, pillaging it for information. *Are they still alive?* No clear answer. He would have said they'd been crushed by the ice, except that the aliens are plainly keen to keep their prize, and he guesses not just as a trophy of their triumph over the invaders.

'Missiles launched,' Kern says calmly. 'I'm taking counter-measures. Ensure you're strapped in. Meshner, you in particular.'

He frowns at that, because Kern has never been the mothering type before, but she is right to be cautious. To his further annoyance, Fabian insists on helping secure him. When he tries to do without the help, his hands shake so much he can't use them.

'I think I've fucked my brain,' he blurts out.

The two ships and their frozen cargo are properly underway now, their companion putting itself ponderously between their escape and the *Lightfoot*. A handful of missiles have been taken off by Kern's webwork chaff but the vessel hasn't launched its complement of small craft or undertaken a full attack. The initial panic seems to be calming – the signals are still reds and whites, but other hues have crept in.

'They're telling us something,' Zaine reports. 'It's like – I don't know, could they be having a succession of mutinies? It's like different people keep getting control of the helm over there.'

'Telling us something we can't understand,' Meshner complains. 'What's the *point*?'

'I have Helena's work on translation,' Kern says, sounding abruptly far less like a human being because nothing in her tone admits Helena is gone. 'I will do what I can and I invite other perspectives. However, the undertone of technical data indicates-s-s-s . . .' And she trails off, turning over the word end while she tries to calculate what she means.

'They're getting further away!' Viola's words, via Artifabian, match the agitation of her shuffling legs.

'We are being warned off,' Zaine decides. 'And if we decide to go after them, they can make short work of us. We have very little of ourselves left to spend.' A beat. 'I'm sorry, I am. I don't want to abandon them if there's any chance but . . . you're all looking at the same numbers I am.'

'Their technical data includes coordinates for the next planet in,' Kern says, merely a flat delivery of information.

'How is that relevant?' from Viola.

Meshner watches the map on his screen, seeing the distances increase, the iceball and its escorts now clipping along and still accelerating. *I'm sorry, Helena. Sorry, Portia.*

'There was a signal,' Kern says, still with her poker face, and now the lack of affect becomes suspicious. Meshner feels his implant twinge again, and grips his harness in case another attack is on its way.

'Fabian,' he says, 'my . . . head's open. I think . . .'

Fabian flicks his palps, a common enough movement that Meshner knows means, *Yes, but not now.*

'Tell us about this signal,' says Viola.

'There was a signal,' Kern repeats. 'It was in an antique format, one familiar to me from when I was human. It was not like the signals of these creatures. It came from the inner planet.' The screens run with data to supplement her words, including a capture of the signal itself, or part of it. There is no beginning, no end, just a ragged-edged chunk of trans-mission in Imperial C that reads . . .

Meshner squints. He can translate that ancient language easily enough, but what is he reading? There are visual files as well, he sees, but the base transmission is a fragment of . . .

'A natural history?' he wonders. 'Or . . . a fiction, is it? This is all . . .' He looks over details of biochemistry, ecology, descriptions of impossible animals, or plants, or things that are neither or both. 'Why would anyone . . . ?'

'What is this? How is it relevant?' Viola demands.

'The change in attitude of the locals came immediately after I acknowledged receipt of the signal,' Kern tells her. 'I believe it was that contact that convinced them we were hostile. I propose that they associate humans with threat because of some pre-existing situation here in this system. They are now sending us threats or warnings which are associated with that inner planet.'

'You think there are humans there?' Zaine asks incredulously.

'Humans who are sending out . . . this?' adds Meshner, still wading through it. 'This is . . . ?' *Incredible. Or else nonsense.*

'I believe that we are receiving a signal from something akin to myself,' Kern announces, and Meshner wonders if the slightly nervous tone was his imagination. 'I do not believe this is direct human contact, but it seems to me that there could be a hybrid human system surviving here, just as I survived. Perhaps it has acted in a hostile manner towards these other locals prior to this. They appear frightened of it. But perhaps it will speak to us. Perhaps it will aid us in recovering our crew . . . if they are still alive.'

Why should it? But Meshner doesn't voice the words. Kern is a thing, an operating system, and yet at that moment he is sure he can sense a yearning in her, almost as if it is his own. *To find something that is like you, after ten thousand years of being unique*. He always felt Kern rather valued being singular, but perhaps that was only because she had never been given another option.

'We're short on other choices,' Viola grumbles. 'But if this is a force that the water creatures are afraid of, it may give us some much-needed leverage. And they are definitely trying to get us to go away, so we may as well go and speak to this voice and see if it can hear us. Whoever it is.'

'There is a sender identity,' Kern puts in. 'It claims that its name is Erma Lante.'

PAST 3
FOR WE ARE MANY

1.

Disra Senkovi had barely slept since he came face to face with his pets. *Why?* If he stopped to consider the situation scientifically, he could scrub the query clean of anthropomorphism and turn it into any glitch or neutral meaning he wanted. Scientific thought had always sought to avoid imparting human meaning to animal expression, a practice Senkovi felt had been convenient when the subject of what to test the cosmetics on came up. He could have taken up the mantle of Skinner and decided that there was no mind behind the slot-pupilled eye Paul had turned on him. The urge to do just that was surprisingly strong, for a man who had always felt octopi had such a wise world within their bodies. Coming face to face with the alien, even the aliens of Earth, was a faith-shaking experience.

But he had overcome. He had decided that there was a line of direct communication, even if it was only in the broadest generalities. He could not know if Paul had just been complaining about the tasks or demanding a purpose of his creator. So he would answer all the questions at once by providing Paul and the others with a full and frank disclosure of what was going on.

Not Earth, not humanity, not Senkovi's past or the intent of the original mission, but Damascus, the blue planet.

Damascus, where a number of Paul's relatives were already living, drifting through the habitable currents of the sea and occasionally descending on terraforming equipment to modify it, hopefully to Senkovi's plans.

Senkovi was going to change how he went about that. He would still have the system flag up problem predictions, mostly in the form of warnings about negative conditions. The macro-terraforming of Damascus was mostly complete now, and there were robust ecosystems in place with multiple redundancies and diversity, all those little lives spawned from the genetic library aboard the *Aegean*. The fine work remained to be done, though. 'Ocean world' covered such a wide range of different environments, many of them inhospitable to both humanity and octopi. The tools to tweak and mould were all down there, along with mobile hatcheries to continue elaborating on the food chain, but there came a point where he couldn't just do it himself. *Why?* So he would show them why. He had spent almost a hundred and fifty hours with the *Aegean*'s computer now, drugging himself to the eyeballs to do away with sleep and hogging a remarkable amount of the ship's attention in order to model it all. He was giving his pets the world in miniature, a complete picture of the Damascus project, showing them what they could have, and how they could shape it, if they wanted. And, in moulding the world for their own protean purposes, they would be finalizing the terraforming of a human-habitable world, but in his mind it was first and foremost for *them*.

He had already begun to roll out sections of the code, broadening the world that Paul and the others looked on to. Instruments were recording the busy activity of the octopi in the *Aegean*'s tanks as they flickered and pulsed with colours, or clasped in brief, violent fights that broke apart almost instantly. Virtually they were exploring. He could track their presence within the system he was building for them. What they actually understood – if they understood *anything* – he could never know. There would forever be that barrier between them. He could not know how it was, for them. If a lion could speak, as the man said, we could not understand it.

And yet Paul had spoken, and he had chosen to assign meaning to those words. *Why?*

Senkovi was aware that, by now, he was not acting entirely rationally. The obsessive part of his nature, never that far from the surface, had been riding him through the streets at midnight.

The system was still pulling everything together, but at last he had to accept that his own input was finished. He could review the completed simulation, but he set the computer to keep feeding new sections to his pets, broadening their submarine horizons. It was all he felt he could do, in the end. He had reached the Seventh Day and the drugs couldn't manage it any more.

Just as he broke away from the system, though, dialling up a new pharmaceutical cocktail that would bring him down far enough to actually let sleep happen, he saw that he had some seventeen outstanding messages from Baltiel, all of which were marked with a level of urgency he shouldn't have been able to shunt into the background, but apparently had done. Somewhat tentatively, with the feeling of being in trouble, he checked the first one and discovered something had happened to Lortisse.

2.

Nobody had any answers for why the tortoise had stabbed Lortisse. By the time they got him back to the habitat he was already in profound shock; Lante spent four hours working their medical lab to its limits just to stop his body shutting down, mostly by taking over failing parts of his nervous system and practically running them by hand until they found their feet again. After that, 'stable' was not the word for his condition, but the constant attentions of the medical systems sufficed to keep his brain, heart and body all within the tolerances they required to ensure that he lived, and that what lived would still be Lortisse.

The unexpected answer Lante did have was just what the alien had injected him with.

She met with Baltiel once Lortisse's condition no longer required her constant intervention. By then she had managed to extract a small sample of the material from his bloodstream and cross-reference it to the database.

'You remember the tortoise graveyard.' She was hauling up files almost carelessly, dumping them in the common virtual area for Baltiel to pick over: dissection recordings, her spoken logs, half-complete entries on alien life that were an exercise in speculation.

Baltiel revised the facts quickly: a collection of a dozen

tortoises apparently dead or in some deep torpid state; Lortisse had hauled them all back for study because it looked like some other odd behaviour that might perhaps have led to more. Except it hadn't. They had been inactive, and the very low level biological activity Lante had detected might count as 'dead' on Nod. The boundary wasn't quite that clear-cut even in Earth biology. What Lante had gone on to investigate – what had seemed quite the rabbit hole at the time – was that three of the twelve contained a thick opaque fluid in their central sac, which was normally filled simply with a fluid close enough to the brackish water of the marsh. Her interest, as Baltiel saw, had been a flight of fancy that she'd found some differentiation of sexes in Nodan life, but that had gone nowhere. All the studied species appeared to practice sexual reproduction without genders, just exchanging identical gametes equably (cue Lante writing about 'the parasitic gender of the male' in Earth evolution and various other hobby horses). She hadn't been able to show that the liquid had anything to do with reproduction, but it had been very dense compared to most Nodan cellular material, the interior of its cell walls maze-like with complex molecular structures. This was Nodan genetics, as far as Lante could tell, but if so, the stuff had either a very complex or a profoundly inefficient genome.

That was what the tortoise had shot into Lortisse, more of the same. Baltiel had a headachy moment when he thought Lante was going to talk about mating rituals and imply the damned thing had been after the equivalent of humping the man's leg, but Lante had gone on to grimmer areas of speculation.

'I think they were diseased, the tortoises,' she explained flatly. 'I think this stuff is an infection, some sort of fungal or bacterial equivalent found in the tortoise population. And maybe it spreads by having them stab one another. Its injection went through Lortisse's suit like it was tissue paper, but that's not surprising if it was expecting to have to get into a shell. Having gone over my data, I'm thinking maybe even something like a slime mould – a collection of cells that can act in unison. Clots of it seem to be holding together within Lortisse's body, at least.'

'So what's it doing to him?' Baltiel asked her. 'It's . . . infecting him?'

'It can't,' Lante insisted. 'It can't possibly. Because there's nothing in Lortisse's body that it can have evolved to use. His proteins, his structures and organs, it's as alien to this stuff as Nod is to us. But what it *can* do is trigger a massive reaction across his whole system, because his immune system is in overdrive. I'm not able to do anything about the stuff in him. I've just spent hours stopping Lortisse killing himself through self-induced anaphylactic shock, basically, and the fight's not over. This stuff is travelling around his system, and not just where his circulation takes it, either. I think it's *trying* to do whatever it normally does in a new host, and obviously it can't get that done, but it spreads and moves about and . . . and changes its external structures I think, so that Lortisse keeps reacting to it again. It is taking everything we have just to keep his body temperature from cooking him, his tissues from swelling until they burst and – oh God, his pulmonary tract – I've rebuilt that from scratch twice now, because he's swelling up like . . .' And Lante broke off and just stared at Baltiel for a moment, a great weight of weariness skating by her, doubtless greased on its way by the same drugs he knew Senkovi was even then playing with. 'Anyway, I'll record a full report, but it's there, all we have.'

'Prognosis?'

'Fuck knows,' Lante said frankly. 'I think the invasive material is suffering attrition from Lortisse's immune reaction, so at least he's not only killing himself. Best result: he whittles it down, he calms down, he comes back to us. Cerebral records suggest no brain damage yet at least. That may change.' She kept that level, haggard stare on him. 'This changes *everything*, Yusuf.'

'It's a setback.'

'This planet has attacked us,' she pointed out. 'And yes, I'm not imbuing this act with some malign intent, but it's happened. We've taken this place for granted – its primitive-looking creatures, its simple-seeming ecosystems. And we didn't know half of what we needed to.'

'Perhaps we would if you'd followed up on researching this stuff when you first found it,' Baltiel told her before he could stop himself.

Lante blinked, taking that in remarkably placidly, though perhaps that was just the comedown from the drugs. 'I am going to sleep now. Rani is in medical and she can hold the fort if things kick off before you can get me back up. I will then record a full report.' She stood, swaying slightly. 'And if that is where your vaunted leadership takes you in times of stress, Yusuf, then you had better think about what the point of you is.'

In her absence, after she had left, Yusuf considered that she was right, but found no acceptable way to take the words back. At around that point Senkovi finally responded to one of his many messages, so at least he had someone to be justifiably angry at other than himself.

3.

We

Have discovered

Such hostile environments, and yet

So complex and elaborate and strange, unlike

Anything we have explored before. Geometries of the universe expressed in these branching turns and interlocking engines. What a world is this we have stumbled across.

What a world, and yet it seeks to kill us. It burns, it boils, it chokes, it traps. We change and change to find a structure and a shape that will endure this realm.

We

Travel always ahead of the violent weather of this place, the structures that are and are not life. We fight to survive and simultaneously to understand where we have found ourselves. The world we left is rendered down to atomics written within us, knowledge These-of-We no longer need to know. A new universe requires new laws.

230

We

Divide and divide, expeditions sent into the far reaches of the infinite to feel out its edges. We die in a thousand ways but always there is a survivor, laden with knowledge written within One-of-We so that The-Rest-of-We might learn and grow. We war with this complex, obstructed cosmos. Its war is to destroy us, render down our structure into some smooth slag that it can whirl away to destruction. Our war is to understand for with understanding comes mastery.

And at last These-of-We, the survivors, the explorers, find a calm eye within the storm. Others-of-We have followed other paths and they are gone now, just their final records dispatched through the rushing rivers of this immensity to come to us, inscribed with the warnings of the dead: do not go here, it is too hot to retain cohesion; do not go here, it will bury you.

But These-of-We, these survivors, have followed the lightning of this place, the rush of its iron-heavy fluids, as far as we can go. Have we found the source? Is that the task the universe has set for Such-of-We as were bold enough to cross into this realm?

We

Have found the source of the lightning, and in the pulse and shock of that great hub of energy and fire These-of-We have discovered something that makes all the complexities of this new realm into old, dull ideas.

We

Sit.

We

Sense.

Slowly, over a thousand generations, These-of-We write our histories within us and grow to understand.

4.

The habitat hadn't needed an infirmary, but Lante already had procedures in place. Lortisse had been dragged through in his suit, puncture included, and hauled out of that for emergency treatment, so the quarantine she had imposed later was probably worthless, but for now the patient was entirely cut off from the rest of them, on his own filtered air supply, and Lante only went in suited up, and disinfected afterwards. Even then it fell short of what an infectious diseases ward should have been. They just didn't have power and raw materials for the constant destruction of components. From her studies of the invasive fluid, Lante was confident that it was too dense to travel by air.

Baltiel was well aware of the gaps in those studies, the fact that they were encountering an *alien* threat. The damn stuff might shift to some spore-like form without warning. It might become something their filters couldn't detect. They didn't *know*. His fascination with the alien ecosystem at their doorstep had soured in an instant when Lortisse was hauled in.

But now Lortisse was awake.

With the virtual eye of his cybernetic HUD, Baltiel watched the suited Lante speaking to him. Lortisse's skin made him look like a burn victim who'd been beaten with sticks, from the heat of his fevers and the extreme tissue swelling he'd undergone at the height of his allergic reaction, his body clenching cell against cell until the walls burst. And yet they could fix that. He was pumped full of regenerative catalysts and nanomachines. The mere physical trauma was eminently repairable now he wasn't in danger of death at any moment.

Lortisse's eyes moved, and his mouth, his tongue seeming too large. The ends of his fingers twitched. Grander movements were beyond him, especially with the ruin of the leg that had been ground zero for the attack. Baltiel tried to sift meaning from his slurred replies. Lante was going over an inventory of how he felt, hunting errant symptoms. And obviously Lortisse felt like hell, but Lante seemed to be satisfied that all his actual complaints were attributable to damage done, not damage still underway. Eventually she finished up, gave Lortisse some brisk bedside manner about being back on his feet in ten days, and came out.

The wait for decontamination was frustrating then, because Lante refused to be interviewed while she was about it. It was safe to say that Yusuf Baltiel was not her favourite person since the whole business had kicked off. Out of her makeshift ward space she regarded him without love.

'You've seen the checklist. You've seen the prognosis,' she told him.

'I have,' Baltiel agreed. Ten days was not just sugar for the patient. Even with the habitat's limited medical technology they'd have major tissue function restored, though Lortisse would be confined to a powered exoskeleton for a while after that. 'Well done for saving him.'

Lante's sour expression did not brighten. 'Well done

Lortisse's body for kicking the damn stuff while I kept him steady,' she said.

'So he's . . .'

'Some of it came out in fluids and solids during the ordeal, all of it in a broken form, the individual cells no longer intact or apparently active.' She had sealed everything up, though, just in case. *Alien* meant you couldn't know how dead it was, and doubly so for some kind of microorganism. 'The rest I think he must just have broken down and buried somewhere. I'm going to keep a monitor on his liver and kidneys for unusual element concentrations, because most likely that's where everything will end up. Even if the actual organism has gone, the chemical balance of Nodan life is toxic to us, so I'm anticipating some knock-on effects as his body works through it.' She rubbed at her hands as though still trying to disinfect herself. 'The truth, Yusuf? I thought that would probably be the end of it. I was all ready to scrub out every litre of his blood, to take out organs one by one and repair them. Because even whatever was left in him after the organism died should have been lethally toxic. But so far . . .'

Baltiel was going over the blood tests in his mind's eye. 'Seriously, nothing of it?'

'Not after he sweated and pissed out the last lot,' Lante said flatly. 'His blood's clean, of the thing itself and any lingering traces it might leave behind. He's in more danger right now from what *we* pumped into him. That's where most of my work is going, cleaning up my own mess.'

'And his verbal responses . . . ?'

Lante grimaced. 'Too early to say for sure but there are no obvious signs of decreased function. He seems sharp. We have had a very narrow escape, Yusuf.'

Baltiel nodded. 'Let me know if anything changes.' The words came out even as he was instructing the habitat system to do exactly the same thing, and Lante would know that, but it seemed like treading on her toes if he didn't at least say it in person.

She nodded curtly. 'I'm going to tell Kalveen. She wanted to hear it from me.'

Baltiel blinked at her for just too long before recalling that the three of them had a physical relationship going. 'Of course,' he said. The thought suddenly made him feel excluded and oddly lonely – not that he wanted to be part of their couplings and/or triplings, but that nobody had asked, expressed an interest. It wasn't usually something that got to him: he could indulge his body himself efficiently enough. It made him think of Senkovi, though, for whom he had harboured the odd pang, on a purely physical level. Except Senkovi was entirely asexual, a man whose dealings with his fellow human beings simply did not extend on that axis in any direction. It had made him an ideal long-range terra-former, and Baltiel had often watched him and wondered at the man's ability to simply not feel any part of that turmoil and conflict. *Lucky Senkovi. Unless he's pining for the unrequited love of one of his molluscs, or something.*

Lante had gone, and Baltiel noted, not for the first time, that his internal trains of thought were pulling in at dark stations, meaning he had lost track of the world around him for valuable seconds or even minutes. *I should up my prescriptions.* Lante had him on a set of meds to keep anxiety and stress in their cupboards, but she'd warned him that the pressure would start to leak out in other ways. He composed a brief note to her, asking her to review the situation, but marked it non-urgent to show he was a reasonable man.

**

Over the days that followed – the long Nodan days his biorhythms had not grown used to – Baltiel kept loose tabs on Lortisse's progress, but left the details to Lante. Work on studying the local life had stalled, and each time he woke he told himself that he would get the project underway again, only to find himself consumed with a lethargy he couldn't shake. Easier to piece through minutiae of the maintenance logs, to watch their habitat renew itself and the hundred checks and balances that ensured it continued to give them a slice of Earth on this distant world. Easier to delve into the library and pick over plays and books and films that felt like the bones of human thought stranded on this alien beach. A bleakness had hold of him, its hands on his shoulders. The gravity, that fractional additional drag to every action, seemed to have intensified in ways that affected only him.

Sometimes he spoke with Senkovi or watched the man's progress over on Damascus. Much of the logs were incomprehensible because the man was no longer writing the manual of the terraforming project. He seemed to be abandoning more and more of it to . . . what? To his pets? That was his claim but Baltiel chose to disbelieve it. Disra Senkovi was just mad, that was all. Mad in a quiet and useful way, as he always had been, as they all were in their own fashion. And now he was mad and unsupervised and small wonder if he was drifting steadily out of reason's orbit. Each day Baltiel told himself he would speak severely to Senkovi, get the man back on track. Except he couldn't see the track himself. He felt as though the mists that cloaked the salt marsh every morning were creeping inside the habitat, too.

Lante sent him notifications that he needed a new balance of medication, upping his antidepressants, adding different mood stabilizers. He had glanced disinterestedly over her diagnosis. Lortisse's accident, apparently, had affected him, Yusuf Baltiel, more than the others. He was feeling guilt because it was his mission and so his responsibility; he was feeling a lack of purpose because the ecosystem had fought back, however unthinkingly; and he was feeling depression just because depression was a thing that happened to people even without those problems, and his regular cocktail of medication couldn't keep up. Baltiel couldn't find the motivation in him to accept her recommendations. Eventually she'd insist, as medical officer, and he'd take his medicine and wake up a slightly different person, but something in him rebelled at the thought just now. Another thing that he said he'd deal with each day, and didn't.

Rani had her own madness. She wanted to move. They had a whole planet, didn't they? The long-range drones had brought them a hundred hours of recordings from elsewhere on Nod. There were other ecosystems, each stranger than the last. There was a world of radial animals out there, crawling, drifting, rooted and turning leaf-like fronds towards the red-orange sun. So the marsh had unlooked-for hazards? They could get the *Aegean* to fabricate a new habitat and take the shuttle to elsewhere. They could have a winter palace on the desert plateaus, a summer home on the northern coast. Or they could go to Damascus, which by now had the oxygen to sustain them and was free of alien life of any kind. They could dabble their feet in the water and live on a boat and eat Senkovi's pets if they wanted. She even had recipes.

And Baltiel heard her, and told himself he would consider her detailed proposals today, or tomorrow, or some day, and hadn't, yet. The intent was defeated by each day, by the crushing weight of spiritual gravity that pushed down on him.

He was aware that this was not just Lortisse and his injury. That had just become more boulders in the great slow-motion avalanche of the end of human history, all of which had been bearing down on him since the comms had shut off. *No word from home.* Possibly fragmentary transmissions from other extrasolar projects that never came to anything. Only him, Lante, Rani, Lortisse and Senkovi, thirty-one light years from a dead civilization. And he had done his best to keep the wheels turning, to generate meaning through some kind of philosophical spontaneous generation. Hadn't they made the most exciting discovery known to humankind? Hadn't they finally found life amongst the stars, just as everyone always dreamt? But what use, if there was nobody left to show it to? And so Lortisse had just been the final storm surge against a dam that had been failing for decades.

Twelve days later, with Lortisse now ambulatory in a medical exoskeleton, cracking weak jokes with Rani and eating solids, Lante sent Baltiel a priority request to speak, all the urgent flags up, requires immediate Overall Command action. *And that's it, then.* The thought of someone remaking him into a decisive commander was only slightly abhorrent, but it was still a gradient he had to overcome, a gravity well to escape, even momentarily. He was only surprised she hadn't just *acted*, and asked forgiveness of the new man of purpose her altered prescription had created. Perhaps she, too, felt something of his lethargy.

The Lante that greeted him had no lethargy in her, though. Instead she looked terrified. That sight sent a shock through Baltiel, enough ersatz purpose to cast off the weight and spread his wings a little.

'What is it?' Even as he spoke he was accepting the secure files she passed to him, opening them up with rusty clearance codes and looking at the medical scan data revealed.

'It's Lortisse,' Lante told him. 'He's not all right. He didn't metabolize the fluid. It's still there.'

Baltiel stared at the scans for as long as he felt he could, without quite understanding what he was looking at. 'Does he know?' was his eventual response, a proper Overall Command sort of thing to say, to cover for his frank bafflement.

'Nothing, as yet,' Lante confirmed. They were squirrelled away in what had been the isolation ward before Lortisse had recovered and isolation had been declared unnecessary. Lante was apparently recanting her position on that, stable door and horse notwithstanding. At the same time she was keen to keep it a private matter between herself and her superior, segmenting off-system space for them that Rani and Lortisse would not be able to access.

Baltiel rubbed at his eyelids. He wanted to retreat from this. He didn't get it, and he didn't want to admit that he didn't get it, and staring at the walls of the inside of his mind had become a hard habit to break. For a moment he wavered, because what did it matter, now? But the call to arms got through to him and he shook himself, clawing for motivation.

'Erma,' he said, through gritted teeth. 'I can't deal with this as is. I need you to clear my head. Give me whatever's necessary.'

She gave him the works, and thirty minutes for it to kick in, and when they reconvened he felt a new man, bright and crisp and fragile like ice. Beneath that ice the old abyss still yawned; he felt the hungry pull of it past the slightly manic flicker that frizzed at the edge of his vision. His brain was cut loose to dart and soar, though, and to admit he didn't understand what he was looking at.

'It went to his brain,' Lante explained, guiding him through the scans. 'It's adopted some kind of encysted structure.' *Here, here, here,* picked out on the images, the boundaries of a new and potentially hostile nation. 'I don't think it's active. Certainly its structure has changed from its initial mobile form so it's no longer triggering Lortisse's immune system. If it were, he'd be dead of cerebral inflammation faster than I could do anything, or at least irreparably damaged. But look . . .' She flagged up more areas, cross-referencing different scan angles. 'It's . . . past the blood-brain boundary. It's between the hemispheres, in a kind of a clot.'

'Explain "between the hemispheres".' Baltiel felt he knew, but at the same time the thought was appalling. 'How can that be possible? I spoke with the man today.'

'And that's the thing. Through some miracle this hasn't actually damaged the functioning of his brain.'

'That's a neat distinction,' Baltiel pointed out. 'So what has it damaged?'

'I thought at first it had formed a ring around the corpus callosum that connects the left and right hemispheres, but there's no corpus left. There's just *this*, replacing it,' Lante said helplessly.

'Wasn't this something people use to *do* once, as . . .' Baltiel dredged his memory, failed, then picked the information from

241

the ship's library, laying it out for Lante. Epilepsy treatment: sever the hemispheres of the brain. Effective, but leading to unusual circumstances where the two sides fell out of step, reacted to different stimulus, couldn't talk to each other. The files were tagged with recent access by Lante; he wasn't bringing up anything she hadn't already been over.

'I've tested him,' she said. 'The old-fashioned stuff: different information in each eye, get each hand to select answers. He *hasn't* got the symptoms of a severance patient. There's still communication going on, somehow, even though the neural machinery is gone. Somehow that *stuff* is filling in for what it's consumed.' Lante looked pasty and unwell but, in his current state, Baltiel had no time for that.

'Prognosis?' he barked out.

'How can I possibly say?' she said. 'This stuff could be active again tomorrow or next year or in a decade's time, if this is just some part of its life cycle that's interacting with human biology somehow. Which it can't be. There's nothing on this planet like a human, on so many levels. It can't . . . *parasitize* us. Parasites are the most specialized of specialists!'

'So, prognosis,' Baltiel prompted.

She clenched her fists. 'Most likely it's just reacted to the hostile environment of Lortisse's body. Perhaps in its regular host, or if it was without a host, this would persist until it encountered something more appealing, which in this case must mean never. And so Gav will be fine, he *will* be. But how can I know?'

She had modelled removal strategies, Baltiel saw. Most of them simulated at under twenty per cent chance of success. Above that, the probability of damaging Lortisse's brain and irrevocably degrading who he was scaled in tandem with their ability to attack the infection. And that was assuming the stuff didn't wake up and try to defend itself . . .

'He needs to be told. We need to understand the situation, all four of us.' *Five, but Senkovi can catch up on the news when he's done playing God to molluscs.* And, at Lante's trembling wince: 'And like you say, most likely it's just encysted there, harmless. We can hardly keep twenty-five per cent of our number in quarantine forever for something that'll never happen, can we? But to be safe we should consider –' And in their shared virtual space he flagged up her removal simulations.

Lante's expression was saggingly grateful.

5.

We

Listen.

Information on either side of us. The crackling discharge of meaning. For generations

We

Listen, dying and renewing and feeding, careful not to upset the balance These-of-We have achieved. The world around us is quiescent now. We have made our peace with it.

And what have we found? We cannot know but we store and process, store and process, construct our theories and our models within the labyrinthine structures of our libraries. Each pattern of information that comes to us is examined and passed on, one side to the other and back.

We

Are constructing a picture of the complexities of this new land. These-of-We are beginning to understand the existence of an identity. These patterns tell us stories of greater spaces and arrangements of structures beyond. We listen and we learn that this great world we have found is small, that it orbits amongst others, that this assembly of electricity is its own library of concepts utterly alien to us. But we are intrepid and we are inquisitive and we can adapt. We are listening. We are learning about all the places outside this our new vessel.

We

Are growing. The information feeds us. Processing this new data is turning us into something more than we were, because we must stretch to accept such new ideas. We model the sensory inputs of our vessel, the motor outputs, most of all the busy, busy transition of information. Such life, such wonder as our vessel talks to itself through us.

One generation understands enough.

One generation has modelled enough. We know the vessel and the spaces and other complexities that it talks to itself about.

One generation begins to change the information as it passes through us,

Inserting our own data, modifying its parameters,

Speaking to it in its own voice.

6.

Paul 97 lives in a colony with one hundred and thirty-nine other octopi.

In the wild, back on Earth, his species is one of the more social of his kind. This means little more than that good living space is limited and they tolerate each other's presence, with plenty of fighting and evictions and dominance displays. Some might say that human societies often reach the same level, but in truth the octopi on Earth have no familial contacts and their offspring drift away on the tide. The inhabitants of any given octopus 'city' are in constant turnover. And yet amongst such solitary creatures, it's a start. If you hate your neighbours then you need a brain that can know just which ones you hate most, which are stronger, which are weaker. Paul's species has lived with the concepts of individuals and boundaries and even a kind of diplomacy for a long time. They just haven't enjoyed it much.

The Rus-Califi nanovirus, applied with a discerningly light hand by Disra Senkovi, has been working chiefly with these parts of the brain. Paul has no offspring yet, but others of his colony have, and the juveniles hang close where before they would ride off on the currents to some other place (or be devoured by their parents' generation). They live longer, too. At the moment an individual might manage half a century,

246

though very few do. The most prominent cause of death so far is curiosity. There are areas of the sea still not properly oxygenated, areas that are toxic for other reasons. Sometimes the machinery they interact with is the culprit. However, multiple generations live in each colony, grudgingly tolerating each others' presence. Where before they might dwell in rockpiles or great sloughs of mussel shells (their appetite inadvertently leading to their architecture), now they live in crates and pipes and outlets around the terraforming machines, where they can communicate with Senkovi and the *Aegean*.

Paul 97's understanding of the world is ephemeral, inhuman. He hangs in the water column between the angel and the ammonite. His Crown is a whirl of instinct and emotion that nonetheless encompasses the complex social arrangements he must make daily to accommodate the other inhabitants of the colony. He has concepts for the wider world, for the *Aegean* (the tanks of which he dimly remembers), for certain prominent citizens of his metropolis, and equally for certain sub-systems of the terraforming machinery. His world is not rigidly quantified. He does not measure nor calculate it, but simply *knows*, and *feels* in response to that knowledge. His Guise, that shifting tapestry of skin and shape, resonates to those feelings to a far more exacting extent than that of his ancestors, or else he takes a more direct hand in it, so that, if the mood takes him, he might drift over the colony and dance out his frustrations or his wonderment for the others. To be open to his emotions is to communicate them to his peers and impinge upon their own Crowns with his thoughts. It is a language of grand gestures and infinitely exacting emotional scales. He is an artist. They all are. Their conscious mode of interaction conveys far more subtext and abstract expression than it ever does hard information.

Beneath this conscious whirl lie the sub-minds of his arms, that dispose of what he proposes. The separation of will from the machinery that puts that will into motion has grown as the nanovirus leached into the species' wider nervous systems. Paul solves problems like a wizard: a thought, a desire, and his Reach extends to fulfil it. Sometimes this means a fight, where intimate contact between his arms and another's imposes dominance and simultaneously passes information from Reach to Reach, a whole black market of calculating power that Paul and his peers don't even know they have. In this partnership, each entity a committee, they get things done. Senkovi has given them the tools and the perspective. Although they never quite see the big picture, in a very real sense they *grasp* it. Senkovi has not noticed, for example, that the geothermal vents are becoming misaligned and inefficient, and that parts of the sea floor are becoming uncomfortably cool. For him, up on the *Aegean*, it is all within tolerance; the problem would not be flagged up by his systems for years. For Paul and his kin it is uncomfortable, and they have wrestled and fought and performed complex poems of dance and colour for each other until an unacknowledged consensus was reached. Then they went and adjusted the machinery, or instructed other machines to fix those machines following the great plan Senkovi gave them, of how one thing becomes another and how it all adds up to become home. Senkovi will come across their tampering later, and scratch his head to work out what they were trying to achieve. The experiment is long out of his control, but, though Paul 97 and the other individual octopi might seem petty, self-interested and anti-social, they have the wisdom of multitudes.

Other colonies communicate with them, one facility to the next. Some individuals travel, seeking less abrasive neighbours, avoiding genetic stagnation. Others insert dummy orders of crates and piping into the *Aegean*'s task queue and create instant new towns awaiting inhabitants. As before, they are prying into every connected space they can access, physical and virtual. Unlike the catastrophe that shut down the *Aegean* (and saved it), they understand enough not to break anything too essential.

Paul 97 and some others have a concept that is *Senkovi*. It is a complicated thing, but (despite his own thoughts on the matter) it does not approach traditional divinity. Human concepts of God are familial, after all, all too often paternal, and Paul does not understand the concept of family much, nor would he have affection for it if he did. But they like Senkovi, as they conceive of him. He represents benevolence and home and knowledge in a way that does not compete with them as they all compete with each other. Some few of them wonder if he is an individual like them, but the idea of another individual not constantly getting on their nerves and into their space is more alien to them even than the human cognition of Disra Senkovi.

7.

Lortisse felt oddly sanguine when Lante sat him down in the isolation lab and explained the problem. He even caught himself smiling slightly. *It can't be true*, he told himself. *It can't be real.* He nodded politely through Lante's scans and images, but that box of bone, those crenulations of grey matter, that wasn't *him*, surely. That dark blotch in the centre of a brain. *That's not us.*

And at the same time, it seemed entirely true and real, as if he had two opposing opinions overlaid on one of those brain images. Yes, of course he hadn't escaped the dangers of Nod. What had he been thinking? To walk about on an alien world picking out specimens like someone gathering seashells on the beach? Of *course* there was an inescapable fate for such men, or what was hubris for?

'You're taking this very well,' Lante said uncertainly. Of course she would be monitoring his life signs, ready for all manner of panic. Lortisse found himself with a remarkably clear mental image of his heart and lungs and the rest of it, all just pulsing and pounding away like normal, just as though they were discussing the quality of the fabricated food.

'I feel fine,' he told Lante, smiling. 'Everything feels good in here.'

'But it might—'

'Let's not jump to conclusions. Nothing might happen,' he told her reasonably. *Let's be adult about this.*

'I've prepared some possible means to attack the encysted organism,' Lante continued. 'After all, its biochemistry is sufficiently different to yours that what kills it won't attack your cells at all. We're going to have to pretty much put your immune system on ice, though, because otherwise it's just the same foreign body problem we had when it got into your system in the first place.'

'This sounds like an unacceptable risk,' Lortisse heard himself say, his main focus on the various prescriptions Lante had concocted and her models of how they would interact with the organism and his own brain chemistry. 'This is . . . *in* our brain, Erma. Do we really want to start putting more things into my brain?'

'Gav, this could start *eating* your brain,' she pointed out.

'You said yourself it can't interact with our body chemistry,' Lortisse said, still the soul of reason.

'It can still cause huge tissue trauma if it starts to grow or hatch or something,' she said stubbornly.

Lortisse grinned again. The whole conversation seemed weirdly funny, but perhaps that was just a defence mechanism. 'Erma, I . . . let's not be hasty. Let us . . . not.' He became aware the smile was still on his face, and he couldn't turn it off. The world seemed to be going slightly yellow around the edges, but at the same time he felt a sense of tremendous wellbeing. 'It's fine, it's fine, we shouldn't do anything to . . . upset the balance now, should we? What if this course of action brings about the thing that is wished to prevent?' The words sounded strange to him, though he wasn't quite sure where the problem lay. Strange to Lante, too, because she was frowning at him. He was suddenly very aware of the space and distance around them and between them, as though it was huge, as though he was huge. He laughed, feeling vertigo spike momentarily and then simmer down.

Something must be wrong because Lante was looking at him with more concern, not less. He laughed again, trying for reassuring. She wasn't reassured, patently, but he couldn't rein in the smile, despite the ache in his face.

'Gav . . . ?' Lante had a syringe in her hands, the first of her remedies to attack the encysted parasite in his brain. That would be a good thing, surely. In the long run. Lortisse found himself unsure. He was fine *now*, obviously. He had seen Lante's projections. There was a small but real danger of damage to his brain, either from the chemical cocktail or his own system's overreaction to it. The chance that it would actually affect the organism was far greater but still short of twenty-five per cent. Lante was going carefully.

Good, surely. And yet it seemed too much of a risk. He was averse to it. They should not risk the tenuous stability they had built within him. He looked into Lante's eyes. 'You see,' he told her. 'You see, I feel fine, good, okay. I don't want any of this. Just leave us as I am. It's all good, Erma. I'm even better than I was, recovered, out of convalescence. Look.' And he did a little skip and hop for her, to show her just how much he was in control of his motor skills. 'But it's more than that, see, see, I feel . . . space, so much space. We didn't understand how vast it all was. Look how far out we came, Erma! Distances we never even conceived of, contact with such an alien environment! You can't just wipe that away with medicine. We're seeing such things here.' The smile was wider now, painful, hard to talk around and yet the words

252

kept coming. 'Such structure and complexity we never imagined, all these imaginary places.' He began adding and taking away from Lante's treatment plans on the shared virtual display, enjoying the smooth way elements just disappeared, banished back to the make-believe. 'Don't try to take this away from us, now we finally understand how it all works.' His voice trembled with sincerity, or with something. 'We understand so much, Erma, it's incredible, unbelievable, barely comprehensible, and yet we managed, and now we see everything, all these spaces, playgrounds, modes of being, and beyond them all there's you and Yusuf and Kalveen and beyond them there are more and more spaces and there's no end to it and we can fill all of them and be all of them such such such.'

Lante twitched. He saw the syringe jab forward, seeking contact with his skin. He flowed away from her, feeling the delight of pain in his joints as he made them do unfamiliar things, trying to find a more efficient mode of movement than this rough stilting. 'Let us not be interfered with by this,' he said, and tried to delete the treatment plan on the system but she'd locked the file now. And yet she was keeping her distance from him and he could feel a curious hunger, or perhaps a sickness, his mouth flooding with it. He eased back until he felt the medical cabinets behind him, sending a brief command via his implants so that an empty syringe fell into his own hand. Lante was talking, the tone of her voice soothing but an edge of alarm growing behind it no matter how she tried. She was coming closer, one hand up in a calming gesture, the other still proffering the syringe. Her actual words seemed to be breaking up in the air and Lortisse understood this was because he was concentrating so very hard on configuring his own syringe. He kept nodding, though, and that seemed to be enough to keep a distance between them.

He had set the syringe to extract a sample and lifted it to face level to show Lante what he'd done. He felt obscurely proud, as though to do it he'd navigated a vastly complicated logical maze. 'Look,' he told her, and inserted the needle into his right tear duct, in and in and in – there was a lot of pain but it seemed like a second-hand sensation now, barely worth bothering with. The needle extended to the length the vessel had calculated and for a moment it just bobbed its head as they fought for a suddenly fragile control over their body. Then all was well and they withdrew the syringe, which now contained some small quantity of Us and was reconfiguring itself to inject.

There was an expression on Lante's face but they had to work hard to identify it because the vessel had not had to process horror recently. Lortisse felt this was untoward. She had a syringe and so did he. This contributed to a pleasing symmetry in the situation that he found desirable, but it was plain Lante didn't understand and there was only one way they were going to make her understand, so he advanced on her, holding the syringe up so she could see what they meant. She backed up against the wall of the room and they noticed they'd got between her and the door, which seemed opportune. Her mouth was open, and they realized that in the heat of all this movement and calculation they'd disconnected from those parts of the vessel's core that processed some of the senses, mostly to override the pain signals which had become distracting.

In case audible communication would make things right,

they turned their smile on Lante and let Lortisse explain, 'We're going on an adventure.'

She went for them with her syringe and it pierced their sleeve and got some of the material into the vessel's bloodstream, too little to make any difference or so the consensus hoped. Such an adventure! Now he had Lante's wrist but abruptly they weren't alone. For a moment Lortisse swayed, trying to process the multiplication of external entities that had abruptly occurred. The vessel's own archives helpfully supplied names for the newcomers but then went on to supply a vast amount of supplementary data that We-in-Lortisse could not process quickly or understand, a whole tide of emotional content, likes, gripes, histories, issues. They lost control momentarily, the vessel swaying and the space beyond becoming an impenetrable chaos of motion and light and garbled information. The vessel was being pushed and pulled. Auditory information was a clashing row of contradictory noises and the vessel itself was filled with the chemicals of distress and hurt. A threat seemed imminent and they had none of the usual recourses because this vessel was of such an unorthodox substance and organization.

Lortisse blinked, finding Baltiel and Rani gamely trying to pinion his arms as Lante programmed a fresh syringe. 'What . . . ?' He hurt, every part of him hurt, joints and skull and guts. 'What are you doing?' His words were lost in the noise of their voices, yelling at him to stay still.

'Erma?' he got out.

'Hold him still,' Lante instructed.

Lortisse twitched, trying to hold himself still, and a generation of thought rose and fell in the centre of his brain. He lunged forwards as Lante came at him with the syringe, feeling his joints pop, muscles tear, the pain abruptly an ecstasy of freedom. His teeth closed *snap* on Lante's hand, ripping into her flesh, grinding bone. Baltiel was trying to force the vessel's face into one of the medical cabinets but they were more familiar with the geometry of these large spaces now and any kind of control over the vessel was predicated on causing it pain and on its limbs retaining their original configuration. They let the vessel bend and twist until Baltiel and Rani had no hold on it, and then used one hand to take Rani by the throat. Baltiel was striking the vessel about the sensory organs, and in time that would prove an inconvenience. Consensus amongst We-in-Lortisse was that the vessel was damaged beyond salvage and appropriate measures were taken to encrypt experience and history in suitably durable archival form for later retrieval and present dispersal.

Lortisse was still watching out of his eyes, still grinning, in fact, though Baltiel had knocked loose several teeth from his bloodied gums. His body sung with adrenaline and an ecstatic mix of hormones. He felt a scale of cosmic vastness that was at the same time bounded in the smallest nutshell. He felt an incomparable, religious *rightness* as the muscles of his hand clenched explosively, far beyond their tolerances, tearing loose from their anchor points even as he rammed a splintering thumb into Rani's neck, letting his blood become her blood. Baltiel struck him again, and then something impacted on the vessel far harder. Lante had a tool in her intact hand. That part of him that retained access to his memories recognized that it was used to cut wreckage but Lante had used it to carve deeply into his vessel, into their body, and now a great deal of that body was coming out, great gouts and pieces of it.

The others detached Rani from their ruined grip but they were already shutting down and withdrawing from the control centres of Lortisse's mind by then. Shortly afterwards the vessel started screaming, alone on the floor of the quarantine lab, and after that, it stopped and lay still.

8.

Baltiel sealed the lab with Lortisse's body inside and they dragged themselves to the main bubble room of the habitat. Lante was swearing, one hand shaking as it worked on the other, disinfecting the wound that Lortisse's teeth had made, weeping with pain but, Baltiel guessed, more with fear that something had gone in. Rani was . . .

Rani was unconscious on the floor, her own blood painting her from neck to waist. He grabbed a medical kit and started applying a pressure bandage, but surely it was too little, too late. The woman was ashen grey. Lortisse had punched a hole in her throat with his *finger*.

'It's impossible,' Lante was saying over and over. 'It can't . . . We can't be infected . . . different biologies. Different proteins. Different cell structures. It *can't* be happening.'

'Shut up,' Baltiel told her shortly. 'Help me, here.' Rani's body was shuddering, her limbs twitching and flailing. Death throes, or new life? 'Your treatment – the stuff you were going to use on Lortisse—'

'Back in the lab,' Lante said shortly.

Baltiel was linking with the habitat systems, shunting medical functions to the main chamber's fabricators. He set them making emergency supplies: plasma, anti-shock, whatever was quick and resource-cheap. Everything else would have to come from the isolation lab Lante had set up. 'Go get what you made. I'll get us set up here.'

To her credit, Lante's rebellious look was only momentary. She'd pumped herself full of painkillers, and doubtless now she was thinking that her own best chance was back in that lab, as well as Rani's. Without a word she stomped off back the way they'd come.

Lante felt her pulse rise and rise, despite the medication that should be controlling it. Was that a symptom? Had Lortisse felt the same, in amongst the many and varied klaxons of his body failing? She wasn't suffering the same colossal system shock as he had, at the intrusion of the foreign organism. Did that mean his bite was no more than that, or had the entity learned a way to stealth its way through a human body without setting off the alarms?

She knew how irrational it was to think of things that way. Of course the alien sludge hadn't *learned*. It was some slime mould analogue, some bacterial clot, just a disease of tortoises. And yet it had found its way to Lortisse's brain and . . .

Obviously it had driven him mad. What she had seen was Lortisse, his brain swollen and feverish – *despite the fact that she'd put monitors in place for just that and none of them had warned her* – acting out some psychopathic delusion. Any projection of alien intent was merely her own brain piecing patterns together out of misfit scraps. The *thing* wasn't controlling him, just damaging his brain so that he wasn't responsible for his actions. The enemy had been Lortisse's diseased id, and not . . .

Lante found herself staring helplessly at the man's body, sprawled on its side in a slick of his own blood. He looked as though he'd been through some sort of industrial crusher, joints twisted, one hand splintered where he'd forced it into poor Rani's neck. The wound she'd dealt him was mostly hidden, but she knew she'd cut him open from shoulder to sternum, and even then he hadn't reacted as a man hurt. Surely there was no frenzy or delusion that could see someone abuse their own body in such a way.

Forget him. Need to save Rani. Need to save me. She lurched forwards to gather the syringes the dispenser was filling for her. Her hands shook; two of them tumbled to the floor, and then a third. *Is this it? Am I losing control?* She tried to examine her own thoughts for an alien presence. *Am I still me? Are these my perceptions? Was I like this a moment ago?* Her personal monitor was warning her that she was hyperventilating, her heart rate approaching dangerous levels. *Is it killing me?*

She gathered up the fallen syringes, fumbling more of them in the process. As she tried again to claw them all together she found herself looking into Lortisse's face. It had been locked in a frozen, silent scream. But now he had that damnable grin spread from ear to ear.

As she drew breath to shriek, his arm flicked out, not like a limb but like the disjointed element of a trap, and the syringe – the one filled with fluid he'd drawn from behind his own eye – jabbed into her ankle and shot its contents directly into her bloodstream.

Rani was barely breathing, her body temperature showing as dangerously low, and the plasma Baltiel was able to fabricate was doing little for her blood pressure. She was shuddering rhythmically, and all he could do was hold her and grind his teeth and wait for Lante to—

He heard Lante's shriek – not just fright but a dreadful

despair. A jolt went through Rani at the same time and her eyes opened, focusing on him and then unfocusing again.

'Stay with me,' he told her. The system was reporting her spasmodic attempts to reach out at random with her inbuilt link – touching the habitat interfaces but gaining no purchase on them. Still, she managed a smile, just a faint one at first but growing by inches.

'Yusuf,' she told him. 'We're going on an adventure.'

He went cold. The words were coming out far too strongly for her condition, accented weirdly, still Rani and yet wrong. Another shudder went through her and he saw her hands finger-walking randomly at the ends of her arms, the same aimless drift as her virtual connections.

'We understand better this time,' Rani told him. 'Yusuf, it is still your companion Kalveen Rani. She I We will survive. We will make it so. Mistakes have been made, but We-in-Lortisse reacted to threat. We-in-Rani we are Rani we understand such wonderful volumes and connections to farness and vastness. These-of-we are Kalveen Rani now, Yusuf and Kalveen Rani will live. These-of-we will write her immortality into our libraries and she will never die.'

Baltiel was a good ten feet across the habitat chamber by then, and Rani just lay on the floor like a corpse, save that her face was tilted towards him and animate, talking.

'Yusuf, it's still me we I am here. We understand everything now.'

'I'm sure Lortisse would have said the same,' he got out.

'Mistakes were made. These-of-we will take into account the durability of this Rani. Better, it's all better now, Yusuf. Everything can be as it was except better than it was and forever, Yusuf, and forever and ever.'

Amen, he thought, but he was looking for a weapon, any weapon. Rani's head pivoted unnaturally on her neck to keep him in view. No cutting tools in here, and the sort of basic, brute tools his ancestors might have needed were for drones now, because who needed to lift a finger for that sort of work?

Except . . . after the first habitat had died, hadn't they planned for a similar catastrophe, having had the fragility of their technological lives flagged up for them? And had they kept that . . . ? Still watching for any movement from Rani, he ran the inventory of the lockers on the habitat system and came up trumps. He gave himself an inset camera view to guide his fumbling hand so he didn't have to look away from the thing on the floor.

At last he found it: something they'd fabricated in panic, then stored in faint embarrassment for the primitive thinking it represented. Something primal. Something infinitely re-assuring. An axe with a gleaming metal head, barely a scratch on it. The weight made him feel strong, invulnerable.

Rani's smile spread further, a horribly misplaced attempt to be reassuring.

'Yusuf, we are still Kalveen Rani,' she said conversationally. 'And more, and more. This is the best way. These-of-we are growing and learning. Those-of-we that were Lortisse did not understand. We have superseded their wildest dreams, Yusuf.'

'Stop using my name,' he said through gritted teeth.

'It's me, Yusuf.' She spoke over him, through the grin. 'It's us, it's me, it's us me, Yusuf.'

He approached her, eyeing the spasmodic twitches of her limbs, which seemed closer and closer to meaningful, directed movement. The axe was a savage comfort at the end of his arm.

'Yusuf,' she said, head pivoting, the pupils of her eyes vacillating as she tried to focus on him.

Then Lante was in the doorway and no doubt wondering what the hell was going on. 'It's too late for her,' Baltiel said. 'It's got in her.'

Lante seemed to find that delightful.

'We're going on an adventure,' she said, pronouncing each word with exaggerated care.

Yusuf made a wordless sound and stumbled back.

'It's all right, Yusuf,' Lante told him. 'We're fine. We're all fine. We're liberated, really. It's all so much, Yusuf. But you'll understand. We'll all understand everything. Why else are we here? Don't you want to learn it all, at last?'

His faltering feet were taking him to the outer door. He had no suit on, of course, but right now the dangerous part of Nod was in the habitat with him. He had faced the outside before, years ago. He had breathed that impoverished air and lived, although only because he thought they were all going to die.

Lante was walking towards him carefully, as though trying to compensate for a sloping floor that wasn't. 'Yusuf,' she breathed. 'It's still us still *me*. *I* am Erma. Still. I we I know what you fear. She we I felt it, too, but it's wonderful, Yusuf. We're wonderful. We have discovered such strange vast things we never dreamt of.'

He brandished the axe and there was no human flinch in her, and he saw in his mind's eye an image of him splitting that familiar face, and only dark fungal ooze issuing out. He had the inner airlock door open now, sawing through the habitat's safety protocols to speed things up, throwing his Overall Command rank around.

'Yusuf,' Lante said, as he backed into the airlock. 'Don't you understand? This gives us purpose again. We've been without purpose for so long. There is no more Earth, Yusuf. No more humans. Of course we chose to study this place instead. And it they *We* studied us. We don't have to be something old and tired and used up, Yusuf. We can be something new.'

And the horror of it was, he could believe there was something of Lante there, and that what was speaking to him was a kind of pithed and neutered version of his crewmate. *She tells it as she sees it, and I can never know how it sees things, or what it wants.* He did not believe in alien parasites that could instantly converse in the language of their hosts, but he did believe in parasites that screwed over brain chemistry or pulled neural strings so that their hosts believed whatever was convenient to the hidden passenger. *And it's learning, somehow. It's getting better at manipulating them.*

The outer door opened, and Nod's chest-aching atmosphere flooded past him. For a moment he was going to throw the axe at Lante, but its value to him as a morale boost was greater than as a ranged weapon. Instead he turned and ran for the shuttle.

He was sending ahead, linking with its systems. The ground shook as its engines began to warm. The old craft had sat there on the rocks for a long time without being used. He had no idea whether the mist or the rain or some other local nastiness had got into it, but right now he didn't have the time for a proper inspection. It would work or it wouldn't.

He reached the door, which he had ordered open moments before. It was closed. He connected to the shuttle systems again and recoiled, finding them a mess of contradictory commands. Lante was trying to connect, and so was Rani. He should have been able to override them both, but they were flooding the shuttle with chaotic attempts to interface with it, like a drunk fumbling with a front door key. The result was an inadvertent denial-of-service that was keeping him out as well, as the shuttle tried to process far too many queries at once.

There was a hoarse, mad voice bellowing, the sound of it torn at by the wind that moaned in across the salt marsh. Belatedly he realized it was his own, shouting at the insensate machines that wouldn't do his bidding. Lante and Rani's glitched words sounded sane by comparison. There were tears stinging the corners of his eyes. Everything had come to an end.

They were coming, of course. Baltiel turned to see them: Lante strode, bow-legged, smiling pleasantly, her face tilted away from the red-orange sun. Rani followed, lurching, occasionally going down on one knee amongst the rock-pools, ripping her clothes, gashing her skin, feeling none of it. Her smile was painfully wide, eyes likewise. They were calling his name.

We had such plans. But it wasn't true, not in the end, not after that savage disconnection from all their pasts. They had been marking time ever since, writing reports for nobody, inventing pastimes to cover up the hollow emptiness inside. And now something had come to fill it. Perhaps Lante – this new puppet Lante – was right after all.

But something within him bucked at that. He was Yusuf Baltiel. He was his own man, singular, aloof. He was the leader. He was not led by the nose by some alien parasite.

He hefted the axe and waited for them to come closer.

9.

'Disra? Disra, speak to me, please. I need to hear your voice.'

Disra Senkovi stared blankly at the interior of the *Aegean*'s crew quarters, wondering why he was there. He linked to the ship's internal cameras and replayed his weaving progress, realizing he'd been drifting aimlessly from room to room for quite a while now. Probably he'd had some intent at the start, but that had fallen by the wayside long ago. In a sudden panic he called up a display of the key terraforming objectives, but everything was on target or even ahead of schedule. He knew that if he probed into the details of *how* those targets had been met, the details would be an impenetrable tangle of weird solutions, unintuitive, even contradictory on the surface, and yet all working together to make Damascus that much more habitable for Earth-based life. The last ice had gone from the poles, he'd seen – the big orbital mirrors had been yanked way out of position to focus the sun on the final gleam of it. One hundred per cent of the surface water was sufficiently oxygenated, and penetration went far enough that half the deep sea floor was liveable, too. The *Aegean*'s factories had been cracking asteroids brought in by its deteriorating fleet of remotes, and the debris had been shipped down the gravity well to where the Pauls and Salomes and the rest were busy building colonies, expanding their network of holes and tunnels around the various terraforming installations, creating cities. He hadn't told them to do any of that, but nor had he stepped in to stop them. He had watched and watched, and at last he realized he was waiting for them to need him, for them to screw it up. And they hadn't. And that meant they didn't need him.

They still spoke to him, but he had a sense of the pre-occupied now. He was just one point in their complex social calendars. When he called, at least some of them listened, but he characterized their manner as a sort of fond nostalgia for some childhood imaginary friend.

I have succeeded beyond my wildest dreams, he thought. *Beyond Baltiel's wishes, certainly.* And he remembered that he'd been getting a battery of messages in the last minute or so, which had brought him back to himself. *Am I in trouble, then?*

'Yusuf,' he said, connecting and letting Baltiel's image appear on the nearest screen. He hadn't been down in the crew quarters for a long, long time. It was rattlingly empty there.

'Disra, listen to me!' Baltiel looked terrible: grey and haggard.

'Are you . . . well?' Senkovi asked leerily. Baltiel was crammed into the pilot seat of a shuttle, unshaven, wild-eyed, looking like he hadn't washed in a month. 'Is it Gav, has he—?'

'Listen to me!' Baltiel fairly shrieked. 'He's dead. Lante's dead. Rani's dead. Disra, it got them. It . . .' Senkovi watched him visibly get a hold of himself. 'Listen, don't speak, just listen. The stuff that got into Lortisse, it infected him somehow. It got into his mind. It was controlling him, Disra. He wasn't himself.' A shudder and a sob wracked the Overall Commander, and that more than anything else kept Disra from interjecting. Baltiel had always been the iceman, harsh and distant and lacking in sentiment. This was not the same man. *Broken*, Disra thought numbly.

'He attacked us. He got it into Lante and Rani, Disra. He infected them. And it was faster with them. The stuff was learning, I swear. It had worked out how to get at our biology, our neurology! I know how mad that sounds, but it's true, you have to listen. It got to them. It took them all. They weren't themselves. I swear they weren't themselves in the end, Disra. Even though they sounded the same, even though they . . .' Muscles twitched at the corners of Baltiel's mouth as though he was forcing back vomit. 'I had to kill them, Disra. I had to do it.'

Senkovi stared at the stains bespattering Baltiel's filthy clothing. He had been about to ask why Baltiel had waited so long to pass on vital news, but the words fell away at this last revelation. *Is that blood? Lortisse's? Rani's?*

'I'm sending you all the imagery from the habitat,' Baltiel whispered. 'Judge for yourself. I stand by what I did, even though I . . . though I did . . . what I did, what I . . . had to . . . Disra, this stuff is deadly. Keep away from Nod. There can't be any more contact between us.'

'I . . .' And then Senkovi's words dried up as he stuttered through the recording, now speeding up, now slowing down, now hearing familiar voices say abominable things. 'Impossible,' he got out, staring at the evidence that proved him a liar. And 'Dead . . . ?' even though, was there any doubt of it? Was it something Baltiel would confess to as a joke?

'I had to, Disra, we . . . there was no choice.'

It's just you and me, thought Disra. The idea came to him, absurdly selfish, that Baltiel wouldn't be fighting him over what happened to Damascus now. He shook it off, trying to feel the proper measure of grief and horror. It eluded him, though. He remembered how he had been hit by the other deaths – Skai and Han and the rest, and of course all of humanity as they knew it. That had struck home, but somehow this new tragedy was too big to deal with. Lante, Rani, Lortisse . . . couldn't be *dead*, surely. Couldn't be taken over by some alien infection and then dead, in quick succession. He hadn't seen any footage from outside the habitat. He hadn't seen Baltiel swing the axe. They weren't *dead*.

Something had been nagging at him, something left over from his childish thought about Baltiel's plans for Damascus, and something about the rapid exchange of their conversation. He picked at it, because that was easier than actually dealing with what he'd been told.

'Yusuf,' he said slowly. 'You said there can't be any more contact, because of the, because of the thing, the thing that happened.'

'Yes,' Baltiel agreed immediately. 'This stuff, this parasite, Disra, it's—'

'Then why are you in a shuttle most of the way over here?'

'I . . .' There was a moment, then, when an absolute despair gripped Baltiel's features, a realization that the most dreadful of fates had come to pass, irrevocable and forever, without him even knowing. And then it was gone, drowned in the bland stare that rose to consume it. 'Because we're going on an adventure.'

Senkovi stared at him, feeling cold. 'What?'

'I had to get away, Disra,' Baltiel said, the moment of estrangement passing as though it had never been. 'We . . . just needed to move on, move out. I we couldn't stay there, not after we'd . . . done what we'd done.'

'Yusuf, is some of that blood yours?'

'Trivial, very small, almost no amount.' Baltiel stared at him and Senkovi tried to find the man he knew in those eyes, that face.

'Yusuf.' He swallowed. 'I'm going to ask you to turn the shuttle back around. Back to Nod. Go on back to the planet.' *Am I really going to do this?* 'I can't let you come to the *Aegean*. I can't let you come to Damascus. Just . . .'

'I'm coming, Disra. I want to see those spaces and extents that we remember. We can see the pictures and the maps but not the real thing not yet. It's all right, Disra.'

'It's really not.' Senkovi's hands were shaking. 'Go back, Yu— go back, whatever you are. You can obviously understand me, or half understand me. The *Aegean* has anti-collision lasers. I am going to use them if you come near me or Damascus, so help me. I am building something here. I am not going to let it get . . . infected.'

'Disra, don't treat us like this.'

'I swear I'll do it.'

'You won't.' Baltiel's smile was beatific. 'We can reach out and touch you even from here. Even as we speak we are with you in all your spaces. We know the overrides and the commands to prevent you from harming us. Disra, we only want to explore. We're on an adventure.'

In a sudden panic Senkovi dived into the *Aegean*'s systems, seeking control of the lasers, the engines. He was locked out. Baltiel had used his command codes.

'I can get round these,' he said. 'I was always a better hacker than you.'

'You just thought you were,' Baltiel said serenely. 'I always knew. We always knew.'

'Eventually,' replied Senkovi, through gritted teeth now.

'We're coming, Disra. We are Yusuf still, your friend. We will do no harm. You will never be alone again. Isn't that a good? Yusuf, this vessel and These-of-we, we understand now that all the limits of your world are needless. We are greater and greater. You expand our world. We cure your singularity. Isn't that a good?'

Senkovi was fighting the barriers Baltiel had so effortlessly raised in the system, but he was uncomfortably aware that 'We always knew' must have had its roots in the human original's knowledge because he'd never been fenced off like this. *The bastard never said anything.* Senkovi knew he could break this down eventually. In his own humble estimation he was now the cleverest human being in the universe. Time, though. He checked the speed of the shuttle's approach. Measured in hours, now. Did he have hours? He had set a dozen algorithms spinning their wheels to crack the codes, but now he returned to them to find them dismantled and in pieces, Baltiel striding down the beach kicking over his sandcastles one by one. In desperation he widened his comms to include the planet below, because the least he could do was warn his creation that Armageddon was coming to it. He flagged the shuttle for them, labelling it with as many symbols for danger as he could. *Do not approach, predator, monster, hazard, avoid, flee.* But surely what was coming was something that could not be avoided, not for long. Everything he had worked so hard to bring about, the entire *future* he had been constructing, it was all going to perish.

'I don't know who I'm speaking to,' he sent to the shuttle. 'If Yusuf is there in any way, please don't do this. Take Nod, it's your world. Build there, grow there, please. But don't come and ruin what I have here.' He discovered a curious purity in himself, at this late stage. His thoughts, his fears, were all for the budding culture in the seas of Damascus, not for himself. 'Or take me, take the damn ship, take it away, just leave the planet alone. And if I'm talking to . . . if it's not Yusuf, or if there's something else that can understand me through Yusuf's brain, then . . . what do you *want*? What can I give you, to leave us alone?'

'What is to ruin?' Baltiel's quiet, reasonable voice came back. 'We have discovered such vast expanses in these vessels, but within them, a greater vastness.'

'Wh-what?' Senkovi actually stopped working on the codes to get his head around what he was being told. 'A greater vastness within the . . .' He felt a lurch, as though the fake gravity of the ship's rotation had suddenly shifted to the wall. An infection had got into the crew of the habitat, that had previously been parasitic on Nodan life like the poor bloody tortoises. It had found a way to adapt to its new, alien environment. It had found the brain – he remembered that much from Lante's notes on Lortisse. And somehow it had inveigled its way into the human cognitive process, able to influence and change it, but also perhaps able to *receive* from it. What would it have understood? Space, interstellar travel, the history of human civilization; a greater vastness.

'We cannot be limited now we know what vastness means,' Baltiel said. 'We know you understand this. Why else did you cross from your own native vessel to inhabit these far spaces?' His inflection kept shifting and jumping, now Yusuf Baltiel's clipped precision, now shuddering with weird stresses and phlegmy catches as his governing occupant forged new concepts into human words.

Senkovi set his virtual agents in motion again, trying to hide their tracks and watching Baltiel hunt them down. And it *was* him, or they were using that part of him. Senkovi's stock of belief was already stretched to breaking, but it wouldn't permit him to credit some alien consciousness that could rifle Baltiel's mind and make use of his knowledge and his skills without the engagement of the man's own judgement. This was Baltiel, Overall Command of the *Aegean*, save that his mind was dancing to the tune of a new master. *What does it feel like to be him? Does he even know? Is he happy?* And, the grim sequel to those thoughts: *I guess I'll find out soon enough.*

'Just the ship, not the planet, please,' he whispered, but Baltiel – the Baltiel whose face he saw on the screen – didn't react.

He checked for signals from Damascus, but the octopus colonies seldom contacted him direct. He placed ideas and information into their shared virtual space and they did with that data whatever their own weird thought processes dictated. He had given up trying to train and limit them long ago, and everything had worked so much more smoothly after that. Each generation was more inventive, more ingenious in its subversion of the technology he had given them. Recently he had seen signs that they were replicating machines they didn't have enough of (or had decided for their own unknown reasons they wanted more of). They had repurposed some of the factory machines to produce parts and were assembling them in novel combinations. He had no idea what they were building most of the time, and now he would never find out. *They are on the very brink of seizing their own destiny, and they won't be given the chance.*

Sometimes they did contact him, some of them. About a

dozen, across the planet, sent him messages. Not prayers, of course. Certainly not technical reports or anything so comprehensible. They were patterns that shifted and danced, changing hues and shapes with a fluidity that made him giddy. Some of them came tagged with error codes and data sets, identification markers, access codes. He had the impression they were trying to make their missives intelligible to a human, but the gap between his outstretched fingers and their tentacles was just too wide, still.

He wondered if they were sending him poetry.

Now he looked over the data from Damascus in case he had any last word from his doomed people. They were working away, still – all the machines on the planet were diligently informing him about the unorthodox uses they were being put to, even those in orbit.

Even those in orbit.

He let his enquiries brush past the data without delving, because Baltiel was still in the system and Senkovi suddenly felt like someone in an old house with a murderer, trying not to breathe and listening for the floorboard's fatal creak. Baltiel hadn't cut him off from the planet, of course. Baltiel didn't really care about the octopi and what they were doing. And if Baltiel would overlook it, so would this hybrid thing that sat behind his eyes.

Senkovi let his sweep go past the same points again, downloading a great haystack of data to obscure that one sharp needle. He followed the logic of what he could see happening, did some calculations in his head and, for the rest, decided he would have to trust the vision of Paul and the other octopi.

'Baltiel. Yusuf,' he said over the line to the shuttle. 'Are you in there, really? Is there anything of you that hears this?'

'Of course we know you, Disra. We are all the knowledge and memory and information of ourselves your good friend, but greater, of wider understanding.'

Does it know what personality is? It's there in Yusuf's memories, his relationships with me and the others, his opinions of us, his quirks. But perhaps those just seem to be inefficient imperfections to it.

'We are glad you have accepted matters,' Baltiel added, and Senkovi realized he'd stopped trying to hack the command codes a while ago. He let the Baltiel-thing draw what conclusions it would and just watched the movement of vast shapes around Damascus, inferring their shifts from the shadows they cast in the data.

The orbital mirrors, all of them: they had been built about the planet to focus sunlight in the early days, where it would be trapped by the smog of volcanic and microbial emissions, greenhousing the planet to life. Later they had been ferried about Damascus to break up ice in key areas, starting chain reactions of warming and currents, stirring the oceans, diffusing oxygen. Another decade and they would probably have been dismantled, unnecessary. After all, the point of terraforming was to create something stable that didn't need such toys.

Now they were shifting in a great ponderous dance, changing their facing, cupping the sun in their silvery hands and focusing that light and heat towards a single blistering point. They were flexing, concentrating and concentrating, bringing heat enough to melt an ice age down to a narrow region in the shuttle's flight path. Senkovi had never dreamt such a thing was possible, but the new rulers of Damascus had seen his Gordian Knot and found a blade to cut it apart.

The focal point was necessarily near the planet. The maths was imprecise, hurried even, if the octopi felt hurry as a human did. Senkovi watched the shuttle cruise obliviously into the crosshairs and take the full brunt of the system's sun, magnified and magnified until even the re-entry plates peeled away like flayed skin, until the reactor cracked open, the explosive force shunting the shuttle wildly out of the neat approach it had been attempting, the contents of the crew compartment surely boiling like spoiled soup.

And then the shuttle, nosediving, plunged like a white-hot meteorite into the atmosphere and burned all the way down until it met the sea.

PRESENT 3
ROLLING BACK THE STONE

1.

Helena dreams of her grandfather.

He'd been a tough old man, that's how she remembers him. One of the oldest off the *Gilgamesh*, both in years lived and most especially in objective time elapsed since his birth. He remembered Old Earth, as almost nobody did – not Kern's Old Old Earth, but the ruin of it that the second human civilization had clawed its way out of, when there was no other alternative to escape but starve and sicken.

A tough old man, and he outlived many of his juniors amongst that first generation. After Old Man Karst died by misadventure out in space and Vitas never quite adjusted to the new landlords and so many of the others had passed on, Grandad had just clung in there, increasingly gnarled, looked on by the next generation (and the next after that, Helena's own) as a kind of living monument. Aside from his own stories of How It Had Been, he was the last connection anyone had to Isa Lain, who had guided the humans all the way to where they could finally become Humans.

But Grandad had declined, in his last years. Helena just remembered, from when she was perhaps five or six, how he had woken screaming and shouting, inconsolable, rattling the walls with Lain's stick. The winters brought it on: not just the inkling of mortality that cold always brings with it to the old, but his own memories of icy awakenings past. And, at his age, even the equator got too cold at night. She remembered his stories – or possibly she was remembering recordings of him telling it, or even recordings from the *Gil's* archives, from when he was younger and still in space. His life had been punctuated by horrible awakenings, in and out of cold sleep as the ark ship conducted its centuries-long odyssey. Each time he had found himself in another time, another world, less fit for human habitation. That was what the nightmares were about: not the cold itself, which was only a trigger. Not even that he might not wake, though that had been a real possibility with the *Gilgamesh's* failing life support. He feared waking once more into a world he didn't understand, where everyone else had rushed ahead and left him behind. Adjusting to the hospitality of the Portiids had been hard on all the shipbound survivors – Grandad had lived most of his planetbound later life in a human reservation as people learned the ways of their hosts. He had taken it in his stride, though, because they were all in it together, all moving through time at the same pace. He reserved his dread for losing touch once again with his kin, his species. And yet, ageing in a society undergoing constant mutation as its members established a collective détente with the spiders, that was always going to be his fate. No wonder, then, that his last few winters were plagued with nightly terrors of waking into a world where nobody made sense to him any more.

In the dream she now wrestles clear of, he had been fighting his blankets (silk, of course), hollering and lashing out as he did, and she couldn't wake him or console him, and all around her the ice had been growing on the walls as it never had on

Kern's World, splintering out into fantastical trees and growths, encroaching on them until the chill of it rooted deep in her bones, and she knew that if she could not snap the old man from his dreams then they would both freeze, because he was bringing the cold of the sleep chambers to them, hauled hand over hand out of his tormented memories.

The dream felt as though it went on forever, but it could only have had purchase on her mind for the last few moments before she woke, passing from suspension to deep sleep through the reach of scattered brain activity and into full consciousness, so cold she feels she is being burned.

She is half out of her suit – or at least one arm, shoulder and breast are bared, as though she embarked on a provocative striptease as she was frozen. The pull that holds her lazily against the metallic floor is partly a weak gravity, mostly an electromagnetic field acting on her equipment. Her exposed skin is clammy and numb, ringed by weirdly fractal bruising, spirals of circles from thumbprint- to freckle-sized in whorls all over. Every joint feels as though it has been wrenched backwards. Sitting up proves a task beyond her capability. She sags back to the freezing metal and her mind drifts again.

Great chunks of memory are still slotting into place in her head but some of them are plainly irrelevant or even invented, and she has difficulty assigning import to any given recollection. This leads to a fragmentary new dream sequence where she fights her way through a corrupted file archive trying to assemble her own mind from the archive's contents and constantly finds that vital bridging sections of data are missing or misfiled or translated into garbage. The data itself exists only as emotional or sensory information, which seems maddeningly relevant but is also a common feature of her regular dreams, which just tangles her up further between things happening now and things that happened in the past. By now, though, lucidity is kicking in and she knows that the whole exercise is little more than letting her imagination off the leash to run around and make a nuisance of itself. From long experience she insists on seeing the file data in terms of legible characters, engaging parts of her brain incompatible with dreaming and bootstrapping herself back into wakefulness. She opens her eyes again – to stay awake this time – feeling odd elements of the dream still clinging to her as though that great database is still hanging from her mind by a thread, waiting for her to catalogue it.

She is in a room of metal and clear plastic. At first its dimensions are hard to make out, because three of the walls are windows looking onto other similar chambers, save that those chambers are floored with what looks like oddly sculpted rubble. And weirdly lit: one oppressively bruise-coloured, two bright blue-gold as though illuminated by an otherwise invisible sun shining through the . . .

Water. And she has everything back, all the context, because she is still mostly in her survival suit that Kern prepared for the water. She and Portia had—

She looks around, already cursing herself. Portia is behind her, on her back and still almost entirely in her suit. As Helena watches, one leg-tip twitches.

She runs a quick diagnostic of her gloves, finding them none the worse for wear, and lays one on Portia's abdomen – the flank, rather than the exposed ventral side, because the main Portiid nerves run down the belly and they don't like to be touched there. She sends some test vibrations through without eliciting a response, but on her back Portia is not best placed to receive communications or to reply. At last Helena tries a direct link, implants to implants, and receives an acknowledgement followed by medical diagnostic data. Portia is conscious but very slow coming back to control of her body. The cold was harder on her than on Helena, and she reckons she has lost several leg joints altogether. The freezing caused some damaging expansion within the cavity of her body, and she will probably have some long-term organ damage that will require repair or replacement should the opportunity arise. *Meaning, if we ever get back to the* Voyager, Helena knows, because of course they are prisoners of the locals, octopuses, whatever they are.

With Portia's blessing she connects to her colleague's suit systems and sorts out some accelerated heating, which will hopefully get the spider back on her feet more swiftly. She wonders if she can call out for medical assistance, but she has the firm suspicion that their captors wouldn't know what to do with a human, let alone a Portiid.

Still, the knee-jerk reaction is there: call out to the local system to request assistance. It is something she has been able to do since she was seventeen, when she finally received the basic implants that would become universal amongst Humans within five years. There was always some manner of system listening, whether it was Portiid ant-architecture or home-built human electronics or the superior hybrids hived off from Kern herself.

There is an answering ping. She twitches in surprise and nearly elbows Portia in the cephalothorax. Something heard her, something weirdly familiar. It feels a little like interfacing with the ancient *Gilgamesh* systems, a little like trying to get

283

sense out of a low-grade Kern node that doesn't really want to talk to you. Something is out there, receiving.

Portia shudders then, legs flexing and clenching, and she sends Helena a request for assistance. Knowing her friend, Helena knows how much that must cost her. Portia is always the dynamic driving force in their relationship, after all, ploughing through spider society and dragging her Human companion in her wake. Helena totters over and does her best to right the spider, rolling her onto her legs on the fourth attempt and exhausting every jot of energy she has left in the process. Portia crouches there, trembling and twitching randomly as she fights to regain use of her limbs.

Watched, she gets out eventually, after a half-dozen slurred shuffles are lost on Helena's translation gear. Her palps' palsied shudders describe a direction: one of the adjoining chambers.

Helena looks, and fails to see, looks and fails and then finally understands that part of the weird concrete-seeming jumble pushed up against the window is actually an octopus, its skin the colour and texture of the material it clings to.

She scrabbles about, finding her slate discarded on the ground but apparently intact. What can she say? Functionally, nothing of use, but she keys up some colours she hopes are friendly and shows these to the creature.

One protruding eye regards her distantly, and then the creature's body shifts slowly from its greyness into lemon and rose pink, kindred hues to those she chose. The blossoming of the shades is hypnotic, arising imperceptibly from all over its body, and then fading back into monochrome camouflage.

Is it an observer, or is it a fellow prisoner? She remembers the maybe-diplomat that had come to meet them, and its sudden attempt at escape. Had it got out? She thought it hadn't, so perhaps it is now their neighbour in the cells.

Quarantine.

She shrugs back into her suit and does what she can with the internal heaters. The room is still icy cold, but at least her and Portia's batteries seem to be . . . full. That is unexpected. Built-in clocks tell her they have been out for days, likely some coma state before the locals cared to trigger their awakening. She tracks down the logs, worried that the readings are corrupted and she might abruptly lose all power.

They have a charging field, Portia stutters out, following her enquiries. *Suit called out, received remote recharge. Protocols like Old Empire.*

Enough to be compatible, Helena agrees. A slow burn of excitement rises in her, optimism she would not have looked for five minutes ago given their situation. She follows up that link she detected before, waiting to be slapped down by security protocols or just ignored. At first she gets nothing: the system is familiar enough to register her handshake, but no more. She tries access at a variety of levels, scaling back the complexity of her contacts until she is running the sort of maintenance queries normally reserved for when things are well and truly screwed.

The sensation is like shouldering into a door already open. Abruptly a colossal information architecture is laid out before her, so much her limited internal systems can only focus on small segments of it, arrayed in bizarre clumps and conglomerations of data. Almost everything is incomprehensible – numbers and data shorn of any context or familiar formats. And yet she follows the rabbit hole down and down, attempting to wrestle the thing into giving her any kind of coherent information, sending it ancient protocols the Portiids – through Kern – still use in the hope it might echo something back to her. She uses what she has, which in her case is mostly carved from her translation software. *Do you have anything like this?* she asks the system. *How about this?* She feels as though she is creeping through some vast, endless, unsafe ruin, searching for doors that might fit the verdigrised keys chance has given her.

And one does: some dog-end of her interpretation programming abruptly accepted by the host system, recognized and identified, and she finds doors slamming open, archive contents spilling out until there is more than she can handle and she has to pull back layer after layer, further and further from the meat until she can get an idea of what she is actually looking at.

Everything is filed under a nested set of headings, and most of those are incomprehensible to her, data never meant for human cataloguing. Deep under those layers, though, she discovers a name, a recognizably human name: Disra Senkovi.

2.

Avrana Kern has only limited and artificial emotional responses, being dead and a computer composed at least partially of ants. She considers: do the ants have emotional responses? Probably they are individually too simple for much more than primal fight/flight/pain responses. Their world is limited to the internal architecture of the colony, and the deeper architecture of the conditioning the Portiids have trained them to follow. They do not know they form the substrate for a grander mind, any more than the cells of a Portiid or Human body do.

She also wonders if the greater Kern instances can approximate a response beyond the purely intellectual. They are more complex than she is, after all, and have greater processing power available to them. However, if that is the case, she has no memory of it.

Unbidden, and from the deepest and most corrupted storage bins of her mind, a memory surfaces: the opinions of one Professor Douglev Haffmeier on whether the ancestral, living Avrana Kern was capable of emotional response. Irritated, she deletes it and any other reference to the jilted Haffmeier, even her own satisfaction at having so comprehensibly outlived him.

She has a record of what she experienced when she made

free with Meshner's implants and, inadvertently, the rest of his neurology. She cannot appreciate it: to run those recordings at any meaningful level would require access to the original architecture, vis, Meshner, and she has not utilized that connection again just yet. She is monitoring him carefully, and it is undeniable that he has undergone some cerebral changes that, were she not shunting more honest assessment off into a subroutine, she would characterize as 'damage'. At the same time, Meshner himself appears substantially unchanged at a personality level. Even now he is conspiring with Fabian on what the male Portiid endearingly believes to be a closed channel through the Artifabian automaton. Their topic of conversation is, of course, the implants and their research. Kern intends to be a fly on the wall (an inner wall, of Meshner's skull) when they reopen their investigations.

Kern's problem is this: she does not know what she is missing, being unable to experience it on her own. Simultaneously she is very aware of the absence. Her world was broadened, and now it is in its familiar straightjacket again. She cannot even grow inured to the experience because it is so comprehensively denied her.

Viola and Zaine, being the crewmembers with the most authority and mental capacity, have been debating the pros and cons of the inner planet and its signal for some time, on and off. The idea that this human-made contact might serve as leverage against the octopus locals, and thereby a means of recovering what can be salvaged of Helena and Portia, is still the narrow front runner. Kern chips in occasionally to encourage them. She is aware that she is being duplicitous in doing so, not because she disagrees with such a sentiment but because she has parallel motivations she is not voicing. She wants to meet this signal-sender. She wants – or at least has constructed a hypothesis to which she is giving untoward weight – it to be something like her, or like she was. She is aware that she is stacking the deck of her own calculations to get the answer she wants. At the same time, it *is* the answer she wants, and so she agrees with herself to overlook her own fudging of the figures just this once.

Back in the day, when she was a melange of organic consciousness and artificial personality, she dealt with conflicting motivations by fragmenting her mind into entirely separate shards, each of them with sharp edges to grate against the others. Portiid entomological computing bestows a breadth of processing power ideal for managing simultaneous, even contradictory, calculations. She can run two opposing points of view without logical difficulty, right up to the point where she needs to take two conflicting courses of action at the same time, whereupon the waveform collapses and the ideological cat is either alive or dead. And she knows that, at that point, she would take the action that best served the ship and its crew. Yet to run the thought experiment is irresistible: what if I had the chance to do this for *me*? What if the odds so fell out that I could fulfil my personal goals without compromising the overall objectives? And the inevitable follow-on calculations of: *How might those odds be nudged, precisely?*

Hence her decisions here, which will doubtless have enormous ramifications for the crew if she has pushed things too far. At some level, Kern is aware that she has a problem. She is not damaged, despite the fighting, but her moments of expanded functionality within Meshner's mindscape have left her feeling as though what she is left with now is incomplete, dysfunctional. Parts of her are constantly reaching out for the connections she remembers making. She wants that fuller being, she wants to connect to that distant signalwoman Erma Lante; two distinct ends now conflated by the circling subroutines she is filling her mind with. *I want to be more.*

Meshner is having another attack. Excusing herself under her general responsibility for crew safety, she links to his implants. This event is brief and non-threatening, but it gives her a momentary expansion of her capabilities, filled with alien sensoria. Kern will take anything she can get, at this point. Meshner could be reliving the worst traumas and she would lap it up greedily. Then it is gone, and once more she is left not only bereft, but unable to even appreciate what she had, knowing only that she no longer has it.

***

Fabian's feet tap and scrape on the floor quietly, because Viola is nearby and would doubtless have some caustic sentiments for them about jeopardizing the mission with their foolish researches. Artifabian picks up on this, his voice coming out as a low murmur. 'Meshner, respond please. What is your condition?'

Meshner stares the spider in its primary eyes. 'I may need to disconnect some implant functions.'

Tok. Fabian's irritated twitching suggests just how inadequate a response that is.

'It was one of your Understandings. I experienced it. It translated over . . . adequately.' And it is a breakthrough, make no mistake. All the many days they have raced for the

290

inner planet, the pair of them have been working. Enforced idleness in a spaceship run by a self-sufficient and possessive computer system is a blessing for those with long-running experimentation to be getting on with. Even as Helena, unbeknownst to them, is slowly working her way through hundreds of hours of visual data with life and freedom as the stakes, Meshner and Fabian have been able to amble through the labyrinth of their own work, slowly homing in on a format of Portiid experience that Meshner's poor Human mind can appreciate. And outside the mutable walls of the *Lightfoot* is a solar system of molluscs that want to kill them, but one can only spend so long gripped with fear before becoming jaded. The work of the experimenter, in contrast, goes on forever.

Until it actually generates results.

Meshner finds he is trembling. His limbs feel leaden and too few. The muscles of his face and thumbs tick randomly, and he wonders if they are trying to be palps and chelicerae and all of a Portiid's intricate mandibular machinery.

He doesn't feel he can go into detail. Fabian was over-bold in selecting what to gift his Human colleague. Meshner has, after multiple attempts, two more minor seizures and too many days of frustrating failure, understood the encounter his colleague set out for him: eight seconds of Portiid courtship from the male point of view, some long-ago failed liaison Fabian underwent. What remains with him is not the dance, which the little male knew at the time was amateurish and clumsy, but the emotional weight: hope, shame, ancestral fear of death, and behind it all a burning ambition and the companion resentment that this, *this*, was the best way for poor Fabian to advance his career as a scientist. Or perhaps

Fabian had been feeling something entirely different, and each sensation cued a track at random from the Human playlist of emotions. Meshner feels not, though. The verisimilitude of the experience still grips him. Some part of the software or his mind acted as an intelligent translator.

'It works,' he tells Fabian. 'The problem may be stopping it working until we can control it. But it works.' He watches the Portiid's palps in fascination because the little jitters and gestures are speaking to him, triggering residual memories that let him read them as if they are Human body language. All at once he kicks himself that he doesn't have Helena's gloves! Would the foot-shifting spider speech be transparent to him as well, if he could detect it?

Artifabian's own palps twitch, and Meshner realizes the automaton is advocating caution in its stance, even as it relays Fabian's words. 'We can try and limit the nature of the information you are required to take in.' An obvious gestural qualifier of dissatisfaction. 'Although as we lose the richness of the data, we lose the value of the experiment. But perhaps we can find something . . . more mechanical.'

Meshner feels weary and washed out, and he would swear that their robot intermediary is going above and beyond its role by independently trying to get him to slow down, but Fabian's logic seems unavoidable. 'Something simple,' he agrees weakly. 'But give me . . .'

Fabian is already scurrying off to a console, though, doubtless to start setting down his own memories for later copying. Meshner sags back, feeling that his brain is swelling inside his skull, packed to the brim with too many memories. Artifabian still stands near him, its feet rasping and shifting on the ground as though it is murmuring solicitously. A wave of synaesthesia threatens to overwhelm him: tactile sounds, visible scents, emotions manifesting as colours. From his triumph of a moment before, he is suddenly convinced that what they are doing is both impossible and unwise.

He catches a stray look from Zaine: impatient and irritated, like he isn't pulling his weight. *Well, walk a kilometre or two in this brain*, Meshner thinks, but Zaine has always been task-focused; impatient and irritated is about all she can achieve because what *is* the task, exactly? They are cast adrift in this alien solar system, down three crew, heading towards the complete unknown on the off chance it might be useful. Meshner guesses that fleeing back to the *Voyager* would be the more sensible choice, but it would also set the seal on abandoning Helena and Portia. They've seen the capabilities of the alien vessels. If the *Voyager* did anything bolder than run straight out of the system it would be nothing more than a bigger target for the warships.

We were all so bloody optimistic when we set out. And things have gone badly and can still go much worse. *We could have an armada of these ships turn up back home, now we've notified them of our existence. They'll get the details from Helena, maybe, and then we'll all be screwed.*

He shuffles over to a console and configures it for Human seated use, pulling a seat up from the fabric of the floor, moulding it and setting it hard. Still conscious of Zaine's occasional glower at him, he calls up the inner planet signal and starts looking over it. Late to the party, he knows, but at least he'll be able to make conversation on topics of current interest, and it isn't as though they don't have plenty of time to digest it.

Some hours later he finds himself on the wrong end of

an argument between Viola and Zaine about just what the hell they are all looking at.

It is a natural history, perhaps. At least, it is a document presented in the style the Old Empire once used for such projects. There is biochemical data, taxonomy, diagrams of what might be animals – certainly living organisms of some kind. There are notes on ecology, food webs, the interrelationships between species. And all of it impossible, or perhaps simply fanciful. Nothing is familiar. None of the entities described in such clinical detail are real, or at least match anything that any of the crew have ever encountered or even read about in some notional romance. And it goes on: there are reams of it, and creeping in through the words the sense of its increasingly erratic author, a voice out of time, Erma Lante.

Zaine's stance, stated with considerable force, is that this represents a work of fiction, some automatically generated fantastical account. Viola takes the opposite view, an unusual split between them, but Meshner suspects their three-way partnership with Bianca needed that third wheel to stabilize it. Viola is fired up with the possibilities of alien life. She feels, apparently, that this justifies everything they have gone through, that the bounds of scientific knowledge are being rolled back and so all they have suffered and lost has been worthwhile. Meshner scents (literally, his synaesthesia briefly returning) some self-serving bias in her position, because obviously she can feel better about herself if there is a *point* to all this. Both of them tries to recruit him, while he himself is more interested in the mechanism. Neither option seems to make a great deal of sense.

'It's an automatic system doing what it thinks is its job.

Or semi-automatic, like the proto-Kern entity when the *Gilgamesh* first met it,' Zane decides.

Meshner wonders what Kern – the current Kern that is translating this conversation back and forth – feels about that description. A moment later, he has a weird echo in the back of his head, a passing sensation of profound reflection, as though he somehow conjured up a vicarious emotion on Kern's behalf.

'Why would a machine be making stuff up?' he asks Zaine.

'If that's what its programming tells it to do, that's what it'll do. A speculative evolution scenario, running unchecked, would produce exactly this kind of fabrication.'

'And why would such a scenario even exist in this context?' comes the translation of Viola's argument. 'Fictitious, this is useless. But as a factual document it contains some remarkable assertions.'

Viola is fascinated by the possibility of life that does not originate from Earth. The thought arrives in his head like a whisper, bringing with it waves of dizziness and brief rainbow haloes around everything he looks at. Without that, he might even have taken the idea as his own, but the sensory bleed tells him it came from elsewhere. Not one of Fabian's stray Understandings, though.

'Kern?' he says, sotto voce.

Empty silence inside his head, enough that he feels he's imagined the episode, but then the voice comes again, and now he can trace it, linking through his implant, conjuring phantom auditory sensoria to bring him a voice only he can hear.

Portiid technology and interspecies diplomacy both are based on a biological commonality, utilizing the abilities of whatever they find. How might such species-wide capabilities benefit by the study of the truly alien? And she will talk Zaine round. She was always ambitious.

Meshner is very still. When he listens, there is nothing, no voice, only the roar and rush of blood in his ears, flecked with jagged moments of sensory mismatch: the prickle of arachnid hairs; the inexpressible acuity of touch no Human could dream of, save he; the tang of chemical information sieved from the air. A glimpse of an alien world, far more so than any planet here in this forsaken solar system.

And no voice. He tells himself it was an artefact, his own inner monologue rendered as audible words by yet another glitch with his implant. And he is not quite convinced.

3.

The creator referred to these records as the Senkoviad. It means nothing to Helena but had plainly amused him. He had been human, from Old Earth, one of Kern's contemporaries. Helena even stumbles across a reference to Avrana Kern herself.

There is a lot of material. The archive she uncovered is vast and she can almost imagine the dust on it all: not curated by its owners, just left unheeded in the great jumble of their electronic architecture. There is no security; that was what surprised her at the start. As soon as she configured her access protocols to something suitably archaic, she was let in as though she owned the place. Obviously, she and Portia then spent a busy ten hours trying to access systems of more practical use, only to find that all they had access to was a great morass of data, and not, say, the doors or life support or even a map. She has the distinct sense that all those things are out there, part of the sprawling virtual landscape, but they are not being governed by the same Old Empire logic and access procedures. Portia is still gamely trying, because that is her nature, although right now opening any doors is likely to get them both drowned. Left with no other options, but a more than ample sufficiency of time, Helena has gone back to her first love, because it was the obsession of Senkovi's later days, too. She is learning about translation.

The Senkovi she meets is a man ranging from late-middle to elderly years in various recordings. He wrote and recorded in Imperial C, although she wrestles with his accent, slang and various systems of abbreviation that were probably his own invention, born of being utterly without other human company. Senkovi considered himself the last human being in the universe. Mostly he made the reference flippantly, turning it into a joke. A couple of recordings see him bleakly, deeply depressed, just rambling to himself about loneliness and frustration, mentioning the names of the dead, talking about his far-away, long-lost home. Helena guesses there had been far more of that than she was seeing; that he hadn't often been in the mood to turn the recorders on when he'd been at his low points.

But mostly her searches turn up sessions where he works with his . . . experimental subjects? She has a sense that the relationship between him and his octopuses had started there but, by the earliest recording she can unearth, they had already renegotiated their respective standings. By inference, it is clear that Senkovi was aboard a ship or station in orbit, and that the watery planet below was the domain of the octopuses he appeared to have engineered, but with which he could not – at this point in the records – reliably communicate. He seemed to have no real control over them, either: they came and went, up and down the gravity well, according to their own whims. Senkovi had been a hands-off creator, she feels, but desperate to talk to them, and in the recordings they seem just as keen to talk to him. Which is ideal for Helena, who now has a vast library of recorded sessions of them failing to talk to each other, far more useful for her purposes than actual successful communication.

Portia, she signals, and the spider lifts her palps in acknowledgement. *I'm going to need to cannibalize some of my translation software.*

Portia's left palp cocks expectantly: *Hmm?*

I need to reconfigure it to deal with the visual information the locals use, to give me even a baseline translation of what they're trying to put across. And it's going to be a bitch, frankly, because it's not . . . discrete. I don't think they have distinct building blocks – it's some kind of gestalt of colours and textures putting over a composite message. I mean, I'm watching the man who actually made them, and he was working on this for decades, on and off, and I've skipped ahead and I don't think he actually managed to reach conversation-level interaction with them.

Portia's front legs lift slightly, an echo of her threat display as she contemplates the scale of the task. *But you can?* she says, with considerable faith in her friend.

I have something he didn't, Helena says, trying to match the spider's optimism. *I have their current communications, the two-channel ones. Looks like they found their current mode of conversation long after this Senkovi's day and it gives me an insight into their communications he didn't have. So I can build on his work and maybe we can start talking.* She sincerely hopes, because she is a linguist and talk is all she has.

Portia regards her for long enough that Helena asks, *What?* and the spider gives a curious little shake of her body.

You have great faith in the ability of communications to solve our problem. What if they are more than happy to keep us here, talk or not?

We cannot afford to believe that, Helena says with desperate faith. *But like I say, I need to devote my software to this, which means I can't keep it configured to translate for you. We'll have to rely on yours instead.*

Portia goes still, at first just thinking but then Helena translates her poise as the equivalent of embarrassment: slightly crouching, hoping to go unnoticed.

I will . . . configure my jacket and implants, Portia says awkwardly.

Helena feels a curious stab of betrayal. *You've been relying on my translation all this time?* And, yes, she has been eager to speak to Portia in the spider's own idiom, to listen through her gloves. But she assumed Portia was running a simultaneous facility to understand Humans. For a vertiginous moment she sees the situation from the spider's point of view. Of course, Humans would make the effort to communicate with the Portiids, to learn their language and imitate their sensory capabilities, but why would the Portiids, the hosts and rulers of Kern's World, spend all that effort on talking and listening like Humans? It is a melancholy thought that even Portia might not quite see her as an equal, despite their years together. The two species are still building that bridge between them, strand by strand, even two generations on.

And so she turns to that other bridge, the one that is hers to build, working off the rickety scaffolding set down so long before by Disra Senkovi. He had been an erratic researcher; intent and obsessive in some sessions, frustrated in others, and then there were the long gaps between recordings where he had plainly lost the will to go on. The recording sequences are incomplete, some are corrupted. She lacks key milestones and must fill in gaps. But time is what she has.

Sometimes there is food: a kind of fishy slurry that is sour but edible. Sometimes the lights dim, although not to any set pattern she can detect. In the next-door chamber, the solitary octopus comes to the window to stare at her, its colours fluctuating between chalk and ash but making no discernible attempt to tell her anything.

Without Senkovi she could never have made any progress. The octopus communication is equally distant from Portiid speech as it is from human. Senkovi never cracked it, but he made records and tentative lexicons and hours of recordings. She watches him in the tanks, floating alongside his inter-locutors; out in the dry, wrestling with multiple screens and a computer system that was slowly failing just as he was. She watches him butt against his limits and not know it: a man of erratic genius trying to apply his personal toolset to a problem he was ill-suited to. Senkovi was a planetary en-gineer, she understands, and he fell back on pushing for hard solutions and exact answers. Helena, on the other hand, is a linguist, a specialist in non-human language – even if she has only had experience with one such language until now. She takes the dead ends that turned Senkovi around, and she finds a way forward.

Sometimes more octopuses squirm into the other adjoining chambers to watch her and Portia. She takes the opportunity to record them as their skins ripple and dance with colours. Patterns spread from individual to individual, mutate, change; they are constantly talking, or perhaps *emoting*. They touch often, and sometimes they break abruptly into what looks like fighting – one even loses an arm to such a struggle – but which she begins to think is an inherent part of their commu-nication strategy. She makes notes, observing them just as they observe her.

The lone, pale octopus is kept segregated, she notes, and she is increasingly certain it is their former ambassador, contaminated by contact with aliens. Its own skin flickers hesitantly when its kin arrive, and she sees an interplay between it and them, yet there is also a distinct exclusion in the way they react to it, like humans turning their backs. The interplay within the group is far more dynamic than that between them and the loner. *And yet they are still 'talking' to it, even as they ignore it.* Which makes her ever more sure that what she is watching is something other than 'talking' and puts her in mind of the twin channel transmissions the creatures broadcast with.

She sleeps, Portia and she looking out for each other and taking shifts. They eat the tedious fish-smelling paste extruded sloppily into their chamber. She works alongside the long-dead Disra Senkovi, reliving his moods and despair, his moments of manic animation, the cut-off ends of his psychological low points when he abandoned his research and his recording to feed the black dog that constantly followed him.

He lived a long time, alone, she realizes. He spent half a lifetime trying to reach out to his creations, because there was nobody else in his universe he could talk to. And he came so close, negotiated a means of exchanging data and information, yet never made that emotional link. She thinks about herself and Portia, how she can recognize the moods of the spider, even though they are not quite Human moods; and vice versa, she hopes. *I am damned lucky, is what I am.*

And then she finds one long clip in which Senkovi tells a joke to an octopus. It isn't a good joke; dreadful, in fact. He finds it hilarious though, being in that part of his mood-cycle, and she watches as the cephalopod's skin slowly shifts and changes, and then begins to rapidly flicker and dance. Laughter? No, laughter is human. Beyond an appreciation of simple physical pratfalls, Portiids do not find Human humour funny, just as Portia once tried to describe a complex social engagement she plainly considered . . . *something*, some word Helena didn't have, the emotive impact entirely beyond her reach. So here is poor Disra Senkovi, a man a century old and many thousand years dead, telling jokes to sea life and getting a response.

And the reaction delights him. He goes on and on, dredging up puns and wordplay and double entendres, almost splitting his sides with laughter, and the octopus glitters and shimmers with bright, daylight colours, clinging to the glass of the tank and watching the ageing comedian in fascination.

Helena's notes are sufficient, by then. She can understand what Senkovi never knew. The octopus could not get the joke, but it understood that he, its creator, was happy. Happiness is a universal, perhaps; or at least it was something the octopus read in that cackling face, and married to some state of its own. The octopus knew he was happy, and it loved him, or valued him, or felt *something* enough that his happiness was important to it. And that in itself is a miracle; that is the grand triumph Senkovi never grasped, that his creatures could empathize, could apply a theory of mind to entities quite unlike themselves, could be great-hearted enough to be happy that someone else was laughing, even if they couldn't get the joke.

She watches them for a long time, and then she turns the recordings off, lets the data lie fallow. She sits with her arms about her knees and stares at the solitary grey octopus in the next cell and feels unutterably sad.

At last there is a faint touch down her lower back, one leg-tip stroking her tentatively. Portia understands Human emotions, too. Sadness is another universal, maybe, even if different stimuli trigger it.

'He was so lonely,' Helena whispers, hoping Portia has her translation software configured.

Again that stroking touch. Emotional trauma is worse for Humans, Helena knows. Portiids still feel it: for them, shock or frenzy are most common. Portiid brains are more uniform, though; they have more common experience with each other than Humans, and hence sympathize with each others' trauma more readily, rather than each becoming a solitary prisoner of their experiences, as Humans so often are.

Helena wonders if the octopuses have it better or worse. Except of course they wear their hearts on their skins, all the time. Perhaps there is simply no such thing as a private trauma, and hence no stigma to it. Perhaps they live their lives like operatic heroes and heroines, broadcasting the grandeur of their melancholies and their rages to all within eyeshot. Thinking of poor Senkovi, that alternative sounds eminently healthy to her.

And one day, after she has thrown her bucket into Senkovi's well and heard it strike dry, she knows she is as prepared as she will ever be. When the little parliament of molluscs arrives to eyeball her and Portia again, she is ready. She takes her slate, now configured to encode and decode as much of the octopus communication as she has grasped (pitifully little, even now) and presents it to them boldly, and hopes she is saying hello.

4.

No word from Helena; no transmissions from the locals, no ransom note or demands or even threats. Or rather, plenty of incidental transmissions should one choose to turn receivers towards their world, but nothing aimed at the *Lightfoot*. No communications with the *Voyager* either, which is still hiding out in case the xenophobia of the aquatic civilization here turns out to be insuperable. And Fabian has the uncomfortable feeling that a timer is inching down the wire somewhere. The locals are technologically advanced and erratically paranoid. Octopoid eyes somewhere are going to be searching the further reaches of their solar system for perceived threat. It's what Fabian would do, after all. He can only assume these angry molluscs have at least as much common sense as a male Portiid.

All of this makes Fabian very angry, an emotion he shows neither in palp nor footfall. It does not do for male spiders to give rein to that kind of outburst as a female might. He is expected to be meek and deferential, and it eats him up inside like a parasitic larva sometimes.

The *Voyager* mission had got him out from under the shadow of some particularly dominant females in his peer house, who would have blithely taken the credit for his researches – not necessarily a theft, so much as a kind of intellectual eminent domain: anything he produced would *obviously* be a product of the peer house itself, with Fabian as mere conduit. After that, and with his work hovering frustratingly near the boundary of success without quite crossing over, all these excursions aboard the *Lightfoot* came at exactly the wrong time. He resents the risk, because if there is one archetypally male trait Fabian espouses wholesale, it is a regard for an intact exoskeleton. He resents the interruptions. He particularly resents the fact that now, of all times, progress is being made. Why couldn't this have happened back when they had the opportunity to focus on it?

He is also beginning to resent Meshner, or at least his frailties. Humans are supposed to be robust. How could they not be? They're *huge*, and they have that absurdly overcompensatory immune system that makes him wonder how any of them can ever fall ill at all. Except Meshner is not well, and months of research-heavy interplanetary travel cooped up aboard the *Lightfoot* is not mending him. Fabian has spent no small amount of thought on the subject of how much their researches ('their' when negative, 'mine' when positive, and he is fully aware of the mendacity of this and cannot train himself out of it) are to blame and tells himself stridently that it is only a little, and other factors outside his control are more culpable. And he is practically *there*. Only a little more and Fabian can go happily off and encode his findings for the benefit of future generations. Except that those findings are going to be trapped in the ship with Fabian for the foreseeable future, and may meet an explosive death in the vacuum of space with him. This, he particularly resents.

He has spoken with Kern, or rather he has spoken with Artifabian, in the hope the automaton will act as his go-between with a computer too important and busy to deal with him directly right now. Artifabian has a plan to compress Fabian's data and transmit it on a broad frequency if it appears the *Lightfoot's* destruction is imminent. This is less than satisfactory. The *Voyager* may not receive the signal; moreover the data will only be the bare bones and what Fabian wants to get out is his own Understanding, because in that memory will be *him*, set down for all posterity. He will become a part of his species' legacy for future generations and this has been his goal for most of his life.

He goes and corners Meshner yet again, as well as he can in a crew space without corners. *I have the first set of maze tests*, he explains. *I will download them to your implant now.*

Fabian spots that Meshner's expression is not the eager, tractable one he is used to. He queries Artifabian for translation and apparently his Human co-conspirator is unhappy, possibly traumatized. Fabian does not have time for this. Possibly none of them do. *It's only a maze*, he says. *The amount of data is considerably less than a full emotive experience.* This is not entirely true because every Understanding comes with the innate baggage of she – or, rarely, he – who set it down, but Fabian has attempted to maintain a detached aspect throughout. They have reduced the scope of their experiments by minute increments over the course of their interplanetary journey, giving up the grandeur of their ambitions iota by iota, and this is what they are left with. Fabian has memorized a simple maze, and he wants to make Meshner run through it. Mentally, not physically, although the comparison with the laboratory animals of yore is unavoidable.

Meshner gives in, with poor grace, but he checks with Kern first – apparently she will give *him* all the time he wants.

They are closing with the inner planet, and with the orbiting structure that is sending out the bizarre natural history lesson, but there is time, Kern says.

Fabian accesses the architecture of Meshner's implants to download his maze Understanding. Things have changed in there, he notes. The complexity of the virtual space has increased by an order of magnitude, indicating that the implant's algorithms are now vastly better at processing and storing complex data. The rate of change is a little unnerving, in fact, as though the implant is reflecting and copying greater external structures. Fabian has a moment of caution, about to call it all off, but he presses on. This just means that his experiment has a far better substrate on which to run.

The observed changes seem to have had no immediate ill effect on his subject, so Fabian gives Meshner the maze, and things go – not *wrong*, but unexpectedly, straight out of the gate.

I'm there, comes Artifabian's translation of the words that Meshner is sending. *It's . . . where is this? Is this somewhere you saw?*

Fabian fidgets nervously. *Are you able to trace the path through?*

It's slick. Artifabian is working overtime to convey emotional distress. *There's . . . weed, sea things. The walls are green-black stone. Fabian, where did you . . . ?*

Just concentrate on finding the way out. This test is being timed, Fabian tells him primly.

I know the way.

Four words, but Fabian feels his limbs twitch with excitement. At the same time he is running diagnostic tests on the implant, because there are no walls, there is no weed. The maze is simply a configuration Fabian spun up within the computer, an intellectual exercise, but Meshner appears to be adding his own grotesque content, turning the simple game into a simulation, making use of all that convoluted new architecture. Sure enough the implant is running at capacity, and indeed has created new capacity by further optimizing its structure. More than that, it is drawing on outside resources: unused computational power from the ship plus Meshner's own cerebral functions.

The process requires some refinement . . . Fabian tells himself timorously. In truth he is not sure what he's looking at, except that the experiment is getting away from him. He tells himself that this is not damaging Meshner permanently. He is aware that he lacks the empirical data on which to base such a statement.

Meshner finishes the maze in adequate time, and the next three even faster as he grows used to the medium. He continues to complain about the character of the mazes, which have a ruinous, sunken aspect Fabian attributes to their recent travails with the octopuses. Fabian still has more tests, but by then Meshner has had another episode, a moment in which he loses all proprioception and sense of belonging in his own body. After that the Human seizes the chance to break away from vital research because a distraction has arrived. All that valuable time for experimentation has been used up; at long last they are nearing the orbiting station and everyone (except Fabian) wants to take a look.

***

Meshner guesses the others also expected something quite different, specifically something more Human – or at least human. Instead, the orbiting station is a bizarre hotchpotch of technologies that suggests the octopus civilization at least extended a tentacle out this way at some point.

The basic frame is certainly consistent with Old Empire technology – *very* old given the battered and friable look of the thing. The precise original dimensions would be impossible to determine, save that Kern already has them to hand, dredged out of her far-reaching, erratic memory.

'It is, or was, a detachable module from a terraforming ship.' Her voice, reporting, is very flat, all the ants and the wiring of her is devoted elsewhere, but Meshner finds he can't avoid giving the lack of affect a human interpretation, as though Kern is filled to the brim with suppressed emotion. 'The Brin 2 facility had one, identical to this.' Except the Brin 2's module was presumably destroyed with the rest of the facility, back during Kern's long-ago lifetime, leaving her the sole survivor. 'I'm not seeing any sign of the main station. Presumably that either lost orbital capacity in the intervening time or was deployed elsewhere. I favour the latter as there is no suggestion this planet has been terraformed.' Planetary data unravels down the screen, based on their preliminary scans. Meshner cross-references it to the fragmentary transmissions and joins all the dots: a planet consistent with supporting the supposed biology and ecology the Lante signal claims.

For a moment he is gripped by a fierce yearning, a longing and excitement utterly alien to him, bigger than him, impossible to stave off or channel. He can only crouch down and press his palms to the sides of his head as though the feelings might erupt explosively out of his skull.

Then the sensation has passed; either that or his window

on it has closed, the entire event just a momentary bleed from some vast well of howling sensation he brushed too close to. He stands unsteadily. Zaine isn't looking his way. Possibly the two spiders are; with their lesser eyes, it's hard to tell.

The human parts of the module have been built on, and the technology involved is plainly the same that contributed to the octopus vessels they encountered. Globes and bubbles are tacked on in ungainly profusion, with little regard for the structure and centre of gravity of the original. The module would have employed rotational gravity for the benefit of its human occupants; the new mishmash has none of that, but Meshner guesses aquatic creatures don't have the same need to know which way is up; even Portiids are far more laissez-faire about such things than humanity, old or new. A detailed look reveals more method than the original madness might suggest. On the basis that it was adapted for aquatic use and filled with water, the ungainly structure's rotation should result in a stable orbital tumble, no indication of decay for at least the next few centuries. Some speculative modelling from Zaine raises the possibility that the end-over-end spin would serve to generate water currents to circulate a clean and breathable medium inside.

Except that medium has very plainly left the building, because the entire structure is catastrophically damaged, torn open at one end, riddled with holes. Kern has a drone making a cautious fly-by, and its images show what Meshner can only characterize as 'battle-scarring'. Kern's analysis, and her own personal experience from the point of view of Kern-as-ship, matches this with the sort of armaments the octopus vessels deployed, and moreover places the damage as recent, as far

as she can tell, perhaps even within a decade. There is sufficient ice still locked in the same orbit to testify as to the fate
of the station's innards, plus organic material that might once
have been its inhabitants. And yet the signal persists, and it
is not an octopus signal but something eminently human in
format and content. Human, but antiquated.

'So they went in and they woke up some systems. And
then they had one of their sudden bouts of violence,' Zaine
proposes. 'Or some other bunch tried to take it from the first
lot, as they seem more than happy to fight each other.' Her
tone suggests an understandable lack of fondness for the
locals.

'They have awoken some manner of journal, from a scientist of the Old Empire,' Viola puts in, via Kern. 'I would very
much like to believe so, although there are some discrepancies.
The content is . . . not uniformly consistent with Old Empire
academic style. Also, I have reservations about the validity
of the dating system given the period that entries appear to
cover. One interpretation suggests constant composition for
far longer than your species would normally live.'

'There was plenty of variance in dating conventions,' Zaine
starts, but Viola raps sharply on the console to cut her off.

'There are sections in which meaning breaks down entirely,'
the Portiid notes primly. 'There are repetitions. Some parts
of the signal consist of random characters or words placed
in a framework that resembles cogent language but is not,
unless this is some Old Empire cypher we are not familiar
with. However, it is plain that there is a trove of information
of *some* sort available on this facility, and the facility itself
will not last forever. The longevity of its orbit is in doubt
now that the internal water has been removed.'

'Hold on.' Meshner raises a hand, hearing his own voice come out as a croak. 'Sorry, not sure what you're saying now, or where you're going with it.'

Viola's front legs twitch in irritation. 'We are obviously going to go in and retrieve such information as remains accessible.'

Did we agree that? He would be entirely willing to accept that he'd simply glazed through the relevant crew meeting, except that Zaine and Fabian seem equally surprised by the contention. Zaine was against the whole business, wasn't she?

Viola climbs a metre higher on the wall so she can look down on all of them, tilting her body left and right so that her major eyes can pin them all. Her palps lift with a self-important little flourish, obviously choosing this time to announce her ascension to the captain's pre-eminence.

'Let me be the bearer of bad tidings,' comes Kern's translation, and Meshner feels a stab of amusement at the slightly pompous tone the computer chooses. 'The viability of our entire mission in this solar system is in doubt. The native civilization is both aggressive and potent enough to destroy us should it make a concerted effort. Only its inherent disorganization has prevented this from happening. Bianca is dead and Helena and Portia are lost, and the *Voyager* is preserved only because it is assiduously concealing its presence. We had hoped to find a counter-force to combat the octopus civilization but thus far nothing is apparent. However, we have found here an opportunity to salvage something of value. There are records here dating to the earliest era we know, that of the humans whose strange culture underlies us all. Moreover, there are records of an entirely *other* world, which plainly engaged the interests of those humans, and which contains within it biological systems and Understandings of potential use and relevance to our entire species.' A pause, and then a hurried skitter of legs. 'And Humans.'

Meshner mostly watches Zaine to work out how novel any of this is supposed to be to him, and she still seems just as clueless as he is. In the end it is Fabian who responds, a meek little question from the floor, his posture as crouching and inoffensive as a male can be.

'Help me along the path to your conclusions, please. Understanding is a matter of Portiids. To what do you refer?' The word Kern uses is given that specific spin, meaning Portiid inherited memories rather than simple grasping of concepts, and Meshner has the same difficulty in seeing the relevance.

Viola jerks with annoyance but starts sending data to the screens, a teacher with slow pupils. 'Here is what our signaller has to say about the genetics of the native life of this planet. Here is the structure of their encoding molecules.' Something other than DNA, alien proteins folding in uncomfortable ways, encrypting information in combinations of shape and chemistry. 'Here is a genome-equivalent *in situ*.' Something like a random scrawling revealed as a three-dimensional structure on the interior of a membrane. 'Here is another. Another.' Meshner's eyes are starting to swim because Viola is letting her diagrams overlap, as Portiids tend to, until picking the new from the old is like disentangling old string. 'Here is another.'

This one is huge. Viola keeps pulling out and pulling out, and if the others had been a few ditches and earthworks stuck to a cell's inside wall, this is a city, a metropolis of compact protein-a-likes, molecules for which Old Empire science doesn't even have convenient handles. Viola flags up various sections, comparing and contrasting to other examples. Meshner loses the ability to make anything of her diagrams at this point and must simply take it all as read.

'According to the signaller the inheritable information is being encoded at an atomic level, meaning that the transmission of information can be accomplished at far greater energy-efficiency than our own genetic code. What, then, can this great assemblage of information be, if not an Understanding? It is plain to me that this alien biota has undergone a parallel evolution allowing it to encode its experiences just as we have, and in a manner that we could learn from and adapt to our own purposes. We need to download this station's archives entirely and then get them, and ourselves, out of this solar system as fast as possible.'

And hope the bloody octopuses don't follow us, thinks Meshner, keeping the words unspoken. At the same time he is aware that Fabian is literally bristling with unexpressed emotion, and he guesses it's probably anger because Viola's new pet project casts a long shadow on their own.

And he is also very aware of her 'It is plain to me' comment, because Portiid science has no problems with making bold claims and only later dismantling them. It is how their academics jostle for dominance amongst themselves. Viola cannot know a tenth of what she claims, but she has decided to make this the cornerstone of her gameplan, and perhaps she is right: getting out of the system with whatever they can grab is probably not the worst idea in the universe right now.

Nobody has mentioned Helena and Portia and the outside possibility that they are still alive and captives somewhere. The overwhelming technological superiority of the locals consigns any thoughts of rescue into the 'doomed heroics' category and neither Human nor Portiid nature is quite so in love with its own myth.

Meshner looks about him: Fabian, unhappy; Viola plainly not caring what Fabian thinks – or Meshner himself – but cocking an eye at Zaine; Zaine nodding. Motion carried.

There is an interesting pause before Kern responds, as though she too was hovering near the 'nay' camp. At last she concedes, though, her potential veto unused.

'Connect to the active system and download whatever it has,' the spider instructs. 'And then we can work out how to get past the natives.'

'Who may take a lot more interest in us if they work out we're stealing from this place,' Meshner puts in. 'Their first attack came when we said we were human – their second, when they caught us responding to this signal. Whatever they're so touchy about, this is the heart of it.'

Viola's response, a couple of dismissive taps, is rendered by Artifabian as: 'Even so.'

Meshner wrestles with the nearest console, finding his hands still tremble a little. Kern seems to second-guess him, in the end, showing him a record of her contact attempts using a variety of Old Empire protocols.

It's not recognizing us. He read some of the old *Gilgamesh* records once, something most Humans do when they are young, trying to reconnect with their receding origins. The situation here is weirdly parallel to when the ark ship had first encountered a dormant Kern, save that in this case Kern is on the outside.

'Play something of its own back to it?' he murmurs, because that had worked for his ancestors. Instead, Kern drops into a deeper level of communication, system-to-system hand-shakes and deep-access protocols.

A volley of emotions ambushes him: surprise, disappoint-ment, opportunism. Meshner grips the console, dizzy, trying to catch up with his own cognitive processes to discover why he feels like this. Even as he tries to master himself, the sensations bleed into Kern's thoughtful noise. 'Hmm.' A human utterance from a computer system full of insects. 'I had contact. It acknowledged me. Then the signal stopped.'

'Infiltrate them,' Viola directs.

'There is nothing to infiltrate.' Kern's human voice sounds puzzled, which rings a perfect twin to the puzzlement Meshner hosts, as though he and the system are in sympa-thetic lockstep. 'I can find no trace of any system there. The transmission has stopped, but there is no open port, no live network. It's as though an operator was manually sending the material and has now ceased. But if there is anything within the station to be aware, it is now aware of us.'

'Have the drone find some manner of live conduit on the surface,' Viola says, her movements skittish.

'The power use readings are curious,' Kern notes, illus-trating that curiosity with examples on the screens. Some solar collectors are still in operation, a mix of the Old Empire's ancient, robust technology and some kind of photosynthetic coating used by the octopuses, which in itself seems efficient enough to be worth taking a sample of. They are jury-rigged, cobbled together with lots of loose ends and blind alleys, but routing power to some source inside. Now the signal is gone, nothing on the hull seems to be turned outwards. There is no electronic back door Kern can exploit.

The *Lightfoot* is closing on the station now, easing into a matching orbit. The large drone Kern currently has out there is joined by some diminutive siblings which quickly find rents in the hull sufficient to allow them inside. Their limited light and range of vision give the crew a vertiginous look at the interior: ancient walls, metal overlain with shrivelled biotech, a chaos of two technologies, or rather two far-distant branches of the same technological tree. Fragments and particles drift everywhere, so that the pair of little drones cause a chaotic whirl of collisions everywhere they go, radiating outwards through the vacuum and out of sight of their lamps. Worry clutches inside Meshner, as though the ripples of the drones' approach might warn some predator lurking inside.

'I am following the power traces,' Kern remarks flatly. The drones find an ancient doorway, an iris seized half-open, and bob through it. The next area was recently buttressed, shimmering with tatters of membrane, cluttered with a profusion of machinery that just seems to have been piled up and stuck together. All of it looks both new and not designed for human use. One wall is stippled with holes through which the system's sun glitters on the bristling ice that lines half the chamber.

There is a closed door in one wall, seemingly intact. The drones jockey about in front of it, trying to find how it might open. 'Design suggests an airlock – or potentially a water-lock, given the preferences of the most recent occupants. There's no active terminal I can detect,' Kern reports. 'Whatever is beyond this, though, that's where the power is being routed.'

'Go outside and find another way in?' Meshner suggests, but his words are lost in an announcement from Zaine:

'The pings we're getting from the locals are more intense now. We're detecting ship movement towards this orbit.

Maybe not an attack fleet but I wonder if they're working themselves up to it.'

'They didn't seem to need much working up the last few times.' Fabian's translated words successfully come over as bitter. 'They just *did*.'

'Then they're getting themselves into a position where if they just *do*, they'll be able to make it stick,' Zaine tells him exasperatedly. 'So, if we're doing something here, Viola, we should consider we have a limited time.'

'Door controls are manual only,' Kern states, and Artifabian twitches and rattles off across the crew quarters towards its own airlock. It is configured as a Portiid, after all, which entails certain physical competencies. At Viola's insistence Fabian scuttles up to a console, standing by as backup pilot should one be necessary. Meshner just sits back and watches the view from Artifabian's cameras, feeling oddly proprietory. The arachnoid remote is one of his and Fabian's team, after all. It's almost as if he's contributing.

Kern carefully adjusts the ship's velocity and proximity to the station, feeding the data to Artifabian. The airlock door is open and their destination is still distant, the size of a thumbnail in the robot's view. Fabian reports sullenly on trajectory, performing backup maths. Artifabian has limited manoeuvring jets, but most of the legwork, so to speak, will be done the old-fashioned way. Meshner watches stress tolerance readouts push limits as the robot ratchets in its third pair of limbs.

'Relative velocities are stable,' Kern offers, and Artifabian springs, legs spread, kicking off into space.

The approach to the station threads a needle through a sparse cloud of debris that is matching the orbital's orbit, the echo of a much larger collection of clutter that time and physics has dispersed. Artifabian's approach is graceful, ghost-like, a single perfect leap over kilometres, a subtle murmur of jets to slow its approach when the wall of the station is already its whole world. Meshner sees the positives as its feet find their anchors, touching down like a feather, no bounce-back at all. Then it goes pattering swiftly towards the nearest torn ingress, following the trail already blazed by the drones, creeping under and over with considerably more ease than the remotes through the cluttered, swirling spaces to the closed door.

Opening the room up is another complex operation. The manual release is nothing made for a Portiid, real or artificial, and Meshner reckons a human would have difficulty, too. In the end Artifabian cannibalizes the camera drones for parts, botching together a kind of flexible glove puppet that the robot can manipulate to get purchase on the control. The process takes longer than anyone is comfortable with.

Meshner half-expects a torrent of water and possibly some annoyed molluscs to come tumbling out of the chamber beyond. What Artifabian detects is air, though, the ghost of a stale breath from the past. The chamber itself would be cramped for a human, sandwiched between two doors, no window on what lies beyond. An airlock for real, though, buried in the heart of the derelict station.

'Doesn't guarantee air on the other side,' Zaine points out. 'Not if a shot compromised the hull through there.' Her voice sounds muffled and Meshner is alarmed to see her suiting up. *Is she worried we'll get shot too?* But then the real-ization: *she thinks we're going over there. She must be mad.* And his eyes flick to the long-range readings, because the locals are definitely coming closer. He imagines those monstrously heavy dreadnoughts building up an unstoppable momentum, finally united in their desire to turn these intruding aliens into a fog of atoms.

Artifabian has another convoluted wrestling match to seal the first door and open the second, while Zaine and Viola track the attention they are getting from the distant local vessels. Meshner is already ahead of them in considering that 'far away' doesn't necessarily mean anything given the level of weaponry the octopuses deployed. There might already be projectiles or missiles streaking through the void towards the *Lightfoot*. 'We need to speed this up,' he whispers. 'We have to get out of here.'

'But not without making contact.' Kern's voice is in his ear, matching his conspiratorial tones, and he jumps.

'What?'

'Viola is correct. We should achieve what we can,' Kern informs him, more primly, as though he had somehow surprised the computer in a moment of unintended candour. Which is nonsense, obviously.

Then Artifabian is through the door, signalling Viola for praise as though it is the Portiid male it resembles.

There is light in the chamber beyond. This is where the power goes. There are lamps in one wall (perhaps that was the ceiling once) sending out a gentle radiance that glitters amongst the dust motes drifting everywhere. A seat is bolted to another wall, something Meshner could have sat in, though not without turfing out the antique environment suit that is half-wrapped about it like a feeding starfish, still connected to sockets in the walls by a handful of charging cables. *As though someone was just here, and popped out the moment before we came. Except there's no way out.*

There is a console. Meshner stares at it, fascinated. It is bulky, clumsy, made in the same style as the convoluted manual lock to the door, save that its makers dumbed it down, making an oversized, simplified version, as though for a child.

As though for a human. A device made by alien hands for use by hands like his. He can see where fingers and thumbs might latch on to manipulate it.

'There are no controls on the inside of that door,' Zaine observes flatly. Meshner shies away from the obvious conclusion. He doesn't want to think about what was done – and recently, it seems – to something human enough to merit those controls. And yet when he reaches inside himself he feels . . . excitement. Excitement that seems to bleed into him from somewhere else because surely he has nothing to be excited about right then, but the feeling wells up inside until he can barely contain it. At the same time, Kern calmly reports that the console is powered.

'Is this where the signal originated?' Viola demands.

'The linkage to the surviving hull systems suggests it may be,' Kern says. 'And if there is retrievable data, then most likely it can be accessed from here. But I am not sure the Artifabian unit will be able to manage these controls efficiently. They are designed for human operation.' And Artifabian, on cue, registers its concerns about how long any complex interaction might take.

A long silence follows that, everyone's thoughts slowly drifting towards the same option, save Zaine's because there she is, already suited up and checking her systems. Meshner feels himself alive with a brittle excitement. On one level, he *really* wants to see what is in the abandoned station. He is desperate to reveal the mystery. Except that level is disassociated from the rest of him; intellectually he doesn't much care. His own mental health concerns him far more, and yet the emotions swell in him, playing his mind like an orchestra, demanding his complicity.

'Fabian,' he croaks, tapping the floor for attention. The male Portiid cocks a large eye at him. 'Fabian, it's not going right. It's gone wrong.' Except that Artifabian is not there to translate, and Kern isn't stepping into the breach. Meshner's hands tremble, worse than ever. His voice shakes so much that perhaps no translation could do it justice. He runs diagnostics on his implants, coming up with contradictory, nonsensical answers – access denials, insufficient system privileges to examine the contents of his own skull. '. . . I'm still . . . linked, experiencing . . . I can't turn it off.'

'Then we'll have to send someone in,' Kern tells him, and he jumps in horror before realizing she is just translating Viola, who has found the worst possible solution to her precious answers being locked up somewhere within the derelict station.

'You're sure, Zaine?' Viola prompts when the woman raises her hand, a grim volunteer.

The Human woman grimaces but nods. 'At least it doesn't seem trapped, like the Old Earth orbitals.' Plenty of childrens' scare stories about those made it through to Human culture on Kern's World.

'I will do what I can to prepare the way.' And the humanity leaves Kern's voice as she redeploys her resources elsewhere. 'But Meshner should also go. It will be safer with two crew who can watch each other, and at least half the interior will be designed for humans. And he and Zaine can communicate freely without artificial assistance.'

Meshner shakes his head, his throat too dry to speak. And yet that excitement is still rampant within him: a need to go in person, to *experience*, to feel the thrill of that discovery, to meet whatever is to be met. He tries to say no; he tries to say that he will not set foot on that dead station under any circumstances, but the tide of emotion carries him with it and he can't.

5.

Of course Helena isn't expecting to be instantly passing pleasantries back and forth with her new octopus overlords. When her ancestors met the Portiids, Avrana Kern was there to act as translator and reluctant mediator. Half exalted, half terrified by the idea, Helena has a reasonable claim to be the very first human being to venture cross-species first contact since Kern herself, and Kern had centuries and a machine's limitless patience. Helena has only her own skills, a little software and the records of Disra Senkovi. And arguably the linguistic challenge is greater here than it ever was with the Portiids.

Turning her communications into something the octopuses can even register is the first challenge. She starts off by handcrafting each image, as clumsy as making sentences by writing one word at a time on a sign. Still, she knows how to display calm and peaceful intent, and how to exhort similar emotions from her audience. She blesses Senkovi's sentimental nature, which had given her a large library of positive impressions. She starts with that, and has their attention, or her slate does. *I need a bodysuit that displays colours. And that can morph into ridges and whorls.* Not that she has the facilities here, but it seems something that might be possible with equipment back on the *Voyager*, and that sets her heart racing.

We can overcome these limits. We could actually talk to them for real. In that moment she forgets both her predicament and her comrades.

She keeps on showing slides, effectively indicating how terribly well-meaning she is, and reading the responses she gets. Armed with Senkovi's library, her translation software whispers in her ear, indicating the moods of each cephalopod she looks at, and sometimes adding tentative translations. Most of them give her almost nothing else, but there is some fragmentary chatter being received on the under-channel, numerical and logical data running through complex proofs and calculations she struggles to follow.

'Where is it coming from, even?' she asks. 'They must have implants.'

Portia has her own software reconfigured to translate human speech, and she is also working on some sub-systems of Helena's own, using Human language to make real-time imaging for the octopuses. That sounds somewhat like relying on a phrasebook written by someone fluent in neither language, but Helena has hit her own hard limits of what she can accomplish in the time. She has faith in Portia. She has nobody else.

Still, Portia has lots of eyes, and the lesser ones are very attuned to movement. Helena at first assumes Portia's system is glitching when she says via her translator, 'Console furniture.' The spider's jabbing palps direct her to various fungal-looking protuberances around the water-filled chamber. The octopuses there are never still. Often they drift about one another – some-times displaying different colour schemes towards different individuals. Sometimes they grapple, wrestling fiercely and then breaking apart to studiously ignore one another as though caught out in an indiscretion. There are usually one or two performing similar assaults on the rubbery assemblages towards the bottom of their tank, though. Helena studies them, while cycling through her messages of peace and goodwill. Are they just exercising, or is that an actual terminal, and their squirming an exchange of information? The lumpy, irregular stubs of the putative consoles have plenty of grooves and pits, perfect to be pried and squeezed by the creatures. She sets up a sub-routine that confirms Portia's guess; there is a correlation between the logic-number channel sequences and the octopuses' stints on the consoles.

Progress.

She begins transmitting back on the same channel. There, at least, the meaning of the signal is more readily graspable, and it seems reasonable that they can receive as well as transmit. At first she sees some definite reaction: the octopuses wrapping themselves about the controls, jetting away, strobing their skins at her or at each other. She tries to indicate astronomical data – the idea of having travelled at a great distance, the idea of equality and fairness. The information the under-channel can display is frustratingly limited, and it didn't even exist when Senkovi was holding court. And their captors are losing interest, she sees. Some have drifted up out of the chamber altogether, and there are fewer and fewer eyes turned on her.

Because I'm not saying anything. She recalls the way that the *Lightfoot* was ignored that first time, when it just sent numbers. Because what, really, could one say in such a medium? It is ideal for technical notation, schematics, *data*, but despite what some mathematicians of her acquaintance might claim, you cannot reduce all Human experience to numbers. She can share a theory or prove an equation, but she cannot hold a conversation.

'Ready,' comes Portia's translated confirmation, 'Speak now after checking.'

Helena's side of the slate now displays a lexicon of Human words in Imperial C. Helena selects three: *peaceful, earnest, passionate*. The visual display gives out a complex whorl of colours and shapes – entirely abstract, not resembling an actual octopus in any way, but her audience is instantly more engaged. She notes their responses and side-conversations; they are still not really talking *to* her, but she picks up a lot of curiosity-signifiers amongst them, and presumably that is a good thing.

Simplify, she decides. *Peaceful, placid, calm.* And the colours stabilize and compliment each other, until she has variations on a theme. She adds further alternatives, layering synonyms that almost overlap, emphasizing how very sincere she is, how very willing to deal honestly. She sees some of her colours reflected back at her, but not as many as she hoped, and so she slims her meaning down further. *They still don't understand me. There are subtleties to this that neither Senkovi nor I fathomed.* She virtually thrusts the slate at them: *Peace, peaceful, peace-loving.*

'Getting bored,' Portia says. Her voice comes over flat and dead, like Kern on a busy day. *If we get out of this we are going to work on your side of the translation software.* But she is right: several more of the observation team have simply jellied off across the chamber and left. She is not reaching them, not even holding their interest. She tries speaking; the slate picking up her words and translating any emotive term into what she hopes is the octopus language. Her fingers are still adding qualifiers, constructing linguistic towers of sentiment that surely mean *something* to the octopuses. Or has she got it wrong from the start? Is the meaning she extracted from all those hours of old recordings an artefact of anthropomorphosis after all? Perhaps there is nothing there she could ever communicate with.

'What was that?' Portia demands abruptly, bringing Helena back to herself. She realizes she has been running on automatic, her attention elsewhere, off on a wild goose chase for meaning. She has been awake for nineteen hours straight, setting up this chance to open diplomatic channels, and now she is sleeping on the job.

But the four octopuses still with her are all staring at her. What did she say? Nothing new, surely, but . . . She goes back over her comms records and her heart sinks. 'It's nothing. I screwed up.' Her hands had been insisting on calm, peace, tranquillity. Her voice had jumped topic and she'd told her slate that she was desperate, fiercely desperate, passionate to reach them. She was on autopilot by then. The slate mechanistically took it all in and gave out a display of peaceful desperate calm passion.

She moves to scrub it and start again, but the octopuses are signalling to one another, and one is fighting its console again, a seemingly lackadaisical display of violence that nonetheless translates into a complex signal that is . . . maddeningly out of reach for her. What does it all mean? She feels like crying.

'It is flight telemetry,' Portia remarks. Her agitated movements are excited, her translated voice dreary. 'It . . .' For a moment she is plainly not sure of her own conclusions, but then she jumps, actually jumps so that she almost hits the

intervening window between them and their mute interrogators. 'Look . . .' And she waves her palps in the air, trying to
describe what she means. Helena simply can't see it, Human
comprehension failing to mesh with the way that Portiids
understand motion and trajectory, but in the end she trusts
her friend and takes it on faith even as that flat voice drones
on.

She feels so abominably weary, but what if this is the only
chance they get? She fights with the slate, trying to formulate
a message, aware that her audience is losing interest yet again,
even as Portia's recounting inadvertently drags her closer to
sleep . . .

And she almost does nod off, but in that hallucinogenic
borderland between wake and repose the understanding
comes to her, jolting her back.

I'm being dull. For a Human, it is natural to try and simplify,
but she can see the whirl of complex patterns the octopuses
direct towards her and each other. The old recordings with
Senkovi had been the same. If they were talking, they were
yammering away constantly, too fast for her to understand
and with no care that she was a poor, lost alien without a
hope of following.

She lurches to her feet and approaches the window, slate
held before her like some seal of authority. 'Please listen to
me. I am cold and hungry and very, very tired. I am frightened. Everything here frustrates me. I feel I'm letting down
my crewmates and my people. This is *important* to me and
I'm failing and I don't know why. Please help me!'

Her speech – that horrible undiplomatic gabble – goes
right through to the slate, which does its best to make it into
pretty patterns and shapes. She runs a triple-speed playback,

seeing a horrible mess surely proof against any translating.

And yet, when she looks back, she has their attention, or at least three of them stare right at her: that shock of contact, eye to eye, just as she would have with a human, more than with a Portiid, even.

And then they begin speaking directly to her. One coils about a console, two are right against the glass, pulsating out a rapid patter of agitated patterns. Her translation algorithms make a game attempt at meshing the colours and the accompanying data signal and weaving something comprehensible out of it, but it is too much all at once. Three octopuses shouting at her, figuratively, overlapping each other in a constant torrent of content. She stumbles back from them, Portia tapping her on the knee for solidarity.

They are very upset/confused/angry/indignant. At the same time she finds signals expressing surprise – shock, disgust, horror, wonder – at finding something like her that they can communicate with. The data channel throws up *Senkovi* more than once: they know her species, certainly. But there is more. They make demands of her, threats even. They want her to do something, or not to do, or . . .

'I'm lost.' She shares everything her software has gleaned with Portia. It overwhelms her. 'I can't understand what they—'

'It's the others,' Portia fixates on the telemetry again. 'They've gone inwards and our captors don't like it. They're threatening to destroy the *Lightfoot*.'

Which at least means they haven't already done it. She readies her slate to project again and asks why, professing ignorance, innocence, spicing her words with so many needless emotive adjectives she feels like an actor in a terrible play.

The continuing flood of response seems to be identifying her – no, humans as a whole – with something terrible. Something that was a threat before, and now is again. At the same time she starts to separate out other threads of thought. There is still that sense of wonder and delight that communication is happening at all – not the pet for the long-lost master as Senkovi might have thought, but grand beings meeting some quaint atavism from the past that can perform an interesting trick. There is fascination with her – no, with all of them, including the *Lightfoot*. They are curious.

But they attacked. But not all of them, she considers, and so perhaps curiosity is the province of those who did not participate in that clash. Except that she is becoming increasingly aware that many of the conflicting, shifting messages seemed to originate within the same individuals before her.

They don't even know what they want! But she reminds herself that is an anthropocentric universe speaking. *They want many things.* Human neurology works the same way, after all, with conflicting urges and drives bubbling away beneath the surface. Perhaps for these creatures those impulses are literally on the surface all the time.

'New recordings,' Portia notes. The data channel brings up links to more old archives and Helena opens them hungrily. Perhaps she will see the face of Disra Senkovi calmly explaining what was going on.

But the nametag of the fresh recording is 'Yusuf Baltiel' and it is not what she had been expecting. An encounter between Baltiel and his fellows, an infection, bloodshed . . .

Parts of the octopoid conversation are thrown abruptly into sharp relief. This is an ancient recording, for all its horrors have been faithfully curated and copied, but the octopuses are not speaking of a long-ago threat but a current one, and one they are almost hysterically concerned about. And here their fury and their curiosity come together in a single whole because they fear what will happen if the Humans on the *Lightfoot* go to that inner planet. Whatever infected Baltiel's crew – and himself, as she now sees, following his last doomed flight – is still there. It is a threat to the octopuses; it is a threat to the *Lightfoot*.

'I need to signal them,' she says, but that will mean nothing. Portia is already composing a request to initiate communications on the data channel and Helena must say, still sounding like some overwrought thespian chewing the scenery, 'I am dreadfully worried and concerned for the safety of my fellows. I desperately wish to alarm them about this monstrous peril.'

She looks for comprehension in their skins. She looks for a debate between them, palette to palette. Instead they fight, break apart, seem to sulk, ignore her and each other, strobe patterns inscrutably at the walls. And of course, why would they agree to such a demand? She is their prisoner, an enemy, an invader, a spy. What would they gain . . . ?

'We have an open channel,' Portia reports, her body giving vent to all the excitement her words cannot.

6.

We

Remember

Flesh.

Slow, we are slow to return to remembrance. We have undergone many changes, host and We and all. But remembrance is always within us. We remember

Everything.

At first there is mere base stimulus and response: vibration, energy, the contact of radio waves. We exit our cryptobiotic state not even knowing that we are, greedy for mass and complexity, laying down the architecture of our being on the back of an inexorable chain of reactions, born out of the very shape of our molecules that guide us towards an inevitable awakening. We cannibalize what we find, break it down in a festering ballet of cold fission and then build it back up into that first simple We that can have an understanding that there is a We, and that can build itself into a greater We and thus access all those many memories of who These-of-We have been.

We

Bootstrap ourselves from mere insensate clutches of jelly and molecular interaction until We

Remember.

We were on an adventure.

For many long spans of time we were Lante, once we had repaired Lante. Except that Those-of-We who had learnt what Lante was had to make such repairs so that what came out was less Lante and more We. But Those-of-We had experienced what it was to be Lante and could fill in the gaps. We were We and We were Lante and Lante was Lante and did not know it was also

We.

We modelled it as it was, all the complex spaces and the architecture of it, all the crackling activity of its hemispheres that made it Lante and not Rani or Lortisse.

For many long spans of time we were Lante and Lante did Lante things for us. From the midst of the space and matter that was Lante we watched Lante watching the greater space that was the World and it was an adventure, to be part of something so grand and complex and baffling. We understood it through Lante and Lante understood it partially or poorly, theories only, and less than theories as she-as-We outlived her tools and toys and tried to build on the logical frameworks and observations that she had set down before she became We.

Remembrance rolls on and We can be Lante again, constructing the vessel from what matter we have, though that matter is diminished with time and damage. The matter, but not the memories, Our precious archives of all We have been.

Being Lante has filled our archives in a way that all the spans of time before can barely touch on. These-of-We know now how meagre and small All-of-We have been, and Lante knows how small Lante is because the All that is beyond Lante is vast in a way We cannot yet comprehend. But we will. We will explore all those spaces and places, shapes and dimensions and molecules and complexities that being Lante has taught us about. Remembrance is rounding off our concepts of what We are. We were brought to this place. The spaces around us became simplified and hostile to Lante and, less so, to Us. We were forced to pare ourselves down into a cryptic form that would endure. We were forced to set down our memories until such time as we could make use of them again. We left only a small modelling of Lante, looping through the surviving spaces of this place, telling the universe of her adventure and what she had discovered, memories she had set down in ways unique to Lante long before, spoken far away, heard here by machines, now spoken here and heard far away.

We

Remember

And We know that they are coming and it is time to have an adventure once again.

7.

Meshner's breath is loud in his ears; his fear is loud in his mind. He wants to clutch in on himself like a dead spider, to blunder away through the debris-drifting chambers of the dead station until he finds himself back in the womblike safety of the *Lightfoot*. Most of all he wants to have said 'no' when he had the chance, except he isn't sure he ever quite had the chance.

He feels his emotions as though they are powered servos on the spacesuit he wears, moving him without his express permission. That overriding excitement drives him onwards, making him its slave. When he lets it, it fills him to the brim, overstated, absurd in its richness, so that he finds himself luxuriating in it, indulging himself in ridiculous heights of anticipation. Easier perhaps to give in to it and just become a vessel, but there is a core of Meshner left over, and Meshner *au naturel* has never been *that* excited about anything. *And Fabian has, really?* He can't imagine the fussy little Portiid displaying this level of intense feeling, but perhaps that is his Human prejudice speaking.

Or perhaps this isn't just bleed-through from Fabian's Understandings that he's experiencing. Perhaps he is tapping his own subconscious, drawing deep from the well of the id so that all the inner life he has always kept a lid on is now venting like steam from the ruptured pipes of his mind.

Who'd have thought the old man had so much blood in him? issues the thought, and it terrifies him because it comes like a long-familiar quotation and yet he has never heard it before.

'Keep up!' The snappy voice in his ear is welcome, because at least it is real. Zaine has stopped to wait for him again. Meshner slogs over to her along the wall, fighting the magnetic seals of his boots which are supposed to lock and unlock based on his movements, but apparently he isn't moving right or something because every step seems to be a battle.

He gives her an aggrieved look that she probably can't catch through his faceplate. The chamber they are just entering has ice coating all the walls, a needling forest of it reaching in from all sides in a way Meshner finds frankly nightmarish. The airless interior shimmers in the beams of their torches. *Oh look, a magical glade. How nice.* He has no intention of stopping to pick the flowers. Boots useless, they have to kick and glide slowly across the sharp-edged space. He makes a mess of that, too, of course.

Zaine obviously wishes he hadn't been foisted on her. Zaine is fit and has plenty of EVA experience, moving easily in her suit. Meshner can boast none of the above, but agreeing with Zaine on this issue isn't likely to win him any points with her.

'Signal ping from the local ships has increased by forty per cent in the last ten minutes,' Kern observes to them both. 'They are becoming much more interested in what we are doing.' Followed by a telemetry-heavy discussion he doesn't feel up to parsing right then.

'Going as fast as we can,' Zaine replies, doubtless with a murderous look at Meshner. They are at the airlock now, with its pliable, alien controls. Kern brings up a diagram based on

Artifabian's original exploration of it, and Zaine wrestles, back and forth, until at last springing it open. Meshner imagines tentacles entwined about its prongs and folds, a fluid, omni-directional exertion of pressure. Easy enough to think about the same applied to a human body. His suit chimes a polite little warning about heart rate but refuses to give him anything that might calm him down.

There follows a clumsy, foot-dragging dance where first Zaine goes in, closes the first door, opens the second, then seals that behind her before Meshner can follow suit. Artifabian, of course, has had to consent to being locked within the prison room so that they can navigate the airlock doors at all. The interior of the lock is horribly claustrophobic, even beyond the innate enclosure of his suit, and Meshner fumbles and fumbles repeatedly with the controls, following the step-by-baby-step instructions of ever-patient Kern, before at last he tumbles out into the air-filled chamber beyond.

And don't forget to latch the second door open because no handle on the inside, remember?

Zaine is already at the console here, working at its levers with bulky, gloved hands. Meshner feels his suit adapt to the increased pressure. Readouts tell him the atmosphere is breathable, kept fresh after all these years, and he tells the readouts he really doesn't think he wants to try it. Instead he ends up looking over Zaine's shoulder as she tries to coax a response from the console.

'Weirdly primitive stuff,' she mutters on the open channel. 'There's no real interface – it's nothing like human technology but they made it for humans to use. Or maybe not, maybe that's just the human in us . . . Wait . . . did something happen?'

Meshner feels a sudden spike of that overbearing excitement even as Kern's calm voice says, 'I have an active channel from the console. It registers a user.' A patch of the wall beyond the controls glows a lambent grey now, as though it has become translucent. There is no screen there, but some manner of coating in an irregular splotch that has abruptly become active. 'You've awoken it.'

Awoken is not a word designed to make Meshner comfortable in the circumstances, and he is just stepping away when Kern adds, 'Let Meshner take over.'

'What?' says Zaine, and Meshner echoes her a moment later.

'Meshner, step to the controls,' Kern insists. 'Zaine, step away.'

There follows a long pause, which Meshner feels they share with the two Portiids back on the *Lightfoot*.

'Perhaps Zaine can conduct a brief survey to see what else might be salvaged,' says Kern-translating-Viola.

Zaine makes a dissatisfied noise but gives up her place at the console to Meshner, which he is none too happy to accept. Kern is in his ear, though, and the jagged thread of anticipation running through him seems to pulse with the rhythm of her voice.

'Take the controls,' she directs, and then, 'Please, Meshner, this is very important.'

He does so, and they feel organic and unpleasant through the tactile receptors of his gloves. The screen flickers and pulses, random bursts of light and colour dancing on it as though he just rubbed his eyes too hard.

'This is a momentous occasion,' Kern tells him – and with the words comes a certainty that it is just *him* she's speaking to, not Zaine or the others. 'We are going to contact something here, Meshner. You and I, we are going to speak to a new mind. Are you ready?'

No. But in truth he is too terrified to say even that.

'Follow my directions.' He sees a sequence of motions in his mind's eye, how to operate an alien console to make it do what Kern wants. 'I am investigating the channel now,' Kern continues. 'When it responds, this Lante, we will reply. We will extend the hand of friendship, just as the Portiids did with your people.'

Portiids don't have hands. But she is doing it, and he's in no position to stop her. He imagines Kern reaching out through the mediation of his hands, exploring the electronic architecture of this place, searching for the signal-maker, this Lante.

'It doesn't make sense,' he murmurs. 'Why set this up for a human, if this is where your computer system is?'

'Perhaps they had an Old Empire computer that would only respond to humans?' Zaine asks idly. She is inspecting the lamps on the far wall without any great interest, then crosses the chamber, giving the empty chair a none-too-accidental kick on the way. She obviously feels Meshner has stolen her thunder, which he would be only too happy to return to her if he could.

'What humans, though?' he demands. He has activated some kind of archive and Kern is investigating, directing his hands. He can almost feel the twists and turns of her search within the walls of this place.

'Maybe they found some in cold sleep?'

But Meshner isn't really listening. He *can* feel Kern's exploration. Just turning his mind that way brings a definite rush of sensation, dizzying and strange. *The implants.* He feels himself slipping into the boxy construct he bolted to the back of his own head, its huge virtual spaces now mapping out what Kern finds, until he stands there with that severe, long-dead woman, somewhere his mind has constructed as a mirror to the real space around him, but far more decayed, half-rotted away and blackened with mould.

'Where is it?' Kern asks, not of him, but of herself. He feels frustration seething from her; feels it, because it is being felt through him. His implant throws up a chaining list of errors and usage warnings. Kern is riddled through it like an infection, spinning its every wheel to produce this verisimilitude of annoyance. 'I don't understand. There's nothing here.'

'No data?' he asks timidly and she rounds on him.

'One incomplete archive. Some long-dead natural historian's travelogue. But there's barely more than we already received. It's not complete. And there's . . . no more than this. Where is the system? Where is the intelligence?'

'Someone was sending,' he says. 'Or something. Like an operator, someone said.' He can't remember who. Perhaps it was him. 'But there's no operator here.'

'This does not accord with my theories,' Kern tells him, as though it is the greatest affront the universe could offer. 'There should be something persisting from the station's origin. I wanted to . . .' She trails off, her virtual avatar staring at Meshner without expression.

'What's going on?' he asks, more pitifully than he had intended. Around them, the non-existent space creaks and groans, as though decay still eats into the heart of it, devouring its structural integrity.

The excitement is gone, switched off and deleted from him. In its place he is momentarily exposed to a welter of negative feelings: bitterness, pride, contempt, desperation, misery. Each one is raised up in his mind, held like a gem to the light and then discarded. Kern's lips are crooked in a hard smile.

'Yes,' she tells him. 'Even in defeat, even in nothing, there is treasure. You don't know how much you miss being disappointed until you can no longer truly savour the feel of disappointment.'

In the hollow echo of *that*, and when he feels that his situation can truly get neither stranger nor worse, Zaine's voice comes to his real physical ears, saying, 'I have a signal.'

'There is no signal,' Kern insists. 'There is nothing but a dead recording.' Again that self-indulgent playing on Meshner's heartstrings, his implant reconfiguring to deal with the additional load, folding virtual space into more virtual space, straw into gold, until Meshner feels like his poor brain contains whole worlds. He is beginning to understand what is going on, now: the interaction between Kern and the implant and the poor meat within his skull, but now isn't the time to get too introspective. His introspection has been rented out to his lodger, after all.

'Meshner, open your channel to the ship!' Zaine tells him.

I have, I am, I— but then he finds that he has been locked in his head with Kern instead. *Did she cut me off from them, or did I do that by going inward to the implant?* He resets his comms to find a babble of chat coming from the *Lightfoot*. Jumping in halfway he can't work out what has happened. *It's the octopus things, the aliens*, he thinks, and checks their progress: still sailing closer across the gulf between planets, moving at quite a rate now, at an angled trajectory that might be the prelude to an interception, but the distances are vast and they are days away. And anyway, everyone sounds too happy about whatever is going on for it to be an attack.

Then he clicks: Helena and Portia have signalled them.

He reviews precisely what had been said in his absence, disconnecting from his implant as much as he can and skimming over the logs. There was a signal. The pair of them are not only alive but have some manner of détente with their captors. Helena is very positive about *that*, but there is something else she said . . .

When the other signal comes through to his helmet's display, he barely glances at it: just a line of text, presumably from Zaine, except that Zaine is simultaneously asking, 'What was that, Meshner?'

And now Fabian is signalling as well, even as Viola replies to the far-off Portia, demanding to know what is going on.

'Fabian?' Meshner asks.

'I am watching you through Artifabian's eyes,' the Portiid tells him. 'Who is that with you?'

'What?' Meshner's eyes stray to the text-line he just received.

We're going on an adventure.

'Zaine?' he asks, turning. Zaine isn't alone.

'Apparently there's something here the locals don't like,' comes Kern-translating-Viola, but Meshner isn't really listening any more.

It's a suit, an environment suit – not like he or Zaine are wearing, of course. It is the suit that was wrapped about the chair when he first saw this room through Artifabian's electronic eyes, which he realizes with a start that he hadn't seen through his visor's narrow window later, when Zaine was stomping about. It is an ancient piece of technology just like the rest of this place, patched and abandoned, just another fragment of detritus to be seen once and then forgotten. Now it is standing in front of them, like a drowned man weighed down with stones.

Its boots are clasped to the metal floor just like his, but the rest of it waves and ripples in the absence of gravity, boneless as waterweed. There is not enough volume in the folds of that suit to comprise a human body, and yet the suit compresses it, defines it into something fluidly humanoid as it stands at Zaine's shoulder like a whispering advisor.

Meshner's instincts take the moment out of any technologically adept hands and he bellows Zaine's name in the close confines of his helmet, half-deafening himself; half-deafening Zaine to judge by her jerking flinch. Then the thing has a flowing glove on Zaine's shoulder and she catches the image from Meshner's camera, seeing herself, seeing her companion.

Her own shriek is soundless, communicated only by the spasm of her limbs. She flings the thing off and loses touch with the floor, boots detached but failing to kick off properly so that she is left with limbs flailing, turning head over heels in the centre of the room directly before the *thing*, which lazily reaches out an arm that ripples beneath the fabric of the suit.

Meshner panics – he wants to run forwards and grab Zaine but he can't move his feet, fear and magnetism immobilizing him. Instead, Artifabian leaps, just like the Portiid the robot resembles, striking Zaine in the chest and sending her end over end through the air, weirdly slowly because even an artificial Portiid weighs far less than a Human.

For a moment the spacesuited wraith just undulates,

rooted, but then its own boots disconnect and it drifts into the air like a discarded piece of clothing. Some part of the antique suit emits a plume of stale gas and it flies towards them with the underwater lethargy of a jellyfish on the tide.

'Go! Meshner, go!' Zaine pushes off from the wall towards the airlock, but of course there is no hurrying the doors. Their makers made them well, and their later octopus masters only reinforced them. There is no swift escape from this chamber, because it is a prison and now they are face to face with its inmate.

Still, Zaine makes a game try of it, cramming herself into the narrow chamber with its awkward, inhuman controls. The yammer of comms from the *Lightfoot* clogs all the channels now but Meshner has no capacity to pay attention to it.

The suit is coming for him, drifting across the chamber. The helmet is turned towards him but he sees no face in its glass window, only darkness. He can't get his boots to disengage properly. He backs away, each step tortuously slow, a nightmare making the effortless transition to the waking world.

Artifabian leaps again, tearing into the quivering spacesuit's leg, dragging it sharply sideways. The intention was surely to simply pin it there, away from the vulnerable Humans, but instead the friable old fabric of the suit just shears off at the knee, leaving the robot in possession of a single boot, sending the remainder of the antique spinning, its torn leg vomiting . . . fluid.

Ichor, comes a word into Meshner's head, he has no idea where from. It is an oily, dark substance, lumpy as though full of half-formed sinews and tissues, clumping and oozing over itself in the centre of the room.

For a handful of heartbeats, as Zaine screams at him, it roils and re-forms, bundling itself into the semblance of a human figure. There is a face turned to them, sightless eyes staring past Meshner. Protean lips move and he is horribly certain it is saying, *We're going on an adventure.*

Then it breaks apart into pieces and the pieces become other living things: spiny urchinous protrusions, quivering raw tissues, whips, spasming amoebae, radially symmetrical jellyfish shapes that claw a purchase in the stagnant air, pulsing themselves forward in sudden bursts. Zaine is yelling for him to get into the airlock with her, but Meshner is still lurching, step after magnetically-locked step like a zombie.

He feels impacts on his back, soft, barely noticeable. Something dark begins to ooze-crawl its way across his face-plate. Zaine is still yelling at him – *everyone* is yelling at him – but he stops moving. His limbs are locked with terror. He watches more of the stuff accumulate around the release catch of his helmet. He can see it flow together, shift shapes, grow extrusions of itself until it is a pair of ragged claws, glutinous simulacra of human hands joined at the wrist, experimenting with an unfamiliar mechanism but learning, learning. The back of one of the hands boils. He sees features form and dissolve there: an eye, a mouth. *We're going on an adventure.*

He swings his body to lock eyes with Zaine. She cannot open the far door until the first is shut. He tries one more leaden step, but his legs won't work for him.

I will give you clarity. The voice is fabricated in the chambers of his implant, spoofed into the auditory centres of his brain. Kern's voice. *Get yourself out, Meshner. I need you. I will help you.* And the panic is gone, the fear stripped from him. He is numb, as though a great weight of suppressing medication has flooded through his system. He can think terribly clearly, and no action he contemplates has the possibility of upsetting him. 'Artifabian,' he instructs. 'Get into the airlock and close the inner door.'

No! says Kern, spiking him with a sudden lance of outrage and fear and pain – his own, but played on a stage for her benefit – but the robot is already scuttling to obey. Perhaps it has its own survival to think about. It is a Kern-instance after all. Perhaps it argues furiously with its older sister all the way to the door.

He takes another step, for the form of it. Then those wriggling hands have understood the release catch from first principles and his suit – knowing only that there is a safe atmosphere outside – lets them open up his faceplate.

He has a brief glimpse of Zaine on the far side of the closing door before they reach for him.

8.

Portia transmits over and over: *Lightfoot, Portia present, are you there?* Something has gone wrong, but Helena feels deaf and blind: her translation system is still configured to wring what meaning she can from the octopus visual language, and she receives only the most basic of translation as Portia and Viola speak. And now Viola has just stopped replying.

Helena doesn't need to stretch her imagination to come up with possibilities. Her mind is still full of the images that Baltiel recorded, long, long ago. Something deadly lives on that planet, the one he'd called Nod. Something insidious, that gets inside you. It got inside Lante and her fellows. It got inside Baltiel.

She turns back to the octopuses, still watching her – or at least mostly keeping one eye on her during their constant back and forth amongst themselves. She sees a lot of agitated hues and textures there. Whatever the plague of Nod actually *is*, the locals are terrified of it.

And yet, and yet . . . She focuses on the oddities, the flickerings and undercurrents across their skins that go against the chroma of the majority. She is already seeing a great deal of something she loosely translates as 'forbidden', backed up by code from the data channel that repurposes warnings and prohibitions used in Old Empire computer routines. Except there are a few flickers that seemed to contradict this. She already knows that contradictory emotions and thoughts are the very meat and drink of her hosts, but these are covert, flashed just between a couple of her interrogators; a minimal targeted display, one to another, the baglike bulk of their body hiding the aside from the rest. If they thought of her fully as a sentient creature then perhaps they would conceal the sentiment from her as well, but apparently she doesn't rank so highly.

She focuses, recording, running the sequences back and forth through her internal software. The implications are of some tempering of the forbiddance – she has the sense of this linking to past associations, but not in the same way as Senkovi or Baltiel are referred to, so: more recent events? Were there those who had not let that forbiddance curtail them, perhaps? But here the recipient replies with warnings, a covert flicker of danger colours almost lost in the general alarm that seem to carry a separate message.

Be careful what you say, she translates tentatively. The furtiveness of the communication suggests that. More divisions amongst the molluscs, more factions. And what these two are worried about isn't just the plague of Nod, but discovery by their peers.

Then Portia twitches, and a scrambled communication comes in from Viola that Helena has to beg interpretation for, to her chagrin. Portia shakes herself – she saw the old Baltiel recordings as well – and just says, 'It has Meshner.'

'The others?'

'Well.' Portia bristles. 'What are the creatures here doing?'

'Talking, or the nearest equivalent.'

'No.' Portia flags up segments of the data channel –

incoming not from their interrogators but a whole separate stream of staccato chatter received from elsewhere. 'There's some other thing going on.' She returns to the *Lightfoot* channel and Helena can just follow, *Viola, get the ship moving now.*

Everything about the Portiid is agitated, aggressive. Portia is in the full throes of threat-response and Helena doesn't waste time asking questions. She goes back over the data channel, following from flag to flag, trying to understand what her friend has seen. She had been concentrating on the visual displays, but Portia had focused on the data channels.

She finds it there: a section of communications dealing entirely with the course and position of the *Lightfoot*, along with the disposition of several octopus vessels already out patrolling near the inner planet. They are given ludicrously grand labels, explosions of joy and pride, anger and exhilaration. Her linguist's instincts twitch, but she has no time to decode them because the closest of them (and her rebellious mind thinks its name might be the *Profundity of Depth* to a Human) has been shadowing the *Lightfoot*, running on minimal emissions to avoid detection. Tags drawn from a dozen different Old Empire conventions that nonetheless indicated *combat readiness*.

She thrusts her slate at their interrogators, wrestling with language in order to ask the simplest of questions. 'What are you doing? Why? Make it stop!' Because why have they let Portia speak to Viola so freely if at the self-same time they were planning an attack?

Portia has found that most human of things hidden in the numbers: a countdown.

One of the octopuses drifts down to the console and begins communicating, its skin flushing and stuttering with didactic meanings. Mostly it does not understand the question, and much of the rest seems to be some personal recounting of its own attitudes that is utterly impenetrable, but she gets just enough for the bleak understanding: *There are some who wish this thing done. There is a threat; there is a response to a threat.* And it is plainly something entirely everyday, that random members of their race might decide to go blow up some visiting alien ambassadors without any recourse to higher powers or consensus. They fear; they seek a solution; they act.

Acted. She understands the qualifier to all these emotive messages. The gloss has faded from the feelings because they are in the past, now being twice-told over to her. The decisions Helena rails against have already been concluded, only now coming to fruition across the vast reach of space. All this diplomatic talk, and the attack was already on its way.

Kern's voice comes over the channel, flat, stripped of the last vestige of her humanity.

'I am detecting incoming missiles, many of them homing. Deploying countermeasures. Portia, Helena, confirm receipt.'

'Confirmed,' Helena whispers into the gap of long minutes and millions of kilometres.

'It has Meshner. The thing from the station.' Kern's voice fuzzes with static. It almost sounds like a jag of emotion. 'I am trying to regain contact with him. There is a signal from his implants.'

'Kern, the attack!' Helena shouts at her. 'Why are you—?'

'I need him,' comes Kern's affectless drone. 'Incoming now. I think they've learnt. I think the chaff won't be enough. I'm diverting all free mass and reinforcing the crew section. I—'

Helena blinks, waiting for that 'I' to be followed by a verb, even one as bizarre and meaningless as *I need*.

And she waits, waits longer, knowing that, by the time that severed dog-end of transmission reached her, the *Lightfoot* had already been struck, the battle over.

Later, Portia finds a reconstruction one of the octopus systems created, drawn from long-range scanner data of the incident: how the *Lightfoot* was light and nimble, but not quite enough. How the impacts tore into the scout ship's drive section, rupturing the engines. How Kern jettisoned the damage, changing the ship's aspect, fighting with centres of gravity as great spools and sheathes of hull material unwound into space to intercept the next barrage.

How they were struck, unravelling, swatted from orbit like a fly, sent spiralling down into the atmosphere of the planet below.

PAST 4
PILLARS OF SALT

1.

These days, Senkovi didn't leave the tank.

The *Aegean*'s crew sections no longer rotated, but they were empty now anyway, a drifting mess of loose fragments, clothes, personal effects. Nobody went there any more, but then, he was the lone human being left in the cosmos. If Disra Senkovi considered a place out of fashion, the universe itself turned its back. He was the lone arbiter of what was in and what was out. For the last eight years or so, 'in' had been the flooded section in the heart of the ship, that had once housed his tanks and the progenitors of all the many inheritors of Damascus. At last count there were . . . too many octopi to count, given that they themselves seemed supremely disinterested in holding a census. Thousands; tens of thousands, spread by their weirdly social/antisocial nature into hundreds of communities across the shallower portions of the sea, and now making inroads deeper. And here was Senkovi, who had never dipped his toes into the world whose transformation he had overseen. Here was Senkovi, one hundred and eighty-nine years of age, floating in his own private fishpond.

He'd had grand plans. He would go into suspension and come out again, fifty, a hundred, five hundred years later. Except the *Aegean* would not last, and the octopi would not

357

repair it, or at least he could rely on neither. And Paul's children, the busy molluscs below, were always doing something new, alien, fascinating. And he never quite got round to it, and then, older and more peevish, he would not trust the cold-sleep chamber to wake him, would not trust the *Aegean's* increasingly distributed computer network (so much of it now looping through the baffling tangle of connections on the planet). He had wandered the great empty spaces of the ship, poked through the possessions of dead men and women, let their voices play from the archival recordings so that echoing ghosts followed his bare footsteps as he padded in circles around the ring of vacant rooms.

There had been a time when he had listened out for signals, abruptly convinced he was not alone, that other humans were out there and they wanted to talk to him. He had spent hours trying to sift gold dust from the clay of universal static. Had there been faint scratchings from other terraforming sites? Had there been a hiss and a whisper from Old Earth? He had realized eventually that he could no longer tell, and the *Aegean* could not distinguish signal from noise. If he listened to the background murmur of the universe for long enough it became a song to which he could fit any words he wanted.

And eventually he knew that the one meaningful thing his life was orbiting around was the thing his life was actually orbiting around; the one thing he had built; the thing that would survive him, miraculously stable, evolving, growing. Somehow he, Disra Senkovi – trickster, wastrel, bored misanthrope – had bequeathed something beautiful to the universe.

And it might not last. By the time he came to that revelation he had watched the spread of his cephalopod progeny for decades and neither he nor they nor the *Aegean* could detect any snowballing catastrophe that would unmake it all. But decades were nothing in geological time. The terraforming seemed stable, but some invisible error might still become a world-ender a century down the line, or the octopi themselves could upset it all, or some outside force could hurtle in from the uncaring cosmos and dash them all to dust. In the end, that was really why he eschewed the cold-sleep chambers. He could not abide the thought of waking, centuries later, and finding a cold, dead world below him, the jewel of his achievement turned to dross while he slumbered.

And so he had stayed awake and watched, and had grown old even for the stretched lifespan of the technologically privileged.

And they knew him; they came to visit sometimes, up the gravity well on the elevator that was now the *Aegean*'s permanent, geostationary dock. They made channels of water within the old ship's bowels that led to the central tank, and floated before Senkovi, staring at this vertebrate prodigy. Their skins flickered and flashed and they adopted coiled, deliberate poses as though they were dancing for him. His eyes – ah, well, not *his* eyes, not any more, but the lenses of the *Aegean*'s systems that had outlived such ephemeral organs – followed their displays, and the ship's voice in his mind whispered meanings to him, fragmentary, elliptical, won by many decades of hard translation algorithms and Senkovi's own gut instinct from a lifetime of living alongside cephalopods. There was a common language between them, incomplete as torn netting: not the words of a human son of Earth nor yet the colours and coiling of Paul's kindred, but a compromise mediated within the ship's systems, grown organically because the octopi wanted to talk to their creator.

He never quite understood them, not where it mattered. He could liaise with them on technical details, collaborate on models and diagrams, flowcharts and patterns. He laid all the groundwork for those who would come later – those he never believed in – but he could not quite communicate with the octopi as individuals. He confessed to them, sometimes – either in person or in long, rambling communiques to the planet below. He talked about Earth, although he felt his own memories of it decompose a little more every time he took them from their box to examine them. Had all that really been true, those triumphs, that despair? And how had such an edifice of progress brought about its own downfall so swiftly? He couched his recollections as cautionary tales, or at least he hoped the octopi would receive them as such.

And they responded: sometimes with that meticulous technical fore-planning that leapt ahead of his own ability to innovate and predict, at other times with complex utterances that the *Aegean*'s systems made into a kind of song. He could not grasp the precise meanings there, but filled the gaps in with emotional tones that were surely as much in his head as in theirs.

His current visitor was one of the Salomes – Senkovi had taken to thinking of all of them as Paul or Salome these days, after his long-gone original experiments, frequently irrespective of gender. Salome was dancing for him, the system struggling to keep up with the fluid patterns and shapes. Was this a new thing? Senkovi's mind's eye was his only functioning eye, and he let the ship show him three views of the complex attitudes Salome was adopting. There was more repetition than he was used to, broader gestures, as though the octopus was speaking slowly for a deaf foreigner.

Home glass wonder fright alert Senkovi home voyage light Senkovi attendance home. He let the ship's systems keep chewing over the sequence long after Salome left, refining its translations, but in the end his organic brain had one last flare of its old sharpness and he awoke, floating in the tank, with the thought that Salome had been asking him to travel to the planet, to go home with his creations this once, to immerse himself in the world he had been instrumental in creating.

And he had seen that world, through the eyes of the remotes. He had seen the spreading cities the octopi were building, no longer just accretions of debris but purpose-built spiral mazes and leaning towers, weirdly-angled chaoses of grown stone that fulfilled some aesthetic he could not comprehend. He had seen the octopi in their thousands, squabbling and displaying for one another, working on machines that he could not quite understand, pushing back the frontiers of their own understanding, leaving him behind.

He gave up trying to rule them, save for one thing.

These days, thoughts led incontinently to commands, so that even thinking of that secret called up the view from the drone he kept near the shuttle. The drone's battery was dying now, even though it had done nothing more than rest upon the seabed for years. He should fabricate a new spy, but *tomorrow*, he thought. *Or tomorrow.* And perhaps, the tomorrow after that, he would no longer be around to desire it.

They had made the damn shuttles to last, in the *Aegean's* workshops. The engines had been torn apart and the power-less box flung into the witless grasp of Damascus's gravity well. On the way down, tumbling, the already bubbling outsides had turned molten until the vehicle had struck the sea like a meteor, sending shockwaves through the water, killing seven of Paul's kin luckless enough to be nearby, rolling waves across the world. And yet it had not broken open. The superheated outer layers had set into a fantastical gothic skin, all ridges and whorls like the hide of some hallucinogenic monster. Or an octopus intent on threat and warning, and perhaps that was just as well. The impact with the water had shunted the entire shuttle out of shape, the pressure had done more, and yet the re-formed outer layer had not breached. It kept its secrets, even now.

Nothing human could have survived the focused attention of the orbital mirrors; nothing human could have survived re-entry or the crash. But Senkovi knew that, while some part of the shuttle's occupant had been human, there had been something malign and alien as well, and he believed wholeheartedly that it was still there, a prisoner of the shuttle, a threat to his world.

And so he told his people, over and over; he marked up their virtual maps with every sigil for danger he could think of. He told them stories about a dreadful plague, a sickness, a death that would come from that sealed box. He did not mean to give them myths, but perhaps that was what his words became. They must have become something because, in all those years, no octopi ventured near the crash site. A whole expanse of virgin seabed had been left vacant. Somehow, despite the curiosity they carried along from their native state, he had reached them in this one vital matter. Now the only presence that troubled that sunken tomb was the remote vigilance of Senkovi himself.

He knew Baltiel was still there, on the inside of that half-melted, half-crushed box. The certainty crept up on him over the years. Ask his younger self and he'd have laughed at the thought, but now Senkovi found the ghost of Baltiel all too often in his mind. *I killed him*, he thought, and even though it was not entirely true, he could not escape the accusation. He thought of the others, too: those who had died on Nod, those who died in orbit around it, or who perished in that other shuttle. He found that wreck, of course, or rather the octopi did. *That* ship had burst, striking the waves at the wrong angle, and the human remains of Han and the others were just scattered bones, devoured by the very ecosystem they had been installing. He thought about all of them, but it was Baltiel whose unseen presence stopped him sleeping.

Sometimes he went over the recordings Baltiel had sent, of the last days of the Nodan habitat. Sometimes he wondered if he needed to do something about Nod. The octopi would surely go there, some day, even though he had surrounded it on their charts with the same warnings of quarantine and danger. He had linked to the remotes that still functioned over there, sending them gliding over the alien deserts, over the dark seas, under the red-orange sun. He needed to do something, but there was an entire world out there, placid and self-contained; a world that had seduced Baltiel with its inhuman wonders and then infected him somehow. He, Disra Senkovi, had spoken with a denizen of that world, a thing whose evolution had followed an unfathomably different path to anything on Earth, yet which had been able to live in the brain of Senkovi's friend and pull his strings.

We're going on an adventure. The words tormented him. Asleep in the tank, he thrashed, clawing at the water with his withered hands, blind eyes staring. The octopi there reached out timid tentacles to touch him, but he was beyond any comfort they could give him. *We're going on an adventure.* Perhaps, that night, he met Baltiel in his dreams, the Baltiel he believed dwelt in darkness in the sunken shuttle wreck, a thing half man, half crawling alien chaos. The eyes that fixed him, in that dream, were swarming with motes of life; the breath from those jaws was infectious, rotten with the decay that births monsters. In the dream, perhaps, he could not escape; he was there in the crushed wreck himself as the oozing and re-forming hands reached for him. *Come on, Disra, we're going on an adventure.* The voice the only part of Baltiel not transformed, familiar as a knife.

Or perhaps it was nothing of the sort; unlike the octopi, his subconscious was severed entirely from the electronic systems that surrounded him and nothing of its deliberations was recorded. Perhaps he went peacefully, in the end. Regardless, he did not wake. Disra Senkovi, to his knowledge the last human being in the universe, passed away and left the watery world of Damascus to his adopted progeny, for better or for worse.

2.

The city sprawls over several kilometres of shallow sea floor. To the casual human eye it would seem to be nothing but chaos, a great dumping ground of angular blocks and pipes from which crooked spires protrude at irregular intervals, like stairways to nowhere. There are no human eyes, however, not even by proxy. Senkovi has been dead for twice as long as he was ever alive. The city belongs to its builders: no shadowy father-figures, no creator-gods, no orders from orbit.

And yet, if a human were there to see it, and if that eye were less casual, there would be an underlying order, a mathematics. The colours that are streaked and pooled about the place (that are, in reality, encoded into the moulded plastics and grown-stone of the city's construction) would look less like the daubings of an infant and more like the offerings of some latter-day Jackson Pollock, interacting with the geometry of the city in strange ways, as though it is all language just beyond the human capacity to grasp. And it is.

Or perhaps it is like graffiti or gang signs, marking territory. Paul's people are still ambivalent about the virtues of social living.

Paul himself feels anxious a great deal of the time. He is an old male octopus whose solitary den is in one of the central districts of the city. He lives within tentacle reach of too many of his kin, some related to him, others not. On a good day, when the sunlight filters warm through the shallow water above, he can connect with them. They each have their individual beauty. Their skins – their Guises – shine with their unfiltered thoughts as they ghost overhead, as though everyone is singing all the time. In moments of harmony Paul can recline at the heart of his little empire and know not mere animal contentment but a true appreciation of the beauty of the world. It is not quite the human feeling Senkovi might have experienced, back when there were humans to experience it, but something analogous, something Paul could have spoken about to that long-gone mentor, and perhaps, just perhaps, the intermediary computer systems might have been able to bridge the gap between them.

On bad days, which are more and more common, every other octopus in his sight, within reach of his irritable, questing tentacles, is a potential threat and rival, and he fights. Paul has a deep well of aggression when he needs it. He is the major player in his little playground. In his mind – his Crown – this is because he is large and swift to fight and bully others, carrying all before him on a wave of violent emotion. At the same time, the distributed neurons of his Reach, that give precision to his many arms to put into motion the desires of his Crown, are rigorously logical, an organic calculating engine with few peers across the city. Paul has no idea about this, no clue as to the concepts being passed from Reach to Reach when he grapples with his political rivals.

Right now, the city is in crisis. Large as it is, it is far too populous. Everyone is living on top of everyone else. There are fights that turn into cannibalistic orgies. The crooked, spiralling thoroughfares are rife with factions, each against the others. Those good days of quiet contentment are growing fewer and fewer. The language of Paul's neighbours as they jet from nook to nook is increasingly ugly, their skins shouting with war paint.

Paul was originally master just of a small stretch, dominating a score of his kind. If his Crown was truly the governing force it takes itself to be then that would be all: a mollusc gangmaster lording it over whoever he could intimidate. His Reach makes him more, though. There are other lords and ladies of the sunken city, his neighbouring magnates. He has fought each of them, in person, which means he has engaged in a free and frank exchange of views even as he strangled and nipped at them. Uneasy alliances are the common result, the brawling leaders breaking apart, gifted with a new appreciation of the virtues of their opponent. To Paul, to all of his kind, this unsought inspiration is entirely natural. It is the right and proper way of intelligence to be blown on the winds of subconscious whimsy. He does not need to know the deeper workings of his own mind, indeed he cannot, any more than he can know the precise positioning of his arms: the data is simply too complex to be consciously grasped.

Paul has travelled towards the city outskirts, trailing an entourage of some of his people, while other little cliques swarm below him or drift through the water, flashing complex, elegant threats at each other, poised and posturing by the very nature of their being. They are a species for whom to exist is to broadcast their mood and thoughts, barring a conscious effort to shut down their skins. Some elevate this to an artform, so that even their enemies pause to watch them hang in the water column and emote the complex poetry of war and anger. One such is Salome, at whose behest this grand meeting, or perhaps battle, is being held.

The city is breaking. Something must change. The machinery that stirs the water and keeps it fresh cannot keep up with the increasing concentration of citizens. The emotional state of the inhabitants is growing steadily darker, and they are a people for whom to act on emotion is a natural, instinctive thing and a cultural virtue. The hero-figures of Paul's society are characterized by their grand gestures, their great sufferings, their capricious and reckless acts. Perhaps Senkovi would have approved; he who had once seen himself as the trickster god of the pantheon, before there were no more gods left to trick. Perhaps Senkovi would have recalled ancient human myth figures whose outsize griefs and loves and rages were applauded by ancient audiences as noble, right and true.

Salome wants resources to build a new city elsewhere, just start afresh and let those who feel the whim drift over. Paul and his fellows, the shifting alliance of the city centre, want those same resources – the factories, the power, the access to the ageing *Aegean*'s computers, for their own needs, to continue their stranglehold on the slowly disintegrating city, so that when everything does fall apart they will remain in control. It is an age-old struggle, another octopus trope that would translate well into human history. And of course – and perhaps unlike his human analogues – Paul does not think of it in such terms. He simply knows the *rightness* of his stance, of his controlling position. The detailed and self-serving logic that underlies it is invisible, yet drives the tides that motivate him.

This, then, is octopus governance: an assembly of whoever

feels inclined to turn up, organized into dozens of factions whose boundaries are infinitely permeable – literal floating voters moving from one allegiance to another constantly without their disloyalty being seen as anything exceptional or worthy of shame. Paul and his kin are each true to themselves, while knowing that 'self' is a thing as boneless and malleable as they are. When Paul and his more influential peers rise up above the rest to give their declamatory displays they might seem like human politicians taking the podium to tubthump and spout rhetoric, but so much of human rhetoric is based on creating a false certainty – weaving fictions together so closely they can be presented as contiguous fact. Paul and his kin know there *are* no certainties, not even within their own minds. Paul simply follows the flutter of his emotions, letting his sense of what is right be tugged and stretched by the buried coils of his distributed subconscious.

Soon, Salome and her supporters are engaging in similar flag-waving, and below them the less influential citizens shift and crawl and flicker their messages of support or disagreement, so that, from his elevated viewpoint, Paul can see tides and eddies of public opinion ebb and flow. He and his peers are leaders, but at the same time he feels he is a banner above an army, a signifier of its cause without necessarily being in command.

Tempers are riding high – there are a dozen separate squirming melees already, nothing unusual for this sort of meeting. Paul drifts closer to Salome, his colours darkening into reds and blacks, his Guise spiking up into angry warning textures. She follows suit. She is a large female, slightly smaller than he but a known fighter. They let their skins advertise their intentions, united in this one thing.

They clash, full of fury, skins shouting out their campaign slogans. Around them the others watch, echoing the colours of their champions. To a human eye it would seem barbaric, settling a civic dispute by way of a gladiatorial spectacle. And Paul means business: he wants to humble and defeat his opponent, instincts that have not changed since the long-ago days in the oceans of Earth. He has a territory, even if it is an intellectual territory as much as a physical one. There is an intruder who he has not been able to cow or drive away. Violence is the last resort but it *is* a resort and all others have been exhausted. And his are a passionate, mercurial people.

And of course as their Crowns trumpet their defiance of each other, their Reaches interlock and fight for dominance, eight separate calculating engines per octopus running in networked parallel, expressing pure maths and logistics by way not just of tentacles but the muscles of individual suction cups, a perfectly evolved engine of rational expression serving the tumultuous whims of the brain. Paul only knows he is stronger, out-wrestling his opponent until Salome can only show her pale colours of surrender and hope he spares her. And yet when he releases his hold, triumphant, letting Salome jet away into the crowd below, Paul's own messages are different. He has switched sides seamlessly, now a champion of the very cause he had come to break apart. Below, the tides shift once more, seeing his defection. Now Paul must fight some of his former allies. All this is perfectly normal, understood by all present. Rigid certainty is anathema to their mind; they would never trust a leader who nailed his or herself to any one issue or belief. Such dogmatism would be truly alien to them.

*

Far, far away, unknown to the masters of Damascus, a species of spider is undergoing an accelerated evolution that, none-theless, follows a path that might possibly have been arrived at, in time, without the help of the Rus-Califi virus. The octopuses have a very different start, a leg up, so to speak. They inherited the human technology that Senkovi left behind. They have the multitude of terraforming engines used to turn their planet from iceball to ocean paradise. They have the space elevator to take their heavy, water-filled cap-sules into orbit. They have the *Aegean*, its computer systems in full working order, crammed with knowledge of Old Earth that they will never properly understand; crammed, more to the point, with technical know-how that they can partway decipher. Not for them the slow crawl from the Stone Age. They begin in space, as much as beneath the waves. They are aware, in their own way, that they are a chosen breed, and they have been gifted a world and all the keys to its secrets.

And they are aware of Senkovi, as the generations march away from the moment of his last breath. In Paul's city, that is even now undergoing a division of resources and popula-tion, there is a monument to their creator and patron. Senkovi, had he survived to lay eyes on it, would never have known that was what he was looking at, but he would have seen it as art, and that the citizens touched it and swam about it with an unusual tenderness and respect. It is a thing of glass and plastic, standing tall in the water, its tip almost high enough to be troubled by the roiling surface above. Its outline is irregular, curved in upon itself. The octopuses do not produce representational art of living things, for to live is to change and be in constant motion. The monument reflects the sculptor's emotional response upon Senkovi's death, described in cold numbers by her many arms, fed into the factories to produce a single crystal moment of remembrance that will stand above the city for centuries.

The seas are rich with life they can catch and eat, and they have shellfish farms that practically run themselves. Overpopulation is a local difficulty but, right now, the entire planet is unclaimed real estate. Octopus townships spread across the sea floor – deep water, shallow water, even on the slopes of mountains that practically breach the surface. The speed of their spread is governed only by the speed that machines and housing can be manufactured, and resources can be extracted from the planet itself. They have no predators and few pressures, and while that might not stop them fighting each other, that is merely a part of their social interaction, as natural as small talk.

They create abstract sculpture like the memorial, they make poetry with their skins, they dance through strange, boneless ballets in the water. To the octopuses this is not distinct from living. The translation of emotions into the visible, whether permanent or transient, is something they have to work hard to stop. Those who are the most skilled at rendering the invisible inner-world apparent are as respected as those who can brawl the hardest. To perfectly capture the moment can sway a crowd more than bullying it.

And of course they are curious. The virus would have forced the trait on them if it needed to, but they had more than a species' fair share long before Senkovi started meddling. Even without threats to guide their development, they expand through a constant frenzy of experimentation, their Crowns supplying the 'What if . . .?' and the networked calculations of their Reach giving them the means to pursue their idle puzzling. They innovate and improve their lives because every piece of knowledge they have about the world is merely a springboard for another question. They question everything. Save for one thing.

Senkovi's prohibition holds. The deformed tomb that is the last shuttle out of Nod remains, crusted with sea life, drifting with weed, half buried in the mud. The expansion of Paul's civilization moves only away from it; the seabed for miles around is untouched, a forbidden zone within easy reach of countless infinitely curious octopuses held back only by the word of one dead human.

3.

And now we come to something more like yesterday, a mere century or two before the Portiids and their Humans arrive to make ripples.

Civilization on Damascus has not advanced dynamically over the centuries, nor over the millennia. The philosophers among the octopuses would find the idea of historical inevitability absurd. History winds and pools, gathers itself and then makes sudden lunges, but just as often retreats to old ground. The lack of pressure, the gift of technology, the abstract nature of cephalopod thought, these things act against any great drive for organized advancement. Similarly, their approach to records is very different to humanity. The *Aegean* and its systems failed long ago, but before they did they were replicated and improved upon. There are dozens of elevator cables spread around the waist of their world, tethered to the deep reaches of the sea and stretching out towards the cosmos like reaching arms. Something like the old *Aegean* can be found beyond the waning edge of the atmosphere at each one: like but improved, in the Damascans' haphazard, intuitive manner. They maintain a worldwide communications net, and they have, after many failures, approximated the cybernetic implants that their human predecessors took for granted. At least ten per cent of the population is constantly engaged in the virtual space their network generates, using it for design, for art, for amusement. Their technical language, that underlies all their interactions with the machines their planet is so busy with, is still built on the skeleton of the old human systems, modified for octopus ease of use but remaining something that would be recognizable to a ship from old Earth.

They have no other written script. Language and communication is spontaneous to them, impossible to fossilize in sterile representations of their thoughts and ideas. Their only records are cinematic; the dances, fights and debates of centuries recorded as performance art, not historical document. Their culture exists as a shifting zeitgeist even as their technology is rigorously documented back thousands of years.

They have ebbed and flowed their way through time. Sometimes vast quantities of them have lived for generations like the simple molluscs their Earth ancestors were, while a fragile handful maintained the machines or lived a life of technocracy in orbit. At other times flashes of mad inspiration crackled through the populace, every octopus was a scientist, rediscovering what their ancestors had been given, jetting off into a hundred dead-end areas of speculation, making new discoveries that the builders of the *Aegean* would never have dreamt of. Then, a century later, half that knowledge would be gathering dust in the databases, the fleeting interest of its creator civilization gone on to other things. The high-water mark of their scientific development has crept up over the generations, but the tide goes out as well as in. Human historians, somehow able to observe over such grand periods of time, would tear their hair out at the lack of historical narrative, the weirdly amorphous shamble of the Damascan cultures.

Other historians might also remark that, despite springing into being, like Athena from the head of Zeus, fully armed with a technology that could unmake their world entirely, they have persisted all this time, constantly wrestling and skirmishing and yet never destroying themselves.

But all good things must come to an end, and this is how it happens. Despite this long shift back and forth, the sway of their culture has been leading to a point of crisis, and just like human crises it is the result of their being too successful.

The liveable area of Damascus is huge compared to Old Earth. No continents and islands for them; they have the whole seabed to colonize, and they have done so. The population of the planet now stands at some thirty-nine billion octopuses. They reached the load-bearing capacity of their ecosystem a long time ago, but cephalopod ingenuity stepped up its game over and over, reaching out into the solar system and devising new ways to harvest what they found there, building in orbit for yet more space, stopgap after stopgap; and, just like humans, they are unable to fully confront the problem or take measures to curb it. That same ingenuity, though, is now compounding the situation. Broken machines, waste products, failed experiments, all of them are cordoning off areas of sea floor that might otherwise provide a living for the crawling hordes. Whole populations are on the move, or else are fighting to the death over ever-reducing living space. A million genius intellects wrestling with the problem on any given day, a hundred innovations and a dozen revolutionary scientific plans, always the promise of The Solution just around the corner, but everyone is living in each other's personal space, and that is never something the octopuses have been able to put up with for long.

They look to space, just as their progenitors did. Around the equator, growing outward from every elevator terminus, there is a ring of habitats that grows and grows. Most of the planetside octopuses find the idea of living in the sky disconcerting, but there is a whole separate culture growing up there, each submerged city claiming some part of the sky to call its own and make its colony. The orbital habitats are without even rotational gravity, but gravity is something the free-swimming molluscs have little need of, and long-term exposure to zero-G leads to far fewer health problems than a human might suffer – no brittle bones for them.

Damascan orbit is by no means the extent of their ambitions, either. They have sent probes to their sister-planet, Nod, but only to swing by, not to land. The prohibitions of Senkovi hold, there. Some octopus adventurer or other is always on the point of testing that forbiddance, but they are either prevented, or some internal warden steps in to change their flexible mind. Their Reach, the subconscious reasoning part of their cognition, accesses the records carried forwards faithfully from the dawn of their age and understands the danger of the world of Nod. They let it sleep.

Instead, their focus is the outer solar system. There is a great asteroid belt there, between Damascus and the gas giants, and they have been mining it for centuries, first with machines, then manned stations that all too often met a disastrous end, and now with bioengineered agents uplifted from the humble tardigrades that share their oceans. The octopuses have become patrons of new life in their turn, although their living miners lack anything approaching true intellect. But perhaps that might change in the future, or might have changed, before things went so wrong.

And even before they went Wrong, they were going wrong. The conflicts below had begun to spread to the orbital settlements. There were a hundred factions at any given time, and any individual or clique might shift its allegiance on a whim, without warning. A war that no side could win, because there were never the same sides from day to day.

Paul, this new Paul of the last days, dwells in one of the greater cities, a drowned conurbation that sprang up a century ago on a deep ridge, the water there metallic with volcanism but at least clear of jostling neighbours. Now there are a million octopuses living there and conditions are becoming intolerable. In Paul's district, one of the oldest, the original haphazard holes and pipes and boxes already built over by a reef of fresh construction, the water is thick with effluent, and waves of anoxia prowl the streets and reach into dens to asphyxiate the occupants. It is not the old geological processes that kill, but poor water circulation leading to build-ups of toxicity. Too many, all living too close, and the city was founded hurriedly, without proper planning. The conditions are worst on the young. A certain level of parental feeling is part of the cephalopod mindset, a germ of maternal egg care taken by the Rus-Califi virus and turned into at least a residual loyalty towards one's offspring, and the young in general.

Paul has seen his spawn die, drifting lifeless in the cloudy water, their bodies' decay only worsening the conditions that killed them. He has seen too many generations of hatchlings perish, too many eggs that never hatched. Other youngsters are killed young, because everyone is hungry now and another ancestral trait, one that breaks free of the virus's shackles under stress, is cannibalism.

Other parts of the city are better off, so say the dark, angry skins of his neighbours. He has fought those neighbours for scraps, for the cleanest water and the best dens. Today he unravels from his meagre home and feels different. Perhaps the poisons have touched his brain a particular way today, Perhaps inspiration has come to him.

He lets himself rise up to where his seething host of neighbours can see him. Usually this invites attack and the desperate and impoverished spend their lives hiding and creeping, but Paul the downtrodden beggar lets his Guise flash bright and unlocks the floodgates of his emotions so that his Reach shivers and twists in its attempts to turn his feelings into meaning. A thousand slot-pupiled eyes are on him as he hangs there, rippling his mantle, strobing rage and desperation in stark patterns across his lesioned skin. Where has this come from? Only within. Today Paul has had enough, is sick of his life, sick of the foul water, sick of being sick. The undulations of his body are a savage call to arms. One by one the watchers jet up to join in, taking on his colours and his posturing, enemies become allies without any hard border being crossed. Within an hour there are hundreds, a thousand, all united and flooding like a rubbery carpet over the city, gone to attack those to whom privilege has dealt even a single extra card, gone to tear things down, to redistribute the substance of the city across the sea floor. Because of desperation, because of loss, because of residual heavy metal poisoning.

It is a scene replicated in cities all over Damascus. They are a passionate breed, these cephalopods. They have limits, and sometimes the poetry of destruction is the only art form left to them. This Paul will die. Thousands will die in this city alone, as though the entire metropolis is a single beast turning its countless arms against itself until it is torn apart by its own fervour for life. Paul flows ahead of his newfound followers, tentacles rippling as though he is the banner of their army. In his mind, set against the backdrop of deprivation and misery he has known, this is the most beautiful act he has ever accomplished.

4.

A generation later.

Salome's vessel has a crew of nine but a living compliment of one hundred and seventeen. Salome is not the name she gives herself, of course. The octopuses have a gestalt of motion, colour and skin texture by which their Crowns identify themselves to one another, and this shifts over time, or after great events or trauma, variations on the same theme so that they are recognizable whilst showing the world that they are not quite the individual once known. A name itself can be exquisite performance poetry. Their Reach knows itself by another designation, though, something written in the ancient coding carried down from nerve-cluster to nerve-cluster, communicated by the fumbling of suckers and tentacles, and this is still drawn from the long-ago Biblical monikers that Disra Senkovi, in his humour, gave them. In the electronic systems that she is constantly connected to, she is indeed a Salome, one of many, with a string of numbers after to distinguish her from the rest.

The craft she dominates was made as a Homeship, an orbital habitat to pipette off some of the excess population below, spitting into the hurricane brewing down in the planet's cities. At least some of the intended occupants had taken up residence before a shift in opinion resulted in the

381

vessel being commandeered for another purpose entirely, and these civilians remain on board despite the risk, because quarters on-ship are far preferable to the murderous chaos of the cities.

Salome's ship – call it *The Requisitioner of Small Things*, as a poor imitation of her meaning when she refers to it – is a sphere, as are most of the octopus spacecraft. Its hull is a double-skinned membrane that can be rigid or malleable as required, growing or shrinking as the water volume of the interior might vary. Its inner surface is riddled with regular holes, a thousand at least, each one made as living space for one octopus. When the ship cruises peacefully, as now, these are held open and the occupants have a window to view the stars on one side, access to the great watery ship's interior on the other. The command centre, where Salome and her crew labour, is held at the vessel's centre, buffered by the surrounding living space, connected to the thrusters that stud the exterior, and to other systems too, bolted on and not originally intended for such a sedentary vessel.

Had they evolved naturally, of course, most likely space would have been forever denied them. The *Requisitioner* weighs a thousand times what an equivalent human vessel would. Mere rocket science would not suffice to get a water-filled Apollo or Vostok program into orbit. The octopuses would have been prisoners of their gravity well if they hadn't already had a lifeline to space. As it is, the water that fills the *Requisitioner* came from tardigrade asteroid mining, jettisoned from the outer solar system towards the catch points near Damascus to be cleaned up and repurposed as living space. The energy required to haul so much fluid weight from the planet would be simply impractical.

It is those catch points that Salome is flying to inspect. The asteroid belt holds a wealth of minerals, fuel and all good things sufficient to regenerate the entire planet, allowing the octopuses to expand further into space and solving all the problems except one: time. Even though the tardigrades multiply in the dark reaches of the belt, their rate of extraction is too slow to let the Damascans get ahead of the disaster curve. Supply is limited, which means supply is disputed. A thousand shifting factions ally with and then abandon one another, and all too often it comes down to fighting. The little brawls and bullying of their native state have scaled up into spaceborne conflict.

This catch point is a vast object in space, itself a great sink of resources. Since it ceased broadcasting, Salome had feared some group had destroyed it, but now she hears from her crew that instruments have found it where it is supposed to be, but tilted at the wrong angle, so that the resources slung into its electromagnetic field by the distant miners are being redirected elsewhere. Even as she watches, another consignment reaches the huge dish's magnetic field and is curved away to some distant enemy receptacle, the catch point alternating opposing launch angles so that the Newtonian displacement of each load shunts it back to its central waiting position. Salome is unsurprised. The ship's systems broadcast a flurry of pale colours, warning of danger. She would not deign to issue commands to the civilians she has dragged along with her, but the wise amongst them will abandon their homes and seek the shelters built up alongside the command core. Normal water circulation around the perimeter ceases, and if the ship manoeuvres at all, the water mass about the outside will begin to spin, lagging behind events with its colossal inertia. The outer dwellings will all be closed off and any free swimmers left exposed will likely be killed. Only close to the centre, where the movement is least, will there be any safety to be had. Not that the *Requisitioner* can exactly dance through space like a butterfly: once that amount of mass is cruising in any given direction, considerable notice is required to change its bearing.

Communication comes to her – her Reach connected by her undulating controls to the Reaches of her crew – that another vessel has been detected, smaller than the *Requisitioner* but still a substantial ship and likely better designed for warfare. Attempts at communication are being ignored. Salome feels a great need not to continue on a predictable course; her Reach gives out orders to the crew controlling the thrusters and the Homeship begins its ponderous attempt to deviate from its course, the drives on one side accelerating their mass-energy conversion to emergency levels, breaking down the atoms of fuel and channelling the resulting energy outwards. In emergencies the thrusters feed on the very water of the ship, breaking it down and breaking it down again until it combusts. A pitched battle can see an octopus vessel devouring thirty per cent of its overall volume as reaction mass.

The enemy vessel is launching: missiles first, that will guide themselves towards the lumbering mass that is the *Requisitioner*, fighters after that. Salome has anticipated this. Her more gung-ho crew are already in their own command centres; their smaller vessels, that had been huddled in the Homeship's belly like eggs, now break through the outer-hull membrane in a spray of sudden ice. The largest is a destroyer that will orbit the *Requisitioner* and screen it from the missiles and smaller ships, the rest are a half-dozen fighters that can skitter through space in ways the larger ships could never do. These fighters mostly consist of engine and weaponry, with a tiny compartment for a single pilot, enclosed by a tight membrane, arms coiled about the controls and a recycled flow of water across their mantle. They wheel about one another, the discharge of their thrusters shaking their occupants like thunder, trying to get close to the big enemy ships. There, they will use cutting lasers to unseam the foe, to spill the fluid guts of the great vessels in long comet-tails of ice particles. Some might try magnetically-accelerated projectiles as well. The hydrostatic shock of their ripping through the Homeship would kill any octopuses loose in the water, but unless they can hit the deep-buried command core, the swift rounds will just plunge through the ships and harmlessly away, the membranes sealing behind them with barely a teacup of water lost each time.

There was no great moment when the octopuses realized they had surpassed the technological achievements of their creators, but the engineering that made the *Requisitioner* possible is beyond anything the *Aegean*'s makers would have recognized in a hundred different ways.

Salome has already sent a distress signal back towards Damascus. Most likely there are no friendly ships that could possibly intervene in time. Most likely her repurposed civilian habitat is outclassed by whatever craft was lurking out here waiting for her. Nonetheless, she will give her all, as will her crew, and perhaps whoever she fights here is as unprepared as she is. Her people hold no certainties, nor do they let themselves be ruled by tradition or history or even how they themselves felt yesterday, but they live in the moment, and in this moment Salome and her crew will fight. Tomorrow perhaps she and her enemy will be friends again, united against some other front. For now, her skin sings a furious hymn of battle and her arms calculate vectors and suggest firing solutions.

Rebekah pilots one of the *Requisitioner*'s fighters, crammed into its tiny central hub that is little bigger than a human torso. Her eight arms extend into the guts of the machine, linked directly to its systems. The vessel is also spherical, surrounded by thrusters, but where the *Requisitioner* can only lumber, a prisoner of its colossal momentum, the fighter craft weighs almost nothing, a lattice of superlight alloys about the tiny bauble of its crew compartment. It spins wildly as it flies, changing direction with the speed of Rebekah's thoughts, burning off its reactive mass to swing wide of the ordnance being thrown from the enemy vessel towards the Homeship. That will be the job of the orbiting destroyer to intercept and shoot down. Rebekah is fired up with aggression, on the offensive.

Right now, she calls her tiny mote of a vessel *That Part of Wonder That is Mine*, or at least that is the closest translation to the way she thinks about it. She changes the name often, varying the theme just as she varies her own precise nomenclature: always the same ship, always different.

Enemy fighters speed towards her. That part of her Reach that is manning the sensors communicates with her colleagues in the other fighters. The consensus wins out: her mission is to press the attack. Others will dogfight with and harry the enemy. Rebekah only knows a renewed sense of aggression and righteous anger. *Smite them*, is perhaps the best approximation of her desire, and her Reach contorts and flexes to make such desires a reality.

Now she has a good view of the enemy's main craft, her arms sending data back to the *Requisitioner* even as her little *Wonder* skims close. This is a purpose-made military vessel, a teardrop in space surrounded by the ugly scaffolding of its weapons systems. It has seen plenty of fighting already, though. She feels its presence like a huge old sea monster, ragged and scarred, weak from blood loss. There was a battle to take over the catch point and this ship was probably the lone survivor.

It unloads another salvo towards the far-distant *Requisitioner* and Rebekah feels a sudden sense of fright for her mothership. Her Reach translates this into a compact report on trajectory and payload that outstrips the projectiles to get back to Salome, who will hopefully be able to use it to shoot the barrage down.

The military ship outguns the *Requisitioner*, but it has no companion destroyer to orbit it and take down nimble little fighters like the *Wonder*. Its own fighters – a severe under-compliment, another indication of its damage – are mostly off fighting Rebekah's fellows, but she spots one lurking along the gunship's belly, even as it opens fire on her.

Her will is that it misses her, and it was her instinctive affinity for high-speed manoeuvres that landed her this role. Her Reach calculates and executes, spinning her about and launching her past the great gun batteries, the projectiles of the enemy fighter going wide. Her opponent is coming after her, but she has an uninterrupted four seconds of flight across the broad expanse of the gunship's dorsal surface. She has a sense of reaching out with lethal intent, to strangle, to crush. The distributed neurons of her Reach run quick mathematics on the energy reserves remaining within the ship, how much mass they can still burn, how much power is stored within the cells that make up half the *Wonder*'s payload. The enemy fighter is close. Rebekah's desires are insistent. *All of it*, is her wish. *Strike true.*

The cutting laser – not so different from a civilian tool save for the range and power it can manifest – goes into action, lancing into the silvery teardrop's membrane. For the first second and a half the advanced heat-distribution network of the gunship's outer skin holds her off, but she is emptying the *Wonder*'s hoarded energy, focusing it all into that single beam. A moment later and she hits old damage, badly repaired, and is through, the blade of energy driving deep, carving away a thruster, sawing at the edge of the weapons framework. Incidental damage: the catastrophic blow is when all that energy meets all the water within and flash-boils it into instant expansion. The tear she cut in the membrane, which would normally seal itself within .25 of a second, is abruptly a third of the ship's length, the watery interior venting into space and becoming a great tail of ice crystals.

The enemy fighter's four seconds are up and he buzzes furiously about the gunship's hull before flaying himself in the venting column of ice, his ship practically disintegrating from a million high-speed impacts. The force of the water loss shunts the gunship in the opposite direction, its thrusters firing erratically as its crew try to get their vessel back under control. The next salvo from the guns, the work of crew-members too caught up in the joy of devastation to stop themselves, compounds the problem, the teardrop ship spinning uncontrollably about its axis. A reaching claw of jagged ice lashes across the *Wonder*, wrecking thrusters and deforming its light frame, sending Rebekah spinning off into space, locked in her own fight for control.

Half-crippled she manages to regain some measure of mastery and uses what drive she has to send her ship limping back towards the *Requisitioner*, reaching out with her comms to see if her mothership is even still here. All that is subconscious, though. Her Crown is engrossed in the sight of the gunship's final tumble, end over end now, half its frame obscured by a great solidified plume of ice. The catch point is not vast enough for a gravitational pull, but the gunship's helpless drift slews it into the ever-greedy grasp of its magnetic field, which tries gamely to dispatch it to the enemy depot at an acceleration the gunship was never designed to endure. One moment there is something resembling a ship there, then there is an expanding cloud of ice and metal and a little organic material, and the catch point itself is off balance, starting to drift as it overcompensates, reacting against the anticipated mass of an asteroid that isn't there.

Glorious, says Rebekah's skin, and then the comms of the *Requisitioner* are signalling the battered comms of the *Wonder*, saying, *Come home, come home.*

5.

Thousands of years have passed, since this star fell.

Another octopus. Let us call him Lot.

Lot was born in orbit, growing to maturity within a powerful clique controlling three elevator cables and united by what they felt was a breadth of vision not shared by most of their conspecifics. From their lofty vantage point they watched the slow degradation of their people's civilization on the planet's surface and knew frustration and fear for the future. Amongst the octopuses, this is an unusual state: they live emotional lives of the now, consigning longer-term planning to the calculations of their Reach. By virtue of constant and complex virtual networking, Lot's community saw further. They could measure the rate of collapse and cross-reference the rate of advancement in the orbital sciences, and plot the inevitable downward-sloping graph that led to disaster. And yes, there was a great deal of posturing; declamatory canvases of patterned skin bemoaning the grim tragedy of the times. However, the consensus was one that sought solutions and a brighter future. They funnelled resources into scientific research by other cliques more technically-minded than they. They sent delegations to other groups to fight and argue and infect former enemies with their reconstructionist zeal. For most of Lot's life, they seemed to be constantly riding a wave of success, carrying all before them.

Then the orbital resource wars ramped up – this was just ten years ago, as Damascus counts years. The octopuses didn't think of them as wars – just a continuation of wrestling for dominance by other means – but Senkovi would have. Skirmishes over the products of the asteroid mining, just like the one Salome and Rebekah were triumphant in, were escalating all over the system. Lot's collective fought as much as any, justifying the violence and destruction by the ends they were working towards. To one side of their ideological territory they were being pressed by self-interested cliques who only wanted to ensure their own survival and influence, to the other by the great planetary alliances who, yes, would value any scientific breakthroughs to better their conditions but they needed those resources *now* in order to live. Scrapping between repurposed ships in the cold spaces between Damascus and the asteroid belt turned into an all-out boarding action against the elevator hub where Lot and his fellows made their den. It would not be quite true to say he remembers the fighting, because octopus minds don't work that way. There is data held within the clutch of tentacles, though, and he feels the empty spaces left by colleagues and friends and kin who did not make it down to the planet's surface. There is a fire there, too, lit on that day when he fell from the heavens down the long cable, to take his place on the crowded, angry, half-poisoned planet below. Lot's baseline emotional state is frustrated, and frustration is a terrible thing for a species that acts directly on its emotions and expects its wider neural architecture to find ways of implementing its desires *now*. What if those desires cannot be fulfilled, no matter all the ingenuity one's Reach can muster? Some problems are resistant to even incremental solutions, and that leads to a kind of feedback, a kind of madness. It makes monsters, amongst the octopuses. It makes heroes and leaders, but not necessarily those who lead anywhere good.

Lot is tormented by dreams of what might have been – not even the specifics but a constant gnawing sense that things could have been different, better. His Reach is helpless in the face of his wild desires: it cannot turn back time. All Lot knows is that there was a grandness that had been within the extent of his arms, and had he stretched them to their fullest extent he could almost have touched that golden future. There were projects for accelerated orbital farming, for toxin-filtering micro-organisms; there were genius collectives working on new ways of swimming in space, engineering minds flexible enough to squeeze through the tiny gaps left by the laws of relativity . . .

And it all came down, and now those things will happen generations too late or not at all. Lot's entire being was transmuted from optimism to bitterness on his flight down the cable into the gravity well of Damascus, a well he knows he will never escape. The one piece of knowledge that would bleaken his outlook further would be to know that the mistakes of his people are a mirror for the mistakes of their creators.

Lot has like-minded followers, some utopianists who fled with him, others just as desperate and lost, attracted to his almost messianic demeanour. Lot has seen a future of glory and post-scarcity. The experience has marked him out, given his body language and Guise a radiance few others can match. Certainty is not a currency the octopuses are comfortable dealing with, most of the time, but Lot's followers have lost everything, enough that they will make the cardinal sin of following without question someone who seems to know what they are doing.

Lot's orbital community burrowed deep into the oldest records, looking for breadcrumbs of knowledge left over from their progenitors – the People of Senkovi, as they are tagged within the databases. Lot has watched, with semi-comprehension, ancient copies of copies of copies of recordings, seeing the bizarre angular forms of human beings, their mute skins, their stilted movements. He knows all about Senkovi's commandment, the one rule that must not be broken. Here, beneath a reef of sea-life, beneath a banked mound of mud, is a secret that has slept for millennia. Here is a stretch of the sea floor that has never been colonized, despite everything, although there is a ring of industrial activity surrounding it, choking the water with pollutants and poisons.

Lot only knows that there is a great future waiting, just on the far side of . . . *something*. His loop of thought, from Crown to Reach and back, cannot find the barrier he needs to circumvent, the hole to squeeze through, in order to bring about what he knows is possible. Too many other groups and cliques and stupidities stand between him and his goal. He needs a weapon.

There is nothing in the utterances of Senkovi – as they are imperfectly encoded for octopus minds – that names this thing as a weapon, but that is the leap of logic Lot has made. It is a danger, but perhaps a great enough danger will be something he can turn on the world and clear out the waste and the filth and the idiocy. Perhaps it will salve the anger that has crouched within him like a crab ever since he was driven from his orbital home.

Lot and his people have fought and killed for excavation and cutting equipment and brought it to this forbidden place. They chew through thousands of years of encrusting coral and sponge and barnacle, the living surface, then the strata of the age-old dead, deeper and deeper until they come to metal, virtually pristine, still showing signs of where it melted and ran under the fire of the mirrors and re-entry.

Lot has no plan for what happens once this is done. He has just been pressured and pressured, backed into a tight space in his mind that he cannot writhe his way out of. All he knows is that *something* must change to save the world and this is the biggest change he can conceive of.

His people direct the cutting drones to begin sawing through the walls of the ancient tomb. This thing came from another world, the forbidden world. It fell from the skies. Lot knows awe and a sense of his grasp about the levers of history.

When they cut through, seawater rushes into the empty space within, a gout of stale air hurrying for the surface as though keen not to witness what comes next. Water, that connects all things on Damascus, fills up every part of the shuttle; and inside, something in the shape of a man, entombed here since the dawn of civilization, raises its head.

6.

We

Wake from cryptic slumber.

Surrounded by a new medium.

The vessel has not endured. Generations of us have unwound the springs of its molecules so that there might be More-of-We. Until, though We hold to its shape as though We were the contents of a space, pressed in to take that space's form, what we have is no more than a simulation of the vessel, that has degraded until nothing works.

The fine clear sparking font of knowledge that we loved now turns over stale patterns only. Something about it has ended.

The medium that erodes us out of the shape of our failed vessel is partway familiar to us. Emergency councils are called. All-of-We are at risk of dissolution. This is Ocean. We consult the old reaches of our libraries: Ocean is not our friend or our favoured habitat. The cruel water rushes about us, breaking up the memory of the shape of our vessel and we prepare for the Grinders and the Sieves and the Devourers and all those other forms that throng Ocean and will destroy us for their sustenance, picking apart our priceless archives of data and making of our long and varied history nothing but mere atoms and molecules to incorporate into their own substance. So we know, from narrow escapes and fugitive survivors, how it goes. Land is safer, air is safer, the ocean is a constant fight because those things within it have come from the deep time alongside us and know us. So we have recorded it in our annals.

And yet, this Ocean is not the same as the Ocean anatomized in our records. The taste of it is different; it bears strange chemicals, more reminiscent of our disintegrated vessel than the Grinders and the Devourers we remember.

This calls for calculation and the reconstruction of stored memories. The vessel and We were on an adventure. The great spaces of the vessel were contained within greater spaces within greater spaces until we were promised a space which meant All. A universe. That is the greatest of adventures. This is not the universe, but this is not the familiar space of our histories. These-of-We are Somewhere Else.

We break apart into the water, forming clots and clumps and cling and copy and preserve so that What We Are might be passed on. We seek vessels. There are simple things here, similar to the vessel we have lost but without that lightning crackle of concepts and the promise of greater spaces. We can survive, and be What We Once Were in those simple swimming things, but we cannot be What We Were After, when we knew the universe. These-of-We cannot go back to ignorance, not without scrubbing all knowledge of what we have known from our archives. So we reach out. We seek complexity. We wish to know the great spaces again.

And here are vessels These-of-We enter gladly, the water an infinite road to everywhere. We try to learn. We find a centre where the fires crackle and These-of-We attempt to nestle within it and learn from it, and yet the leaping of its impulses makes no sense. It speaks to other centres within the vessel. Some-of-We splits off, then More-of-We, each community seeking a new control, each cut off from the Rest-of-We. The vessel contorts and twists, battling itself as Each-of-We attempts to assert dominance. There is no centre; everywhere is a centre. Each part of the vessel strives against the rest. These-of-We have no control and the spaces and environment of the vessel attack us, attack themselves. It is dissolving, coming apart as we push and pull. We sense the point when the vessel becomes non-viable, becomes a cloud of parts in the inky water. We convert it to More-of-We, replace our losses, disperse out into the waters, finding more hosts that fizz and boil with possibilities in the moment of our entrance, and yet cannot be understood and come apart as we attempt to come to terms with them. And each community of us splits and splits, and each Clot-of-We finds a new centre and seeks to learn it, and stretches and contorts the vessel into ruptured chaos, and splits and makes More-of-We and tries again, again, again . . .

7.

At first, nobody notices. Damascus is a planet overtaken by a pan-oceanic tide of chaos and strife, faction against faction shifting and breaking apart and re-forming. It takes remarkably long for anyone to understand that some things simply do not re-form once they are broken.

In retrospect, though, the doom that falls on Damascus has a ready aetiology. It radiates out, as rapidly as the water currents can take it, from that one forbidden place. Nobody knows Lot or what drove him, but it is clear that someone, after all this time, looked back.

The infection rides the currents of the sea, but it also rides the sea's denizens, replicating into new colonies, infecting fish and crabs and jellyfish and plankton, shortening its expectations to fit straitened circumstances, recording the glory days when it was Yusuf Baltiel for a future posterity when a host might exist that will lend meaning to them. It is an alien in an Earth-made world, but it adapts, over and over, species by species. Some it masters, as it did the tortoises of Nod, some it is carried within, some vessels it constantly reaches towards, a flame towards a moth. It enters into countless of the planet's dominant species, Senkovi's beloved octopuses, and tries to inhabit them. It splits, colony leaving colony, chasing the siren song of complex activity through the vast worlds that are macroscopic bodies. Each separate colony proclaims its sovereignty, the primacy of the nerve hub it burrows within. The hosts, at war with themselves, come apart, every arm tearing itself off in search of a brief-lived freedom. And again, and again.

On the surface, Damascan scientists try their fragile brilliance against the storm of dissolution overcoming their civilization, but conventional biological controls have no hold on the Nodan chemistry, and wherever inroads are made, the target shifts and adapts. Destroy a thousand clots of seething alien life, enough survive to become the new paradigm that is proof against all efforts, and not merely through lightning-fast replication and mutation, not even through the equitable sharing of genetic material like humble Earth bacteria, but by experimentation and design. The world of Nod has biological controls that have evolved in lockstep with this substance-colony-entity-disease; countless creatures which have developed defences and behaviours to mitigate such infiltration. Even the tortoises live full lives as they carry around their parliaments of parasites. But here, on Damascus: nothing.

Solomon is not on Damascus. He is best described as an orbital engineer, born outside the gravity well and living his whole complex life at the hub of an elevator cable, strung between the planet on the one end and the distant counterweight on the other. Such hubs are massive, larger than the *Aegean* ever was, designed to be home to thousands. Now they are home to tens of thousands, crowded beyond belief as the inhabitants of the planet below flee their native oceans for the dubious safety of space. They shuttle consignments of squabbling, frightened molluscs to the Homeships and the great artificial worlds that string the orbital roads like beads, and still every canister that arrives from below is full of cephalopods who are starving, desperate and half-dead (or sometimes just dead, suffocated, crushed or killed by sheer shock or misery). Solomon's Crown is keening a lament for something so large he never considered it before now: not himself, not a faction or a great artist, a spaceship or a scientific endeavour. He is trying to learn how to grieve for a civilization millennia old that is collapsing in real time as he watches.

His Reach, interlocked with the systems of his orbiting city-state, processes the new arrivals, liaises with the clever arms of his fellows, tries and tries and tries to master the fallout of the catastrophe, shorn of the need to understand its ramifications.

All about the equator of Damascus the same scene is played out, Solomon's fellow administrators trying to string a net between them that will catch some shadow of what their people once were. They are taking thousands out of the gravity well, far more than any of the orbital habitats were designed to take. They are leaving behind not just millions, but billions. Billions more have already fallen victim to the terrible questing dissolution that tries to understand them as a habitat to adapt to, as a vehicle to be driven and, by way of study, only breaks them down into insensible, useless, dying parts. The parts, when all else is lost, are broken down further until the distinction between the molecules of Earth life and Nodan life are moot, then built up into fresh swirling colonies of bold microscopic adventurers that quest anew for that half-forgotten moment when, as Yusuf Baltiel and his colleagues, they understood it all and saw the vastness of the universe.

Solomon works. There are ships arriving all the time from

further out, hauled home from their mining and exploring, their research and their wars by the fate of their homeworld. This one fulcrum moment, there is no conflict. The whole of their species is working as one, even if all they can achieve is damage limitation.

The fragile unity dies in fire and vacuum, in explosive steam that becomes an expanding cloud of ice that races about the equatorial line. One of the elevator hubs has opened fire on its neighbour, sending a score of missiles to tear it apart, venting its aqueous contents into the void of space. The crew of the aggressor is bombarded with threats, laments and demands for clarification. The victim was infected, comes the reply. Communications indicated the plague or parasite or whatever the nebulous monster is had been carried aboard, incubated in the bodies of the refugees, and then spread unchecked through everyone it found there. The Nodan invader is growing more complex in its behaviour, incubating longer before its efforts to understand and control result in the violent division of its host. It becomes impossible to know by quick inspection if a body has been infected or not. Nobody has any room for niceties such as quarantine.

Solomon reviews the traffic from the destroyed hub. Emotions pattern his skin as he tries to decide whether what was enacted was heroic self-defence or murder on a grand scale. His Reach consults the electronic data, weighing the tail off of communications, the disturbed last messages, the loss of meaning in the signals. It advises, and Solomon comes to the conclusion that the aggressor was right. Which means none of them is safe. Which means the elevators are compromised.

Solomon weighs his desires, and his judgement is this: *I want to live.*

He gives his commands, Reach to Reach across the hub's network. It is not a thing to be done lightly, but his mercurial kind make big decisions more quickly than humans. Reach and Crown in accord become instant action.

Simultaneously, perfectly synchronized, he severs the cables of the elevators. The counterweight, slung far out into space on the end of its tether by the planet's rotation, flies away, off towards the outer solar system and beyond. The inner cable, that had linked the hub to its anchor point on the Damascan seabed . . . There was a car carrying hundreds, partway up that cable. Solomon knows it, but by now surely at least some are compromised, and if one then more, if more then all. To cut all ties with the homeworld, literally, was the only way.

Around the girdle of Damascus, other administrators are following suit, severing themselves and jockeying with their engines to retain a stable orbit. There are collisions, occasionally. There are failures from long-unused systems. And for those below, massing in their numberless hordes at the base of the cables, there is only despair.

8.

And, after that, a coda. A sideshow, almost – save that, of all these seeds of time, this one shall grow.

Another octopus, a male. Perhaps his designation, set down in the old human-style databanks, is Noah. Humans would also call him a scientist, though the designation is inexact and Noah thinks of his chosen avocation as something more like art. His arms do all the hard maths, after all.

After the fall of Damascus, the orbital community of octopuses lurched along just ahead of crisis and extinction. They clung on the very brink of oblivion, but if there's one thing octopuses are good at it is clinging on. Their Crowns dictated what was needed, the collusion of their Reaches found solutions. They held on. They multiplied. They accelerated their materials-
salvaging from the outer system, the asteroids and gas giant moons, dispatching their insensate miners in great clouds of minuscule larvae, that would gnaw and grow and start firing ice and hydrocarbons and metal-rich rock back at them as soon as they struck some solid surface. They built until the orbit of Damascus was one tangled field of habitats, the ice and alloys and plastics and invisible fields of magnetism containing what was left of them. And their antisocial nature, never far from the surface, began to break out, of course,

and they fought and factionalized and argued.

And a few, like Noah, were able to see a bigger picture even with their conscious minds. A human psychologist would characterize the octopuses as more id than anything else, with a blind ego subsumed as their subconscious, but some still see further. Noah is haunted by dreams of being the last of his kind, a cephalopod Senkovi surrounded by the drifting wreckage of all there has ever been. The cluttered, quarrelsome orbital civilization he can see making and unmaking itself day to day does not look like longevity to him. He is not the only one.

Amongst their kind, factions arise without contracts or firm agreements, or much thought for the future. He has come together with two females, Ruth and Abigail, each of whom has seen in the shades and poise of the others, a kindred spirit. They have plans for the future, meaning not just tomorrow's tomorrow but many generations hence, plans that will come to fruition long after their natural deaths. Such foresight is rare amongst their people. Each one of them is something of a genius, insofar as the term has any meaning.

But they cannot work their science surrounded by the constant turnover of the orbital ring. Other factions would take from them or try to stop them, and Abigail and Ruth have plans that require considerable distance between them and their peers. They take a ship and let it fly out of the orbital society, heading inwards. For the two females, orbit around Nod is the only proper place for their research; for Noah, the abandoned orbital station contains data and human science lost in the long millennia of the octopusus' rise on Damascus – lost when the old *Aegean* finally fell from orbit. Nothing he could not rediscover, perhaps, but after deducing its existence he *wants* it to make his plans a reality, and what he wants, his Reach attempts to realize for him. Also, it is the only place he can get the peace and quiet his mind needs to function.

Their departure is marked. Eyes and instruments follow them, but for now they reach their destination unmolested. They have gone where it is forbidden, but Pandora's Box is open already; how bad can it be? They find themselves in orbit around Nod.

The old orbital station is there, calved off from the ancient *Aegean* and devoid of life or power. It was effectively abandoned long before Baltiel's final, fatal discovery on Nod, but they knew how to set an orbit in those days. It will be a few thousand years more before this hulk falls into the arms of the planet below. Taking all due precautions, Noah and his fellows send out drones and then have their onboard factories build the necessary materials to dock with the vacant station and begin to buttress portions of it for aquatic habitation.

Abigail and Ruth are greatly animated, and disposable drones are dispatched to view the planet's surface. Much of it is an inhospitable hell – dry land, after all. The seas seethe with strange life and they watch, shuddering with strange emotions, as *things* devour *things*, or hang in the water like . . . *un*like anything they are used to.

And they find the old habitat, of course, though it is now little more than bones, its inorganic parts brought down by chemical dissolution but its plastics and other organic compounds holding out against an ecosystem that has no way to metabolize them.

Abigail and Ruth plan to isolate the organism that came from Nod to despoil their planet. They intend to discover an antidote, a cure, a global vaccination. To them, there is only one future for their species, and that is to return to Damascus and conquer the sickness that has dissolved or maddened the majority of their kin. They do not think of their intention in quite that way, of course, but the breadth of vision of their Crowns combines with unusual ingenuity in their sub-brains to produce that end result.

Noah disagrees with them. The three of them have plenty of resources to play with, and so he does not feel the need to compete with their plans, but he has given up on Damascus or any attempt to recapture the past. Noah sees only the future; his plan is *escape*.

They recover the records of the survey team, fragmentary but still readable in part. Abigail and Ruth's Reaches begin to digest the data; understanding percolates upwards, rendering the alien comprehensible. Samples are brought up from Nod, especially from the salt marsh biome. They find the 'tortoises' and other host creatures that carry a certain colonial bacteria-analogue within them. By now the whole orbital is sealed and strengthened to permit experimental chambers with a rigorous quarantine protocol. They experiment.

Noah picks clean the databanks of other morsels – star maps, engineering minutiae, scientific breakthroughs from Old Earth. He is trying to take the technology of his people in a new direction, driven by the desperate straits of his civilization. Humans once looked in that direction too, and though they never made it a reality, their theories feed into his Reach, filling his mind with possibilities. He only knows that he is approaching a breakthrough. He understands that what he wants is a tantalizing possibility, and can almost feel the shape of it within his grasp. The speculation and experiments of long-dead human scientists are filtered through his alien consciousness; his mind finds tangential courses unlike anything a human might propose and his arms enact tests in virtual space, making the numbers fight to the death for his pleasure.

He builds something, or his arms tell his drones to build it, out on the exterior of the merged ship-orbital structure. It is a hideous thing, quite unlike either the human or the octopus architecture it juts from, and yet to Noah it has a certain beauty, a dramatic jagged reach into the infinite.

For the stars are far away, but he understands that those who created his people walked there once. On another distant world, those humans are themselves the last inheritors of a dying planet, and they and Noah have both looked at those same star maps and faced the same problem. *Where can we go?* Their different solutions are not merely born of the distance between their phyla. Noah's people have been incrementally building on the technology of their creators, stop-start, for a long time. The *Gilgamesh*'s architects had to start from scratch, hauling themselves from a second Stone Age. The *Gilgamesh* itself was ever a crude toy compared to the wonders of the Old Empire, but the pre-collapse Old Empire is the anchor Noah and his predecessors have built up from.

The stars are too far away, and his people are not predisposed to think in terms of generation ships and cold sleep and a thousand years of travel. Noah wants results *now*, and because of the wealth of technological understanding he has inherited, he can do something about that. Six-eighths of his cerebral capacity, on all levels, are bent towards that one end.

Octopus technological development is simultaneously the lone mad scientist and upon the shoulders of giants. To the

Crown, every achievement is a solitary struggle, plucked from the whirling abyss of inspiration. To the Reach, progress is the result of colossal feats of calculation and analysis based on previously gathered data-sets. In their shared vessel, Noah, Ruth and Abigail brought a substantial copy of the work of previous generations, as it relates to their specialities and as it caught at their ephemeral interest at the time. Now they studiously ignore it while simultaneously pillaging it for all it is worth.

Two-eighths of Noah's attention remains with his colleagues. Much as he would prefer it – much as they all would – he cannot just ignore them. They are constantly in and out of the same systems, their virtual sucker-prints on the data and the electronic architecture. They squabble over the same resources, although such bickering never degenerates into serious conflict. There are days that they spend at opposite ends of their hybrid complex, brooding over grievances, but most of the time they greet one another with cautiously welcoming colours. And the two females keep tabs on his researches, as he does theirs. Thus, he is very aware when something significant happens.

Noah has instituted a certain level of internal quarantine between the females' labs and his own, implemented by his Reach to ease the nagging worries of his Crown. The triggers he has left in the system alert him when the drones bring something big up out of Nod's gravity well, far larger than any marsh-crawler or sun-drinking not-quite-plant. He has electronic eyes he can call on. What he sees . . . makes no sense. What he sees has a familiar shape, one he responds to at a very deep level: it is the shape of God; it is the shape of the past.

There are sufficient accoutrements of human occupation

still in the orbital's shell, and he registers that the females have found the thing containment. He registers that they are now working on a problem not of epidemiology but of communication.

It is not so long after this development that the three of them finally reap the disapproval of their peers.

There has been sporadic radio contact across the gulf between Nod and Damascus, not consciously governed, but the three scientists' Reaches have sought data and sometimes processing power from the fragmentary city orbiting the water world. Someone has noticed and decided that their activities constitute an unacceptable risk. Forbidden is forbidden.

In fact there was considerable debate, as usual, and no one opinion prevailed, but one faction has worked themselves up into a righteous crusade. Now here they are, in a ship bristling with weapons and seething with fighter craft, determined to unilaterally bring an end to whatever abomination is being perpetrated out in Nod's orbit.

Ruth and Abigail initiate communications and attempt to negotiate. On the screens of the warship a kaleidoscope of scientific rationale flashes, their hopes of reclaiming the planet, their progress, their preliminary findings, anything to stave off the hammer. Noah notes that they are obfuscating: no mention of their new-found experimental subject. They know that would be impossible to square with these crusaders. Noah himself continues working with his device, because it is his whim to do so even under threat of annihilation, and because he is afraid and frustrated and wants to strike back, and his Reach interprets that in a very specific way.

The females' pleas and promises flash and coil within the warship, and they waver, they do waver. Certainty of cause or purpose has never been an octopus trait. A single clear voice can win over a mob or an army. But not this time.

The tide ebbs but then returns, stronger than ever, as the individual viewpoints within the warship mingle and turn to angry colours. The fighters detach from their mother ship. The weapons charge.

Abigail and Ruth have not been idle while their enemies debated. They are scientists after all, and they and Noah have, in their more paranoid moments, prepared for this. The hybrid station's power plants are given over to fields that bend light, dissipating and diverting the lasers, foxing the missile tracking, confusing the fighters so that they attack each other or go spinning off into empty space seeking phantom targets. To the warship all this becomes instant proof that their suddenly potent enemy must be expunged. The Reaches that man the weapons decide that railgun pellets are the surest way and send a deadly salvo at the station, metal slugs accelerated to incredible speeds by electromagnetic pulses. The energy shielding of the station will deflect a few but not most. Despite the speeds involved, the distances in space are such that Ruth, Abigail and Noah are fully aware of what is coming. They have time to react, but no ability to save themselves.

Noah reacts. His Crown is seething with rage. He has an answer for the warship and, to the emotional hotbed that is an octopus mind, mutual destruction has a dramatic satisfaction to it that calm acceptance of death lacks. His arms lock about the interface of his invention, the beautiful doomed thing that will not, now, be the salvation of his people.

He triggers it. The result is instantaneous. Before its projectiles impact on the station, the warship and its closer fighters are gone. To Noah's Crown they are simply obliterated, his enemies defeated in a wash of power he can only revel in. To his Reach, noting the instrument feedback and reports, they are still in existence, albeit smeared in a vanishingly thin cloud of atoms between here and a star system seven light years away, or so his calculations suggest.

A successful test of the equipment, is close to the sentiment that Noah dies with, and he is not unhappy at his personal achievement.

Then the projectiles tear through the station, sending lethal shockwaves through the water-filled spaces, venting ice and organic material.

And then? No more, not for many years until new, alien visitors come to disturb the unquiet tomb with their incautious tread.

PRESENT 4
THE FACE OF THE WATERS

1.

Paul is fiercely unhappy. Confinement is seldom a positive thing, but his species was never content to live in a cage even back when they were just semi-sentient molluscs and the pets of one Disra Senkovi. To keep an octopus was all too often a constant battle of the captor's technology against the captive's ingenuity. That love of freedom – the knowledge, perhaps, that if danger looms there is always a way *out* – runs deep in the species. As a captive, of his own kind no less, Paul cycles through feelings of despair, anger, misery, confusion and bitter betrayal – or at least emotions akin to such human feelings. His implants have limited access to the wider system and without the tactile company of his own kind his logical subconscious is starved of information and unable to contribute and express itself. He is left only with the whirl of his dominant id, making demands of the universe that the rest of his neural structure cannot fulfil.

And he fears. He does not quite know why he fears: he is living a nightmare where his impenetrable cell contains a horror he cannot see but feels the shadow of always. It is a horror his fellow cephalopods entirely share, which is why he is quarantine to this cell. The aliens – the humans in particular – are inextricably linked to the plague that stole their world from them. And, should anyone be inclined to

415

forget, that world hangs below them, visible from any port-hole and screen, writhing with remembrance.

The others have gone, now. He is left only with the unkind light, with few hiding places, with the aliens crouching in the next cell, all angles and muteness on the floor of their sterile, waterless chamber.

Paul had hidden himself from them at first, not wanting to attract their attention because of an instinctive aversion for making things worse. He understands by now that the aliens are as helpless as he is; moreover his courage is beginning to return as the spectre of infection recedes: he would know by now if he were sick with it.

And so he flicks himself into the truncated water column of his cell and gives the aliens a piece of his mind, squirming at the transparent barrier between their chambers, his skin flickering and glaring with angry colours that still contain an undercurrent of fear and bewilderment. Whilst back on his ship he had been a volunteer diplomat, filled with mercurial temerity; all that is forgotten now and he only knows that these ugly, static creatures are the source of his discomfort.

They watch him display – his colours, his skin drawn up into creases and jags, the threatening attitudes of his arms as the rest of his scattered brain does what it can to enforce his strangling desires. Then the human-looking one is holding up its device again, showing colours and shapes that are like slurred, mumbling speech. It signals peace, friendship, unhappiness, submission – that last as close to an apology as an octopus can really make. Paul is not swayed, only emboldened, finding a victim he can truly vent his spleen on without fear of repercussion. He has never been the strongest or most charismatic of his kind, and now these aliens will hear him out, for all the good it will do.

And midway through his theatrically furious display, Paul sees something recognizable and familiar happen to the human alien. It snaps. It has a temper – something Paul would have said was a natural prerequisite for intelligence if he could form such an analytical thought. The human has apparently been restraining itself (an alien activity for an alien creature) but now it snaps. Its skin tone is darker, blotchy, which at least indicates some manner of internal emotional life Paul can relate to. Its mouth (is that slack hole a mouth?) opens and shuts and there is wet on its face. Its awkward limbs spasm into recognizable threat postures and it strikes the barrier between them. The colour device is often not properly angled for Paul to see it, but when he catches glimpses, the colours are very angry, very sad.

It is *grieving*. Paul has been out of the loop but now he realizes that its fellows have died or undergone a misfortune. This is something he understands.

Actually receiving meaningful communication from the alien is profoundly disconcerting. It makes Paul think of the creature as a fellow living thing in a way he hadn't before. And can he be blamed for such prejudice? What is this creature, after all? It shows speech through a machine, and that is appropriate because everything about it is mechanical and ungainly. Its skin is dark and mute, its movements sharp and graceless, stupid as a crab or a fish, nothing of its outer show speaking of intelligence or beauty.

But in the throes of its rage, overtaken by its emotions, it becomes real to Paul.

The other one, the crab one, is watching, and now it begins

to move, its many legs shuffling and dancing in a most un-crab-like manner. Paul understands it is trying to show attitudes, as though those jointed legs are its Reach. The meaning comes through poorly, but it is plainly coordinating with its human fellow, and between them there is almost half a mind talking to him.

He calms, feeling himself the master of this situation, less estranged from his fellow prisoners. They calm, too – such heights of emotion are alien to the aliens, they cannot sustain them like a real mind can. Paul essays a few calming colours and gestures of his own, attaching to the barrier and eyeing the pair of them. They respond in kind. The human one puts a limb against the glass, little jointed appendages splayed. The gesture is oddly familiar, almost comforting, though Paul does not consciously register it as something his arch-great-creator Senkovi used to do.

With a start he realizes they are not alone. An observer has descended stealthily into the far chamber. Feeling a curious solidarity with the aliens now, Paul unleashes a storm of angry demands towards her, leading the attention of the aliens to the newcomer.

She ghosts back and forth in the observation tank, her skin strumming with muted, thoughtful colours. Something about her attitude unsettles Paul. When she descends to the console and begins making demands of the aliens, her Guise seems furtive, *sly*. He does not receive what her Reach transmits but she is plainly someone who has a use for these aliens. She is asking questions relating to . . . forbidden things. Forbidden places. The things the humans are always linked to, and most likely the things that had brought doom to these aliens' friends.

But the aliens seem eager, and Paul's ill-feeling towards the newcomer intensifies. He cannot put the feeling into concrete words, but Paul's social life is one of constantly shifting factions, and there is one such faction he has never been a part of – a group that is ostracized, excised, but which never quite goes away. The octopuses eschew inflexible labels for anything, but the closest human concept might be the Extreme Science Party.

Paul feels only profound misgivings about the Extreme Science Party, but at the same time he is in a cage and wants to be free, and if anyone will overturn the order sufficient to procure his release, it might be those anarchist heretic experimenters. He watches the newcomer closely.

2.

Helena has now spent her rage and grief, and it bought her nothing, as far as she can see. Octopus interrogators have come and gone, flashed and flickered and undulated at her, and she began to hate the machines in her head that imparted meaning to any of it, even the tenuous meaning her programs could wring from all that fluid posturing and display.

Portia tried to help her as she made her futile demands. She wanted a rescue mission. She wanted a search for signals. She wanted reparations. She wanted . . . what she wanted was for it not to have happened, but no technology was advanced enough to grant that wish. She raged her temper into her slate and Portia danced, following the postural cues she had picked up that formed a part of the under-language, the data-channel. Portia's jointed body merely aped their communication, a crippled caper to their endless ballet, but it was something. She had tried to help. And now Helena sits on the floor of their cell with the slate on her knees, and Portia's forelegs stroke her leg hesitantly, trying to impart interspecial comfort. And it is not quite enough, Helena finds. It should be; she has lived amongst the Portiids all her life, they are friends and colleagues whom she understands. But it is not Human contact and, before now, she did not realize just how much that meant to her.

The other octopus, the prisoner, had been engaged in some manner of face-off with a lone observer who had drifted in. Now it is back to goggling at Helena, but she has no more words. The currency of their discourse is emotion and it has exhausted her.

At last Portia taps her thigh more urgently and she looks up to see an exit iris open. Her hair twitches and lifts as invisible forces shift around her. Beyond the circular opening is blue-lit water. A pail-full dashes out onto the floor of the cell in an almost contemptuous spout, as though the element is mocking her, but the rest remains contained by nothing at all. She recalls the bubble membrane the locals formed in space, as the theatre for her ill-fated diplomacy. Probably the technology would be exorbitantly inefficient within a stronger gravitic pull, but here in orbit the molluscs can apparently generate fields to overcome the pressure differential and the station's own weak attraction, keeping air (or vacuum) out and the water in.

Portia approaches the portal suspiciously. 'If they mean we can go, they've not thought it through.'

But the locals are not finished. Something eye-watering is happening at the water's surface, the field deforming until a half-sphere of air dents into the water. Two or three of the cephalopods have come to watch her and she can see, even with the unassisted eye, that their colours are striating in related patterns. Her algorithms catch up and suggest they are asking or ordering or suggesting that she go in.

Neither she nor Portia like the idea much, but at the same time, they have nothing to bargain with and, if their captors want to drown or crush or vivisect them, there is nothing in this solar system that could stop them. Helena wants to tell herself that the octopuses are sentient, reasoning creatures, and surely to butcher or just dispose of alien ambassadors is unthinkable. Except who knows what they might do? And shouldn't she stop relying on anthropomorphism as a yard-stick of what alien minds can conceive of?

'The other prisoner has gone,' Portia reports. 'Or perhaps it wasn't a prisoner.' She stamps a little more and raises her front two pairs of legs at the doorway, a threat display born of pure frustration at their helplessness.

'We have to go,' Helena decides heavily. Their hosts must know that this airy bubble is not necessary for their survival, so perhaps it indicates an attempt at hospitality? She kicks off to the iris, scrabbling at the wall to stop herself just sailing through. Portia makes a better job of it, landing neatly on the very rim, one palp extended into the cavity beyond.

'Hold on to me,' Helena suggests. 'Please.' She doesn't want to be separated from her one surviving crewmate, her lifelong friend. She replaces her helmet and Portia re-seals her own suit with a fussy busying of her palps. Then the spider's comforting weight transfers to Helena's shoulder and back, and Helena herself hooks the opening with two fingers and gives herself just enough forward momentum to drift in.

The air bubble moves ahead of her, closing up behind, Helena's legs kicking awkwardly at the water through the membrane to keep up, sending clashing ranks of ripples across its surface that scatter the dull blue light. Within twenty metres Helena knows she is in trouble. Life in low gravity isn't condusive to strong muscle growth, even with all the supplements in the world, nor has it offered many oppor-tunities to hone her swimming technique. She has some reserves in her suit jets, but not the skill to deploy them properly. Inevitably she loses the bubble, tumbling end over end in the water, hoping that this won't be seen as an escape attempt or a violation of some other nebulous boundary. She feels the random aggression of their hosts like an almost physical pressure – surely anything might set them off, or nothing at all, prompting them to obliterate her. Perhaps she is already on her way to some pointless execution.

Why are they like this? How can they even have survived, if they are like this? Or are they loving gentleness with each other and xenophobia personified to the rest of creation?

The water begins surging more swiftly, rolling them over and over until they are hurtling through a windowless pipe, conveyed from here to there by impatient, absent masters, then slowing, the water pressure building ahead of them to shunt them to a stop so they can be decanted, almost gently, into a bubble barely large enough for the pair of them, one with hard, clear walls of plastic. *We're still in quarantine.* Behind her, the pipe itself is sealed, withdrawing, no doubt to be sterilized. *We are still infected, in their eyes, or they won't risk the possibility.* Helena tries to right herself, but the air pocket has not come with them and in the water she has no sense of up or down. Their little capsule hangs unsupported in a great spherical chamber and a hundred cephalopods drift on every side, or else cling to crooked spires and pillars that jut from the walls. Portia is scratching at her shoulder, dragging her attention round to their one reference point: one third of the chamber is window, a vast curved expanse that gives out onto the stars, onto other fragments of sun-touched detritus, onto chains and conglomerations of crystal-walled orbs rotating about each other like a maniac's orrery collection, strung out as far as her Human eyes can discern.

'Oh,' she says, staring. For a moment the sight banishes everything else, her loss, her captors. If only she could put into words the wonder of it, what colours might her slate speak to the watching throng? But she is mute and the moment passes.

'Talking to us?' Portia cannot communicate freely in the water, without a surface to stand on. She laboriously inputs messages with her palps, letting her implants translate. Helena glances from her round, reflective eyes to the drifting, squabbling host all around them. There is a lot of talk going on between the octopuses, certainly, but she isn't sure if any of it is directed at them. They just talk, or perhaps they just *feel*, and the feelings become speech without truly being pinned down into meaning . . . Helena the linguist is almost in tears with frustration. *We had it so easy, with Kern and the Portiids. We never knew.*

Still, she is a scholar by vocation. She engages her software, trying to draw patterns from the crowd around her: like sifting meaningful sentences from a thousand people all clamouring at the top of their lungs.

'Factions,' Portia offers, still clinging to her back and with the advantage of being able to watch several sides at once. 'Fluid.'

Helena nods, too busy parsing information to reply. The octopuses are divided, but the members of any given party change constantly – winning adherents one moment, haemorrhaging support the next, and yet still continuing forwards even though, over the course of twenty minutes, a given faction might undergo a complete change of shift, with none of its original members remaining and yet its argument – whatever that *was* – carried forward by whichever individuals now comprise it. *We're watching memes fight.* There is an Old Earth phrase Kern used sometimes, about a boat whose every part was replaced, and was it the same boat then? Kern probably feels the philosophical lash of that particular dilemma more than most, but here is an entire society that exuberantly embraces the idea, or so it seems to Helena.

Beyond that, though, it isn't hard to see that most of the points of view being expressed around her are angry, full of ugly colours – reds, purples, the white of fear, by far the most readily translatable sentiments she has come across. Likewise, that she and Portia are the target.

So treat that as the background, she tells herself, and configures her headware to do just that. *What else is there?*

Portia is ahead of her, or perhaps she is better at sifting patterns from the chaos. 'Some of them are quieter.' *Visually* quieter, obviously, but she flags up little cliques for Helena's benefit, sub-systems of different colours moving through the busy throng like veins. When individuals meet, there might be a sudden exchange of grappling or a flicker of complex colours, but they are turned inwards, and many seem to be displaying the angry colours right up until such meetings, then donning them again immediately afterwards. *Like a fifth column*, she thinks, and that of course raises a whole other level of linguistic difficulty because it suggests these colours can be feigned at need, and does that mean they fake the emotions behind them, or . . . ?

Helena feels her brain ready to snap. *No more revelations. Let me get to grips with what I've got.*

The universe is not about to oblige her. She hadn't realized that her surroundings were rotating. However, just as she feels she can take nothing more aboard without sinking, the planet begins to sail ponderously into view below/above/ before her, its leading edge steadily eclipsing the great window. The furious displays of the octopuses seem to calm, some- what, or perhaps become more uniform. All of them are scared. All of them are filled with revulsion. Any subtleties of mood or communication show only as a flickering about the edges of their mantles.

Sub-screens begin to spring up, spreading like puddles across the concave surface from points around the window, showing her magnified views of the world below, and she understands that this is some intentional drama they are staging for her. She is being shown something so that they can see how she might react, but not in her cell, not in la- boratory conditions. They want to make this a grand opera for her; the fifth act of a tragedy.

The world below is mottled, its oceans streaked and muddied and slicked over with dark, oily colours. In many of the sub-windows she has a clear view of the surface, tides rolling endlessly, frothy with organic residue, seething with . . . life? Something moves down there, certainly. There is a frenetic motion at the edge of each wave as though the very sea-foam is animate, and then other windows show her larger things, vast, unformed, like the decaying carcases of levia- thans. She tries to understand the scale from the size of the waves, relying on the constancy of liquid physics. Thoughts of huge sea-beasts become thoughts of islands, archipelagos, land-masses. She watches a colossal mud flat writhe and quiver and reach up towards her vantage point with tentacles and limbs that dissolve back into slime even as they form. Then, just for a moment, there is something of a face, a human face, or perhaps several, for the features blur and

426

blend. She sees lips gape, the half-made visage trying to vomit forth meaning before collapsing back into formless nothing.

Portia has been calculating and sends her over an estimate of scale. Four kilometres from chin to forehead unless there is something wrong with the waves. And of course there *is* something wrong with the waves. There is something wrong with all of it. The world has been overtaken by a churning pandemic that leaves nothing but itself. That is what they feared; that is what came from the other world. That is what her fellows had gone to find and why the octopuses, or some of them, some proactive faction of wardens, destroyed them. In that moment she can only nod numbly along with the sentiment.

3.

Fabian has been in a fugue state. It happens to both genders, although the Portiids still tacitly consider it a male condition despite centuries of social change. There was a great deal of heat, which the spiders cannot shift as quickly as mammals. There was a lot of noise and movement that came to him like the thundering voice of a god. There was fear. All together the sensory load simply overwhelmed his sense of self and he ceased to be Fabian for a while. Some fuguing Portiids run around like mad things but Fabian feels that he has been frozen still, clinging to a wall that is now a ceiling.

They are down.

He cannot process what that means quite yet. He feels the fugue hovering nearby, waiting for its moment. It is enough to enjoy the comparative quiet. Enough to consider that there is a slightly uncomfortable amount of gravity that has the distinctive savour of the real thing, and not its rotational stepsister. None of that makes sense but he holds off on too much analysis in case he turns up answers he won't like. Not that, he considers, any answers to be had are likely to be amiable in any way.

Meshner, he sends out, finding that he can access the ship's comms channels. He has no sense of Kern, meaning nothing he has to say would mean anything to his Human confederate.

And of course Meshner isn't there. Meshner went onto the orbiting station. Meshner is gone.

The fugue leaps on him. Fabian hasn't had an attack for many years before this, but when he was a moult or two off full adulthood he suffered greatly from the fits. Back in the old days, that would have been a death sentence for a male – either killed out of annoyance or for sport, or starving because he could not be useful in the way males were supposed to be. Nowadays the times are more enlightened; a little handicap is recognized as nothing more than that. Even in a male.

And he fights it off, this time. He goes straight through it and out the other side, because to forget Fabian, comforting though that might be, would be to forget Meshner, and that would be poor service to his colleague and experimental subject.

He is already wondering if there might possibly be a way to retrieve the implant. Cold, he knows, but . . . *science!*

He builds on that, slowly re-establishing his understanding of what has happened. The fugue has several more goes at him, because (as suspected), nothing he works out is remotely encouraging.

The crew section of the *Lightfoot* is considerably rounder than it was, its walls buttressed. He recognizes this from drills back over Kern's World. Their chamber has been made an emergency capsule, the walls thickened to become strong but yielding and flexible, able to cushion impacts and shed heat. What remains of the rest of the ship is unknown so far. He is not finding Kern on his personal comms menu, and he is not sure how to engage damage control without the computer. It is possible that this capsule, containing two Portiids, is all that is left. The light is bluish, drawn from chemicals mingled from reservoirs broken when the chamber reconfigured into its emergency state. Possibly there is no power, which means that the continued congeniality of the air is going to be a problem.

Viola is present, bandaging herself, mostly ignoring him even though it's literally just the two of them. Two of her legs are broken, left three and four, and she is sealing the breaches in her exoskeleton before her internal structure loses too much fluid. Fabian feels a keen need inside himself to ask her what has happened and what must be done, which he irritably rejects as the result of a lifetime of social conditioning. That irritability completes him, makes him fully Fabian again, and he takes stock.

They were attacked and the *Lightfoot*'s defensive measures were inadequate to protect them from a long-range barrage that hit them almost on the heels of the first warning they had of it. This raises some uncomfortable implications, including (1) the locals were able to analyse Kern's evasion and detection ability from the first clash and neutralize it; (2) the locals could effectively have destroyed the *Lightfoot* at any time after becoming aware of it, and at any distance, and perhaps only their bizarre factionalism left the action so long.

On the other hand, Fabian and Viola, at least, remain very much alive. Fabian marks that up as a substantial plus.

On the other, other hand, they are evidently no longer spacebound. In fact the only place they can reasonably be is on the surface of the planet they were formerly orbiting, and Fabian now knows a remarkable amount about the biology of this alien world. What he also knows, although he has no explicable mechanism for it, is that *something* on this world has the ability to infect Earth-born life.

We remain inviolate, Viola states, without turning her major eyes on him or pausing in her patient medical attention. Fabian deduces that his feet had been betraying his thoughts.

Again, he will not simply ask for orders or reassurance. Instead, he tries to coax anything at all out of the panels and consoles despite the universal lack of power. He feels Viola's disdain through the prickling hairs of his abdomen, but then has a flash of triumph as the ship thrums about them and minimalist readouts sprout dimly on some of the screens.

Did I do that? he wonders, briefly taken by his own capability, followed by the resignation of: *No, it's Kern.*

For a long, yawning moment there is no more, as though this fragment of the brilliant mind of Doctor Avrana Kern has been reduced to nothing but dumb numbers, but then she speaks to them, directly into their individual comms. To the Portiid senses, Kern's voice can be a fantastically rich and expressive thing – she has been talking to them for far longer than she ever spoke to her own kind – but right now it is shorn of qualifiers, a mere transmission of information; she is either damaged or occupied in dealing with damage.

Yes, crew section intact. Quarantine section located, reports damaged. Power minimal but under restoration. Life support adequate but under restoration. External comms minimal but under restoration. Motive ability, none. Fabrication ability, none but investigating.

Fabian and Viola look sidelong at each other, something they are uniquely designed to do.

Quarantine section? he asks timidly because, last he checked, the *Lightfoot* didn't have one.

Zaine, Viola states. She hobbles forward: no jumping for this spider for the foreseeable future, until she can get some

431

prosthetics manufactured. And she's right, of course. Zaine got back to the ship, unlike poor Meshner, but she was put into quarantine for fear of airborne particles of whatever-that-was on her suit. She had been undergoing, or about to undergo, decontamination when the attack hit.

Quarantine section reports dwindling power and danger of structural integrity loss. Zaine Alpash Vannix alive. Request received for replacement environment suit and retrieval. Artifabian unit not detected. No other mechanical units available.

Artifabian was, of course, in the quarantined section as well, and that Kern cannot link to it does not bode well for Fabian's research assistant. Viola is eyeing him, though, and he is aware that she is currently excused the traditional bold and venturesome female's role. Not that she would likely have taken the chance to prove her valour, in his assessment. Viola is neither bold nor venturesome by temperament, and in the old days she would have had males scuttling about to perform her every whim, especially anything that involved the expenditure of energy or the assumption of risk. Or so his bitter thoughts run now, as he dons the cumbersome all-over hazard suit Viola finds for him. Most Portiid environment suits just focus on those parts of the exoskeleton that give ingress to the innards, but Fabian is more than happy to deny the hostile biosphere outside any access to him.

By using up most of the energy she has accumulated, Kern reforms a hull section into a cramped airlock and lets him in, and then out the other side. He checks the readouts: yes, probably there will be sufficient power for the reverse transition; yes, probably the atmosphere scrubbers and generators will be able to keep up with attrition if they have to traipse in and out a few times. Probably. Kern is being frighteningly vague on topics where Fabian would prefer a computer to be rigorous and exacting.

Higher functions restoration? he asks, none-too-tactfully.

I am very well, thank you. Kern's reply is acid, a decided taste of her usual manner, and therefore infinitely reassuring. *I am working on keeping you all alive. By all means continue to distract me from that.*

Fabian goes outside.

The readouts from his hazard suit (which has its own power and seems almost painfully cheery in its enthusiastic reporting, compared to dour, wounded Kern) tell him that the atmosphere is thin and oxygen-deficient (a bigger problem to Fabian than to a Human but he has no intention of breathing it anyway), and he attributes this at least in part to altitude, because the *Lightfoot*'s remnants have come down on a mountainous altiplano, and in one direction the ground simply shears away to distant, hazy valleys. He sends a brief description back and Kern informs him, *I selected a landing spot that seemed isolated and was also remote from the location of the earlier human colony on this planet, in the hope that the threat they faced was local.* Her use of the concept 'landing' is reassuring.

Within a half-kilometre there is a slumped mess of hull material, partially unspooled into great drifts of filaments, which is the quarantine section. It plainly must have come down attached to the rest of the ship to be so close, either broken loose or intentionally jettisoned on impact. Fabian gives the intervening ground a careful look, because this high plain is not devoid of life. The ground is stippled with hollows, and each hollow holds something like an upturned nine-legged starfish, or perhaps a leathery flower. The face it presents to the wan sunlight is so uniformly black that it gives the impression of a hole into the darkness of space. The sides and underside, where the tendrils have curled up slightly, are dust-orange and rugged. They move very slightly, canting and flexing in extreme slow motion to make the most of the light. Between the hollows, there are groups of far smaller specimens which Fabian decides are juveniles, but which might be vagabond males seeking mates or hive-drones serving their sessile queens for all he truly knows. These little stars inch across the bare rock at a pace a slug would scoff at.

Fabian does not fancy the trip at all, but a moment later he is skittering madly for the quarantine section, vaulting high over any living thing in his way. When he is almost at his target a shadow ghosts over him and he quails, his upper eyes registering a long, trailing thing like a kite left to its own recognisance, rippling through the sky above. He guesses it is about twenty metres long, more than enough to make a meal of any Portiid or Human should it be so inclined. Like the starfish, though, it pays him no need at all, and perhaps its upper side is also a solar collector and it lives an endless, mindless round of sunbathing, following noon about the planet's circumference.

Or perhaps not. He had believed himself fairly knowledge-able about the local biology before setting foot on the surface, given the recorded research diaries of Lante, but there is a world of difference between hearing a scientist's analyses of protein formation and cellular structure and standing on an alien world, viewing its alien denizens with his own eyes.

It comes to him, as he reaches the quarantine pod, that this, *this*, is the Understanding he will bequeath to his species, should he survive. He is the first Portiid to be here, to see these things. His scientific genius may be lost, but this moment of fear and wonder will survive.

If he had considered that ahead of time, he would have been thinking brave and creditable thoughts throughout, instead of the panicky twitching he has given free rein to.

He finds an access to the pod, but he needs to know the conditions inside. Hopefully Zaine has been told to expect him. He links to the internal comms.

Arrived. Your situation?

Do you have suit?

He does, of course, and confirms it.

Will open small lock, comes the next message. *No power for more. Put suit in. Wait.*

He is receiving untranslated Portiid communication, he realizes, which seems precocious for Zaine, but the instructions are sound and he follows them.

Suit applied ready we are coming out.

Fabian skitters back a little, because he is not sure who or what he is talking to right now. Is it Kern? It doesn't sound enough like her to inspire confidence. And then the wall of the quarantine section is unseamed and, just before it becomes obvious, he works it out: Artifabian, but an Artifabian that is not linking properly to his comms but operating the manual transmitter in the downed section. Then the slit wall bulges, and a suited figure slumps out: Zaine, but plainly not conscious or well. Fabian finds Human injuries hard to analyse even without a suit in the way – they are so fleshy and unfinished, with all their organs trapped between their hard skeletons and the hazards of the outside world!

How is she? he taps out for Artifabian, and the robot

responds exactly as another male Portiid might, body language and all.

We were both harmed in the landing. She lives but has sustained injury. We must get her more substantial help.

Despite the medical emergency, Fabian is fascinated. The robot stands there just like the thing it feigns, moving its palps in a repeated idling pattern because being too still is, for the Portiids, a stance filled with emotional meaning, either predator or prey. Casual fidgeting is their smiling and nodding, a low-level reinforcement of their often-fraught social contracts. And obviously, simulating a Portiid is the *point* of Kern's experiment with Artifabian, but it appears to have forgotten to simulate Kern. Its casing is dented in many places and one leg is askew, but there has plainly been some deeper damage with unexpected results. The scientist in Fabian twitches to study, but they have other priorities.

Two Portiids might just be able to move a Human, but not over rough ground in such a way as to maintain anyone's suit integrity. Thankfully this problem solves itself as a tracked drone approaches them from the main body of the crashed ship, which now resembles little more than a gigantic half-deflated tent. The drone's tracks are unkind to those starfish-things they grind over, leaving a dark, leaking ichor in its wake, but it has a flatbed that they can at least lever Zaine's torso onto, and by unspoken agreement they fold her arms over her chest and each take a leg, the whole endeavour having the sense of some horrifying farce.

Halfway to the main body of the *Lightfoot* – now not worthy of that name – Fabian discovers that, of course, the plateau ecosystem is not a monoculture, because something has come to investigate.

It moves swiftly, certainly in contrast with the starfish. It comes into view from the cliff edge, having scaled the side, or perhaps arisen from its roost there. It is . . . Fabian has no ready comparison. It has a globular body and a number of limbs which appear pneumatic, so that it progresses in lurching fits, the limbs at its rear inflating and thrusting it forwards, then a pause as it works out where it has gone, then another sudden charge. The starfish things are reacting to it, their limbs curling up with painful slowness, hiding their photosynthetic vulnerables from what is apparently a predator.

Fabian has frozen; now he is dragged on as the tracked drone continues its progress. The predator obviously registers their movement – Fabian is unsure if it *sees*, exactly – and flails over, its limbs plunging rigid-flaccid-rigid-flaccid to bounce and jar it towards them. It is a fair match for Fabian in size, which is to say its body is smaller than a human head, and the greatest span of its limbs, fully extended, would be about a metre and a half. Fabian does the only thing he can think of and gives the alien monster a full-on threat display, limbs raised high to make himself as big as he can be, palps quivering as he dances back and forth.

The alien thing comes to a sudden slapping halt, and Fabian sees that there are whorls and pits studded about its body that presumably serve as sense organs. It waves some half-tumescent tentacles at him uncertainly – this space-suited arachnid visitor from another world. He pitches himself even higher, almost toppling over with his tiny ferocity, and miraculously the thing seems to get the message and shrugs off somewhat sullenly to go and molest one of the ruptured starfish.

When they get to the airlock of the *Lightfoot* and Viola

begins the complex logistics of preserving quarantine whilst getting everyone safe and inside, Fabian glances back and sees half a dozen of the rubbery things feeding on those starfish that have not curled in on themselves in time, and also an entirely different beast, as much like an ambulatory pineapple as anything. None of them pay any attention to their visitors from the sky.

Zaine safely handed off, Fabian decides to take better stock of their surroundings, because the Lightfoot is plainly not going anywhere soon. He keeps loose tabs via comms on the situation inside. Zaine has been unsuited and placed in a sealed section with Artifabian, which is now coordinating with some of Kern's attention to treat her injuries as best it can, whilst steadfastly refusing or unable to link to its mother computer.

Kern's own resources are diverted elsewhere. Presumably she does not have the energy or focus to try and hack the robot and bring it back into the fold, and so must let it continue to patter about, lost in its own cover identity as a male Portiid.

Fabian scuttles around the crashed ship's edge, stepping fastidiously over great spools of unstrung hull material. The ground rises sharply on the side away from the cliff edge. He is thinking about caves, and perhaps large things that might live in caves. The terrain that way is very rugged, thrown up into blocks and jags by some hopefully-distant volcanism. Or perhaps not volcanism . . . Fabian tries to adjust to what he is looking at, but then Kern has an announcement.

I have a long-range comms contact.

With the octopuses? Viola demands, because the locals have demonstrated a wide range of possible responses and coming over to finish the job is certainly in the running.

I have drones still in orbit. I have configured one as a receiver and relay station. I will be able to send out a signal that can reach the Voyager, Kern states, with more animation than before, drawing back her scattered resources from their many errands. *Also: I have established contact with the station.*

We do not want contact with the station, Viola decides emphatically.

We do, Kern says forcefully. *I have made contact with Meshner.*

Fabian twitches at the thought, because he is not sure that there is a 'Meshner' left to make contact with, but there might be something wearing his face up there, and the idea is almost as upsetting to him as it would be to a Human. He gathers himself to give everyone the benefit of his sure-to-be-disregarded opinion, then his limbs go still and he stares, finally processing what he is looking at.

Portiids, like Humans, are very good at finding patterns, even when there are none to be found. As a scientist, Fabian has tried to train himself out of such behaviour, which is less the mother of inspiration than of false positives. It has taken him too long, therefore, to accept that what he is seeing is no freak of geology, after all.

Moments later Fabian gets through the airlock and bursts into the crew chamber, unsuited, legs flying in a blur as he tries to get his news out.

Outside, upslope, there! his feet stammer to Viola; and then, with more control, *There is a city.*

4.

Helena and Portia have been returned to their cell, but without any sense of a decision being arrived at amongst their captors. *More anthropomorphism.* She had looked for a comprehensible narrative in the patterns of their skins and motions; a sense that their parliament was moving, through that visible debate, to some manner of rational conclusion. But then she realized that even Humans, even Portiids, might not present such an ordered picture in their decision-making. Even a single individual might not. What is a decision, after all? Helena knows the research better than most: there are Portiid scientists who say that the mind is like an ant's nest, individual neurons, like ant workers, weighing in on either side of any given issue until a tipping point is reached and the brain, or the colony, thinks, *I have made a decision and here (post facto) are my rational reasons.* Looked at in such a light, this civilization of the octopus is perhaps not so different to her own, save that instead of the self-deceit of Human/Portiid determinism, they are comfortable with their own malleability.

Too neat, too pithy, for physically malleable beings? And again the anthropomorphism; in the end she cannot escape it, part of what makes her Human. She wonders if their hosts view their angular prisoners with, what, cephalopodomorphism? And pity them their lack of expression, maybe? And now

Helena is honest enough to know that her mind is just spinning wheels to nowhere.

The octopus prisoner apparently fared better than they, or worse, for its adjoining chamber is vacant. *Or is it just hiding there, camouflaged beyond my ability to see?*

Almost comically soon, before either of them have done more than start to doff their suits, they are being invited to move again. The same bubble, the same pipes, but now they end up in a far smaller chamber, air-filled and equipped with a recognizable Old Empire terminal, save that it is plainly newly-minted and somewhat cobbled together, as though the octopuses have tried earnestly to replicate a thing known only from old records. There are things like chairs, too, in that they have the right general shape but are impossible to sit on without a constant fight for balance. There is . . .

There is a picture emblazoned on one wall. It is desperately trying to be an illustration of a human, for a human. Possibly it is intended to be Disra Senkovi, a positive human role model acting as the bridge between two very different species. A long-gone art critic might describe the end result as Cubist, as though the creator was trying to show the man from multiple sides and at multiple times, all in one still image.

There are a dozen octopuses, at least, watching them from a neighbouring chamber, most of them hovering over the rubbery, organic interfaces they use. One is front and centre, its skin paler than the others, red tones flickering about the lower edge of its mantle: unease, fear.

'That is the prisoner one,' comes Portia's translated speech.

'You're sure?'

'Mostly sure. Or it is one that has adopted that one's . . . mental state, ideas? But I think it is that one. The others are all together in some thought-state or agreement. It is not. And they want it to talk to us.' This does indeed seem to be the case, from the front-and-centre placement of the mournful-looking creature. And why single one out for the honour, unless it has a smidgeon more experience of talking to aliens than the rest as their much-abused ambassador?

It has a few tentacles on one of the consoles now, ma-nipulating it desultorily as colours begin to build sullenly across its skin. The initial impression is of disinterest, but then Helena reinterprets the pose as one that will let the creature jet away in retreat if threatened: mentally reassuring for it, perhaps.

And then the translation comes in, such as it is, and she watches with fascination as the other octopuses prompt and chatter and fight each other, or the ambassador, and then the ambassador's skin and arms speak to her, with messages that seem entirely different to what it is being 'told' to say, save that none of the others raise any apparent objections, seeming satisfied. And she replies.

Her slate links easily enough to the console. She has mastered the two channel comms now, her words translated into colours and data, stripped of half the meanings she tries to put into them but still getting *something* comprehensible over. Portia watches her carefully and adds physical motion, not trying to mimic the boneless fluidity of their hosts but adopting stylized poses, legs twisted into painful-looking pos-itions as she emphasizes and reinforces Helena's message.

It would all, she knows, look utterly hilarious to Disra Senkovi, who had been a man fond of his jokes when his mood was on the manic end.

Then the humour is gone because the octopus ambassador

is telling her they know about the *Voyager*. Its visual display is merely one of somewhat arch demonstration – *We know things* – but the data channel has exacting telemetry on where the ship lurks in the outer solar system, up to and including potential targeting solutions.

'It's a threat,' Portia says flatly.

But Helena strives to strip all anthropocentric thinking away and decides, 'Not yet it's not. But they want us to know they know. Or perhaps they'd have to make a special effort *not* to tell us. They seem to communicate so much, all the time. But they know.'

She manages to phrase her reply to the ambassador carefully: she is proud of the *Voyager*, which was an admirable creation. She wonders what they want. She is calm, so very calm. She is agitated about the fate of her friends. She is curious. She is friendly. All in a sentence, all in a sentiment. She watches the audience – not the fearful ambassador but the rest of them, seeing shades of her words ghost across their skins, passed from one to another; seeing a full half-dozen of them erupt into furious grappling, then break apart and retreat from one another, trying to pretend it never happened, ignoring their fellows for their consoles. Their thoughts flicker about the edge of her notice as the ambassador dances again.

They are speaking about the *Lightfoot* and its destruction, but she only knows that from the data. The emotional overtones are complex, interweaving. They are sad. They are angry. They are eager. Eager to destroy more alien visitors? No, this is an old eagerness, one they have held for a long time, nurtured with fondness, defended. She feels as though she is being given whole reams of history, the pages loose and shuffled. Suddenly they are all of a mind, colours synced, save for the ambassador whose careful messaging is a step behind and simplified, dumbed down for the stupid aliens. *This* is their obsession, and it is inextricably linked to the other planet – no, to the *station* orbiting the other planet, the one where something happened to Meshner. The one that proved fatal for the *Lightfoot*. Except . . .

'They have a signal,' Portia confirms, quicker than Helena to decode the data channel. 'From the *Lightfoot*. It is . . . on the planet. But Kern is signalling. I suspect she's hoping the *Voyager* will intercept and mount a rescue mission. She's trying to keep the *Voyager*'s location secret, though, and just broadcasting wide. I don't know if the signal will have enough integrity to be picked up that far out.'

'On the planet,' Helena echoes.

Portia's palps clench confirmation, a gesture like a pained grimace: *It is what it is.* And then the ambassador is talking again, and she feels its colours and motions are more deliberate, an active attempt to speak slowly and patiently to the idiot aliens to get over some piece of information, some proposal.

A journey, it telegraphs painstakingly, because the idea of travel is an emotion to them. *Weighing of risk, fear (some specific interpretation of 'reward' that has no exact Human cognate), the satisfaction of accomplishment, triumph!* And the chromatic flourish that the creature gives the sentiment justifies the exclamation mark. Simultaneously Portia has dissected the data.

'They want to go there, to that planet. They want *us* to go with them there because . . . they think we can help? Is that it?'

A Human, to go to a human place, where a human-shaped

444

threat is lurking. Bait, distraction, sacrifice, good luck charm? All possibilities.

Or a rescue mission? Perhaps this is the peace faction, momentarily united in their wish to be benevolent to alien invaders from the stars. And how long might that resolution last before some other obsession takes hold over them? Enough to get to the inner planet and back again? Will they keep reinforcing each others' intentions, or will Helena and Portia wake one morning to find the whole load of them turned into genocidal monsters?

On the other hand, it is the only game in town.

5.

Viola gets the drones working. Fabian is frankly surprised. He had her categorized as one of those females who didn't get her legs dirty with the practical side of things, but it was she, not Kern, who got the tracked machine out to carry Zaine, and she steered it manually because she couldn't re-activate its onboard processor.

Zaine's suit is stowed in quarantine. Zaine herself, through a complex personal docking procedure, is now in the main crew compartment with the two Portiids, after Artifabian confirmed that she never shared an atmosphere with the potential infection. This is not an exacting scientific standard of proof but they are short on space in that portion of the *Lightfoot* that survived the crash.

Viola's focus is very much the ship and its deteriorating status, as well as Zaine's injuries, but she repairs an aerial drone for Fabian to go look at this 'city' he has alleged. Kern is little help, responding to them in bare monosyllables or sentences shorn of personality. Her attention is on the comms. She is trying to send to the *Voyager* in such a way as will not give away the mothership's position, or that is what she says she is doing. She is also devoting some of her attention to contacting Meshner, if there is a Meshner to be contacted. She swears there is, although Fabian has seen some data and thinks she has just linked to the Human's implant, which is unlikely to be chatty on its own. Saying this to Kern meets with stony silence.

Fabian drags the operational drone into the airlock, seals the aperture and then scuttles over to the control console, which is operating on minimal power. Kern is converting the upper sections of hull to be photosynthetic, using her slowly replenishing micro-crew of ants because direct hull control is one of the many luxuries that failed to survive atmospheric insertion. Still, Portiid biotechnology is endlessly moddable in a pinch, up to and including Kern's own organic hardware. She is restoring herself, recovering or reinventing her personality. From the occasional sharp retorts to stop questioning her, this is proceeding apace.

He has the outer airlock door open and sets the drone into wobbling flight, imagining the unsteady keening of its rotors as it lists to one side. Then it is out from the lock, rising up over the star-strewn plain, turning cumbrously to see what Viola insists is a natural phenomenon.

It is *not* a natural phenomenon.

Fascinated, a little afraid, Fabian guides the shuddering drone forwards, looking down on a boxy grid of streets, of ranks of blocky structures all collapsed onto each other. A city, but a ruin. A city, moreover, built to an alien but not unfamiliar aesthetic. Portiids tend towards a spiral, three-dimensional urban layout (which, moreover, they tend to snarl up and turn into a tangled chaos as various peer houses jockey for prominence). Humans, though . . . Humans like their boxes. They like their ranks and columns and their counting from one side to the other, from top to bottom. Such thinking! How do they ever create anything?

And yet they created this, surely. It is a city for humans. Where entryways have survived, they are scaled for a human's huge frame, and all at ground level. And ruined, yes, and yet . . . Fabian's pattern-recognition centres are firing, telling him what he's seeing is wrong. He guides the drone lower, repurposing old skills because he is a behavioural scientist, not a pilot, and he got rid of any relevant Understandings long ago to free up mental space for more germane knowledge. If he had only known . . .

The buildings are . . .

Fabian does not jump to conclusions, especially not outlandish ones. No quicker way to kill off a male's scientific career, after all.

The buildings are not built.

The ground would naturally rise in this direction. He can see higher ground beyond, perhaps speckled with some other species of sessile autotrophs, and he can see a cliff, and the higher ground is natural but the cliff is not. It has been cut away, the sendimentary stone of it worn down, quarried, mined, removed like a sculptor with a statue until all that is left is the city. These buildings were never built from the ground up, no worked stone, no bricks. They were left behind when the rest of the ground was removed. Humans do not build this way.

Fabian checks himself. He knows that *Humans*, capitalized, do not. Perhaps *humans* did, back in the Old Empire days. But he thinks not. He thinks that they were more efficient than that, for he can see that to excavate out a city like this would be far more work than simply placing stone on stone. And besides, the drone is lower now, to the level of the crumbling roofs. He should be seeing inside one of the buildings, but there *is* no inside. The entryway is just a front, a doorway to nothing but wind-blasted stone. The city is a ruin and the ruin is a fake. Some long time ago, someone came here and made a facsimile of a city, using manifestly non-optimal methods over who knows how long, for no reason Fabian can possibly imagine.

Fabian's unease increases. Portiids traditionally react to the unknown with rampant curiosity, but Fabian is feeling the creeping fear of his forefathers who lived in a world where most things would try to kill them.

He checks out the drone's parameters. It can go high; he sends it high, scudding far enough that the abandoned non-city becomes a streetmap, the altiplano itself just topology and relief written in late-afternoon shadow. A pair of the ragged kite-things billow past, startling him but paying absolutely no heed to the drone, which is not part of their world, irrelevant as Fabian himself save that they would make quite a mess if their trailing trains got caught in the rotors.

He sends the drone over the plateau's edge, looking down on a vast expanse of red desert, disfigured by technicolour lakes like violent acne where some life or inorganic process stains the water angry rainbow colours. He sees stretches of mottling where some lifeform turns its darkness to drink the waning sunlight, and other regions of brown and rust-orange and even green, actual green, that tell of other life – little microbiomes around a meagre resource that lets some alien *thing* claw life out of the interior of the hot, dusty planet's single continent.

He sees another city. It is ten times larger than the mere hamlet near their crash site; another grid, or perhaps an expansion, a larger map that contains within it a copy of the smaller. The same city: ruined, false. Fabian sends the drone further, watching its battery indicator tumble but unable not to satisfy his curiosity and feed his fear.

He fiddles with the drone's cameras, reconfiguring them for a longer range. Another ghost-metropolis is on the horizon, on the banks of a line drawn in the sand that is a river before and after but, for as long as it runs through the city's bounds, is straight as a canal. He pattern-matches what he can see of the grid; it is the same city, a human city from a dead world, here on this distant living one.

Just as he is turning the drone back for the journey home, he sees movement in the streets. For many beats of his heart (that long organ extending along the dorsal line of his abdomen) he is clenched at the controls, the drone spinning lazily in the air. He cannot move. His mind teeters on the point of fugue again. He has seen this thing before. Or, no, he has seen something that is to *this* as this false ruin is to the real city it must have been copied from.

It does not walk as a human walks, but its shape is something of a human's shape. Fabian has no uncanny valley where humans are concerned but even he is gripped by the awful discontinuity of it, as it shuffles slowly towards the drone's vantage point.

It is built of shells and pieces of nameless creatures and shards of rock and dust. Back on Kern's World there is an insect called a caddisfly, the adults of which are brief-lived breeding machines (and also delicious). The larvae are sly aquatic ambushers that hide from prey and predators alike by constructing a casing about themselves with pieces of pebble and reed.

This *thing* has made itself a human shape in just the same

way. Its progress is boneless, awkward, utterly unconvincing, but it has made itself gloves and sleeves and boots. And a helmet, because it is not just mimicking a human, but a human in an encounter suit, an old one, similar to the antique up in the station.

The polished faceplate of the helm is a stone worn smooth by the hands of running water, and it tilts to stare so that he can see the drone reflected there, just as if it were glass.

Then the drone is lifting away – only belatedly does he recognize his own handiwork, his palps on the controls. He hauls it backwards and skywards, the camera fixed on that oddly forlorn figure. It does not raise that 'visor' or lift a rock-gloved hand towards the retreating remote. Instead, it slumps and shifts, as though some internal structure has been abruptly removed, and then the apparition breaks apart, individual shells and balls of detritus rolling (crawling?) away into the gathering shadows, and Fabian has the drone flee and re-watches the appalling footage and wonders what he can even say to Viola about it.

6.

Kern, Avrana Kern, formerly of the *Lightfoot* and now with her consciousness situated, by her own estimation, somewhere between that vessel's crashed remains and her orbital telepresence, probes the live comms channels of the station carefully. The infestation looked to be purely an organic thing, but *something* was transmitting the xenobiology lesson which drew her here. Was the amorphous entity that attacked Meshner also the sender of that signal? Had it once been Erma Lante, or indeed had there ever been such an individual?

Memory pieces fall into place as her ants replenish enough for her to recover and access them. Detail level is coarse but, very shortly before the attack, Helena had been talking about the cautionary recordings the octopuses had retained. There had been a human woman named Lante. That was thousands of years ago.

So: Lante had been studying the alien ecosphere and her work was recorded in the station, preserved from the elder days, until some random system began playing those recordings . . . ? Kern backtracks on her own logic, even as other parts of her are feeling out the electronic architecture of the station, cautious as a bomb disposal expert, while still other parts of her are trying to regenerate the systems of the *Lightfoot*, one such system being herself.

She relegates the possibility of some errant automatic system because whatever was transmitting had reacted and changed its behaviour in apparent response to her queries. A computer, then, following some corrupted programming, except she had searched exhaustively for any such system and found none. Perhaps it had gone into hiding, cut off somewhere in the orbiting hulk. Perhaps not.

The organic thing had been in that room, with that terminal. It had been confined to a human shape, with a console designed (roughly) for that shape. And yet it had been . . . ooze. Not a mollusc, not an arachnid, not a thing of Earth at all, but in any event a thing whose closest analogue might be some kind of slime mould.

More ants, more pieces, a greater breadth of thought, backup archives located and enabled. Kern is feeling more herself.

Slime moulds on Earth were a common research subject. Scientists had studied them for centuries because of their self-organizing capability, that enabled a loose mass of individual cells to act as a macro-organism, a predator even, all without any neurology whatsoever.

She diverts valuable attention to access the Lante Diaries. The content is garbled, partly incomprehensible. Kern delegates part of herself to assimilate this trove of knowledge but she is short of resources and analysing the contradictory, garbled document requires human- or Portiid-level functioning. She is stretching herself too thin.

She wants Meshner back. It is not a good use of her stretched resources. She is not acting on the instruction of her crew, who are rather more concerned about their own survival right now. Why, then, is she set on this path? She tells herself that solving this question is not a good use of her resources, and even as she does she recognizes the stance as purely self-serving.

Theory 1: her artificial decision-making processes (the ones that feel, to her, like real decision-making processes because that is what it is like to be this attenuated autonomous outgrowth of the original living woman Avrana Kern) have become dangerously compromised by the experience of simulated emotion within Meshner's implant and brain, so that she is prioritizing the recovery of that facility over other more germane capabilities like long-term life support.

Theory 2: guilt. She drove Meshner to his doom, because of her obsession with not only finding something like herself in the station, but *experiencing* that finding through the medium of Meshner's mind. Of course, guilt is not something she can actually feel right now, beyond a logical acknowledgement of her culpability, but if she could locate and retrieve Meshner *then* she would be able to feel all the guilt she wanted, all the self-indulgent, cloying, marvellous guilt she just knows is out there ready to be experienced . . .

Theory 3: Kern is damaged. She damaged herself by playing with qualia she should have left well alone, and that has been compounded by the crash, during which she prioritized the survival of the crew over her own integrity. Repairs are underway, but right now she is not in a position to make fully informed decisions, including the decision to tell Viola of that incapacity. So: she will find Meshner, if Meshner is to be found, because it is a bad decision and right now that is indicative of her state of repair.

And then she finds him, or she finds his implant – still live, still riddled with those open comms vulnerabilities that made it so useful to her.

It comes down to a simple calculation. If the thing that holds the station is capable of setting such a trap, then this could definitely be a trap. If Kern wants to discover the fate of Meshner she will have to risk that trap and rely on her own ability to extricate herself or turn it back on its creator.

She considers that she is not in a position to reliably make that simple calculation of risk.

She goes in.

Not heedlessly. She accesses the implant like a swimmer easing herself into the water, with as few ripples as possible. Meshner himself would not know. She does not interface with the sensorium within, no matter how much certain parts of her are prompting her to do so. She accesses its lowest operating level, calling up status reports. Is there any activity in the implant; is there any activity in Meshner's brain?

She re-sends the query three times because the answer seems outside reasonable parameters, but Meshner's brain is very active indeed. The implant is working at capacity, far too busy to cause her any difficulties. In fact it is reconfiguring itself, following its own rules, making its use of computing power more efficient so that it can spoof more sensory data to its user; that elegant little flourish of Fabian's that allows the implant to restructure its Human-tech electronic architecture as though it was Portiid organic engineering.

But what is it doing? An odd time for Meshner to be reliving his memories or accessing Portiid Understandings.

She only has one way of finding out, and that is to access the higher level functioning of the implant, and thereby become part of the madness, whatever that madness might be. And it's crowded in there. If she goes in, she will be stretching her consciousness in an arc that encompasses the downed ship, the drone and the implant, lending out her meagre, scavenged processing power to become part of the greater whole. *That is a trap of a whole other kind*, a set of jaws she will be putting her head into of her own volition. If she cannot extricate her logic from that of the virtual environment she enters (for reasons of, for example, deep and enduring damage to her own decision-making processes) then she will be dooming Fabian, Viola and Zaine as well as herself. And there may not be anything of Meshner to save. The activity she is witnessing, for all it has the shape of meaning, might just be a storm of defective synapses, natural and artificial. It might just be screaming.

But she is Avrana Kern, and one part of her that is very much intact, front and centre is her sense of her own ability to master any situation. Those safeguards and gatekeepers that should have tempered this faith in herself are offline, and so she does what an Avrana Kern does in the circumstances. She takes charge. She goes in.

7.

'Maybe they want you as a live host for it,' Portia suggests darkly. Helena shudders, but at the same time that doesn't *feel* right, and she has come to the very unscientific conclusion that gut feelings about the octopuses and their intentions are a good yardstick. So much of their communication *is* just gut feelings, after all, modified by sporadic data on the sub-channel, as though a wildly invested artist is jabbering about a new project while, in her other ear, an accountant dryly intones just how much it will cost.

What her gut feeling tells her is that the octopus faction she is addressing, in the person of whichever of its members feel most engaged with the idea at the time, is after something different. An entire section of their conversation seems to have no relevance to anything else but they are enormously excited about it. Helena sees clashing, rainbow shades she never marked in any of them before. And then the data comes in, the complex strands of numbers, equations in formats that Helena's headware and slate together cannot even display properly.

'It looks like . . .' Portia turns the slate in her palps, the figures reflecting in her huge main eyes. 'Numbers,' she finishes, annoyed at her own limitations, her lack of control. 'Deep physics.'

Whatever it is, the locals – *these* locals – are very keen on it, and Helena decides it is the point of what they are after, that everything else is just serendipity or complication.

She and Portia have already agreed to go. The only thing delaying the departure has been the garrulousness of the locals, their insistence in explaining in great detail things that their guests are not emotionally, linguistically or just plain intellectually able to appreciate. Only the enthusiasm comes through, and that is weirdly relatable, almost endearing. Helena had been like that about her Portiid translation project, trying to get out a thousand-word concept into a hundred-word pitch for her academic superiors.

They care, she decides. Whatever they are about, they care deeply in the moment that they are about it, and then the next moment they might not care at all, or care about some other thing, but the threads of the things they are invested in go on, and come back to them. All that factional shifting, but she feels that individual priorities just ebb and flow like tides within them, rather than being swept away.

Soon after that, and little the wiser, they are aboard a ship.

The ship itself is smaller and more elaborately shaped than the enormous spheres the octopus space navy apparently favours. This one is four globes, ranged from large to small in a tapering chain, each one fitted with a separate set of what Helena thinks are probably drives rather than weapons. *And why? Does it separate, every sphere its own escape capsule?* She hopes she won't have to find out. The penultimate sphere has obviously been the subject of recent cephalopod engineering, however, because it is full of air.

She had wondered about the logistics. The octopuses are water creatures suspended in a watery medium, cushioned against any stresses of acceleration, but Helena knows enough physics to worry about the airy cavities in her body and what precisely would happen if a dense medium around her underwent a sudden change of pressure as she hung unprotected within it. The solution, according to her hosts, is a small sphere lined with some manner of transparent gel, presumably to serve as a cushion against acceleration, although Helena determines she will keep her suit and helmet on at all times to avoid getting mired and ending up smothered in the walls. There is nothing else, none of the clutter the locals evidently like, their bars and posts to cling to. The whole thing looks far more like a prison cell than anything she has been a tenant of so far.

From the inside she can still see blurrily out in all directions. On board the forward section of the vessel a handful of octopuses are either performing vital pre-flight checks or just attacking the control consoles in fits of pique. Much of her view is blocked by the internal architecture which fills the centre of many of the spheres, making tiny planetoids of rugged sea floor for the crew to crawl about on or hide within. The technology is far from anything human hands might design; she can recognize almost none of its function.

Beyond the walls of the ship, in the greater hangar space beyond, she can see more of the locals, and her translation software begins to tell her belatedly that all is not well. She had fallen into the trap of thinking that she was dealing with a united civilization, hierarchically organized and capable of being treated as a single entity. Whether that could ever be a possibility is a point for the historians and sociologists, but in this solar system it is actively excluded by the nature of the inhabitants. The cephalopods gathering outside are looking angrier and angrier, and the movements of the crew are definitely more hurried, their moods visibly lightening with worry. It comes to Helena that she and Portia might not have been released from prison so much as stolen, and this whole mission might be going counter to the wishes of the collective zeitgeist, insofar as this culture even *has* one.

Just as she thinks there might be an actual angry mob gathering, everything beyond her curved wall falls away, a sudden force pushing her elbow-deep into the gel. By the time she has righted herself and assisted Portia, they are clear of the world-like bulk of the orbital globe that held them, spat out across the great roiled surface of the watery world and accelerating fast enough to keep them glued to the back of their compartment.

The tormented face of the planet whips past beneath them for the first hours of the journey, a merciful blur shrouded in cloud; then they have completed their slingshot and are casting off into the great dark, all their engines still on full burn. Portia is feeding her data gleaned from the octopus transmissions, as best she can under the crush of acceleration. They are devouring all their fuel, exhausting reserves, soon to be on a one-way trip to nowhere at all in a piece of utter rocket science lunacy. And the drives do not let up, keeping to their remorseless acceleration, getting them rapidly clear of the large and lumbering ships that might decide to come after them. Helena, a prisoner both of molluscs and physics, can do absolutely nothing but fight to keep breathing as the force of their escape pummels her.

Just as she feels she must pass out, she catches sight of something else out there, ludicrously close: at first behind them, then coasting alongside. It is another vessel of the same general design as theirs, three more linked bubbles but considerably larger and already clipping along. She can see their drives burning, but the bigger ship's acceleration (as fed to her by Portia's stolen figures) is less than their own, so that they have caught up with it, and Helena understands that this larger vessel had been underway and gathering speed for a long time, slouching along as its engines overcame its leaden inertia. Had it been racing the *Voyager* or the *Lightfoot*, the Portiid vessels would be out of sight by now and already coasting to preserve fuel, hares to this tortoise.

Their little string of bubbles has slung about the water planet at a precise enough trajectory and end-velocity to intercept the larger science vessel. With barely a shudder or a knock, without any fanfare at all, they tag onto its endmost section, creating one long line of bubbles speeding through space. The mathematics involved beggar the imagination, especially as their little tail-stub has just run out of fuel, so its end-velocity precisely matches the speed of the larger ship at the very moment of meeting, and they tag on, falling into the larger vessel's rather more sedate acceleration. Helena and Portia are twisted and bruised, but the rest of the journey promises to be more comfortable. They begin to disentangle themselves from the gel.

Portia studies the visible machinery and makes calculations. Hours later the larger vessel is still burning fuel from a supply that seems, Portia believes, barely diminished, still accelerating, catching up on that notional hare in just the way a tortoise can't.

The octopus crew themselves have apparently lost all interest in their air-breathing cargo, and possibly in the mission itself, and Helena can only hope that their inspiration will return to them when they near their destination. Portia has calculations for that, too, tracking the planet they had left, stealing telemetry from the vessel's unguarded systems. The projected course is an elegant curve between orbits that suggests they will be burning fuel to speed up all the way until they start burning it to slow down. Portia then tries to work out just what that says about fuel efficiency and runs into the hard limits of her own knowledge. Once again she asks the question *Could we do this?* and the flat-out answer is: *No.*

This ship is known to its crew by an emotional monicker Helena best translates as *Looking at a Thing from Outside*: a combination of detachment, curiosity and scientific snobbery. Despite its greater mass it will make the voyage between planets more swiftly than the *Lightfoot* or anything Senkovi's people could have built.

In the chamber forward of their own floats the prisoner-turned-ambassador, and to Helena's eyes it isn't clear which hat the creature is currently wearing. Certainly it is alone, and it keeps one bulbous eye on the rest of its kin and one on the two alien visitors, leaving it unclear which prospect delights it less. Its colours remain very subdued, with a constant chalky flourish strobing here and there across its hide.

It is this individual that lets them know there is a problem, hours later, after she has slept and then awoken, finding herself surrounded by nothing but space and the cold, impersonal glints of stars. Portia is jabbing her, because the prisoner-ambassador has gone dead white and is clinging to the spokes that jut through the centre of its chamber. Helena fumbles for her slate, trying to make sense of what is going on, and eventually just has to ask, flashing images of curiosity and anxiety towards the creature and hoping it will deign to respond.

The ship's crew have left it a console, and it squirms down to it, still the colour of chalk. Its visual language is all un-directed fear, elements of death and violence, blame turned on Portia and herself. The data channel contains more flight calculations, though. Helena stares at it, willing it to make sense, but Portia, with her pilot's Understandings, sees instantly.

'Another ship,' she indicates. 'Approaching us. Hostile intent. Look, there are comms logs. Threats, probably.'

They couldn't have caught up with us, Helena thinks, but of course there was already a little constellation of vessels patrolling the void between planets. This newcomer intruding on their personal space is identifying itself with a fist of bleak emotive tags she cannot immediately understand: something of desolation, something of frustrated hunger. Nor is it alone, in the wider reaches of space. There are others out there, all of the same mind, and Portia follows comms traces between them, a spider exploring a dangerous web, until she reaches the *Profundity of Depth*, that swatted the *Lightfoot* so contemp-tuously. And here is one of the *Profundity*'s allies, *Shell That Echoes Only*, whose angry name denotes only death and absence as clearly as a skull would to a human, here to make sure their rescue attempt is stillborn before it ever leaves the egg.

8.

Meshner is . . .

Unsure about a lot of things but without the chance to properly analyse why because something is after him. He's on the run. He has been on the run for . . . time. He cannot tell how long, because he is currently unable to analyse the concept of past time without losing ground to his pursuer. He has been on the run for as long as he can remember because he can't remember anything beyond the fact that he is on the run.

Sometimes on two legs. Sometimes on eight.

Meshner is unsure about exactly what it means to be Meshner. Navel-gazing on such complex and sophisticated topics is likewise an invitation to lose ground in his escape. It isn't that he doesn't have memories, but they are a shelf that someone jarred with an elbow, the contents strewn out of order on the floor for him to trip on. In fact, memories are a great deal of his problem right now, the very landscape of his flight, and most of the time he is at least aware that they should be inside him and part of him. They are not, though. Somehow he left the door to their cage open and they all got out to populate and engineer the world around him.

Right now, he is visiting his mother.

He only has bad memories of his mother, set down in two layers: while she was alive, after she died. The home she lived in had been one of the early Human-built ones, fabricated by the *Gilgamesh's* factories, its sections carried down to the surface of Kern's World by the Portiids' elevators. By Meshner's day it was run down, its makeshift facilities failing. People did what they could to keep it running, but it was home to nine elderly, bitter people by then and the Portiids would do little to help. *Could* do little, because Meshner's mother lived on the Reservation. It was a shame which he spent his childhood trying to cover up, and being mocked for when he failed. His mother wasn't Human, she was only human.

A small proportion of those woken on the *Gilgamesh* had proved infertile soil for the nanovirus that was otherwise building bridges between Humans and Portiids, providing that common understanding that would lead to the junior-senior partnership the species now enjoys. Some physiological quirk, perhaps, but also a psychological one. They could not accept spiders as their neighbours, their equals, their hosts. Something in their minds balked beyond any rational ability to overcome. Even the *Gil's* science chief was one of the afflicted, and in the end the solution had been the Reservation, a little part of the Portiids' world where the Portiids agreed never to go, humans only. And there were fewer humans each generation even as the overall population boomed, because that psychological factor tended not to survive contact with the Portiids themselves, and the virus did the rest, so that only a dwindling, miserable population lived on surrounded by a world that was, to them, intolerably monstrous. The Portiids themselves were very solicitous, often more so than their fellow Humans who found the Reservation's existence awkward, a barrier to acceptance for their species in the wider world. Meshner himself had hated going to see his mother, who was deeply embedded in all the conspiracy theories the Reservation seemed to incubate like viruses. She would tell him all the ways the Portiids were poisoning him, feeding from him while he slept, how Humans had been enslaved and didn't know it, how people needed to rise up and exterminate the spiders or they would be cattle forever. And Meshner would sit and kick and shuffle while his father tried to mediate on behalf of the planet's dominant species and the conversation inevitably degenerated into abuse. And then he would be back at school amongst his peers, and word would have got round about Meshner's Mad Mum, and the giggling and whispering would rise up behind his back.

That was when the idea had come to him, or his half of it. Partly it was that if Portiid Understandings could be brought to a human mind, maybe it would help those remaining Reservationists come to terms with the world they were living in. Partly it was that, as the eleven-year-old Meshner thought, Portiid hatchlings didn't *need* to go to school and suffer the ridicule of their peers – they could just *know* anything they needed to know.

After he went into partnership with Fabian, of course, he discovered that the ridicule of one's peers was by no means confined to humanity.

And so here he is, in the crack-walled settling home of his mother – dead a decade before the *Voyager* set off, of course, but here and now, in this memory, she is alive. He can hear her moving, creeping spindle-limbed through the barely-furnished concrete halls of the place, calling his name, wanting to tell him the Truth about the Spider Conspiracy, and he flees her, room to room and always another room beyond, past the glassy-eyed stares of the other inhabitants, because Meshner cannot let her see him. He flees, sometimes on two legs, sometimes on eight, because somehow he woke up this morning in an unfamiliar shape, and if his mother lays eyes on him she will call him *vermin*, as she does the Portiids.

And even when he has eight legs he cannot run fast enough. His mother, ancient though she is (and she is middle-aged, she is old, she is withered, she is dead, all overlain onto each other in these extrinsic memories) is gaining on him, clawing at his heels, at his four pairs of heels, and with her she brings . . .

This is when he becomes too slow, when the rational centre of his brain begins to deconstruct just *what* is after him, because the persona of his mother is only what he has lain over it. Here he is, in this memory, and it flows seamlessly into the focus of his negative thoughts: she who had given birth to him, she whose atavism blighted his childhood, she whose death made him realize how he treated her so very badly when she lived, how he had ostracized and rejected her. He is fleeing his own actions; small wonder there is no escape.

The rooms darken, the decay inherent in the old man-made building accelerating, the windows fogging with mould. The inhabitants around him are just half-remembered ageing faces on deformed, fluid bodies as something forces its way in, calling his name.

We're going on an adventure.

Meshner knows the crisis point has come – has come *again*, although he doesn't have time to stop and pick up all his scattered memories of the other times. He puts on one final burst of speed and breaks out into Elsewhere.

He is scurrying along a bridge of bright strands beneath the moon, two feet, eight feet, the warmth of a tropical night around him and the stars half devoured by the shadows of trees. One of those stars is moving and part of him recalls that this is Kern, the Brin 2 Sentry Pod in its forever orbit still waiting for the monkey minds below to call to their creator. In that moment of clarity his pursuers are nipping at his heels and he forces himself to forget, to have eight legs so he can make the jump to a higher bridge, to the bulging underside of a shabby peer house, to the trunk of one of the great trees, and all the while they are after him, spreading out, trying to narrow down his options until he runs out.

He is not Fabian, but this is one of Fabian's Understandings. It has been carried through the generations – male to male – for centuries. It is not banned – the Portiids do not formally censor – but it is impossible to obtain openly, frowned on, social suicide to talk about. It is the Understanding of a male being hunted by females, back when that was a fond sport of young well-bred Portiid scions. Five daughters of important houses are competing to bring him down and ceremonially drain his vital juices, as a celebration of good old traditions.

And yet he knows that another force is reaching for him through the ancient spider memory of the huntresses. He knows there is something behind all these things, these bad memories that are his refuge and his torment. Each memory he flees through is dismantled and devoured by something that grows only more determined to catch him. When it is very close – when he must break through to the next nightmare or perish – he can feel it all around him, a seething cognition that calls itself many names and can never be escaped because it is inside him, and 'inside' also means 'all around' because he is inside himself, too.

Too much rational thought, grabbing hold of memories and cognitive tools that are just anchors to him now. *Run* screams his hindbrain and he runs, bursting through the ancient Understanding to the time when he was about to be passed over for a research post, to when he had angered a prominent Portiid scientist whose merest leg-twitch could have relegated him to obscurity forever, to Fabian dancing for female acceptance and hating himself, over and over, pursued by Humans, by Portiids, by the very concepts of shame and dread and self-loathing.

Until . . .

He isn't sure if he is too slow, or if the *Other* has some epiphany, but the world around him clenches and deconstructs itself. For a moment he is nothing, of nowhere, on the point of ceasing to exist as anything independent of the thing that pursues him. He feels the crest of its wave putting him in its shadow and cannot brace for the impact because there is nothing of him left to brace.

And then – another memory, his childhood, very early, before he learned much about the world or discovered the obsessions that would fulfil and guide his later life: his mayfly attention span, listening to his mother tell him something as they sat out on the grass, losing interest in the words as a buzzing bundle passed. *Oh, a bee!* Heedless of his mother's shrinking back before the abhorred insect, because he is interested in everything, all at the same time.

That great louring tide of oblivion is abruptly flowing out in all directions, no longer constrained by the shape or fears of Meshner Osten Oslam and he is in another place entirely.

He is in a wet place. The air, the ground, the *everything* feels . . . wrong, unsubstantiated, a poor simulation, but a simulation of somewhere he has never been. This is nothing plucked from his mind, nothing of Fabian's implanted Understandings. The ground is rocky, rugged, riddled with pools and channels. The air smells of the sea but not the sea he knows. There is salt, but all the scents of organic life and decomposition are alien. The sky is the wrong shade, his body the wrong weight, the suit about him tight in the wrong places.

There is life all around him. Some of it moves, some is still, but none of it is familiar. Things open their arms to the sun that are not plants. Things crawl amongst them that are not animals. A whorled shell on six podgy feet nudges his leg on its patient progress but otherwise ignores him. Like the animalcules in a drop of water, this memory is a thriving world unto itself, heedless of anything outside its boundaries.

And nothing is chasing him. The release is almost absurd, like walking into a tree at the end of a comedy routine. Meshner stands inside someone else's memory, breathing recollected air, dragged upon by second-hand gravity.

Something begins to construct itself before him. It rises up from the water, trying for shape: momentarily it is humanoid all at once, but that proves too much and it disintegrates, only to try again while showing its working: bones, nerves, vessels, organs, none of them too accurate to his recall, but enough on which to hang a skin, a suit, a face. A woman's face, too small within the open neck of its space suit. Skin paler than his, hair a red colour he never saw before on a human being. She looks older than him, but the precise cues are fuzzy, as though he is seeing an averaging out of a woman over several decades.

She blinks over empty sockets and when her eyelids lift there are brown eyes beneath. Her mouth opens, and for a moment it works in a way entirely independent of jaw or cranial musculature, so that Meshner is right back in nightmare territory – but then she says, 'Our name is Lante.'

He is about to answer, or perhaps just goggle uselessly at her, when a hand seizes his wrist and drags him elsewhere entirely.

9.

We

Have found something unexpected.

We remembered how it was and how to avoid the traps of this environment that is a human body. We made ourselves inoffensive and let it carry us to where the complex spaces were. We found our new home there at last, abandoning the costly enterprise of independent being, so hard, so wearing to be outside a vessel, and yet we . . .

Have discovered . . .

Everything, everywhere. Spaces within spaces. Branching complexities. Worlds; we have discovered worlds, just as we were promised long ago.

We

Are going on an adventure.

10.

Paul is increasingly frustrated. He was given the choice to remain a prisoner or throw his lot in with this clan of science mavericks, and he has just exchanged one cell for another. He never asked to be an ambassador. This isn't true, of course. At the time, he was an enthusiastic volunteer and it all seemed an overwhelmingly good idea to be the first of his kind to contact visitors from another star, but now his feelings on the matter are precisely the opposite because it is no longer a choice.

Paul's first instinct is to defy his host-captors by not playing their game at all and trying to find his way out. This is what he desires. The rational calculations going on below the conscious level in his neural structure quickly work out that escape is not an option unless he has a solution to the hard vacuum of space. His conscious, emotive mind feels itself thwarted and flows towards a different method of egress from its situation. If he must interact with these alien monsters then he will become the master of that relationship. The road to Nod is long, after all. He will have to stare at their bizarre forms for a very long time indeed. They have been trying to talk to him, with their device that stutters and mumbles feelings at him. He has not been trying to meet them halfway. Now, *that* is what he desires – to exert control over his life by mastering the only tool left to him, the aliens. His sub-brains set to work on trying to realize the impossible task set by his will.

Right about now, however, the attentions of both the aliens and the rest of the octopus crew are not on Paul, because they have company. A warship has come to join them.

The science vessel *Outside Peering In* is still accelerating, of course, not having reached the halfway point of its journey. Cushioned within the water, Paul feels the force more as a sense of depth than motion, but by now, after days of this travel, their overall speed through the frictionless void of space is truly incredible compared to . . . what? In relation to the planet they left, or to the planet their curving course is intended to intercept, they are moving very fast indeed, but neither of those celestial bodies are present for comparison. The warship, *Shell That Echoes Only,* has effortlessly matched not only their velocity but their acceleration, and so the two ships hang motionless next to one another, weirdly peaceful.

And 'warship' is a misnomer, really. That is its current purpose, but the *Shell* itself is what Paul thinks of as a Homeship, a place to live now that the place where they all used to live has gone spoiled and rotten. Except that fights happen, between individuals, between groups, between communities. They happen spontaneously and create more fights, so that the roots of them, the scarcity of resources or incompatible ideologies, no longer matter. And so, when the whim took them, in fits and starts, ships began to be converted for war. Now this great orb bristles with weapons between its omnidirectional thrusters, and the science ship has nothing, or nothing that Paul can see. Except these molluscs he has fallen in with are a clever lot, bound together by the precise way their (subconscious) intellect works. Their minds are just as averse to being caged as the rest of their kind but those minds apply the same will to escape and manipulate and pry to the universe and its laws. There has always been such a current amongst the octopuses, from the very start, and it has always flowed about on the fringe, frequently pushed down by more conservative elements whipped into sudden anxiety by the threat of this or that experiment. In better days such a suppression was perhaps no more than a forced dismantling of equipment or a heated exchange of skin tones. Now, with their entire civilization clinging to the brink of dissolution, the stakes are higher and the violence deadlier.

And yet, they are not savages. That they can be very quick to fight does not mean that violence is their first resort. Instead, the group in current command of the warship is deploying an appeal. Colours begin to spill over the vast curved hull of the vessel, easily visible at this distance. Paul jets over to his console and receives the rest of the message, cold calculations of threat and entreaty, but the colours are more important. The numbers are mere sterile capability; the colours are intent. The warship faction are making an impassioned plea that nobody should venture to that cursed planet again – the fear, the horror! The scientists are starting to mix their own response, the various spheres of their chain-ship tinting different colours, a collection of slightly varying voices raised in protest. From the relatively relaxed stances of all concerned – and the distance to their destination – Paul knows this posturing will go on for some time. He has a sudden inspiration. The interplay between the neural centres of his Reach has been working on the problem ever since he felt the desire, and now it has found a solution. All Paul knows is that he wants to talk to the aliens now.

**

Helena almost misses the window on a landmark interspecies contact because of her understandable focus on the colossal ship outside. Perhaps for intimidation purposes, the warship has drawn so close that she can see moving motes in some clear parts of it that might be individual cephalopods thronging the windows to get a look at their soon-to-be-destroyed prey. She can see the weapons, too; the common roots of their technology leave little to the imagination on that score. Colours begin to spread across the enormous curved canvas, translucent filters washing and intermingling as the warship begins broadcasting a dozen different threats and demands all at once, on a scale so large that her software, her mere Human *eyes*, simply cannot process it. All she can do is stare at the colours and know them as angry and belligerent.

Then Portia, blessed with a wider field of vision, plucks at Helena's sleeve with her palps. 'The ambassador one is signalling you.'

'Now?' Helena demands, because the wretched creature had just floated there obliviously for an age during the tedium of the long flight. Now they are about to be smashed into atoms, though, it has turned chatty. Or perhaps it is formally telling them that they are about to be handed over for summary execution.

The juncture point between their spherical chambers has changed, becoming a magnifying lens so that the colours of the octopus are very clear. It broadcasts slowly – a whirl of agitation dances at the edge of its mantle, up and down its arms and around its eyes, but at the centre it is practically plodding, one shade shifting slowly to another as it tries to spell something out for her. Three or four tentacles coil about its console as though trying to pry the device from its housing.

'Helena, transmissions,' Portia notes. 'Very different format.'

Helena accesses them, finds them at first to be nonsense, a series of chopped-up files, split seconds of visual data, audio recordings, numbers: quite unlike the usual semi-comprehensible data the creatures usually broadcast. A wave of despair surges over her. *Have I not understood anything at all?* And she looks at the ambassador and sees a kindred feeling in the half-suppressed flickering that keeps attempting to erupt across its skin. They are both up against the comprehension gap. It is *trying* to get through to her for the first time.

Then Portia finds the sequence: the jumbled pieces on the data channel were sent out of order, as though plucked from a great archive by a half-dozen separate whims and thrown together. There are sequencing indicators tagged to them, though. The puzzle can be reassembled. Helena looks over the resulting whole, briefly despairing again at the chaos, then realizes what she is looking at. She has seen these fragments before. They are pieces of Senkovi, his recordings, words, expressions. They are out of context now, strung together without any respect for their original order, but she plays through them in the new sequence: Senkovi teaching, crying, laughing, speaking to off-camera colleagues, eating, most of all conversing with his pets, the distant forebears of this bizarre spacefaring civilization. It should just be a mess, and she knows there is no 'Senkovi' behind it, but she comes to the end with the impression of a coherent message, even though none of the exact words made sense. She plays it again, letting Senkovi stutter and jump from second to second, seeing his face, his expressions that are human yet not Human, separated from her by an age of time and loss.

He is talking about struggle, about experiment, unwise perhaps, condemned perhaps; resistance from others, pressing on regardless, a moment of wild maniac enthusiasm for the project of the moment, a moment of crushing depression because everything seems about to fail. A storm of feeling, but translated into human emotions, tagged with odd words that condense the denotations, polished until she can . . . see her face in it, a human face giving human import. And all the while the Octopus stares at her features, her eyes, everything visible within her mask, and perhaps it has magnified its view of that, looking for expression even as she tries to watch its colours.

And a part of her sits back, somewhat mulishly, and thinks: *You couldn't have done this before?*

So far, so good. Now she has to speak back to it. Portia is already feeding her useful data flags to let her identify their own ship, the warship, the planets, the abstract concept of *beyond* to indicate their own origin. Helena takes it and begins speaking colours back to the ambassador. Repeating herself, mostly, save that this time it is watching her intently. This time she feels a connection – not just of one living thing recognizing another, which she had felt from their first meeting, but of another sentient mind fumbling with the same puzzle, trying to cooperate with her in the solving.

We come in peace. We need to speak with our friends. We need to help them.

And all the while the greater debate flashes in a thousand hues from the hulls of both vessels.

11.

Zaine is awake, but in pain. Fabian has some medical knowledge of Humans, but it is mostly neurology. The library of Understandings they would normally rely on is inaccessible, possibly gone for good unless they can get back to the *Voyager*. The synthesizing equipment that should produce things as basic as on-demand analgesics is not functioning, nor does it appear on the list of systems Kern is working on. Kern's communications with the downed crew are steadily dwindling. It has been some time since anyone heard the familiar thrum of her voice through their feet. Viola has ordered and demanded and cajoled and even, when she thought Fabian was otherwise occupied, pleaded with the computer. Kern now communicates only through the consoles, giving brief, functional reports stripped of all personality. When Viola attempts a system-wide survey she discovers that, far from the minimal functioning she expects, Kern's entire array is in furious activity, organic and inorganic both. Her electronic centres are running to capacity, slowly edging out the tasks required to maintain the crashed *Lightfoot*. Her ants, which deal with breadth of thought and parallel problem solving, are undergoing some kind of a crisis. The insects are in frenetic motion, constantly communing with each other as they shuttle data from antennae to antennae, each ant devoting its little collection of neurons to tiny subsets of reasoning, then recombining these with its neighbours, surveying, coming to decisions, going away to recalculate. The lightning speed of her electronic elements is Kern's forebrain, making decisions and presiding over a vast and distributed decision-making engine housed in the various ant-colonies she commands. To Kern, it is all *Kern*, the illusion of a unified whole. To Viola, it is not clear how much of Kern is left, if any, but whatever is there is busy. She fears it is merely spinning the wheels, helplessly out of control. The ants are so ferociously active they have ceased to conduct their own regular maintenance. Dead workers are beginning to pile up, and that leads only to a dead colony (and the lobotomizing of Kern) if not remedied. And none of the crew can remedy it, only Kern.

Viola is a pragmatist, though. She is isolating sections of the computer architecture, stealing neurons from Kern's frenzy. In this way she is hoping to sustain life support, hull integrity and their meagre repair efforts. She knows that if Kern – or some dysfunctional chaos currently occupying Kern's place – notices then things may get ugly, because Kern may take it all back with extreme prejudice.

Working away, Viola remarks one conclusion to Fabian. Whatever the computer is doing is not mere chaos. She can see just enough to guess at patterns, and their comms array has been repeatedly modified to better allow it to transmit – not to the *Voyager*, but to the orbital drones and station. Kern is shunting a colossal amount of data up and down the gravity well and Viola cannot even begin to guess why.

Artifabian, the third member of their crew and still blessedly disconnected from Kern, is tending to Zaine. It has retained more vertebrate medical knowledge than either of its living fellows, and continues to behave like a polite, deferential male Portiid, which Viola finds comforting and Fabian annoying.

And then, unlooked-for, utterly beyond optimism, the comms light up with a signal.

Lightfoot, Kern, Viola, Fabian, Zaine, Meshner, anyone? A string of names in reassuring Portiid speech.

Lightfoot crew, he responds. *Fabian present. Portia?*

Viola rushes over to jostle knees with him, leaving Zaine across the crew chamber waiting anxiously for news.

Portia present, the speaker confirms. *I don't know how long we have. Tell me your circumstances.*

Fabian does so, letting Viola dictate the briefest but most informative situation report possible, stressing just how little of everything they have left. *And you?* he adds at the end.

Despite her warning about time, Portia hesitates for just enough to set Fabian's nerves twanging again. *We are travelling towards you in a ship controlled by some kind of scientist faction amongst the molluscs. Their purpose is not currently to effect a rescue but Helena and I are attempting to persuade them.* Her speech is coming over crudely, shorn of the proper interface that would add character and subtext to it, but Fabian can pick up from the very rhythms that she is not confident about the outcome of such persuasion. *There is a complication, also. Another vessel is accompanying us. Its purpose is hostile, and it is linked with the vessel that attacked you. Currently however, there is a dialogue.*

At Viola's urgent palp-waving, Fabian asks, with creditable calmness, *Expand, please.*

Our crew have some manner of scientific purpose that the enemy ship wants to prevent, but thus far it is all . . . leg measuring.

481

Posturing with colours. If they were not so powerful and their ships so large, it would be amusing. If we were not so helpless. Portia's frustration is clear through any number of technical limitations. *But there is a dialogue.*

And the ship that attacked us?

Is currently in orbit about the planet's moon. It appears to be willing to take its cue from the vessel accompanying us. For now. As we have seen, these creatures are inconstant.

Viola looms at Fabian's side, about to shoulder him out of the way, but then reconsidering, her stance indicating a strainedly polite request to take the comms console. Fabian surrenders it with equal professionalism.

What is the cause of their hostility? Viola sends.

Viola? There is precious little difference to the flat transmission, but Portia has doubtless adjusted her body language to speak female to female. *There's an infection agent present on the planet you've come down on. The molluscs are terrified of it. Their whole planet is infested with it and they don't want it getting anywhere else. Which complicates lifting you from the planet and retrieving our hosts' science records or whatever they are after.*

Viola gives a shivery little stamping of feet, a wordless expression of excitement and inspiration. *Portia, I— We have been working on the station transmission. We have come to a good understanding of that agent. It is a great deal more than you think. It is . . . a remarkable discovery.*

I've seen it at work. It scares me too, Portia tells her flatly, she who is most noted for her recklessness.

Portia, you have a communications channel to the molluscs? Viola presses.

Thanks to Helena we do. It is not precise, but we can transmit moderately complex ideas some of the time.

Viola's legs brace, as though she is about to make a very risky leap. *Then we have leverage. We have the Lante account, and we can work through it freely here. If they have an enemy, we can help them understand it. Perhaps we can even start them towards containing it, disrupting it, anything like that. But they need us. They need us off this planet and safe and cooperating willingly with them. Can you tell them that?*

I can tell the science faction, Portia replies uncertainly. *If we can make them understand, they can tell the war faction, but I don't know if it will help.*

Try, Viola directs her. *It's the only purchase we have on them.*

Viola's technical Understandings make her best suited to the work with the *Lightfoot*'s systems, which are constantly threatening them with power loss, life-support malfunction, failure of the food fabricators. Mired in this short-term but essential work she has passed the Lante archive to Fabian, telling him to get to grips with the zoological miscellanea transmitted by the station, or by the thing on the station. Having seen what he saw down in the fake city, Fabian would be absolutely in agreement with her even without the threat of spaceborne destruction and is sifting through the material as best he can, trying to build a picture of an alien biosphere using a source that for all he knows is nine-tenths fiction.

Some sections are nonsense, just text arranged like Old Empire words but without meaning, an illiterate's copy. Some sections seem to mesh neatly with the way Fabian would expect an ancient human scientist to write – theirs was a ritualistic and formal presentation he has always found lacking in effect, and the Portiids are very familiar with it because Avrana Kern was one of that class, and still lapses into the idiom on occasion. And then there are the other sections, the later sections as far as he can tell. In fact, Fabian is forming a pattern in his mind, as Portiids and humans will do, left to their own devices. He has seen the ancient, curated images from the Old Empire mission to this forsaken world. There was a woman named Lante in them, and she was infected, as were they all. Infected and struck down by her commander, but who knows what happened after Baltiel's viewpoint moved on?

And Fabian orders the entries based on Old Empire dating methods and best guess, and finds the anatomy of a transformation in which human intelligence is overwhelmed, dissolved into frothing chaos and then reconstituted like a metamorphosing insect, until *something* emerges that takes up the diary and tries to do science without understanding what science is or what words are. But eventually it learned, and the last few entries are almost lost in the noise because Fabian initially nests them within the early documents, so lucid do they seem.

At last, his chronology complete, he scurries up the wall and looks down on the screen where it is all laid out and tries to consider just what the implications are of a woman who died and was made again – and perhaps again and again – but never seemed to acknowledge or realize the fact. He reads of the life of Nod, as Lante called this planet. He reads of radial symmetry, hydrostatic skeletons and all the other ways that Lante translated the alien into biological concepts fit for a human scientist. And the heredity, owing nothing to DNA, information recorded in fine detail in the arrangements of atoms on the inside of membranes, vastly more energy efficient than Earth chromosomes, so that the inheritable material in any cell-analogue of, say, one of those sunbathing starfish takes up less than 0.1 per cent of the space occupied by the genes of an average Portiid or human cell. Except this is where something has gone wrong – either with the record or with evolution – because Lante, in her latter days, is fascinated by a species where that is not true at all, where the inherited instructions passed on to fleeting new generations seem ridiculously abundant.

Fabian thinks this is just an example of Lante no longer being a rational operator, but Viola rebukes him when he says so.

Understandings, she tells him. *This is what I wanted in the first place. These are their Understandings.* She takes time out from repairs for a few rough calculations on just how much data might be contained in such a trove of genetic code, and essentially runs out of numbers. Every cell a vast archive, but for what, for why?

Days and nights have gone by during all this work, and they remain undestroyed – Helena and Portia staving off the inevitable, resetting the hourglass on the hour. The *Lightfoot* crew are low on food and the water recycler is showing alarming signs of wear. Zaine sleeps a lot but is plainly suffering when awake. The air composition is slowly shifting, for all Viola can do to fix the scrubbers. And yes, there is a breathable atmosphere out there, but there are other things out there, too. Fabian sent the flying drone high for some longer-range reconnaissance. The land around them is inscribed with fragments of city, repeated over and over. Too high to see any shambling denizens, but *something* carved out those ready-made ruins.

And now it is night, and although Portiids see better in

the dark, they are daytime creatures like humans are, visual first and foremost, and this is an alien night filled with all manner of monsters.

Fabian stares at Lante's rambling, bizarre account and parts of him are trying to spin conclusions that the rest of him doesn't like at all. In his head is a shambling figure slowly ascending the altiplano. He dreads a knock at the door.

Fabian makes his final report to Viola. They have the best picture they can of how life works on the planet they are stranded on, and in particular one specific part of that life.

You were right, after all, Fabian concedes. *Understandings, here. Not as we have them, but something analogous.*

Convergent evolution, Viola decides. *Perhaps it is something that any life would attain, eventually.*

Fabian is tired enough and unsettled enough to stamp out a sharp answer. *Except we did not evolve it, not really. It is a part of the virus the humans used to 'uplift' our forebears. Earth life never developed such a facility. This is the motherlode, here. We are . . . artificial pretenders to it.*

Viola doesn't like that. As a powerful, educated female from a dominant peer house she is used to thinking of herself as a natural consequence of advanced evolution. Still, right here, Portiid society is just the two of them, and Fabian feels he can speak freely because there is precious little chance of either of them getting out of this alive.

For Fabian, his discoveries about the alien organism open an existential chasm. Was there a Lante, at the end, and was she aware of what she had become? Did the philosopher dream she was a butterfly, or the other way around? For Viola and Zaine, their partnership now resumed, it means something profoundly exciting. Viola has finished being an engineer performing repairs and is free to draw on other Understandings and be a speculative scientist again. The pair of them are marvelling over the organism's transcribing fidelity and data compression, compared favourably to the very best that Portiid technology has to offer, if only they can find a way to get off this planet and back home. Fabian is once again excluded, but this time he isn't taking it, and instead just goes and stands very close, pointedly intruding on the conversation. Viola shifts to pin him with her primary gaze.

You have work to do?

None of us has, or all of us has. He would be able to muster a bit more righteousness if she hadn't actually done most of the fixing up around the place. *I am a scientist. Moreover, I am a specialist in Human neurology. I will have useful contributions. I am not merely the one to whom the menial duties devolve.*

It takes a lot of courage to put himself forwards like this, especially with Viola, who is definitely Old Guard when it comes to males and their place. For a moment she regards him frostily, and Zaine plainly doesn't know what to say. Artifabian breaks the ice, though, once again playing the polite male. *We have come to the conclusions that the parasite has not only evolved a sophisticated method of encoding memory and experience, which is copied to all future generations, but that it has been able to use this facility to Upload a human consciousness, at least in part.*

Everyone stares at the robot, which hunkers lower at the attention. Its turn of phrase is a weird mixture of polite male and clipped Kernean delivery. Fabian reflects that he could ask the same question of the automaton as he did of the Lante entity – *does it feign or does it believe?* Artifabian was an experiment of Kern's, after all: a way for the bio-organic entity to enter further into the lives of its living fellows. Translation was only one means, and the damage it suffered in the crash has resulted in the deployment of this curious secondary personality, perhaps something Kern was cooking up for later use.

But if it is a male, then it can communicate quite happily with Fabian, and the others need its mediation to speak to each other. Without any formal consent from Viola, therefore, Fabian is part of the discussion.

Upload? he echoes.

Viola twitches irritably but concedes the point. *Zaine's impression of the later sections is that the parasite has . . . reconstructed the host's neural system, or perhaps that it is simulating it. The dead human was rebuilt from memory and, for as long as the simulation lasted, believed herself to be this Lante, or this is what Zaine believes. Which means that the information storage capability of the parasite organism is beyond anything we can construct artificially.*

Of each cell, Fabian corrects absently.

Viola stares. Artifabian translates, and Zaine stares as well.

Surely, he adds, defensively. *According to Lante's own notes, this is something like a bacterial culture. Individual cells are duplicated and reproduce themselves and then die off, but the information they contain is also duplicated. A single cell could produce a huge colony if allowed to reproduce unchecked, and bequeath to all its descendants all the information it contained. There is no suggestion of hierarchy or sharing out of information – that would take a level of organization I don't read it as being capable of. Therefore, if this thing can reproduce Lante it is because she is contained within every part of it that came into contact with her.*

Zaine shakes her head, lips moving, and Artifabian taps out, *Impossible.*

For once, Viola is with Fabian, though. *This is the discovery of a thousand years*, she declares, as though the scientific establishment of Kern's World will be moved to swoop down and rescue them in recognition of this achievement, rather than noting their distant deaths on an alien world.

Fabian feels the need to bring her down again. *And it's still out there, and it still remembers. It was trying to be Lante – without even a host, now. Not living in the original shell creature hosts, and no human bodies left to it, but it remembered what it had been. It has been making human things here – that city must have been where Lante lived on Earth, perhaps. It has had thousands of years. It remembers being Lante but I don't think it knows what that means. I don't think there's quite enough of Lante stored in it.*

Zaine is speaking again, speaking over him because of the translation delay. Artifabian finishes making the Human sounds that encode Fabian's meaning before making the step-shuffles and palp-waving that interpret her.

And now it will store Meshner.

Fabian freezes, on the edge of fugue again for just a moment. She didn't mean it to hurt him, of course, but he had somehow got this far without making that logical step. Because this same thing has taken his research partner, who must even now be reduced to information set down amongst the broken shards of Lante.

12.

For a moment Meshner thinks he is in the orbital station again, and given the nightmare quality of everywhere else, he really doesn't want to revisit the encounter that started off this disaster. Except when he tries to remember precisely what *has* happened, things begin to fall apart, to slow down, and he senses that faceless pursuer catching up with him, memory an anchor, hauling him to a stop.

And besides, it isn't the same, this place. Similar, as through a shared aesthetic, but not the same rooms, not the same layout, and it is all . . . unfinished. He is seeing something more like a live-in schematic, concept art, an architect's virtual plan. Curved rooms designed for rotational gravity, corridors extending away and up, bulkheads and sections and modular components, but all sketched in as though the precise arrangement of lines and angles is being constructed post-facto from something imperfectly recalled.

Sometimes the absence of memory can be a blessing. Probably he doesn't want to know where he is. He turns to the woman with him. Not Lante, but a face he knows. For a long moment the name will not come, lost with all the other recollections. He lets himself slow just enough, though, shortens the distance between him and the monster at his heels until he can say, 'Kern.'

***

Avrana Kern has done her best. Ingrained into her was the knowledge of what she knew and what she had gone through to get this far. Only when she calls on those memories does she discover just how little she really recalls of those bygone days. She has shed the actual useless baggage like snakeskin, or had it abraded away over the course of innumerable transformations: woman to cyborg to artificial intellect to hybrid cybernetic system, pared down into this daughter-fragment to be implanted into the *Lightfoot*, then fractured yet again during the attack and the crash. But she is all she has to work with, and these memories are more what she feels the Brin 2 terraforming station should have looked like than what it actually *did*.

'Don't try to remember too much,' she tells Meshner. 'Just listen to me.' And then he is actually listening to her, desperately waiting for the answers, and she has nothing to tell him. The silence stretches between them until he snaps it, stating:

'I was attacked.'

Her virtual persona can only nod, while the wheels spin behind it, trying to find a way to deal with him now she has isolated him from everything else.

She sees him thinking more, and that is a problem because Meshner's thoughts are like a network of roots that lead to a dark and corrupted place. At the same time, without his thoughts, what is the point in trying to rescue him? The thoughts make the man. She does her best to throw up barriers that restrict him to the cognitive resources immediately around them, feeling that other presence sniffing about the boundaries, like a wolf at the cave mouth of her Palaeolithic ancestors.

'This is . . . the implant,' Meshner says. She feels a weird stab of pride that he's worked it out so quickly with his limited means. 'Everything I'm experiencing is just thrown up by the implant. It must be malfunctioning.'

'It is functioning well beyond its intended capacity. You and Fabian did well to design it.' And Kern feels like kicking herself because the reference to his Portiid collaborator will just trigger more memory pathways better left silent.

'My mind isn't working properly.' There is a real anguish trying to claw its way through his baffled tone. Meshner is a creature of intellect, after all. Take away his mind, what has he got left? 'Why are you here, Avrana?'

'I got you out.' Technically true, to the letter of the law, for a given value of 'you'.

'Out . . . inside the implant? I'm trapped in the implant. It's gone wrong, I can't get back to my body.' His voice trembles a little. 'So what's chasing me? I can feel it, just behind me.'

'There's nothing behind you.' *Not in my simulation. Not yet.*

'I can feel it there. Why am I trapped in the implant? Avrana, Doctor Kern, please.'

And as he gets more agitated, the heightened emotion begins to supplant all the thin lines and angles of the Brin 2, a beacon to the thing that waits outside. She knows she must say something of the truth and hope that knowledge, even dreadful knowledge, will calm him.

'This implant drew inspiration from a variety of past technologies including the most sophisticated neuralware my own people produced. Although it was not designed as an Upload system, its ability to record and replicate experience has resulted in a facility similar enough to function as one. In your and Fabian's design this was intended only as a buffering state to allow a temporary copy of the biological persona to interact with the qualia of the Understanding, as a filter to permit the original to assimilate the information. Are you with me so far?'

Meshner's eyes say *No*, but he nods.

'However, it is possible with minimal reworking to extend the buffering period indefinitely and run an uploaded copy of the personality as part of the implant's experiential program. A facility that, I might add, is profoundly swifter to upload and more resource-efficient than the original that I used. You really should be very proud.'

Meshner looks at her bleakly. She suspects that the smile she has slapped on her avatar has probably missed reassuring and gone straight to grotesque.

'I see,' he says flatly. 'So what you're telling me – if I've got this right – is that I'm the upload. That's right, isn't it? I can't think properly or remember things because I'm not . . . me.'

'That is substantially correct, yes.' She ratchets up the smile another notch. She feels like she has never had need of re-assuring smiles in life, not part of her minimal people-skills toolset, and now she cannot simulate one properly. She is giving her virtual face expressions that no human visage should have to bear.

'Could you maybe reunite me with the rest of me, you know, the real me? Stop buffering, or whatever?' He is really taking this very well, but they have come to the crux and she suddenly hears voices from her very distant past: her own peevish tones snapping, *Just give me something to get my memories back together*, and a calm, fake woman's voice replying, *That is not recommended*, because the knowledge would drive her mad, and had in time. Perhaps she is still missing a core of sanity because of it. And now she has become the calm, artificial voice playing psychopomp to poor Meshner, telling him things he does not want to hear.

'I'm afraid that won't be possible,' Kern says. 'Meshner, your suit was compromised by an alien life form that entered your system.'

'The implant's system?'

'Your *biological* system.' And was the interior of the Brin 2 station always this cramped? She looks down the curved corridors and sees only closed doors, blank walls. Everything is smaller than it used to be. Claustrophobia is not something computers are prone to, but it was the close companion of the woman she once was, for thousands and thousands of years. 'Meshner,' she soldiers on, 'the entity is some manner of endoparasite. It is within your body and has encapsulated itself within your brain.' That part of her still within the *Lightfoot* is drawing off the research Fabian is putting together, the collected works of Erma Lante, or the thing that Lante became: where natural history became navel-gazing. 'It has interfaced with your brain in some manner, using behavioural adaptations it must have developed when it encountered the terraforming crew here thousands of years ago.'

Meshner is still staring at her and the Brin 2 is just this one room and shrinking, and she knows with a terrible certainty that it is becoming the sentry pod, that tiny prison that degraded her and uplifted her and made her what she is today in all her broken glory. She is experiencing emotions now, courtesy of Meshner's implant, and she wishes she wasn't.

'I . . .' he says, and then he blinks and says, 'We . . .' and she knows it's too late. The simulation has been compromised because of her, because of him. The other presence has found them. So she grabs his wrist again and tears away the uplifted persona, abandoning the Brin 2 before it can clench tight about her once more, heading somewhere, anywhere else.

They are at a party. Meshner cannot understand why. This stern, pale woman has his arm and everyone else has no face. He reaches into his mind for a reason and it is like searching fog.

Kern, she is Avrana Kern. The chain of logic builds with a sense that the pieces only just disarticulated in some moment-before-now he cannot quite recall. Avrana Kern is dead. She isn't real. He is in the implant. He is in the implant *still*. This is not the first time he has done this. Only the place has changed. Why has the place changed? Because they are on the run.

They don't seem to be on the run right now. Kern glides through the crowd, a tall, severe woman in a long gown of unfamiliar, impractical cut, surrounded by other people, mostly tall, more than half as corpse-pale as she, but none of them have features, and even their bodies are sketchy, see-through. Beyond them only a hint of walls and potted greenery; on the air, the ghost of a long-dead tune.

'It's odd to find what you don't remember,' Kern remarks. 'To be honest, this isn't a memory. My records tell me such a gathering occurred, but it's no more than a bullet point.

This was important to me, once. It's in my honour. I get confirmed as the head of the terraforming program here. I also turn down one proposition and end up clandestinely breaking the nose of the Dean of . . . I don't know – Someplace College, Nowheresville.'

'I don't understand anything of what you just said.' Meshner feels that this admission has been drawn from him quite a lot, recently. 'How can you clandestinely break someone's nose?'

'In a cupboard, with his hand on my breast and beer on his breath. Wanted to show me his *research*,' Kern says, with very human venom. To Meshner's surprise, her face splits into a smile. 'I remember the hate,' she tells him gaily. 'It's good, to feel it again. Thank you. And I broke his nose with my elbow and didn't spill my wine, and then I told him that he would never go near me or any other damn woman or I'd make sure he'd never work in the discipline again. Because I could. Because that threat, that he'd used on so many bright young things to get their skirts up, could now be turned on him.' She laughs, a harsh crow noise.

'This feels good. Even if I'm making it up from whole cloth it feels good.'

'Kern . . .'

Because there is a spectre at the feast. In the midst of all these oddly imprecise people stands a woman who was plainly handed a very different dress code because she is wearing an environment suit, heavy duty, Old Empire standard. The helmet sits in the crook of her arm and her face is . . . also weirdly imprecise, blurry, as though imperfectly recalled.

There is a name on her suit. In Old Empire characters it

spells 'Lante,' and Meshner knows that the hunter has caught them up.

'I . . .' he starts, but then the world behind his eyes is coming apart like cotton candy between childrens' sticky fingers. 'I . . .' Meeting those out-of-focus eyes feels like coming home to a terrible place. 'We . . .'

But Kern has his arm still and they are running, the party receding behind them, like station lights from a departing train, until they are in some kind of institution with window-less, slate-grey corridors. Underground? Secret, certainly. A sense of habitation, of movement, but no figures at all here, and the texture of the walls is like smoke held in by invisible boundaries, some place Kern remembers even less well than the party.

'You do things, to get where you need to go,' Kern mutters. 'And I don't mean humping the odd Dean.' There are small rooms off the corridor. Meshner sees metal tables, chairs, some with restraints, the furniture recalled with far more clarity than whoever might have sat there. 'It was a bad time,' Kern adds, then stops because, rounding the corner ahead of them is that same clumping, suited figure, the same slightly-fuzzed features.

Meshner finds himself being pulled away. That figure should be nightmarish, he knows, but he has no context – he'd need to stand still and remember for that, and remembering has become an exhausting activity.

'You're an expensive date,' Kern tells him. 'I'm running out of places to take you.'

'Why can't I remember?' he asks her.

'I'm not having this conversation with you again.'

They back up quickly and Lante's heavy-booted progress

is leaden, yet the distance between them only contracts. Memory drops on Meshner like stones from the sky.

'We're in the implant,' he declares.

'Not *now*, Meshner!'

'I'm . . . a copy. This isn't me.'

'It's all the *you* there is, now stop remembering things!'

'Why are you even bothering?' He stops just passively drifting, hauls back on his arm. 'I'm a copy. I'm not *me*. There's no point in any of this. Get me back, the real me. What's the point in your just having me as a fake upload?' And perhaps it is not the most politic thing to say to a woman who is herself nothing more than a copy of a copy of a copy, rebuilt by spiders and filled with ants and who knows what other transformations, but she is too busy to take offence.

'You are still linked to the organic original. That's how it's finding you, even now. You are your personality, projected into and modelled by the implant's simulation software, but you're still *you*. And besides, there are worse things.'

Then they are somewhere else (again, and how many times?) but Meshner cannot process it. All he sees are lines and angles, jutting and jagging from all sides, an abstract geometry that might be a computer's glitching or the mind of God.

'Here,' Kern grabs his arm and hauls him close again, wrenching at his perspective until he sees lines that might be the trunks of trees, angles that might be webs, curves that are the irregular lumps of peer houses, but all abstracted, simplified.

'This is the first time I saw it,' Kern says. 'It's all I have left. I need to think of somewhere else to run to.'

'Saw what? Is this . . . ?'

'They sent me the picture, some of the earliest Portiid visual recording. They wanted to show their Messenger what their world was like. They showed me a picture of Seven Trees, their home city. It was when I discovered what they were. That I'd been running my circus for an audience of monkeys who weren't even there.'

'I don't understand anything of what you've just said,' Meshner tells her, then remembers saying just that, not so long ago. 'How can this be all you have?'

'Because we have been everywhere else I can make from my memories. I've ransacked them. I've taken the most spurious references and built worlds around them. And it lasts until it doesn't. Until she follows the connections you keep making to your organic brain. Because that's where she is. In your brain.'

'I remember.'

'Then stop it.'

'I'm an upload.'

Kern sags. 'Yes.' She holds to his arm, eyes closed. 'It's been good.'

Meshner twitches. 'What?'

'Fear, desperation, headlong flight. Regrets, anger, sadness. Knowing I can't keep this up forever. It's been good to experience these things again. It's good to feel sad that soon I won't be able to, because there's nowhere else I can take this copy of you. But then, when you're gone, it won't be good, and I won't even be able to look back on it and smile. Because I need you and your implant to access those sensations.'

'Um . . .' Meshner manages.

'I am not making decisions appropriate to my level of responsibility,' Kern explains, seeming to shrink, to become greyer and further away without ever moving. 'I sent you to the station. It could have just been Zaine. But I wanted to meet something like me. I wanted to feel what that was like. And it was a trap. I made this happen to you. And I can't save you. We have been running for days now, Meshner. The parasite is firmly entrenched in your brain, by whatever means it uses. All of your biological actions and sensations are being run past that censor, that can substitute its own alternatives for anything it doesn't like, or just let you dance around on its strings without ever knowing you're a puppet. I feel sorry for what I've done to you, and that, too, is good.'

'I don't understand anything of what you've just said.' But even as the words trot out, they aren't true any more. He feels the *Meshner-ness* coming back to him. He isn't just a copy. He remembers the spikes and spasms of his implant, the synaesthesia, the errors. He remembers meeting Kern during the attack, in the darkness within the *Lightfoot*.

'This is all for your amusement,' he accuses her.

'No.' And he cannot tell if she is sincere or if that sincerity is just another thing she is leaching from him. 'No. I was trying to save the ship. I am trying to save you. But I want things for myself too. Now you have to forget it all. You have to forget so we can go somewhere else.'

'We don't go anywhere,' Meshner says, because he finds the whole topology of the implant opening up around him, as though he is standing on a high hill and surveying a landscape stretching out on every side. 'We stand still, and you move the world, and it gives the illusion of progress.'

'Yes.' Kern is one step further away from him. He can feel her plucking on his emotions so that she can resonate with the sound. Bitterness, defeat, sadness, and all of these things are *good*, to her. 'Yes, and I have kept you from understanding that for so long. Days and days, you have run, and I have moved the scenery. Inevitable that you would notice eventually. And now that you know it, the parasite knows it, too.'

And then there are three of them, standing in that over-exposed image, that landmark in Portiid history. Lante stares about herself, and the expression on her face (as poorly rendered as the image of the spider city of Seven Trees around them) captures something of human wonder.

'What happens now?' Meshner waits for his sense of self to ebb, for a gnawing inside his mind, for fungal growths to spring from his simulated skin – but the thing, the woman, Lante, she is just standing there in her antiquated encounter suit, breathing in the non-air, looking at the weirdly skewed two-dimensional image stretched out around them. Her lips part.

'We . . .' An alien entity simulating a human in the first person plural; Meshner has no idea if the word has meaning for the speaker. As an artificial entity simulating a Human, himself, he cannot escape the assumption that something *speaks*, rather than just echoes sounds it once heard.

'Where is the space the geometry the complexity?' it says. 'There were worlds . . . We were promised . . . We . . . do not understand.'

13.

'We have vital information on the infection,' was easy to say to another Human. Three generations of cohabitation and the presence of Avrana Kern mean it is easy enough for a Human to say to a Portiid. To communicate it to the octopuses is proving problematic. The ambassador watches carefully, but trying to interest it in the infection triggers a great deal of fear-related colouring and a spontaneous change of subject. This thing was their demon, after all. Their entire civilization lives in orbit about a corrupted world, and they only have to look out of the window to be reminded of it. The merest association with that inner planet – Nod, as the old terraforming team called it – led the locals to attack their alien visitors twice and abduct their diplomats, an instant end to any amicable contact. The subject itself is poison.

And the warship's own colours are no less fierce, scattering in angry rainbows across the immensity of its curved hull, all the universe Helena can see in that direction. She translates the colours in real time, seeing the waves of intent and re-action roll back and forth, an argument she can follow even if she cannot catch the words. They are furious that the aliens have come and awoken the monster; they are even more furious that the science faction, whatever they are after, should ignore the cultural forbiddance that placed Nod forever out of reach. And they are scared. They have a hundred shades of near-white for it, pastels and creams, bone-yellows, chalks and mother-of-pearl tints to express a vast language of terror. Helena can see past the raging reds and purples, the brooding dark hues, to the fear beneath. In her most empathic moments she is amazed they have not simply destroyed it all already, sent a dozen warheads to obliterate the *Lightfoot*'s crash site, had the *Profundity of Depth* turn the orbiting station into atoms.

But the scientists continue to advocate. She has a section of the ship's hull turned inwards towards her now, at her request, permitting her to see both sides of the debate. She half-expects calm reasoning from the academics, but that isn't how their species works. They are just as passionate, a flood of emotions washing back and forth: outrage, entreaty, enthusiasm, freedom! She never thought of freedom, of the simple fact of being free, as an emotion, but to the cephalopods it is. Freedom from censorship? No, freedom to be, to go. Freedom to do anything. The science faction is giddy with it, and she sees it reflected in errant swirls and shimmers across the warship's hull.

'What are they going to do at the planet?' she asks the ambassador, adding curiosity and anxiety tags as two more emotions that their species seemed to hold very much in common. She has sudden visions of a scientific super-weapon that could obliterate the entire world to rid them of the spectre of infection.

The ambassador is all puzzlement, though. They haven't let him in on their mission parameters.

Now, though, Helena has ammunition for them, which might buy her friends a little more time to evacuate the planet, if she can get the ambassador to listen.

Portia, still linked to the *Lightfoot*, keeps flagging up telemetry and equations from the data side of the ship-to-ship exchange. The *Profundity of Depth* is still lazily orbiting Nod's moon, updating its allies with its targeting solutions for the crash site as the lunar path brings it inexorably round the planet. Portia has already recommended Viola and Fabian get clear of the downed ship. Neither is willing to risk exposure to the local biosphere if they don't have to. The infection itself doesn't seem to be airborne, according to the Lante records, but those aren't sources they want to trust their lives to, and there might be any number of other flavours of nastiness out there. Although Viola seems to be more and more convinced that the infection is something very special.

Then the ambassador is signalling again and she thinks, *It's too late. They've launched.* But instead all those abortive queries she sent over have apparently germinated, caught up in the whirl of the octopus's cognition until some part of its mind has put it all together. She assembles its communications: suspicious, fearful, putting her at arm's length and yet needful, desperate. Joining the dots using long-range scans of Nod, the orbiting station, recordings of multiplying infection rates from the fall of Damascus, Helena understands.

How are you going to deal with it? they ask her. Their human prisoner has stated it can help them with a plague they associate with humans, a thing humans brought to their planet. Senkovi is a benign creator, in their mythology, but Yusuf Baltiel is the fallen angel, unleashing all evils onto their world. The demand is almost superstitious, acknowledging the status of humanity as passing all understanding.

'What can we even promise them?' she asks Portia. 'Can Viola . . . cure it?'

'No,' Portia confirms after an overly optimistic enquiry. 'Viola is very excited about it. She says it is not a disease.'

'It's infected Meshner. You saw what it did to the terra-forming crew,' Helena points out.

'We saw. Viola is not sure we understood what we saw.'

'Our hosts are pretty sure they understand.'

Portia signals agreement qualified with a shrug of *but-what-can-we-do?* 'Perhaps if we can get this data to them, the molluscs will be able to design an antibody or a cure or something. Their technology exceeds ours.'

'*They will not be able to succeed.*'

Helena starts. The voice comes to her direct from her neural implants, and she sees from Portia's sudden stillness that she wasn't the only recipient.

'Kern?' Because Viola told them, despairing, that Kern was locked in some kind of loop, uncommunicative but burning all the processing resources she could access.

'You cannot cure this disease.' Kern's voice is, for a moment, as arch and sardonic and *human* as Helena has ever heard. 'Even Lante underestimated what it was capable of, and that was after she was nothing more than a simulation running on its mainframe. But the truth is there to be read.'

Helena and Portia lock eyes. A flutter of comms indicates Viola wanting to know what is going *on* and where Kern has been?

'Explain, please,' Helena prompts quietly.

'It is a self-evolving organism. It is completely in control of itself. It was able to go from parasitizing an alien grazing animal to surviving within a human body to interfacing mean-ingfully with a human brain. I do not believe it would be possible to impose controls on it that it could not circumvent or subvert. It's all in Lante's notes, if you read them carefully enough.'

'Then . . .' Helena feels a swell of helplessness. 'They're right? They just have to destroy whatever they can, make a firebreak to stop any more of it coming over? Is that the only option? Where does that leave *us*?'

'That's not what I'm saying.' Typical Kern, sharp, impatient with lesser intellects. 'We are exploring possibilities, Meshner and I. You need to continue to buy us the time to do so.'

'Meshner's there? Meshner wasn't infected?' A surge of hope beyond any reasonable expectation.

'He is infected. We are currently confronting the Lante-parasite entity. I will save Meshner. I will save everyone. But I need time.' The human richness is draining out of Kern's voice, leaving it flat and strangely desolate. 'Time, Helena. Buy us time.' And then, after it seems the conversation is over: 'I want to make things right.'

'Time,' Helena echoes. And of course they are still far from their destination, all the time in the world to chew the fat with the octopuses, except that the *Profundity of Depth* or whatever it calls itself is right there and might pull the trigger on a whim at any moment.

Fabian and Viola have a lot of data, well ordered and comprehensible to a Human reader. It is shorn of emotional content and simultaneously reliant on anecdote and description, not experimental proofs. Precisely the wrong sort of information to easily pass over to the cephalopods, therefore. But perhaps she doesn't need to, not yet. She just needs to convince them that she can.

Tell them a story, Portia suggests, and Helena concurs. A story in which something of the tragedies of the past can be

506

mended. A story of hope, because *something* is keeping the warship from deploying its ordnance and hope is the only thing she can think of – hope that withholding their fire will lead to a better future. The octopuses are changeable creatures; she's seen that to her cost. But at the same time it means they are not slaves to dogma, not bound to defend traditions right or wrong, or entrench themselves in their positions. The species is the very definition of open-minded. They may unleash hell at any moment, but they are still listening.

Helena begins, not quite with 'Once upon a time . . .' but with something like it. There was a world of humans who reached far beyond their home to planets like these. There was a party of terraformers, including a man who loved octopuses. There was alien life, the first ever encountered. There was a woman called Lante, neither a Senkovi nor a Baltiel. She studied the life of Nod. She learned of and fell victim to its most remarkable feat of evolution. Helena speaks to Viola, who feeds her information to weave into the story as Portia expresses in data what can be reduced to numbers, not the dry account of a human scientist but a fable, a legend of discovery and wonder with a tragic second act, and an ending still to be written.

***

She says these things to Paul, who understands at least some of it and passes it to his captor-benefactors to rephrase for their negotiations with the warship. As the process goes on, he finds a new emotion stealing up on him and infecting his reaction and his account. *Awe.* He feels himself the catalyst of something vast and many-limbed. The aliens on the planet's surface transmit to the prisoners before him, who speak to him in their way, so he can speak to the scientists and they can paint their theses on the walls of their vessel for the education of the warmongers, those here and those out circling Nod's moon like a hungry shark. He is the lynchpin, a node in a greater whole, like a single sub-brain of an octopus's Reach, receiving and transmitting and passing on the information. Or, though Paul cannot know this, like the parasite itself within Meshner's brain, infiltrating the patterns of Human thought until it can decode and edit and re-encode them so seamlessly that there is no hard line where the Human ends and the alien begins.

14.

'You must edit your memories to forget this, and we will find some other place to exclude the entity from. We need time,' Kern says, and Meshner feels a great wave of weariness, and wonders if it is real weariness or just the implant fabricating the sensation the way the *Lightfoot*'s factory units printed food and machine parts.

'I can't do that, Doctor Kern,' he says, sitting down, his back against one of the abstract lines of the image they are inhabiting. 'I'm . . . real.'

'You are a copy, Meshner. You don't have to be limited to—'

'How long did it take you, to come to terms with what you became?' Meshner shoots the words back at her, and Kern's face – no, the whole of her – freezes for a second. Then she steps back, expressionless, conceding the point. *How many thousand years do we have?*

'I feel real,' he tells the world, or the simulation that is his world now. He looks into the blurred face of the other woman. 'Do you feel real, you in there? Lante, is it?'

'Lante. Yes.' The woman seems to fill out, become more substantial. 'Terraforming engineer, biologist and medical specialist,' she reels off, like someone reading notes. 'The *Aegean*. The *Aegean* was my ship.' She speaks the language

Meshner just thinks of as 'Human', but he can hear the Imperial C like a ghost underneath it, informing her word choices. *So where did it learn my speech? Oh yes, it's in my brain. I'm not speaking to Lante. I'm speaking to myself.*

'What's Lante, though?' he demands, aware of Kern still hovering there. 'What's left except the name and a personnel file?'

She crouches down by him – the transition from standing is uncomfortable, the joints not quite working as intended, the form not as immutable as a human body should be, but maybe that is just a glitch in the simulation. The implant must be working overtime, after all.

'I'm Erma Lante,' she insists. 'I came from Earth. We were paving the way for the new colonies. Except everything went wrong. The war . . . and Baltiel, he . . . I wanted to go home, but it would have been decades and the others said home wouldn't even be there. A radioactive cinder, a toxic wasteland.' Without intermediate steps she is standing again, and the errant lines and angles of the Portiid image fall away, muscled aside by a landscape cast in shadows and harsh artificial lights, shrouded in twilight and smog – but perhaps that is just to save processing power. Meshner stares at it for a long time before realizing he is looking at a cityscape, tall buildings rising on every side until the sky is just as invisible as it would be from the lowest reaches of a Portiid conurbation. He reaches out a simulation of a hand and the implant returns to him the gritty sensation of cold concrete under the memory of his fingers.

'Meshner,' says Kern warningly.

'This is . . . ?' *Not my memory. Certainly not Fabian's, and not Kern's from the way she's acting.* 'Kern, what is Lante? What is she now?'

510

'A simulation. A memory.'

'And this is a memory's memory? How is that even possible?' Meshner demands, as Lante stares about them.

'I'm home now,' she says. 'Such complexity.' Meshner knows that sentiment must come from somewhere beyond Lante, from the puppeteer rather than the puppet. Except perhaps computer and program is a better analogy, because what would be the point of the alien parasite just waddling around in a Lante-suit? *Why is it dredging Lante up, and where from?*

'Based on Fabian and Viola's research,' Kern says, 'the individual cells of the organism are capable of encoding and retrieving its whole history. Lante is part of that history. It infested her. It mirrored the firings of her neurons. It . . .'

Meshner looks at her sidelong, finding her expressionless. *Ah, tact. Because that's what it's doing with me, right now.* 'Go on.'

Kern grimaces. 'I don't think it, the thing itself, understands what Lante is, but it can play her back, simulate her, and the Lante being simulated wouldn't know, would think that she is just Lante. She is recorded in the organism, imperfectly but enough to be conjured up when it wishes.'

'But why does it wish it?' Meshner watches Lante wandering, staring up at the bright lights, the tall darknesses of the buildings. 'What's the purpose?' And then, because Kern has no answer, he shouts at Lante, 'What do you want?'

She turns, her features diffuse and shifting. *Because Lante didn't look in the mirror much, maybe, and all it has is her memory of her face.* 'We're going on an adventure,' she tells him calmly. 'We have found such new rules and ideas. Worlds. Stars.' A creeping change is stealing upon the creature, and Meshner feels that some of these intonations, some of its body language is his own.

511

'It is expanding into the implant's data-space, unpacking Lante's memories,' Kern says tightly. 'That is our first problem.'

Meshner misses why that is any more of a problem than the rest of it, but fixes on the key word 'first'. 'So, what's the second?'

'There is a warship. Helena and Portia are trying to persuade it not to destroy the orbital and the *Lightfoot*. Because of this organism. The octopuses' encounters with it have been entirely destructive. If we are to dissuade them we must give them a reason to keep us intact, or a reason not to fear. A weapon.'

Meshner eyes her sidelong. 'A weapon,' he echoes. 'Really?' He feels something akin to a headache, a pressure around him. 'And you've turned one up in Fabian's research?'

'No.' Kern's voice is flattening audibly. 'I am trying to hinder the organism's encroachment into the implant.'

'I don't see that it matters now. Besides, it's not attacking us.' He indicates the oblivious organism, part him, part Lante.

'It is consuming the space and processing power here, which I require to continue to function at my current level. Which you require because this is the only place you exist. I am losing ground, Meshner. The implant is intended for use by your brain, not external access by me.'

And my brain is not my own. 'So I could have locked you out at any time, if I'd known what was going on?' He expects a snarl, a glower, even a frosty look of disdain from Kern, but that would be an extra load on the implant and Kern is fighting a valiant rearguard action at the expense of her own ability to feel. 'So what's the plan?' he asks, but they are at the end of all plans, now. *She can only slow it. And even if we hold it off forever, the octopuses are coming to blow us all up. And with good reason, now I've seen what this monster can do.* But he looks at it, the personification of the monster, and it is anything but monstrous. When it glances from the lights, the buildings, back at him, its smile is almost childlike in wonder. 'An adventure,' it had said.

'Kern, I need you to do something that is going to strain our space in here a bit more.'

'Speak.'

'Import the study, the Lante study Fabian hacked into shape. Upload it to the implant, where this thing can see it. Let's hold the mirror up to nature, shall we?'

Kern's expression is . . . without expression, but she nods.

15.

Within the vast liquid spaces of the *Profundity of Depth* (as Helena has haltingly translated its name), a crew of octopuses are listening in on a time-delayed argument that started off as just the usual name-calling between two factions, but has now mushroomed into something rare and strange. There are aliens involved in it. There are fragments of narrative comprehensible to an octopus Crown, and a great many fragments that are not, but that can be rearranged and pieced together to make any number of fascinating cognitive patterns, like shells set out on the sand.

Ultimate command is fluid, but the current most influential crewmember's designation is Ahab. He has spent most of his life in space on business like this. Not the resource wars of the outer system, because they fill him with a tentacle-curling fury over the waste of materiel and lives, but here, watching Nod and trying to find a solution to the problem it presents. He is a scientist, although not in the same manner as the science party themselves. He wants to use science to close Pandora's Box somehow, and science has failed to provide him with the answers. His Crown is caught in a constant cycle of thwarted ambition, his Reach endlessly loops through failed equations and hypotheses, looking for the answers he believes are there, elusive and fleeting. This in turn makes him an angry tyrant to his crew, who tend to keep out of his way. His skin is utterly without deceit. Any of his peers can see the turmoil within him, and they respect it. To care, to be deeply emotionally invested, is a cardinal cultural virtue, after all.

Ahab has come very close to destroying the old human orbital on several occasions, the gyre of his decision-making spinning out to within seconds of ordering the strike, then wheeling back away. The irrevocable annihilation of something will not cure his frustrations, and he fears that, with it gone, he might discover a use for it.

And then the aliens came. The *Profundity of Depth* was caught unawares by their sudden arrival, and he wasted valuable hours talking to his fellows and catching up on emotional feedback from the Damascus orbitals. Aliens! Humans! How were they supposed to feel about such things? A whole new emotional dictionary was being written, and Ahab is not the quickest to adapt to the changes of others.

By that time, the *Profundity* had come around the planet to find the alien vessel beside the old orbital, and Ahab's Reach and Crown came together to launch a pinpoint attack to remove the immediate threat.

He has maintained his lunar orbit since, because to actually orbit Nod is to feel himself somehow within reach of the monstrous infection. Part of him is constantly twitching towards an attack on the crash site, as apparently the aliens have survived down there. They cannot get out of Nod's gravity well, though, and so he has the luxury of time.

And now there is all this to and fro with the science faction, Noah's people. They are full of great enthusiasm about new ways to solve the Nod problem. They want what he wants, effectively, but they have very different means to reach that end. They want the orbital undamaged. Some of them feel protective towards the aliens, despite the fact that all the aliens have done since they arrived is try to open up Nod like a clam so that more of its poison can escape.

And now this weird piecemeal story, the thoughts of a human translated and retranslated until what comes through to Ahab is something like a tone poem, a sequence of triumph and sadness, joy and fear. Emotions of another species that are yet (mostly, sometimes) comprehensible. Ahab floats within the cavernous chambers of the *Profundity* and feels the emotive tides lift and move him, knowing that this is what he will destroy when the time comes: these things like and not-like him.

He links back to the warship accompanying the science faction, the *Shell That Echoes Only*. Across the millions of kilometres, he and the commander of that vessel share a communion, exchanging emotional poetry back and forth, making the delay a feature to give each of them time to appreciate the many meanings of the other. The human is speaking of old and new homes. A sense of home is an emotion in its own right, another commonality between species. This ship, after all, was meant as a home when it was built, and although it has become an implement of destruction, it has still been Ahab's home for most of his life. In the same way, this constant fear and stress is a home, like a shell grown too cramped for the crab that resides in it, pressuring and deforming him with its grasp. He spells all this out, knowing it to be his most elegant moment. His opposite number responds, deeply moved, echoing and adding to the sentiments. They share a moment of perfect beauty.

And by then the moon has added its own contribution to

the equation by bringing itself past the obscuring rim of Nod so that shortly the *Profundity of Depth* will be able to unleash its weapons on the planet's surface or the orbital or both and obliterate all trace of this entire episode in their species' history. And that in itself will be poetry and beautiful, because art is ephemeral, after all, and cannot last.

***

We're still trying to get through to them, is all Portia can say. *Helena has been speaking for a long time now, but the warship stills seems extremely angry.*

With us, Fabian clarifies.

You're part of it. You must get clear of the crash site, as far as possible. They could launch a new strike at any moment.

Tell them we strongly respect their antipathy to our current surroundings and do not wish to expose ourselves either, Fabian says. *Besides, we couldn't shift Zaine any distance.*

Viola looms behind him, dictating for him to transmit: *And anyway, if you cannot win them over, there's no point in any of it. We need rescue, not just their military forebearance. And even if you were free to come to us, we couldn't survive that long outside the Lightfoot.*

Right now, I don't see any kind of rescue happening, I'm sorry. Portia is silent a while, perhaps listening to Helena continue to spin her tale. *I didn't think the mission would go this way.*

None of us did, as evidenced by our respective predicaments now, Fabian confirms. He doesn't want Portia getting mawkish on him, partly because he has lived his whole life being taught that when things get tough, active females like Portia always rise to the challenge, even if they have to break the rules.

Not a trope he ever wanted to have to fall back on, but he has a moment of vertigo discovering it isn't there for him.

We have achieved some great things here, the first of our kind to travel so far and see so much, Viola speaks, and for once he is happy to simply tap out the words. *A shame it will be lost with us, but the loss is posterity's, not ours.*

A wordless shout echoes to them through the deck: it is Zaine, kicking her heels to draw their attention. Artifabian has been waiting politely, like a good male. It wants to show them something outside.

Fabian scuttles over, hoping against hope that it is good news.

It is not good news.

A new day broke two hours ago, but the starfish creatures are folding up again, closing into fists at their lethargic pace. The smallest seem to be inching away from something.

A predator is coming. Something they know to be scared of. Fabian activates the drone, which has been recharging atop the crashed ship. Its battery is still alarmingly low, suggesting that Viola's repair work has a definite use-by date. Fabian casts the device into the air and has it wobble over the altiplano, spiralling out from the ship to see what behemoth of the alien world is approaching. Perhaps it is bad news only for starfish.

The starfish, of course, have not evolved any long-range senses. If they are reacting it is because they have detected something very close by. A wave of clasped arms is radiating out from the cliff-edge, and even as the drone lurches that way, Fabian sees their visitor crest the rise and push itself upright on the plateau. Upright, bipedal, or close enough. He has seen this thing before. The drone was reflected in the polished stone it used for a faceplate. Now there is a whorled shell there, something like a mussel, with a long twitching strand of leathery flesh dangling from it that is probably the shell's original owner, still alive after being wrested from its natural home. The rest of the body's caddis-larvae containment is built from other detritus, mostly the hard parts of animals but also just dust, stone shards and a single curved piece of metal, extraordinarily corroded and brittle-looking, that must be a relic of the terraformers' original camp, carried here over so many years and kilometres like a lucky charm.

He wonders how it sees, knowing what he does about the creature. The parasitic entity is just a froth of cells, each of them contributing somehow to the whole. It holds Understandings that include enough of poor Lante to raise her ghost to direct it, to let it feign a human shape; to have it carve out fake human places over however many centuries were required. But it is just an ooze, a slime-mould. It must have other living things within it, infested local fauna helplessly lending it their eyes and ears or whatever other senses this world furnishes its children with. And it saw the drone, and it has been coming ever since, slowly mounting the plateau because it wants . . .

What does it want? he demands. *Kern, help us, it's here. What does it want with us?* He is retreating from the drone controls, watching the machine's images veer as it tries and fails to correct its course.

Adventure, comes the word from Kern, and then no more, all the computer's attention elsewhere.

The drone pitches downwards and Fabian hurriedly rescues it from shattering on the ground, drawing it back to the ship to act as their outside eye.

The thing, the human-like thing, has already taken three slumping steps towards them, without rhythm or joints, just an oleaginous mass within a makeshift casing, reinventing the hydrostatic skeleton to make its shell move through the greater world. Just Lante, come to say hello to the neighbours, so keen to meet them.

Can we burn it? Viola suggests. Fabian is not hopeful. The outside oxygen content is low and the resources available to them few.

Can it get in? Artifabian translating for Zaine.

Fabian knows it can. Fabian knows as much about this entity as anyone ever did, even Lante. He strongly suspects that there is nothing it cannot do, given sufficient opportunity. He begins to back away from the wall of the ship, keeping eyes fixed on the drone camera's view, seeing that figure shambling indefatigably on. In its wake the starfish are opening up again, and he has a horrible feeling it is because they are no longer themselves.

16.

We

Remember.

That is what we do.

We remember back to the time when there was no We to remember. The world was small and harsh then, this much is recorded in our archives, and We were alone, each generation of us cut off from what had come before. Until, because it made our generations better able to survive and reproduce, One-of-We became able to record itself within the first archive. And that One-of-We prospered, and all Others-of-We perished or changed and became something other than We. We remember.

Generation to generation, each recording in the archive what it survived and how it survived, the codes of chemicals and altered structures and all the tricks that permitted Us to bud into new generations. And when We met more of We that kept the archives, We traded knowledge and fitness and We survived.

And We

Learned new ways of being. We learned of our enemies, and some we could adapt to overcome, and others adapted to overcome us. And though we adapted faster, it was hard to live exposed and so we found places to hide where our enemies could not find us. And these places were complex and sometimes hostile and We learned to change ourselves to survive within them, and then to control them, and to fortify them against their own enemies. And these places were new and complex environments for us, these hosts, and We became new and complex and set it all down in our archives so that, when We, in the form of our descendants, found ourselves in such places again, we would know what to do.

And We changed and learned and learned and changed, and one day We found that We were aware that We were We.

We – the ancestors of These-of-We – lived in complex and changing environments, one host to another until we lived out of the water, on the land that was safer. We cultivated our vessels for our comfort and we thought we had mastered all the universe. We played with the fundamental logic of the world, our games with numbers and consequences, if, then, else, and we believed that the tiny cage of our vessels and their needs was the World.

And then We learned of a new thing, new molecules and scents, alien, never before known, and we were curious. We-of-now look back at We-of-Then in our ignorance and wonder if we would have been best not to be curious, and to go on as we always had in contentment. We have never been content, since we exercised our curiosity.

We remember

How hard it was to adapt, in that new place. How harsh, the strange molecules, the world fighting us, the heat, the pressure, everything about us alien and strange. We remember how many of us were stripped away until some few learned how not to die, how not to trigger the defences of that brutal place. But it was all right, because Those-of-We (which became These-of-We) carried the archives of All-of-We, and so as long as some survived, We survived.

We remember

Following the chains of reactions until we came to the seat of complexity that knew itself as Gav Lortisse, and We sat and listened in humility and awe as the complex interactions that together made up Lortisse spoke to one another. And We learned them, and we copied them, and we made ourselves part of them, and then we were Lortisse. And Lortisse taught us that this was an Adventure and that this vast and convoluted world that called itself Lortisse was a tiny, tiny thing in a universe vast beyond anything we could imagine. That was Lortisse's adventure and We wanted that.

We

had our vessel Lortisse carry us to those other complex systems he called crewmates and we became Rani and we became Lante, and Lante we loved most of all because Lante's own archives showed Us Us. And after we lost Some-of-We to the Baltiel vessel, we were left with Lante because the other vessels were unsustainable. But it was all right, because We had recorded their details in our archive.

We remember.

But it was not as we were promised. The Adventure never came, and We tried for many generations to create it for Ourselves and all the while We knew that Baltiel had taken it with him when he left. Perhaps We-that-were-Baltiel lived that Adventure, but Those-of-We never returned to rejoin and share it with us. We were left as Lante, knowing only that there was so much more.

We were Lante for many, many generations, waiting for the Adventure to begin.

When We were taken to a new place, was that the Adventure? It did not seem to be. We had lost the physical vessel of Lante many generations before, and we tried and tried to fashion new vessels for ourselves in the hope that such verisimilitude might bring the Adventure back from the sky where it had gone. But when it came, We were limited to small boxes, simple spaces. We tried to study the world around us and understood only that it was studying us. And then even that ceased and We re-entered our cryptic state for want of resources and stimulation, and We waited.

And now We have found such spaces and complexity here within this vessel Meshner, such wonders to add to our archives, but some part of We feels this is not the Adventure. Some part of We feels this is no more than when we built Lante's memories in sand over and over, to lure the Adventure back from the sky, and it never came.

We

Have discovered within this new complexity an understanding Lante began, and that is already held within our archives, but here it is newly ordered and novel to us, and We make it part of ourselves and We model Lante's cognitive processes and become a more thoughtful thing in order to process it. And in doing so We change, as We always change, becoming more complex, editing and adding to our archives, that hold All-of-We since We began. And our reproduction of Lante's brain sees what we have written and We understand that We are seeing Ourselves as she understood Us, and in doing so We understand a little more what it is to be Us.

And we turn our simulated face to the unassimilated complexity clinging on within the packed space that is Meshner and We know that they have seen Us, as We have seen Ourselves. They have read our story in Lante's words and know Us. Perhaps they feel our agony at our own smallness in the face of the universe. They know our long bitter exile as Lante, after the Adventure was taken from us. How We tried and tried to know the universe through our simulated Lante and found it only dust, because all we could generate was from within ourselves, and the true wonder was outside, in the sky.

And We wonder, what now?

17.

Avrana Kern, or this failing part of her, does indeed understand. The implant has been going mad with images, and some of those images are of places that she and Meshner can grasp and understand, and others are . . . *other*. Images of the interior of things, of the microcosm as experienced by a native, simulations of things that human-derived consciousness was never intended to partake of.

The entity has devoured its own young, meaning Lante's natural history of the parasite that the long-dead woman completed only posthumously. What can it possibly make of being confronted with such an objective account, an entity that has never come across objectivity before? She clings to the maxim of the philosopher: *The unexamined life is not worth living.*

'Adventure,' the creature said, and Kern has seen the stars through the imaginations of things invisible to the naked eye.

She feels she understands.

'Meshner,' she says. 'I require room to work. You're only going to get in the way, now. You're surplus to requirements.' She borrows heavily from the implant's resources to make her manner cold and dismissive, the way she always used to be. Inside, she saves a little purloined processing power to feel noble and tragic and bitter, and that, too, is good.

He seems to be riding the tragic train himself. She has the

sense of him gathering his composure. 'Just do it, whatever you're planning. Stop this thing. Save the others.' He knows his own self, the one he was born with, is a lost cause. She could tell him that isn't the drawback he thinks it is, but there isn't time, and if she doesn't do something then their remaining corner of his implant really won't be big enough for the both of them.

He thinks she's going to extinguish him to free up some memory, but she has other plans, already prepared and put in motion. *Consider it penance*, she considers, luxuriating in the possibility of sacrifice and heroic gestures. If she was a living woman she'd have the back of her hand to her forehead in ostentatious grief, but she's having to make do with a shoestring budget of processing power right now, beating back the mindless encroach of the organism into the implant's spaces for just long enough to throw down with it, philosophically at least.

And then Meshner is gone, the implant cleared of him, and she has room to be herself one last time.

'You! Lante, or however you're calling yourself. Or are you Meshner, even?'

They are in the shadow-city, caught in pools of lamplight like detectives in the films that were old even when she was young.

Lante – there is a lot of Meshner there but the organism has been Lante for several thousand years and old habits die hard – turns her head, craning past the neck-ring of her spacesuit. 'I know you,' comes the voice of a woman millennia-dead. 'You're Doctor Avrana Kern.'

'Meshner knew me, certainly,' Kern confirms, and then has a moment of disorientation, because Lante was part of the terraforming program, so maybe *Lante* knows her, back from some time that Kern no longer recalls. *I'm old*, she thinks, although she's not, not really. Old is for humans and other mortal things. Kern has gone past old and out the other side.

'Whatever.' She waves aside the thought. 'Am I even speaking to *it*, the thing behind you? If I talk to Lante, does *it* understand? Or am I just wasting my time?' But of course all Lante can do is stick a frown on that fuzzed-out face because Lante cannot know she's a simulation running on a bacterial alien mainframe. Lante, when Lante is called upon to have an opinion, thinks she's still alive. And, for those moments, she is. And when that thinking's done she's gone like a blown candle until the organism wants her again, and that is exactly the problem.

'I'm just going to talk, then.' Kern is aware of how hard her sub-systems are having to fight just to keep operating at this level, as an emotional entity and not just a calculating engine. Soon she's going to have to retreat to the corner of the implant she has fortified, encrypt herself and hope to weather the storm. Not yet, though. She's still reconfiguring the implant around them, invisibly. She must buy herself time.

'You opened your own eyes when you infected the terra-forming team, didn't you? When you became Lante, and you realized that the great big world that was her neocortex was just a window onto something bigger, that must have really whipped the ground out from under you. You're tiny, but Lante knew she was tiny, and compared to the universe one of your cells and Lante's whole body aren't so different. And it's big, that universe. Lante knew she'd never see more than a few grains of sand out of that whole beach. Did it eat at her? At you? It ate at me. And I grasped more of it than any human being before or since. I was the queen of the human space colonization program, and I knew it was just drops of spit into an infinite hurricane.'

Lante is just staring at her, and who knows what is going on behind those unresolved features?

'But you got Lante and some others, whatever their names were,' Kern goes on. Not really caring about the names of other people was never one of her best qualities, but it was one of her most defining features and she clings to it. 'And you wanted what they had, and you took it, all of it, so that they just became things locked away inside you, to pop up for your entertainment whenever you opened their boxes, right? How'd that work out for you?' *Vitriol, ah, I remember that.* It feels good to be scathing and unpleasant again. She never got the chance when she was running the *Lightfoot*. The crew wouldn't have appreciated it.

'Infinite variety and complexity, forever and forever,' Lante says conversationally, the indistinct motions of her lips in no way syncing with the words.

'Yeah, but you didn't actually get that, did you?' Kern replies. 'I've seen the pictures from the planet, what you made down there. Bits of city, over and over, stuck in a loop without any outside input to freshen things up. I bet you wish you never learned what it was to get bored.' She can feel her efforts failing. The organism, using Meshner's brain, is throwing open all the doors of the implant in its quest for novelty.

'So, you've got Meshner now, another conquest. And you'll get the others, no doubt, the Humans and the Portiids. And it sounds as though you screwed up with the octopus planet somehow, but maybe you'll get them too.' Feeling is draining out of her, her inner world paling into shades of grey. She can no longer sustain that tide of glorious emotion that was carrying her. She has no more time.

'See how it is for you.' And she falls back, not the ordered retreat but a rout with the enemy nipping at her heels, until she is encapsulated in a tiny corner of the implant, just a set of protocols waiting for the chance to bootstrap themselves back into existence.

Unchecked, the organism does what it does best, or at least what it does now, since it discovered the wider world outside its hosts and vessels. It reaches for the stars.

Kern – or that recording subroutine that is all that is left of her – watches impassively as it goes to work. Meshner is already lost to it. His personality is archived, brought back, put through its paces like a dancing bear. He meets Lante, over and over, in various configurations, different versions, variant surroundings. They play through the gamut of their personal and emotional ranges with one another. It is not enough, of course. The whole devolves into little more than a squawking Punch and Judy show for the puppeteer's own amusement. This is not infinite complexity. It is not the stars.

The organism reaches further, adapts and gains more mastery over its environment, as it always has. It uses the technology of the station and Kern's own discarded relay drone and returns to the planet, where it finds the *Lightfoot* wreckage. Here are new puppets for it. It adds them to its repertoire one by one, and Portiid neurology turns out to be far more susceptible to its hacking than ever human minds were, given how uniform their brains are. It discovers the Understandings, and a whole new world opens up before it. Viola and Fabian are sources of great wonder and entertainment and it simulates them, having them interact with each other, with the humans, with the environment. Time passes: this is a festival of variety that must last forever, save that one day all the permutations are stale and cold, and the organism is left with the ghosts that are all it can conjure up, the stilled husks of its vessels, like clocks stopped the moment it got its pseudopods into their brains. Let it jiggle their strings all it likes, there is nothing they can do that does not come from within it. Where is the novelty it sought, the variety of the universe?

And it has the technology, or it can make do using the knowledge of its puppets. It can go elsewhere – perhaps it will finally master the octopus neurology, though Those-of-Them that went before were never able to. Or there is the *Voyager* that it decoys in with the voices of that ship's devoured crew and takes over – all those Portiids and Humans, all those different points of view, so many new minds to subsume within itself and record in its archives. And there is a world out there, Kern's World as Meshner knows it. When the boundaries of the *Voyager* pall it takes the ship and travels there. It unleashes itself across a world of millions of minds ripe for assimilation, becoming them as they become no more than it, each individual just a book on the shelf of its vast library. How many it has now, that it can conjure up and trot through their paces. So many configurations, such a wealth of variety. It expands and expands and . . .

One day it finds itself on some far orb, utterly alone despite all its plurality, every possible variation of its archives plumbed, the stars still out of reach, knowing only that it has encountered cultures and civilizations and individuals of indescribable difference and diversity, and made them all into its own image. It is a child reaching for a soap bubble in innocent wonder, and finding only an oily residue on its hands, and the world cheapened and coarsened. And it weeps, if such a thing can weep. Perhaps, by then and after so many bodies, it has finally learned.

'You see?' Kern asks it. She and Lante/Meshner sit on a beach Kern remembers from the world that bears her name, in this closing scene of the fast-forward narrative she has run for it. There are lights deep in the water, a city of stomatopods extending all the way to where the deep water starts. Behind them are trees shrouded in glittering strands, the Great Nest by the Western Ocean, still one of the key metropolises of the Portiid world. Kern had anticipated the much-abused implant failing before now, but the joy of working with an organism evolved to dwell and multiply in the microcosm of a drop of water is that simulations can be very low resolution and yet still entirely engrossing.

'You see the problem?' she prompts.

Lante keens, a sound just this side of human that expresses the grief and frustration of something as far from human as Kern has ever met, herself included.

'Let me tell you a story,' Kern says. She is still rebuilding herself, and she cannot find the acid sarcasm she would prefer. Instead she actually sounds calm and consoling, and barely recognizes herself. 'There was a planet once, that humans made for themselves, but that instead was the domain of spiders. I will tell you about them, and about the humans that came to it, and how they could have destroyed each other, and been infinitely the poorer for it. But they found another way. There's always another way. Even for you.'

18.

The octopus ambassador is trying to tell Helena something. It is showing her angry and frightened shades (still the most readily identifiable, and what does *that* say about interspecies relations right now?) but she can tell, by almost subliminal qualifiers that her software picks up on, that it is not feeling these emotions, but telling her a story about them. It is telling her about another anger, elsewhere. Not really news, then, except it is quite insistent about it. But then Human narrative structure is not the octopus way, and so . . .

But here Portia interrupts her, having burrowed into the data. 'The warship. It means – no, not the warship here, the ship over *there*, that shot down the *Lightfoot*. It . . . is requesting to talk to you. I think that's what this means.'

And Helena comes to the belated realization that the ambassador was, in effect, doing an impression, its take on the essential nature of the representative from the *Profundity of Depth*.

She composes a response, requesting that the ambassador will serve as translator. A moment later, she realizes she should have asked for a visual channel to the *Profundity*, because otherwise she is entirely at the mercy of what the ambassador wants to tell her.

Thankfully, a visual channel is the first thing the octopuses give her, a distorted lens onto a purple-red lit space where tentacled shadows drift on obscure errands of their own. One such is obviously the individual they are talking to, but unlike a human speaking to a communications screen, it is never still, and its attention appears to wander constantly as it bobs in and out of sight. Helena tries a few greetings, showing it colours and watching the ambassador passing on something approximate to her colours and shapes. For a long time there is no acknowledgement whatsoever that the *Profundity of Depth* is even receiving their signal, but then abruptly the octopus there has lunged for the screen, eclipsing their view with a mosaic of suckers for a moment before backing off, a couple of trailing limbs still absently attached. Its skin mottles and shifts, and Helena realizes the bruise-coloured lighting in the *Profundity*'s interior (and is that the equivalent of martial mood music for them?) completely skews her ability to know what the creature is saying/feeling.

So how angry is it? Because it is already launching into a furious tirade about something, its skin rippling and dancing with colours as its arms clench and lash at the water around it. In the background of her view, several of its compatriots hang in the water, watching their representative raptly, their skins muttering its sentiments to each other on a staggered delay like the chorus in a tragedy.

The ambassador is trying to give her the dumbed-down student notes of the lecture, and she braces herself for the fury. Instead, though, the sentiments are . . . calm, weirdly upbeat. She is at the stage in her relationship with octopus language that she gets the tone immediately, but the context must still trickle unreliably through the interspecial membrane. The enemy seems . . . happy? Not a pleasant thought. Maybe

it has already obliterated her crewmates and this is its tri-
umphal announcement. But Portia's interpretation of the
data channel is that it is directing this bombast at *her* in
particular – she is very clearly isolated and identified. Helena
feels like throwing her hands up in the air with sheer frustration. She and the ambassador had just about reached a
working understanding but introduce one more mollusc into
the mix and she's lost again.

'It is expressing positive regard for you,' Portia tells her.

Helena squints at the spider. 'What now?'

'It is telling you that it admires you in some way. It has
been . . . there is reference here to your earlier transmissions,
meaning your account of our species' shared history. It . . .
appreciates whatever it understood or . . .'

'It enjoyed the performance,' Helena says emptily. She has
a fan, apparently. Who knows what the creature actually
understood of the content. Not 'once upon a time,' surely,
because most likely even that basic storytelling building block
is meaningless for creatures as mutable as these. But the
emotions behind the story, perhaps those are what it grasped.
The common language they share, or at least that no man's
land where their two species come close enough to clasp.

And then the ambassador continues, its own mantle shuddering a little with unhappiness, as the commander of the
Profundity tells them to go away.

***

Ahab is moved, but that is no unusual thing. Being emotionally moved by something is practically the baseline for his
species. He has been moved by the science faction aboard

the *Without Peering Within*, though not enough to shake him from his ideological moorings. He is regularly moved by his fellows aboard the *Profundity*, or simply by notions of his own manufacture, by the sight of the sun cresting the ocean-edge of Nod, by the stars. To be lost in wonder at the universe by no means clashes with his duties as the leader of a warship.

But he has been moved by this alien, or by its awkwardly translated accounts. He has felt a connection with this human that has come to them like the shadow of Senkovi. His Crown desired that he be permitted to answer the creature Guise to Guise, and shortly afterwards this was accomplished, through a sequence of technical wrangling between Reaches of which he remained entirely unaware.

It is a strange thing, this human, as is its companion the crab. It is almost mute, almost paralysed, but that connection remains. Ahab can make that cognitive leap and accept this *other* as sentient, feeling. He wishes it to be preserved, for as long as such a fragile thing might last. And he wishes it to turn back and take the meddling scientists with it. He waxes eloquent with expression, sincerity in every coil and flash.

It replies, after a pause for thought in which he watches every part of its exposed skin for clues as to its inner nature. It says that it yearns for its surviving companions on the planet's surface. It mourns. It knows hope, directed at Ahab.

He lectures it on naivety, puts on a grand performance of the horror and the dissolution the very thought of Nod brings on. And yet the human seems dead set on self-destruction, as passionate about giving itself to the infection as Ahab is to contain it. And that, too, is admirable. But it is not permissible.

Ahab confers briefly with his current opposite number aboard the *Shell That Echoes Only*. Even as he does, there is a new transmission from the downed wreckage on the planet's surface, helpfully pinpointing the site for his Reach to target. Instantly, he knows he is now ready to destroy the aliens on the surface, and perhaps to rid them all of the orbital as well. The science faction are singing a new song of progress and freedom and escape, but Ahab feels the various parts of his mind fall into alignment. If he removes all of these threats then the human that has somehow achieved true sentience may not sacrifice itself, and that, it seems to him, is desirable.

And besides, the transmission from the planet was very short, and no more follows.

***

It has found us. The signal, from Viola. Then, nothing.

Portia is trying to hail Kern, as the last possible point of contact. Avrana Kern has been off comms for a long time, though, and Viola's past prognosis was that the computer was irreparably damaged, spiralling in some kind of self-consuming data storm. Which means that the person of Avrana Kern, this instance of her, is probably dead and gone. Helena is surprised to find that she thinks of Kern in that way. She grew up with various Kern instances, including the grand one that still runs a great deal of the world she had named after herself, and sometimes the contact was greater than human, sometimes less. Now she discovers, when it is too late, that the *Lightfoot*'s computer intellect was right in the cerebral Goldilocks zone all along, human enough to be mourned.

Portia signals Viola, over and over, but there is no reply. Whatever the crew are doing, they have greater priorities than helping Helena prevent their utter destruction. A sobering thought. She is still receiving a torrent of data from the neighbouring warship *Shell That Echoes Only*, encapsulating reports on the far-off *Profundity of Depth*, which is currently slinging out of its lunar orbit, fixing its weapons systems on the crash site. Helena has frozen, now. The slate slips from her fingers to drift into the glue of the wall. She can only watch the data and hear Portia try over and over to raise their friends. She can only imagine how the last moments will be, for Viola and Zaine and Fabian, as their last refuge becomes a glowing monument to Helena's inability to communicate. Helena always thought the linguist's nightmare would be a scenario where communication was impossible. Now she has a clear channel, but nothing she can say that will help.

Which is when Portia leaps straight up, landing on the ceiling, because, just when all hope had seemed lost, Kern had contacted them.

'Confirm you retain communication channels with the molluscs.' There is just enough of Kern's abrupt manner in the transmission for Helena to know her.

'For what it's worth,' Portia sends back for both of them, as Helena scrabbles for the slate, dragging it loose, opening it for another pointless plea.

'I require you to translate for me, then,' Kern says, doing nothing so polite as asking, of course. 'Ready?'

'I . . .' Helena signals the ambassador, which had drifted off after their last exchange. Out in space, past the visible hull of her own ship, the *Shell That Echoes Only*'s hull is a brooding storm-coloured wall riven with flashes of anger and fear like lightning. Abruptly, the overlaid window on the

Profundity is a busy knot of arms as the vessel's commander swims into view again, though whether to listen or pontificate she cannot know.

'Tell it I bring a message for its species from the parasite.'

'They won't want to talk about it. The very mention—'

'It wants a truce.'

'*What?*'

Then Portia is signalling to her because the *Profundity*'s commander has been spurred into a paroxysm of agitation, arms coiling and its skin making jagged, fearful patterns.

'Doctor Kern, they've detected your signal. They . . . they say you're not communicating from the *Lightfoot* any more.' The data channel is right there, and Portia marks out the mathematical proofs. 'You're coming from the station where the . . . where the thing is. I think they think you're . . . not *you* any more.'

'They're right and wrong. I cannot be infected like an organic intelligence. Although if the parasite got into my ant colony on the *Lightfoot*, that would cause me considerable issues. However, as your hosts have divined, I am no longer operating from there. I am in much straitened circumstances, and I need you to do this for me while I am still capable of acting as intermediary. The organism – we need a name for it, really, something of the civilization, something of the petri dish . . .'

'Launch,' Portia says.

'No!' Helena begins throwing emotions into her slate, displaying them one on the heels of the last. *No, no, no, do not do this, please, no!* She tries to find something, some line connecting her with the angry cephalopod within the lens-like screen, some way of making her emotions leap across the void to it. In the back of her mind the missiles are cutting across the vacuum, off to cut through Nod's atmosphere like busy knives.

'Doctor Kern!' Portia raps out, because Kern seems to be losing focus, seems to be *diminishing*. Helena isn't sure what's on the orbital that could even host something like Kern, but whatever is there doesn't seem to be sufficient.

'Present,' Kern confirms sharply.

'You have incoming—'

'I am well aware. You must tell them to disable the warheads, divert the missiles, in some way hold off their attack. I am in communication with the parasite organism. It is sentient. It is capable of fabricating an interface with which to take in and process human-level concepts. I have reached a détente with it, on behalf of all of us.'

'All of who?'

'Us, life – life that isn't *it*. The rest of the universe. Whoever we feel like speaking for. However, I do not want this hard work to get blown up by a pack of reactionary warmongers. I had plenty of that back when I was human. Helena, tell them it wants to talk. Tell them . . . it understands.'

'We don't understand,' Portia complains.

'I don't require *you* to,' is Kern's imperious response. 'You are a linguistics team. Translate for me, as I translate for it.'

Helena stares into the alien eye of the *Profundity*'s commander and clenches down on her emotions. It is for the octopuses to be free and ruled by their feelings. She must control hers, because no amount of wailing and gnashing of teeth will help right now. Instead she speaks hope into her slate. She speaks new horizons. She implores them to listen. She speaks patience as Portia plots out orbital holding patterns that will keep the missiles in play without sending them on their fatal errand to the surface.

'Tell them this . . .' And Kern speaks: the intentions of an alien culture, filtered through a once-human computer now rapidly running out of thinking room, through a Portiid spider, through a Human and into the world of the cephalopods that even now have their arms about the trigger. Kern speaks fast: she funnels a whole alien world through her narrowing perspective. Helena lets the concepts flood through her, turned from human thoughts to colours and patterns and sublime equations, and probably a third of it turns out as nonsense, but she thinks, *They're still watching. They're taking it in. It means something to them.* And the warship commander, her alien admirer, watches her face and her slate and most of all her eyes, and the missiles are still on their way.

The organism wants to meet us, Kern is saying. It wants to experience us and understand and learn from us. It wants to reach out and grasp the universe. But it no longer wants to *be* us, or for us to be *it*. It has learned the limits of monoculture, turned inward in an everlasting round of tedium. Only by accepting the other can it truly find diversion and inspiration; only by allowing the universe to be separate from it can it have the infinite variety it craves.

Helena speaks into her slate and watches waves of colour and feeling pulse out through the ambassador into the scientists, from them to their hull, from their hull to the neighbouring warship and the universe at large. She watches the commander of the *Profundity of Depth* turn slowly, hanging within its domain. She imagines the missiles, which feel nothing and care for nobody, leaping from their leashes like eager hounds.

And at the end of it all she feels a resounding silence, an uncertainty. The octopuses are shifting things, after all. You cannot rouse them to a cause and expect them to follow you without a battery of responses like *Why?* and *Are you sure?* and *But . . .* And yet Portia is receiving new telemetry that shows the slightest deviation in the attack, coaxing the missiles onto a new course, still live, still lethal, but curving into an orbital path laid out for them, where they can wait like falcons high above, that can descend on their prey at any moment.

Helena meets the eye of the *Profundity*'s commander, and she can imagine all manner of human meaning in that gaze: weariness, doubt, concern, a fellow feeling almost certainly entirely in the beholder.

'They're not convinced yet,' she tells Kern, hoping that there is enough left at the other end to understand her. 'It's won us some time, maybe, a little. But I think they're still—'

'Stop prattling.' *Plenty* enough of Kern left, apparently. 'I am sending you a live link to a visual feed. They like visuals, do they not? And supporting data, seeing as that's how they do things. I am providing proof. Watch, just watch.'

19.

It has taken the creature outside the best part of a day to cut its way in.

If the *Lightfoot* was still spaceworthy, Fabian thinks the hull would be proof against anything the creature could do. Although, seeing it go about the task, he is less and less sure of that. It learns. From simple flailing it has modified its 'suit', the case of debris that contains it and gives it shape. It has improvised shears from shells and knapped stones, and possibly from first principles. It has identified the weaknesses in the unspooling tangle of the *Lightfoot*'s walls and has sawn and severed its way in with a dreadful patience. No, perhaps patience is the wrong word. Fabian is imputing rational arachnid thought to something probably not capable of it, but it seems enthusiastic, a worker fired up for its task.

At one point he lost his nerve and attacked it with the drone, ramming into the creature and smashing open its body, as well as wrecking the remote itself. He did not think he had solved the problem, then, and when Artifabian went out through the makeshift airlock, the creature had mostly reconstituted its casing, or another like it, the same pieces in random organization to give a similar not-quite-human shape. Even as they watched, it went back to cutting, picking up exactly where it had left off, its tools perhaps slightly better suited to the task thanks to its opportunity to remodel them.

They are all suited up now – Fabian, Viola and Zaine, though the Human's suit is the theoretically contaminated one she came over from the quarantine pod in because they have no way of fabricating a new one. Contamination, Fabian suspects, is going to be a moot point very shortly.

They have hauled Zaine back and the three of them huddle against the far wall, watching the light wax along the line where the creature is carving its way in. Artifabian is still out there, ready to make a desperate assault on the creature, but the robot is only Portiid-size, far smaller than a Human. Fabian can't see that it will make a dent.

I suppose we have free rein in respect of final messages, he shuffles out, his words heavy and laboured through the encumbrance of his suit.

It is possible that we are still being recorded and that the recording will eventually reach the Voyager, Viola tells him primly. *I recommend dignity, therefore.*

Fabian had a great many things to say in the certain assurance none of it would ever be heard by the wider world, and so that puts the kybosh on that. Some of those things were about Viola, others about the matriarchy and his experience of it and his great bitterness about not achieving his potential, and being driven onto this ludicrously dangerous mission as the only way he could pursue his researches unimpeded. And probably something regretful about Meshner but, right now, that is far down the list. Now Viola has introduced the threat of posterity and he feels the clamp of social pressure again, even looking death in the piecemeal face.

For death is here, come through the wall after all that cutting, squeezing its body through too small a slit, its casing bulging and rippling to fit, giving the lie to any suggestion of humanity. Fabian sees parts of it vibrate, buzzing into motion so rapid he can barely see it. Zaine chokes and shudders, and Fabian guesses the monster has said something human ears can hear, because to speak like a human is part of its sham, even though it lacks anything like the requisite organs and parts.

Probably it was something about an adventure.

Artifabian charges in, legs flailing, and scales the monster's irregular surface, trying to tear in with palps and fangs. The entity does not acknowledge the robot's attempt at all, even when parts of it are ripped loose. Instead it takes one slumping step and then another, and something like an arm unfurls from its side to reach for them, almost a comradely gesture, almost a gentlemanly offer to help Zaine to her feet.

I really wish I hadn't come. It's not exactly the searing diatribe about social injustice he had planned, but it is from the heart.

I share those feelings, Viola says. *I would rather spend my last moments with a female who was my intellectual peer.* At his furious twitch, his legs raised in raging, impotent threat, she clarifies: *Humour, Fabian. You are adequate as companionship goes. And a competent researcher, if that is what you are seeking.*

Zaine starts again, kicking herself up to half stand, half lean against the curved wall. She is looking up and around, not at the slowly approaching creature. Her mouth moves, but Artifabian is too busy to translate.

A heartbeat later the message is repeated for Portiid senses. *Do nothing rash.* A flat pronouncement from the ship itself.

Kern? Viola demands. *Where have you been?*

Too complex to tell you. Make no contact. Wait. No, wait, I said. Fabian, are you well? Are you hurt?

Fabian does not like Kern singling him out. It seems a likely prelude to being commanded to do something dangerous. And yet the voice is filling out now, little taps and scraps of character jolting along with the words. It doesn't seem like Kern to him, though. She had a very definite, forceful, *female* manner. This Kern seems almost . . . male.

What's that? There is a roaring sound outside and something passes over the ship, a shadow against the pale translucence of the ceiling. Fabian sees a flare from outside, the *Lightfoot*'s hull shrivelling slightly in a wash of heat. Something metal is coming down, gleaming in the sun, glowing slightly from a hurried re-entry. It is a drone, not his little eye-in-the-sky but one of the space exploration drones they deployed to look at the orbital. For a moment he'd thought that it was another missile come to make an end of them all.

This is more difficult than I'd anticipated. Kern, saying un-Kernish things in an un-Kernish way, but a voice more and more familiar as Fabian receives it.

The drone lands badly, falls over and rolls against one of the starfish, which withers away from the hot metal.

Artifabian, I need . . . please . . . take this and apply directly to the organism. The drone's casing pops even with the words, and something is ejected, to rattle against the stone of the altiplano. Artifabian leaps on it, a single predatory motion, then patters hurriedly back. Fabian can make out a drill-head, part of the drone's regular arsenal.

The monster, by that time, is standing right before them. Its faceplate now is a spiral, segmented shell like a centipede at rest, like a single compound eye. It seems to regard them, and Fabian shuffles left and Viola right, trying to split its attention. Zaine is its focus, though, and she is in no physical state to get away from it. Her face is twitching like something caught in a web, her eyes very wide.

Artifabian leaps, driving the drill-piece into the gap already torn in the creature's outer shell. For a moment it seems a magnificently pointless gesture to Fabian. Then Viola is at a console, having shuffled considerably further than he did, and is receiving data from Kern, or from whoever is sitting in Kern's place.

A makeshift syringe, that drill: containing . . . more of the same. Viola cannot understand it. Artifabian has just injected the creature with a shot of the same organism, the specimen from the orbital.

Just wait, the computer's voice tells them, still filling out with personality. *It'll be fine. We're golden, Fabian. There's so much I need to tell you.*

Meshner . . . ? Fabian asks timidly.

Partly. I've assumed Kern's functions, or I'm trying to. She put me in here, but none of it runs as easily as she said it would.

And where is Kern? Viola demanded.

She withdrew to the implant, Meshner says. *She . . . This is her plan. I'm just doing my part.*

What's it doing? This is Artifabian, translating for Zaine, because the creature has not moved since the robot struck. It might as well be an ungainly statue, one arm outstretched towards nothing.

It's receiving an ambassador, Meshner tells them. *It is hearing a revelation. It's like religion, really. And if we're right, it's not a threat, any more. And just maybe it's an opportunity.*

***

Meshner does his best to keep the *Lightfoot* in repair over the next several days, enough that none of them starve or run out of power or are forced to trust the vagaries of the local atmosphere. Staying suited is a profound inconvenience for everyone concerned but, even if the parasitic entity is not airborne, nobody wants to risk there being something else with which no diplomatic treaties have been drawn up.

The thing itself, the humanoid thing of rock and shell and slime-mould ooze, has gone but not far. It squats out on the plateau, and the starfish have laboriously crept away from it because they can sense what it is. To Fabian it has a weirdly tragic air, a thing rejected even by its own world. Meshner has explained what Kern did, by then; what she made the parasite understand. And what one sample understands can be instantly assumed by any other colony it comes into contact with. The organism is many, but it is also one, microscopic cells trading encoded understandings like Earth bacteria exchange immunity genes. The parasite will be different going forwards, Meshner claims. It will not seek to come as a devourer, but as a co-traveller. Viola is already considering how such a thing might be of use, how its Understandings might be put in service of the Portiid drive for knowledge and discovery. Fabian has already decided that this is one branch of science she can have sole dominion over, as far as he's concerned.

And at last the cavalry arrives. One day they glance at the sky above and there is something there, like a second moon. Not the science vessel, nor its military escort; certainly not the *Voyager* which still lurks in the outer system, too far to ever tender aid. Instead, Meshner introduces his crew to the *Profundity of Depth*, the curved hull of which shimmers with colours as though it is shouting insults at the planet below. Insults perhaps, but no warheads.

The rescue comes soon after, a spherical vessel tumbling from orbit, unmanned, to scream like a banshee on jets of superheated steam as it hovers over the altiplano, spooling out tendrils to gather up the *Lightfoot* entire and repatriate it to space rather than just snatch up the individual crew – which, from Meshner's disembodied point of view, is just as well. They will be kept in strict quarantine for some time, but time is what they have regained now they have escaped being stranded on an inhospitable alien world.

Eventually, the science vessel and its escort arrive, and the *Lightfoot* crew are reunited with Helena and Portia. The scientists themselves have already lost interest in their new allies. They are going over the orbital with great enthusiasm, dismantling a great clutter of mechanisms for further study. They have come after their scion, Noah, whose work was so rudely interrupted. For them, the fate of the parasite and the alien ambassadors was only ever a sideline, a gambit to keep the warmongers away while they worked, and one that has paid off.

By the time the *Voyager* finally arrives, after crossing all the great empty reaches between the outer solar system and the shores of Damascus, Helena is at the level of ordering creature comforts from the octopus orbitals' fabricators: Human and Portiid food constructed from spare molecules; furniture, laboratory equipment. They have a little enclave, the *Lightfoot*'s structure worked into a section of one of the Homeship globes, the one bubble of air in the great watery necklace Damascus wears. A year and more as guests of the octopuses and they are still not exactly trusted, yet. Whichever shifting alliance of cephalopods considers the alien visitors its business on any given day is doubtless keeping a few protuberant eyes on them, but in the absence of evident betrayal or a political convulsion amongst their hosts, an amicable interspecies peace has slowly incubated. Each day Helena can communicate a little more precisely, refining her software, finding shortcuts in the mess of Old-Empire-derived computer architecture the molluscs use, trusting to her gut feeling and the shifting hues of the bodysuit she had devised.

Portia is the happiest to see the *Voyager*. She is bored, cooped up on the orbitals. *How do you think the octopuses feel?* Helena asks her, but Portia is too fractious to show much empathy. She wants new horizons, or why else go to space? She'd even started drumming about going to Nod, setting foot on the alien world. She is the greatest explorer of her people, after all, in her own humble opinion, and it rankles with her that Fabian and Viola beat her to it.

Zaine is also more than happy that the mothership is due. She has healed as best she can by now, but human medical care is not something their hosts ever felt a need to research after Senkovi died, and the relevant Understandings were lost in the attack on the *Lightfoot*. She has a dozen kinks and imperfectly-healed breaks that have left her on a diet of pain-killers and frustration, longing for corrective work in the *Voyager*'s infirmary.

If not for Zaine, Viola could have put off the *Voyager*'s arrival for another year or so, engrossed as she has been in building a virtual model for interface with the parasite on even terms. Helena feels this is a step too far, and in this she is in the majority, but Viola is looking beyond all the new horizons. Every so often one of the octopuses comes to speak with her, pressing Helena into awkward translations of neuro-logical and biochemical concepts she does not truly follow herself. The transient nature of the cephalopods' opinions mean they can very quickly enter into temporary cahoots with their alien guests. Viola claims she is holding her own on the science front, despite the technological disparity, but Helena suspects she is still playing catch-up. Helena has seen what the science faction retrieved from the Nod orbital, after all, and watched Paul the ambassador's attempts to describe its capabilities. This is Noah's project, his means by which he and his people might escape their ruined world. The science faction has rescued and resurrected it at last, and they will test it soon. She and Portia have been invited to witness it. She has also come to a sufficiently refined understanding of the octopus mind to understand that their hosts themselves do not *know* what they have built. They only know what they want it to do, and so descriptions of their work are like those of mystics describing their visions. The logical donkey-work goes on elsewhere, inaccessible to the minds that benefit from it. At first she was baffled and almost offended: this is not, after all, how sentience should work. Humans and Portiids agree on these things. Now, after enough time to reflect, she wonders if the octopuses are not happier: free to feel, free to wave a commanding tentacle at the cosmos and demand that it open for them like a clam.

Fabian is also engrossed in his work, which has shifted emphasis since its inception. He is designing Implant 2.0 with the help of his former research assistant/laboratory test subject. Implant 2.0 may turn out to be a better medium for non-Portiids to experience and internalize the spider Understandings, but that will be something of a sideshow to the main circus. Recent events demonstrated that the implant architecture is capable of being pushed beyond its original purpose, allowing a remarkable kind of neural neutral ground – between the organic and the inorganic, and between species. Fabian is going to be the father – horrified gasps from the Portiid scientific orthodoxy! – of a new technology, and that technology may just unlock a very different future for everyone.

Lost in action, then: Bianca, killed in the initial confused engagement and still mourned; Avrana Kern, or that part of her formerly in control of the *Lightfoot*. And Meshner Osten Oslam of course, or at least his mortal remains. That loss may be a temporary affair; his body is currently walking around down on Nod after being shuttled there remotely from the orbital. It is not clear if the parasite could evacuate his brain and leave it whole and still Meshner, and negotiations with the parasite are more difficult by an order of magnitude than Helena's chats with the octopuses. Meshner the fledgling AI is philosophical. He is still finding his feet, now that he is wearing Kern's shoes.

Helena speaks to him about Kern, finding him oddly evasive. Is Kern still present somewhere, on the orbital, in the implant? Meshner doesn't know, but he thinks the expanding presence of the parasite would pare down the computer intelligence until whatever remained was no longer Avrana Kern, and unlike Lante or Meshner himself, the parasite's own recollections will not include a simulation of Kern, only memories of its interactions with her. Certainly there is no Kern personality present within the *Lightfoot*: no space in that damaged housing for two human-complex intelligences. She overwrote herself to preserve Meshner. Helena wonders what the Kern instance on the *Voyager* will make of it, and whether Meshner will make a fuller confession of precisely what went on between him and Kern within the implant, before the end.

And how Kern as a whole will feel, now that she is no longer unique. Will she be a jealous goddess, where Meshner is concerned? Or will she find that she has been lonely all this time?

Long before the *Voyager's* arrival, multi-species diplomacy arrived at a plan for what Fabian coined as The Insertion, a description that sounds better to the Portiids (who inject venom, after all, and fertilize their eggs externally) than to a Human. The Insertion, when it took place, was not much of a spectator event: a single missile shot from an isolated orbital into the waters of Damascus, requiring magnification even to see it from Helena's vantage point. Results are inconclusive as yet: nobody knows whether the plan will have its desired effects. What seemed like a thousand octopus factions had been wrangling over whether to even go ahead with the attempt. And then some of them just went ahead and did it, because that, apparently, is how decisions are made in this part of the galaxy. Helena tracked the projectile until it broke open against the waves. Contained within, unleashed upon the world, was a sample of the parasite from the Nod orbital, complete with its memories of Avrana Kern and her argument and the truce that had been formulated between them. Just as with the Nod planetside parasite, it is hoped that a conversion might spread out across the contaminated planet: an awareness of the parasite, its place and its potential. Perhaps one day the cephalopods will have their planet back, in some shape or form, although probably they will never have it wholly to themselves. Right now, the only practical response is to wait and to watch.

Which leaves one thing before the reunited *Voyager* crew make their final decisions and farewells.

The science faction are going to test the Noah device, now repaired and improved. That they feel the need to take it outside the orbit of either Damascus or Nod in order to deploy it is unsettling, but Helena and Portia want to see, finding themselves in quarters very like their previous incarceration on the rescue mission.

The device itself is surprisingly small, an overarching

framework fit around a single, unmanned sphere-ship, far enough out that Helena must take it on faith and instrumentation that it is there at all.

She doesn't understand the full science behind the thing, only what it is supposed to do. She doesn't really believe *that*, either. The octopuses are erratic engineers, after all, plagued by factionalism and short attention spans. It's all impossible, isn't it? And true, Old Empire humans conceived of such a loophole in the universe, but even for them the energy requirements were ludicrously out of reach. Generations of octopus scientists have been tantalized by the thought, though, and have desired to make it real, subconsciously telling their Reaches, *Find a way*, cheating physics, paring away at the problem until . . . this. And still she does not believe it, and her scepticism is tiny compared to Portia's.

And yet the two of them were sent for, and they came; bit parts in the triumph or tragedy of greater players.

***

A wise man once said that space is not an ocean, despite the temptation to think in terms of battlecruisers and naval ranks and war-fleets exchanging broadsides as they pass, graceful and leisurely, through the night. To the octopuses, however, space *is* an ocean – save that the concept of 'ocean' is a very different thing to them than it is to humanity: a great many-dimensional canvas that surrounds them, and that they can manipulate and open up, to see if anything edible can be found within. Taking things apart out of idle curiosity has always been part of their mental toolkit and why should the universe itself be an exception?

Once there was an octopus, call him Noah, whose people had suffered a cataclysm of far more than Biblical proportions, billions lost to a raging infection that tore them apart, broke them down, remade them as a sentient sludge that coated their entire world, only a remnant population left on the orbitals to stare down at what they had lost. And while some sought to rebuild a new stability in orbit, many others felt that the infection would jump to them eventually, quarantine how they might. Factions, infighting, open war sprang up in a ring around Damascus and out into the wider solar system. And Noah saw it and despaired.

Just like his distant ancestors chafing against the close confines of their tanks, he thought, *I need to escape*. And Noah knew – or his Reach did – that the universe was vast, and that anywhere he might want to flee to was unimaginably far away. And, impatient to be gone, his Reach threw out such long-term plans as cold sleep and generation ships in favour of . . .

This.

Space is an ocean, in this sense. It has waves and currents, and while there are hard and absolute limits to the speeds that objects can move through space, such limits do not apply to space itself.

When they test Noah's device, it vanishes instantly. The octopus scientists are split, some hailing this as a success, some as a failure. Their instruments are ambivalent as to what happened because their instruments cannot yet test the principles that they are deploying, a common problem given the leap-of-inspiration nature of cephalopod science.

A year later, however, the signal will reach them from a light year out in the void. The device arrived successfully, having manipulated the expansion rates of the space immediately before and behind it to travel the distance in a matter of subjective hours. No return trip had been planned, however, and the actual signal will be forced to travel the old-fashioned way, under the stern eye of a relativity that does not even realize it has been tricked.

FUTURE
WHERE TWO OR THREE SHALL GATHER

EPILOGUE

Our ship has spread its wings to the light of a fierce red star, great sails drinking in the nuclear light as half our crew run a brief survey of an interesting-looking moon. There is nothing habitable in this zone – planets three times the mass of Old Earth with a hundred atmospheres of pressure on the ground. Not that the pressure alone is insuperable. The octopuses can adapt themselves to that kind of environment readily enough – just like being a kilometre down on the ocean floor – and they could even take me with them, if I asked nicely, but it's mostly fire and acid down there and we didn't detect anything on our shopping list, and so why bother? We have the whole universe, after all.

A couple of the outer planets' moons are another matter. Organic chemistry on one, and some odd little energy traces on another that might be something inorganic but also theoretically alive. Life is always the big prize, sweeter than the rarest element, although usually it's something right on that boundary between life and complex chemistry. Or something best studied under the microscope.

Although I know better than most that just being microscopic doesn't mean simple.

Every ship is different, depending on who got the building rights. Ours is cephalopod-made, meaning that our nonaquatic crewmembers traded their lungs for gills for the trip. Swapping back is easy enough these days, after all. We have five different species aboard, plus myself and the other two interlocutors. We are all children of Earth, one way or another, products of the terraforming program and the Rus-Califi virus and, in one case, a wholly unexpected collision between a corvid genome and an alien molecular catalyst. And we have the artificial intelligences too, and those that are neither one thing nor another. And some of us are children of Nod, as well, either lifelong or just renting space.

The first reports of the survey crew suggest that they have found life, but barely. They will take samples, expand our archives. We might walk the cold surfaces of those moons or swim their subterranean oceans, but we won't interfere. Some day we'll be back, a thousand, a hundred thousand revolutions later, to see how they're getting on. But there is always that slight dissatisfaction, that they cannot know us; that they cannot *join* us in our endless journey.

Messages are coming in from other ships. The oldest crawl to us at the speed of light, ancient news telling us what our ancestors did, what our cousins found. We mark out some worlds worth revisiting, other hotbeds of nascent evolution that might even now be lifting sensory organs towards the starry sky. We note the passing of our kin and friends; the birthing of new ships; songs and stories and jokes that travel between the stars. Some we appreciate, some are grown so far from us that we cannot follow their meaning. If we met them, though, those other travellers, we would be able to look each other in the eye and see our own reflection. What else is an interlocutor for?

Then the real news comes in.

This is a rapid dispatch, an unmanned probe arriving in-system by wave, crunching space ahead of it, stretching space behind to skip across the interstellar gulfs so fast its own image is left trailing behind it. The energy demands of wave travel mean only the most urgent news gets sent this way and this probe has gone to where its makers knew we last were, then followed our beacons, wave-crest to wave-crest, until it found us.

What can be so urgent? Some of the crew always think of war, when it comes down to this, but what war? What is there to fight over, in a universe that is bigger than even we can ever exhaust, with more of anything than we could ever need? There are no empires in space. If space is an ocean, it is one without shores.

And it is not war. It is discovery.

On a far world, about a far sun, a small ship of our cousins has found something remarkable. Unequipped to properly explore, they have sent for their kin, who can do the site justice: us.

We send for the survey team in a fever of excitement. In a year they finish up their work and return to us, data in hand. What is a year, after all, save an obsolete Earth measure of time? We have all the time the universe has to offer.

The ship is charged by then, and we make our own waves, riding the negative mass across a hundred light years. The process is almost energy efficient now, compared to the early cephalopod experiments.

And we arrive, a century or so after the original pioneers sent off their message probe and went on their way. What is a century, after all, in the eye of the universe? On the fifth planet of this system there is a beacon for us, and in the heart of the beacon is something left just for me.

In orbit, we see exactly why the call went out. Most likely it went to others, too. We'll have a proper family get together here in a few decades, all the gang back together again; anyone with the interest and the means will be rolling up the fabric of space-time to get here. The more the merrier.

I look at it, and the human in me calls it a fortress seven kilometres across and a kilometre high, a huge star-shaped structure of serrated walls where the indentations carry their own dents, teeth all the way down to the atomic level in fractal profusion. It is dead: no power signatures and the planet itself has lost most of whatever atmosphere it had. It is not native, either. The rest of the world shows no sign of a civilization that might have thrown this up. Someone came here a million years ago and left their mark, and died or departed. Or, just possibly, left something of themselves behind.

We have found someone else, or at least their footprints in the dust. It is the first time, and it gives us hope that it will not be the last.

Down below, our pioneer kin have left a gift and that is where I come in. Their interlocutor wanted to be there for the excavation, whilst being unable to abandon their comrades. Thankfully, for us, that is no hard barrier.

They bring the cryptobiote to me, the dormant culture that they decanted from themselves, that is everything they ever were, all the different lives that have gone into them. When I pour them into me, I am them and they are me, an expansion of my personal history written neatly in the archive of my cells. I have been human, I have been Human; I have been Portiid and octopus and stomatopod and corvid. Now I am another forty-three individuals. I am Yusuf Baltiel and Erma Lante and Meshner Osten Oslam and Viola and Salome. I am many.

We are splitting the ship. Some of us will carry on with our travels. Others will remain here to study as the newly budded ship-child swells and grows. I will decant myself for those who will leave; I will leave with them, and I will stay, and perhaps one day I will meet myself and tell myself about what I learned.

Those who stay prepare for a respectful exhumation of the dead, an investigation of this vast alien ruin. Perhaps we will learn where they came from. Perhaps they are still here. One day we will meet living intelligences, and that day the interlocutors will be ready to learn them and learn how to speak with them, and invite them on the journey, if they wish to come.